Vengeance
Is
Mine

Vengeance
Is
Mine

Helen Sanders

Little Red House Press
Rich, Mississippi

Vengeance Is Mine is a work of fiction. Any references to real people, events, establishments, organizations, or locales are intended only to give the fiction a sense of reality and authenticity. Other names, characters, places, and incidents portrayed herein are either the product of the author's imagination or are used fictionally.

Little Red House Press
5965 Coahoma-Rich Road
Rich, MS 38617 USA.

FIRST EDITION

Library of Congress Catalog Card Number: 2002227695

ISBN 0-9711276-0-3

First Printing: January 2003

Author's Note and Acknowledgements

The settings for most of this story are real but in order to make it more believable, I have altered certain facts. For instance, MSCW does not have separate housing for the members of social clubs. Also, freshmen were not allowed to have cars on the campus in 1963. I hope that you as a reader will bear with me whenever you encounter such "fictional facts" and that they do not detract from your enjoyment of the story.

There are many, many people to whom I owe a debt of gratitude.

First to Ree Holley. Without your help and encouragement this novel would never have been completed. You were there from the beginning. I deeply appreciate all the time and effort you put in to make our work a success.

To Margaret Hubbert. Thanks for your honest criticism and for being such a loyal friend. You made the difficult journey a lot more fun.

Special thanks to Dr. Charles Hubbert whose mind is a plethora of knowledge. You helped to make Geoffrey come to life.

Additional thanks to the authors of Writer's Digest Books. Without those resources, I would never have been able to complete this novel.

To the many authors I have met along the way, either in person or on the Internet. Thanks for your advice and support.

A special thanks to Mark Holley for taking your valuable time to read this manuscript and offer helpful comments.

To our "sales rep" Kevin Holley. Thanks for all the help you gave in finding just the right people to guide our book in the right direction.

To my editor, Ann Kempner Fisher. Without your encouragement and pursuit of perfection, this novel would have never been published. Any errors are mine and not yours.

To my fellow teachers and students at Lee Academy. Thanks for putting up with me while I struggled to complete this work. You are the best.

And last but not least to my family. You have been totally supportive even in the worst of times. Without your patience and understanding I would never have been able to fulfill my dreams of being a published author.

For my Family

Vengeance

Is

Mine

Prologue

August 1944

"Sister, the pain—I—can't take it anymore. You have to do something."

"Ssh, Teresa, it'll all be over in a little while," the nun said as her assistant wiped the sweat from the young girl's brow. "Just one more push. I can see the baby's head now. Come on, you can do it."

Teresa La Porte forced herself to make one last concerted effort to expel the foreign being from her womb. Savage pain ripped through her body and her scream permeated the room. Her guts felt as if they had been turned inside out. Finally, the baby's head forced its way out of her body. What sweet relief.

"Oh my, Sister Mary," the nun's assistant gasped as she stared in amazement.

"What—? What is it? Is something wrong with my baby?"

"No," the nun said with a laugh. "But you have twins. There was another one hiding behind his brother."

Teresa bit her lips and tears rolled from the corners of her eyes, not so much from the pain she had endured, but from the knowledge that she would not be able to keep her sons. Her parents had forced her to come to New Orleans to have her baby because they were too embarrassed for the townspeople to learn the awful thing their daughter had done.

Two days after the babies had been born, Teresa received a curt note from her mother.

Teresa, thank you for calling us the other night. I hope you understand why your Dad and I had to send you to New Orleans. The promotion at the office was so important to him, and we couldn't let anything stand in the way. Everyone thinks you're a counselor at summer camp. When you feel well enough, just give us a call and we'll come down there and pick you up. Once you get home everything'll be just like it was.
Love,
Mother

Teresa slammed her fist in the pillow. "Yeah, Mother. I know just how you and Daddy feel. My pregnancy was just a little bump in your road to success. Well, don't worry. I won't be in your way any longer."

Teresa leaned over and got a pen and several sheets of paper out of the dresser drawer next to her bed. She wanted to hurt her parents so badly for the way they had treated her.

Mother, I've made up my mind that I'm going to keep one of the twins. I realize I can't take care of two babies, so the nuns have made arrangements for a wealthy couple from Little Rock to adopt the other baby. I know you don't approve of what I'm doing. But don't worry about me showing up on your doorstep carrying your illegitimate grandson. I wouldn't want to embarrass you and Dad. I'm going to live in a convent in Poplar Ridge until I can find a job and earn enough money to support Geoffrey and me. Geoffrey is a beautiful baby. I know you'd love him under different circumstances. I'm sorry I've been such a disappointment to you and Daddy.
Teresa

A month later, Teresa La Porte boarded a bus for the

Mississippi Gulf Coast, clutching to her breast a precious bundle wrapped in a blue blanket. Taking the window seat right behind the driver, she unfolded the blanket and looked lovingly into the mesmerizing gray eyes of her tiny son.

The bus lurched to a stop. A tall, lanky young man wearing the dress blues of an Air Force officer got on and took the seat beside Teresa. She was still crying and fumbled for a tissue.

"Use this," the young man said as he handed her his handkerchief. "I'm Paul Bockker. Is there something I can do to help?"

With a rush of emotion, Teresa unburdened her troubles. When she had finished, Bockker said, "I'm stationed at the Air Force Base in Poplar Ridge. Maybe we can get together after you and Geoffrey get settled in."

For the first time in months, Teresa La Porte smiled and relaxed.

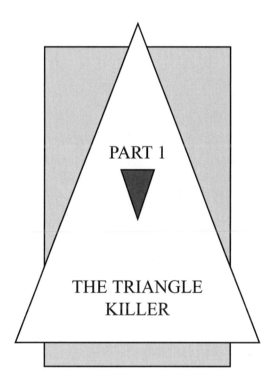

PART 1

THE TRIANGLE
KILLER

1

September 1963

The Delta Social Club at Mississippi State College for Women was holding a ceremony celebrating the acquisition of its new pledges in the Carrier Lodge, just outside Columbus. Twenty-two miles away, a young man was planning revenge on four members of the club. Rage boiled inside him like a festering sore.

I don't even know their names! How can I punish them? Wait a minute—Danny Browning's annual. Why didn't I think of it before? He grabbed his car keys and burst out the front door of the old farmhouse.

Fifteen minutes later, Geoffrey Bockker pulled up in front of the Kappa Sig House on the Mississippi State University campus. Steeling himself, he walked up the sidewalk and knocked tentatively on the door. A fraternity member opened it.

"Hi, is, uh, Danny Browning here?" Geoffrey asked. "I need to see him."

"You and every other horny guy on campus. His room's on the second floor, third door on the right."

Geoffrey bounded up the stairs and knocked on Danny's door. He opened it before Danny finished saying "Come in."

"Danny, my name's Geoffrey Bockker. Pat Overton and I have a couple of classes together and he told me you're called the Kappa Sig Casanova 'cause you keep a scorecard of all the goodlookin' 'W' girls in an annual. If it's true, I'd like to borrow that book."

Danny's bright eyes glistened at the mere mention of his famous possession.

"Yeah, you heard right. But you gotta tell me why you want it. I just don't loan it out without a good reason."

"I spotted this gorgeous chick at the movie in Columbus, and I need to find out who she is. She's really built and I sure would like to date her."

Danny grinned. "That's a good enough reason. Just don't lose it. It's better that a little black book. I've got my special rating system. It's based on a baseball game. First base means she'll make out on the first date and—"

"I get the picture."

Danny smirked and dangled the annual so high above his head that Geoffrey had to reach up for it.

"Give me the damn book," Geoffrey said as his gray eyes flashed with anger.

"Sure, man, I was just teasing. But you do have to pay me a fifty dollar deposit first."

Geoffrey reached into his wallet and pulled out the money. "I'll bring this back to you in a couple of days."

"Sure, just guard it with your life."

As he was driving back to his house, Geoffrey ran his fingers over the raised letters of the cover. He desperately wanted to tear through the book until he found the names he was looking for. Although sweat popped out on his forehead and his breathing became labored, he refused to give in to the temptation. Sharing his discovery with his girlfriend, Angie, would make it even more meaningful. When he reached the front door, his hands were trembling so badly he could barely get the key in the lock. Once he was inside, he sat down on the sofa and nervously thumbed through the annual until he came to the section labeled Social Clubs. Displayed prominently on a page underneath a huge triangle was a photograph of four girls holding the college softball trophy. Their arms were raised in conquest and a broad smile was plastered across each face. Under the picture it read: " 'Big Four' (Suzanne Yates, Barbara Flowers, Arlene Harris, and Janine Walton) lead juniors to victory over freshmen."

"You damn bitches! What gives you the right to smile? I lost the two most precious things in the world because of what you did." Geoffrey spat the words out.

He copied the names of his intended victims in a spiral notepad, underlining each name twice.

The next morning, Geoffrey awoke with a start when sunlight cast its beam across his face. Surely the events of the day before hadn't really happened. But the notepad and the annual lying beside him convinced him that his fears were grounded in truth. The desire for revenge coursed throughout his entire body, but he forced himself to remain rational. His heart pounded—it felt like it might literally explode out of his chest. He took several deep breaths to calm himself and walked into the bedroom and stared at a group of pictures on his dresser. The events of the day before and snippets of the horrors he had endured began to flash through his mind.

There was the phone call from Angie telling him to get to Columbus as fast as he could, her diatribe against the Delta Social Club, especially a group known as "The Big Four," because they hadn't given her a bid, and finally the revelation that she was pregnant—these visions all seemed to run together in a jumble. Then the tempo slowed down and Geoffrey was forced to relive in excruciating detail the terrible events that occurred after Angie had rushed to her Thunderbird and gunned it out of the parking lot.

Geoffrey had raced to his car and jerked open the door of the Chevy Bel Air. Peeling off, he left a trail of rubber behind. He had a good idea where Angie was headed and sped after her, doing his best to keep up with her as she raced down College Street and took a left onto Fourth. He managed to keep her in his sights and screamed out when he saw her take the ninety-degree turn off onto Old Bridge Road without slowing down. The Thunderbird fishtailed and he watched in shock and horror as Angie's body was flung against the window like a rag doll. In the next agonizing moment, the car crashed through the barricade at the end of the road and became airborne. A sound like that of the keening at an Irish wake erupted spontaneously from his throat. He pulled to a halt in front of the broken boards and jumped out of the car. He stood there, momentarily stunned, before he dared to look over the edge. The car had careened down the steep ravine into the empty creek bed and was enveloped in flames. He crawled through the remaining pieces of broken board and half-ran, half-slid down the side of the ravine. The heat from the car was unbearable and he couldn't get close enough to see inside. He knew he had to get help, so he started back up, his fingers clawing into the dirt and loose gravel. When Geoffrey finally reached the top, out of breath and sweating, he ran back up Old Bridge Road and onto Fourth Street where he flagged down a motorist.

"Go...to...the nearest...house and phone...the fire department...an accident, the end of Old Bridge Road," Geoffrey gasped to the astonished driver. "Hurry! My...girlfriend's down there, trapped in her car!" Geoffrey turned around quickly and raced back toward Old Bridge Road, praying that Angie was still alive.

After what seemed like hours, a wailing of sirens signaled

the arrival of the Lowndes County Fire Department. Geoffrey waited anxiously while the men scrambled down the treacherous bank.

They dragged the canvas hose as close as they could to the car. Working feverishly, they were finally able to douse the flames. Then they moved in to free Angie from the wreckage. By the time Geoffrey pushed his way to the front, one of the firemen who had been kneeling over Angie looked up and said, "I'm sorry. She's dead." The sweat-streaked men wrapped Angie's body in a sheet and placed it on a stretcher. As the group trudged up the hill, Geoffrey clutched the side of the stretcher until they reached the top.

One of the firemen put his arms around Geoffrey's shoulders. "Son, I'm Chief Summers. I know this is hard for you, but we need to know exactly what happened so we can write up our report. Y'all weren't drag racing, were you?"

Tears streamed down Geoffrey's cheeks and his voice broke. "Oh, no sir, Angie got real upset over something that happened at the 'W' and took off in her car, driving ninety to nothin'. I was trying to catch up with her, but I guess she forgot about the barricade at the end of the road and plowed right though it. Can I go now? I've gotta call her parents."

"Okay. Take it easy. But I need your names to put in the report. I'm sure the police will want to question you, too. How can they get in touch with you?"

Geoffrey responded perfunctorily and walked to his car. He shook his head and cried silently. "Angie, you can't be dead...and our baby...why didn't you tell me about him instead of handing me that damn lab report? We could've worked something out."

2

Geoffrey's throbbing head brought him back to reality. Taking deep breaths, he calmed down enough to dial the number of the Cooper Funeral Home in Poplar Ridge.

"Baxter, this is Geoffrey. Could you please tell me when y'all are going to have Angie's funeral. I can't find out anything here and I sure don't want to call her parents."

"Geoffrey, I'm real sorry about what happened. We're not sure yet about the funeral. The Lowndes County Coroner's office just finished the autopsy this morning and Angie's daddy and Mr. Cooper are on their way home with the bod—Angie."

Geoffrey let the phone drop into the receptacle.

God, he'd never thought about an autopsy. He imagined Mrs. Burrell's reaction. She'd go berserk and say that Angie had ruined the family's reputation. He reached in his jacket pocket and pulled out the pregnancy report that Angie had shoved in his hand just before she ran to her car. He wanted her family to think she'd never found out she was pregnant. They had to think she'd killed herself because she didn't get a bid to Delta.

Geoffrey flung his suit and duffel bag into the back seat of the car and slid in behind the wheel. This was one time he dreaded making the drive home. Whenever he realized that Angie wasn't snuggled up next to him, tears formed in his eyes and he had to blink hard to clear his vision. Every time he breathed deeply, he could sense the fragrance of her perfume. It reminded him of the very first time he saw Angie.

He had been standing outside the foreboding white brick structure of his new school, the fifth one he had attended in five years. Suddenly he became aware of the presence of someone standing next to him. He could smell the faint scent of roses and turned to see the face of a young girl who looked just like one of the porcelain dolls his mother had kept in a curio cabinet in their living room.

"Hi, my name's Angela Burrell. What's yours?"

"Geoffrey...Geoffrey Bockker," he stammered.

Angela took Geoffrey's hand in hers and led him to a nearby bench. "Let's sit here and talk a while. The first bell doesn't ring until eight. By the way, my friends call me Angie."

A warm feeling engulfed Geoffrey. Maybe things were getting better. His new family, the Holleys, seemed to like him and a pretty girl wanted to be his friend. After that first meeting, Geoffrey and Angie became inseparable. They were kindred spirits, united because both were pariahs. Geoffrey had lived with a series of foster families after his mother's death when he was eight years old, and Angie knew that she could never live up to her mother's unattainable expectations. As soon as her parents allowed, the couple began dating and the romance continued throughout high school. In fact, the only time they had been separated was when Geoffrey went off to college.

When the outskirts of town finally came into view, Geoffrey was relieved. He rolled down the window and breathed deeply. The familiar odor of salt air wafting in from the Gulf welcomed him home. He turned onto Ancel Street and pulled into the circular drive in front of a building that had been the home of one of the area's most prominent families in the early 1800s. As a child, Geoffrey had often ridden by the house on his early morning paper route.

Set in a group of spiraling live oak trees, the old two-story house was accented by huge Doric columns across the wide porch. Spanish moss draped from the limbs of the oaks like icicles on a Christmas tree. The house, which was so elegant that it had often been the subject of picture postcards in the '30s and '40s, had been turned into a funeral home by the Coopers in 1950. Geoffrey had worked there during the summers in high school and still had his key, so he drove around to the back and went in the door used only by employees. He hoped the Burrells were still at their house because he didn't feel like facing the barracuda or her milquetoast husband just yet. He wanted to be alone with Angie.

When Geoffrey rounded the corner, Joseph Cooper was coming out of his office. Instinctively, he put his arms around the boy's shoulders. "Geoffrey, I know you must be devastated about Angela. We got back with her about an hour ago. I'm getting ready to prepare her body."

"Could I please see her, Mr. Cooper? I almost broke my neck getting here. I know you're not supposed to do this, but as a favor to me—"

"Geoffrey, I don't think it's such a good idea. She doesn't look like any of the bodies you helped prepare. Remember, she's just had an autopsy performed on her."

"I understand, sir. But it's real important to me."

Cooper felt sorry for Geoffrey because he didn't think the boy knew what he was letting himself in for.

"Under the circumstances, okay. But just for a little while. Then we've got to get her ready. You understand?"

"Yes sir. Thank you."

"She's in the embalming room. You know where it is."

It took all the courage Geoffrey had to enter the room. He had been there many times before when he assisted with embalming, but this was different. His beloved Angie would be lying on the cold metal table.

He paused and willed his hand to clasp the white ceramic knob and gradually turn it a few degrees. Although he quickly let go, the motion had been enough to allow the door to swing open. The beams from the lights in the ceiling cast an eerie glow on the sheet-covered body lying on the embalming table. He breathed in slowly and walked with measured steps toward the table. Taking the rough muslin sheet by the corner, he pulled it back slowly until he could see Angie's face. He stepped back in horror and emitted a blood-curdling scream when he saw an open cavity where her nose had been and an exposed left cheekbone where the skin and flesh had been completely ripped away. Her head had been shaved and behind one ear and over the back of her skull ran a scar sewn up with thick twine, like the stitches on a baseball.

When Cooper heard Geoffrey's scream, he knew he had made a mistake allowing the boy to look at Angela. He ran into the room and quickly covered her face before Geoffrey had a chance to see the other atrocities caused by the wreck and the autopsy.

Holding tight to the shivering boy, Cooper tried to comfort him. "Geoffrey, I was afraid this would devastate you. I'm sorry I didn't stop you."

Geoffrey's body heaved with sobs and he could barely speak. "It's not your fault, Mr. Cooper. I…I just had no idea what she'd look like. Can you fix her up?"

"We're going to do the best we can. I'm not sure whether the Burrells are going to want an open casket, but I hope they don't. It's better for folks to remember Angie as she looked before all this happened. Geoffrey, why don't you go on home now so Baxter and I can get to work. Don't worry. We'll do the best job we can."

At that moment, a disheveled woman ran into the room, barreling past Geoffrey and Cooper.

"I want to see my baby! You and Walter wouldn't let me go with you to identify her body. Now get the hell out of my way!"

"Carrie, no! You don't want to see Angela until I've prepared her. I haven't had time to do anything yet."

But his words did no good, and Carrie Burrell ripped the sheet from her only child's body. In addition to her disfigured face and mottled skin, the condition of the body caused the horrified mother to gasp as she stared open-mouthed at what looked like a deflated balloon. The organs had been dumped back into the open body cavity and the chest plate had been laid back on her body and sewn with twine, forming a Y-like pattern. In anguish, Carrie Burrell struck out at the first person she could blame. She sobbed violently and pummeled Geoffrey's chest with her fists.

"This is all your fault, you goddamned son-of-a-bitch! The police said she must have been going at least ninety miles an hour when she ran through the barrier. Y'all must have had a fight for her to have been that upset!"

Geoffrey had never particularly liked Angie's mother. Whenever she drank too much, she tried to compete with Angie for his attention. Besides, if she hadn't pushed Angie so damned much, the miserable girl wouldn't have felt guilty about not getting into a social club. Now that he was backed into a corner, he wasn't going to hold anything back. To hell with her feelings.

Geoffrey clenched his teeth and replied, "No, m'am, there was no fight. Angie didn't get a bid to join the Deltas or any other social club. She knew she couldn't face you, so she ran off in her car and deliberately killed herself. Her blood's on your hands, not mine."

Her face red with anger, Carrie Burrell spat out her words, "I don't believe that! I never pressured Angela into joining a social club. I just told her that she'd make friends with a better class of girls if she did."

"That's bullshit. She told me all the time about how you used to brag about getting into Chi Omega at Ole Miss."

By this time, Angie's father had entered the room. "You two, stop right now. For God's sake, can't you show some respect to Angela's memory instead of fighting like a pair of alley cats?"

Cooper interrupted, "I think all of you need to leave so that I can get my job done. Go on home and get some rest. I'll call you when the body's ready."

Geoffrey and Angie's parents walked out into the hall. In a way, Geoffrey felt relieved. He knew that if her parents had learned of Angie's pregnancy, her mother would have lit into him with both barrels.

"I'm sorry, Mrs. Burrell. It's just that I'm so upset about Angie. She was my whole world. I don't think I can live without her," Geoffrey cried.

"It's okay, Geoffrey. We understand, don't we, Carrie?" Angie's father pleaded.

Carrie Burrell mumbled something, pulled out a cigarette and nervously lit it, staring icily at Geoffrey the whole time.

"Geoffrey, Mr. Cooper's right. Let's go home and wait until he calls us. You're welcome to come to the house, if you want to." Walter Burrell extended his hand and Geoffrey clasped it firmly.

"That's really nice of you, sir. But I think I'll go on over to my house and wait. I'll see y'all later."

The Burrells walked toward the front door and Geoffrey

turned down the hall and went out the back. He sat in his car a few minutes, trying to decide what to do.

I've got to leave town before the funeral. When the autopsy results get here, Mrs. Burrell will raise holy hell. I can't let anything screw up my plans.

During the long drive back to Starkville, Geoffrey became livid when he thought about the way "the bitch" had treated him. She had some nerve asking if there had been a fight between him and Angie. She knew he loved Angie so much that he would have died before he so much as uttered a cross word to her. When a vision of Angie's mutilated body lying on the embalming table forced its way into his mind, it brought back memories of his own mother.

Geoffrey had stood in the stuffy funeral parlor, stroking his mother's cheek as she lay in the coffin. Tears streamed down his face. "Mommy, mommy, please come back to me."

Paul Bockker leaned over and placed his arms tenderly around his adopted son. "I know how you feel, Geoffrey, but nothing we can do will bring her back."

At the funeral service, Geoffrey clamped his hands over his ears to keep from hearing the monotone voice of the minister as he droned on and on about God's newest saint. But the worst memory of all was standing over his mother's bronze coffin in the cemetery, with the rain dripping from the edge of the funeral tent, as he told her goodbye forever. They had been devoted to one another and now he would have no one to tuck him in at night or to kiss away his "boo-boos" when he fell and hurt himself.

Geoffrey heard the honking of a horn and realized that his car had swerved into the other lane, forcing the driver to slam on the brakes and pull off the road. Geoffrey rolled down the window and screamed, "You son-of-a-bitch, watch where you're going!" His heart pounded and he gripped the steering wheel tightly until he was able to calm down.

About two in the morning, Geoffrey finally arrived at his house. He opened the car door and trudged up the steps. Later, overtaken by exhaustion, he collapsed on his bed, but his mind was racing so fast that he couldn't get to sleep. Stumbling into the kitchen, he made a cup of instant coffee and carried it back to his bedroom. As he sipped the steaming coffee, his eyes shifted from Angie's pictures to the page of smiling faces of the Delta Social Club.

3

By nine in the morning, having been unable to sleep all night, Geoffrey was so antsy that he had to get out of the house. He got in his car and drove around aimlessly until he came to a discount store. As he was browsing up and down the various aisles, he noticed a display of votive candles. A vision of a shrine formed in his mind, and he selected about a dozen of the candles. On the way to the checkout counter, he passed the toy section. His heart ached when he saw a group of vinyl baby dolls. They reminded him of the child he would never get to hold. He reached down and picked up one of the dolls and caressed it in his hands. His eyes glazed with anger and he snatched up three more dolls.

When Geoffrey got home, he arranged the candles in a semi-circle in front of Angie's pictures. After wrapping each doll in a soft white handkerchief, he laid them in front of the candles. Using his switchblade, he carefully cut out the picture of his four enemies in the shape of a triangle and laid it on the dresser. He sat down in a chair facing the dresser and grasped the knife firmly. Leaning forward, he laid his left arm on the dresser and made an incision from the tip of his ring finger to the first joint. He held up his arm and blood dripped from the wound onto the picture. Like a voodoo witch doctor, Geoffrey dipped a toothpick in the blood and wrote "Killer Bitches" across the smiling faces of the four girls. When he couldn't get the bleeding to stop, he wrapped a handkerchief around the wound like a tourniquet. A terrible throbbing pulsated in his temples and he kneaded his pounding head with his knuckles to alleviate the pain. The monster, which he had managed to chain in the far recesses of his mind so long ago, fought to break loose.

Its seductive voice pleaded, "Free me and I'll help you destroy these four abominable creatures."

"No, I won't let you out. You'll only bring me misery and pain like you did before."

"Remember how good you felt after you set fire to your foster parents' house. Relax and we'll savor those memories together."

Geoffrey put his head down on the desk and his mind became a movie screen on which the events of that fateful night in 1951 were projected.

Please, God, don't let her bother me tonight.

The little boy had prayed silently as he lay in his bed. The creaking of the steps, however, made him know his entreaty had been to no avail and soon he heard the familiar scuffing of her slippers on the hardwood floor as she shuffled down the hall toward his room. His heart fluttered like the wings of a wounded sparrow when he saw the knob on his bedroom door turn ever so slightly.

"Alright, little man, Mommy's here to play our game again. But remember, you must be quiet or Daddy might find out and make us stop. We wouldn't want that to happen, would we?"

As soon as she had eased her corpulent body underneath the cover, he lay as still as he could, praying that the ordeal would be over quickly. She turned his head toward her and kissed him on the lips. The odor of whisky and cigarettes on her breath repulsed him as much as the kiss and he had to fight to keep from getting sick. He jerked his head away from her and stared out the window. "Now, little man, just relax and give me your hand."

When she finally left, only then did the little boy allow himself the luxury of releasing his pent-up emotions. Tears rolled from the corners of his eyes onto the pillowcase.

Mommy, why'd you have to leave me? I hate these awful people. I'd rather be dead and in heaven with you than here in this horrible place.

From somewhere deep inside his soul, a voice, unlike any he had ever heard, called out, "If you listen to me and do what I say, I will help you destroy these evil people."

In the early hours of the morning just before daybreak, the little boy crept out of his bed and went downstairs to the laundry room. He reached up on the shelf beside the ironing board and picked up a can of cleaning fluid. Then he walked through the kitchen and down the hall toward his foster parents' bedroom. He hesitated in front of the door, but then resolutely turned the knob and pushed it open just a hair so that he could see inside. The odor of stale cigarette smoke and whisky greeted him. His foster parents were snoring heavily, and he knew he must make his move soon because one of them might gasp for breath and wake up. He opened the door just enough to get inside. He quickly tiptoed across the room, dribbling the cleaning fluid from the edge of the sleeping couple's bed to the door of the bathroom. He went inside and turned the knob of the space heater as high as it would go. Then he pushed the drying rack full of clothes directly in front of the heater and tiptoed out of the bathroom, past his sleeping enemies, and back out into the hall. Closing the bedroom door behind him, he tried to control his labored breathing as he stood guard outside.

The crackle of flames and the odor of burning clothes caused his heart to race with excitement, but he still didn't try to escape. He had to make sure that the fire would destroy the two people in bed. Finally, when the smoke snaked from under the bottom of the door and rose up to the ceiling, he knew it was time to leave. He raced out the door and across the lawn to the neighbor's house. Gasping for breath, he mashed on the doorbell repeatedly until someone came to the door.

"Son, what's wrong?" John Cavett asked, as he looked down at the terrified face of the pajama-clad child.

"Please help me, Mr. Cavett. I woke up and the whole house was filled with smoke. I tried to reach my parents' bedroom but the fire was so bad, I couldn't get in."

"Martha, call the fire department and come down here right now—the Ashleys' house is on fire! You take care of Geoffrey while I go over there to see if there's anything I can do before the fire trucks arrive."

Martha Cavett rushed down the stairs, putting on her bathrobe on the way down. "Oh, you poor baby. Come here and sit with me. I'm sure your parents will be alright."

The boy stiffened when Martha Cavett enveloped him in her arms, but he didn't try to pull away. He stared blankly ahead and didn't even budge when three fire trucks pulled up in front of his house.

After an hour, the blaze was finally under control. Only then did Martha Cavett take Geoffrey outside.

One of the firemen came over and knelt down in front of the child. "Son, I'm sorry, but we couldn't save your parents."

The little boy didn't say a word. He just stared into the face of the fireman with his piercing gray eyes.

4

Geoffrey's finger throbbed and he jerked his head up from the desk. He glanced at his watch. "Oh, God. I must have fallen asleep," he mumbled to himself. He still had to figure out a plan for punishing the four bitches. He grabbed his spiral notepad and pencil and stared in amazement as the words of a perfect plan seemed to take shape on the page in front of him. When he had finished writing, he paused to genuflect in front of Angie's shrine for reassurance.

"Angie, when I get back tonight, I'll have one of them with me and you'll get to see her punishment."

He picked up his switchblade from the dresser and rummaged through his house, carefully choosing the items he would need for his sacred mission: duct tape, a piece of ski rope, and the handcuffs he had stolen from Ray Karsten, one of his foster parents who had beaten him half to death one night.

The anger Geoffrey still felt toward Karsten, compounded with his hatred for the four girls, was enough motivation to send him on his crusade without worrying about the consequences. He drove to Columbus in an almost zombie-like trance and entered the back gate of the campus. Angie had proudly pointed out the house where the members of the Delta Social Club lived, since she was sure she would be a member one day. He pulled up behind the two-story ante-bellum building and got out of the car.

I think I'll wait back here until I spot someone who can help me.

Soon, a petite brunette rounded the corner. Geoffrey's eyes were drawn to a triangular pin on the collar of her blue shirt-waist dress. He knew she could tell him where to find the four girls. When he stepped out from behind the bushes, the startled girl gasped.

"Sorry," Geoffrey said with a friendly smile. "I didn't mean to scare you. I'm Paul Phillips and I wanted to surprise some old friends of mine. I think they belong to Delta. One's named Barbara Flowers. You know her?"

"Yes, I know Barbara. She's one of my social club sisters, but she's not on campus right now. She and her roommate, Suzanne Yates, left just yesterday to practice-teach in Tupelo. By the way, I'm Kate Whaley."

Geoffrey, who was momentarily stunned by Kate's reply, felt an uncontrollable urge well up inside him. He casually put his right hand into his jacket pocket as if he might be reaching for a stick of gum. "What about Janine Walton or Arlene Harris?"

"Gosh, Paul, looks like you're out of luck. They've gone, too. None of them will be back on campus until the end of the semester. I'm sorry I can't be more help."

Geoffrey grabbed Kate and clamped his left hand over her mouth so tightly that she could barely breathe, much less scream for help.

"Be still and don't make a sound, or I'll slice your throat," he hissed as he pressed the button on his switchblade and held the razor sharp blade along the edge of her neck, just underneath her chin. Then he released his hand from her mouth.

"Okay, but please don't hurt me," Kate begged, her eyes bulging with fear.

He lowered his hand and placed the point of the knife into the small of her back as they walked toward his car. Jerking open the door, he shoved her in the front seat. He put the switchblade back into his jacket pocket and got in behind the wheel.

"Lie down." Kate, terrified, did as she was told.

Geoffrey's face flushed with anger. He chewed on the inside of his cheek as he cranked the car. After they had gotten out of town, he pulled off onto a deserted road and stopped the car. "Sit up, bitch."

Kate was shaking and crying as Geoffrey taped her mouth and put handcuffs on her wrists.

"Lie back down, and don't move or I'll cut you to pieces."

Geoffrey never said another word until he reached his house. He ripped the tape from Kate's mouth with such force that she let out a gasp of pain. "I told you to keep quiet," he said fiercely.

They got out of the car and walked up to the front door. Once they were inside, he took the key from his pocket and unlocked the handcuffs.

Only then did Kate get up enough nerve to speak. "You bastard, I never did anything to you. Take me back to the campus right now, or I'll scream my head off."

"Go ahead. Nobody's anywhere around. The nearest neighbor is three miles away. I think we'll listen to some music." He walked across the room and flipped on his stereo.

"Why'd you get so mad when I told you your friends weren't on campus? That's crazy," Kate persisted.

"Your precious social club refused to give a bid to my girlfriend after y'all made her think she was getting one. She got so upset she ran off in her car and killed herself."

"You mean Angela Burrell? I heard about what happened to her. I'm sorry. Paul, you know she was just a little overweight, and Ole Miss has 'owned' the Miss Mississippi pageant for so long that this year we were ordered to get pledges who looked good enough to win beauty pageants. That way the 'W' might finally bring a halt to Ole Miss's monopoly."

"Damn, is that all y'all care about? Winning some beauty pageant? That's a crock of shit. Listen, you bitch, Angie told me about four girls who seemed to run the club. She blamed them for her not getting a bid. Now, I know all you Deltas are to blame. So every single one of you'll have to pay the consequences, starting with you."

The look in his steel-gray eyes let Kate know that his was not just an idle threat. She wheeled around to try to escape, but Geoffrey grabbed her by the back of the collar. Her dress ripped, and she fled into the kitchen and jerked open a drawer underneath the countertop, her fingers desperately fumbling for some sort of weapon. Just as she grasped a butcher knife, Geoffrey clubbed the back of her neck with both fists. The knife fell harmlessly to the floor as she collapsed in a heap. Geoffrey reached down and flipped her over on her back.

"Now, bitch, you're going to pay for what you did to Angie and our baby."

By this time, Kate had regained consciousness and Geoffrey stared at her menacingly as he pinned her down with his muscular body. She flung out her left arm, trying desperately to reach the knife, but couldn't make contact. She struggled to thwart off her attacker, but Geoffrey's strength was too much for her. The voice in his mind cunningly suggested that Kate represented his evil foster parents and he needed to punish her sexually for what they had done to him. He tore off her dress and underclothes and savagely raped her. Kate screamed as the pain shot throughout her entire body. "Stop it, you bastard!"

At first, Geoffrey's only responses were pig-like grunts and moans of sexual fulfillment. Then he wrapped one hand around her neck and snarled, "Why should I stop? Angie didn't have any way to relieve her pain and torment."

At that moment the "Triangle Killer" was born. Geoffrey wanted to humiliate his victim by using Delta's symbol as an insignia of his revenge, so he pierced Kate's forehead with the point of his switchblade. Bringing the knife down slowly, he carved out the shape of an equilateral triangle as carefully as if he were peeling a piece of delicate fruit. As an afterthought, he jerked the skin from the flesh. Kate screamed and bucked, trying to throw Geoffrey off balance, but she was no match for his physical prowess. Geoffrey caressed the piece of skin with his fingers and rubbed it against his cheek. A scowl spread across his face and he threw the skin down on the floor. Wrapping both hands around the handle of the switchblade, he raised his arms and brought the knife down with such force that it penetrated Kate's supple body all the way to the hilt. The sucking noise of the knife being pulled out of her flesh and the blood rushing from the wound sent Geoffrey into a frenzy, and he repeatedly stabbed Kate until her thrashing finally ceased.

Afterwards, Geoffrey stood up and took several steps backwards to admire his handiwork, alternately sobbing and gasping for breath. His skin was covered with beads of perspiration, glistening in the fluorescent lights, and he wiped the sweat from his forehead to keep the salty liquid from burning his eyes. He trudged into his bedroom and tenderly picked up one of the baby dolls. He walked back into the kitchen and crammed the doll as far as he could into Kate's vagina.

"This is just a reminder that you Deltas destroyed our unborn baby as well as Angie."

After what seemed like hours, Geoffrey wrapped Kate's

corpse in an old blanket and carried it outside. He placed the bundle in the trunk of his car, hoping that the blood wouldn't soak into the rubber matting. During the drive to Columbus, the fact that he had actually murdered someone with the strength of his own two hands hit Geoffrey full force. His head began to spin and he thought for a moment that he was going to be sick. He rolled down the window and breathed in huge gulps of fresh air. In a few moments, a feeling of calmness came over him. Angie's vision crept into his mind and he knew then that he had done the right thing. He reached over and turned on the radio and hummed the tunes of the songs the DJ was playing. When he arrived in Columbus, he took the back way to the campus and dumped the naked body behind the Delta house. In the balmy stillness of the night, Geoffrey looked toward the building where his enemies lived and shook his fist. "This ought to scare the hell out of you Deltas." Like a thief in the night, he left as unobtrusively as he had come.

When he arrived home, Geoffrey sat down in front of Angie's shrine to receive her blessing. Caressing one of her pictures in his trembling hands, he cried out, "Oh, Angie, I killed her just for practice. I promise you one day I'll get the four responsible for taking you and our baby from me."

His eyes glazed over and red from crying, Geoffrey plodded to the kitchen, totally oblivious to the blood all over the floor. The triangular piece of skin caught his eye and he bent down to pick it up. *This can serve as a memento of my revenge.* Rooting around in the cabinet under the sink, he finally found what he was looking for, an empty quart jar which had once contained some of his grandmother's homemade fig preserves. He filled the jar half full of water and let the skin fall from his fingers, smiling as it kissed the surface of the water and floated like a leaf. He replaced the lid and held the jar up to the light, turning it around and nodding his head in approval as he did so.

Geoffrey continued staring at his souvenir until the clanking of the air conditioner's compressor brought him back to reality. With the same gentleness that a father puts his newborn back in his crib, he carefully placed the jar in the refrigerator.

Showing no remorse, Geoffrey calmly cleaned up the bloody kitchen with warm water and a strong cleanser. He rinsed out the mop and the cleaning rags in the sink and laughed as the red water swirled down the drain. When he passed the laundry room, he realized that he had one more chore to do: wash the bloody clothes and the blanket. Afterwards, sated by his kill, Geoffrey didn't even bother to rinse the stench of blood and sweat from his body but lay down on his bed to record the events of the day in his notepad.

5

The next morning a student on her way to work in the dining hall discovered Kate's body. The horrified girl's screams brought campus security. Since there had never been a homicide on the campus before, the local rent-a-cops knew they were in over their heads and immediately notified the Columbus police and called for an ambulance. When the ambulance arrived, the attendants poured out and raced to the body. They grimaced at the ghastly sight. Although the victim's chest area was covered with purplish stab wounds and blood, their eyes were immediately drawn to the area on her forehead where the skin had been ripped away, leaving a dried crust of blood in the shape of a triangle. They checked for vital signs and finding none, immediately attempted mouth-to-mouth resuscitation. All their efforts were in vain so they notified the county coroner and waited for the Columbus police.

Officer Bertram Barron was in his patrol car cruising down Seventh Avenue when he heard the orders from the dispatcher. He set his cup of coffee on the dash and flipped on his siren. He made a U-turn at the next intersection and raced to the campus. By the time he arrived, the campus police were trying to calm fifteen or twenty hysterical girls, all screaming at once.

"Coming through," huffed the overweight, balding police-man, whose short stature and barrel chest made him resemble a bantam rooster.

The girls stepped back, but their wailing continued. Even a seasoned veteran like Barron was not prepared for what he saw. "Jesus, what happened here?" Almost gagging on his words, he looked toward the campus police questioningly.

One replied, "This young lady discovered the body about seven this morning on her way to breakfast. Says the victim's name is Kate Whaley. What do you make of that patch of miss-ing skin on her forehead, Bert?"

"I dunno—maybe some kind of friggin' ritual. You know a bunch of the kids around here are rumored to be involved with some sort of satanic cult crap. Maybe they did this. It's pretty evident she wasn't killed here since there's no blood anywhere around."

As Barron spoke with the campus cops, several more police cars pulled up and one of the men began cordoning off the area. Finally, Ellis Braxton, the chief of detectives from the homi-cide division, arrived to take charge. Braxton, a tall, thin, sandy-haired man in his early thirties, was filling in for the chief of police, who was on vacation.

"Found out anything, Bert?"

"Not much. Kid's name is Kate Whaley. Someone found the body here this morning. My guess is the killer somehow got her in his car and took her off campus and murdered her and then brought her body back here. Look at that place on her forehead where the skin's missing. Forms a perfect triangle. I've never seen anything like this before. Got a real weirdo on our hands."

The conversation was interrupted by the arrival of the coun-ty coroner, Franklin Thomas "Doc" Jamieson. Wearing his usual attire of khaki pants and shirt and cowboy boots, he ambled toward the two and gave his customary tug on his left ear as he drawled, "Well, boys, let's have a look. Get those damn squalling girls away. I can't think with them howling like tomcats."

Methodically, he took pictures of the body as he began his preliminary exam. A more detailed one would be done in the morgue later.

"She's been dead between four and six hours because her body feels cool, and rigor mortis has set in only in her neck and jaw. Plus, her wounds have already begun to indurate. Whew, the sonofabitch must have really wanted to hurt her. All those stab wounds and that weird mark on her forehead."

After examining the body a few more minutes in its initial surroundings, the coroner decided it was time to take the remains back to the morgue.

Jamieson arrived at the Lowndes County Morgue and headed to the autopsy room to begin his now familiar but always unpleasant task of performing a detailed examination of a corpse. He glanced around the sterile isolated room and drew a deep breath. After he had pulled on his latex gloves and looked down at Kate's body lying on the stainless steel table, he shook his head. "How could anyone do this to somebody so young?"

When Jamieson had finished the exam, he signed the temporary death certificate, listing multiple stab wounds as the preliminary cause of death. At that moment, his assistant, George Fletcher, walked in with a terrified young girl.

"Doc, this is Ginger Prescott, Kate Whaley's roommate."

"Ginger, I'm sorry to have to ask you to come down here, but we needed someone to officially identify the body before I can get started on the au—uh, procedure."

The girl appeared to be in a complete state of shock even before she saw Kate's body lying on the table. Trembling from both the icy cold of the room and from the unpleasant task she knew she had to perform, Ginger glanced at the body and quickly averted her eyes. She burst into tears and mumbled, "That's Kate," and ran out of the room, gagging and crying.

Jamieson followed and gently put his arms around her. "I'm sorry you had to do this. George'll drive you back to the campus now."

As Ginger and the deputy coroner were walking out the door, Jamieson called out, "Don't worry. The police will catch whoever did this to Kate."

After the two were out of hearing range, the coroner slammed his palm against the wall in anger. "You're damn right they will, and the son-of-a-bitch'll get what's coming to him!"

Jamieson sighed. It'd been a rough week already. First, the car crash victim and now this. The poor girl in the car had been six weeks pregnant. He was glad he hadn't told her father the truth. It would have broken the man's heart. Of course, it had to go into the official report, but he'd decided to put off mailing it until later.

He took out his camera and photographed Kate's body from various angles, then weighed and measured it. He recorded these measurements on a form labeled Case Number 85-45898, Kate Whaley. After the customary tug on his ear, he reached up and flipped the switch of the overhead microphone and intoned, "This is the body of an eighteen-year-old Caucasian female." Thus began the detailed external examination and internal dissection of Geoffrey Bockker's first murder victim.

The external examination was progressing smoothly until Jamieson began probing the pubic area of the victim. He quickly reached up and turned off the microphone. His fingers had touched something slick. Grasping the object, he pulled until it protruded through the vaginal opening. He eased it out and stared at the vinyl doll, momentarily shaking his head. He had never come across anything like this in his work. He flipped the switch back on and made a note of what he had found. He laid the doll in a sterile tray and continued with the rest of the examination.

Jamieson was ready to begin the autopsy itself. He placed the scalpel at Kate's left shoulder and carefully made the first incision. He drew the blade down until he reached the midpoint between her breasts. The procedure was repeated on her right shoulder.

As gruesome as the autopsy was, the hardest part would come later. Kate's parents would have to claim the remains of their child, an agonizing experience even the veteran coroner did not look forward to. George Fletcher walked in just as Jamieson finished the autopsy. Jamieson immediately showed George what he had found.

George stared at the little vinyl doll. "What the hell does it mean?"

"Damned if I know, but Ellis Braxton needs to see this right away."

The two men gently laid Kate's body on the stainless steel mobile cart and rolled it around the corner to the room next door. There they placed Kate in one of the sliding drawers in the refrigeration unit until her parents and the funeral director could arrive to take her body home.

When they got back to the coroner's office, George Fletcher placed the call. "Ellis, Doc wants you to get over here right away. He's found something that'll blow your mind."

6

Although Geoffrey was so exhausted that he had slept all day, he suddenly sat straight up in bed, petrified from fear and gasping for breath. His skin felt clammy and his clothes, drenched with perspiration, stuck to his body. He had been reliving over and over the moments right after Angie's accident. Instead of being carried up on a stretcher from the wreck, though, Angie was walking up the side of the ravine. Her entire body was charred and covered with oozing blood. A huge gash ran diagonally across her once beautiful face. Her head tilted so far sideways that Geoffrey couldn't understand what kept it from toppling over. She held a bloody infant in her outstretched arms as she called to him, "Just look what they did to me and our baby." Afterwards, a mist enveloped her entire body and she disappeared.

Now that he was fully awake, the urge to kill raged through Geoffrey's entire being. Kate's murder had whetted his primal appetite and he knew he had to strike again. The pounding in his head and the blinding lights returned and his inner voice urged him on with its litany, "Kill them now! Kill them now!" He knew, however, that it was not feasible to go to the campus

until later. To ease his tension he took a quick shower and put
on a pair of navy blue slacks and a madras shirt that Angie had
given him for his birthday. He lay down on the bed and opened
Danny's annual. The faces of the Delta Social Club taunted him
with their incessant smiles. He slammed the annual shut and
shifted his gaze toward the picture he had cut out of the book.
What right did any of these bitches have to be happy? "Before
I'm through with you, I'll slice those damn smiles off your
faces," he snarled.

The monster in his soul now bellowed and raged and
Geoffrey knew he couldn't put off his mission any longer.
Realizing that it wouldn't be as easy to subdue his next victim,
he went upstairs and rooted around until he found the bottle of
chloroform he had used to kill bugs for his biology collection.
He put the bottle and a package of gauze pads in a sack and
came back downstairs. He picked up his switchblade and his
car keys from the dresser and headed toward the front door.

During the twenty-five minute ride, Geoffrey mapped out a
plan of action. He knew that the girls would be suspicious of
strangers, and he chuckled when he devised an almost fool-
proof method to gain their confidence.

His red and white 1957 Chevy Bel Air certainly aroused no
suspicion when he pulled onto the campus because most of the
"W" girls dated State boys. He parked in the woods behind the
Delta house and got out, watching for girls wearing the now
familiar triangle. Like a hunter lining up the sight on his prey,
Geoffrey drew a deep breath when he spotted a beautiful
blonde and moved toward her. When the girl looked up and saw
a stranger approaching, she recoiled in fear. With the devious
mind of an already seasoned killer, Geoffrey quickly acted to
allay her fears. "Hi. I'm looking for my sister, Angeline Carter.
You know her?" Before the girl could answer, Geoffrey moved
his left hand into his jacket pocket and said, "First Kate, now

you!"

The girl turned to run away. Geoffrey's right arm snaked out and grabbed her by the wrist. He twisted her arm behind her while he clamped the dampened gauze across her face with his left hand. After a few seconds, her head slumped forward and her body went limp. Geoffrey put his arm around her shoulders and walked her to his car. He opened the door and shoved her inside. He reached into the glove compartment for the ski rope and tied her hands together. With a smile of satisfaction, he closed the door, got in the car and drove off.

In a few minutes, the girl stirred and moaned when the effect of the chloroform began to wear off.

"What's your name?" he asked brusquely.

"Cassie Franklin," the girl mumbled.

Geoffrey's overwhelming desire to punish Cassie could wait no longer. He drove the car off the highway and onto the shoulder of the road. He reached over and pulled her close to his body. She could feel his hot breath on her face and shuddered when she looked into his cold, steel eyes. Geoffrey grabbed Cassie by her hair and jerked her face toward his. He forced his tongue so far into her mouth that she began to choke.

"What's the matter, bitch, haven't you ever been French-kissed before?"

"No, I hate it."

"A little goody-two shoes. Okay, baby, I'm going to show you something that'll make you feel real good."

Cassie trembled with fear. Geoffrey pulled her head toward his lap and the thought of what he was going to force her to do made her nauseated. She closed her mouth tightly and swallowed hard.

"Oh, shit," Geoffrey mumbled as he leaned over and opened the door just in time for Cassie to vomit. He angrily rubbed his handkerchief over her mouth and slammed the door.

"Baby, I'll finish what I started when we get back to my house. You'll get to meet my Angie there."

"Who's Angie?" Cassie asked meekly.

"My angel baby that you Delta bitches wouldn't let in your precious social club. You're the reason she's dead."

"Oh, that poor girl who ran off into the ravine and got killed? I'm sorry. I really liked her a lot. But I had only one vote. The older members didn't want her in. They said she was nothing but a fat whore."

This insult to Angie's memory infuriated Geoffrey and he wanted to kill Cassie at that moment, but the sound of tires crunching on the gravel thwarted him. He cursed when he looked in the mirror and saw a deputy get out and approach the car. He pulled out his switchblade and cut the ropes from Cassie's wrists. "Keep quiet if you know what's good for you." He pushed the knife against her body for emphasis.

As the deputy flashed his light in their faces, he asked, "Son, young lady, is there a problem?"

"No, but thanks anyway, officer. My date wasn't feeling too well so I pulled over for a few minutes. She's better now so we'll be on our way. We want to try to catch the nine o'clock movie."

The deputy nodded and spit out a stream of tobacco juice on the ground. "Okay, son, but watch out. Y'know there's a killer loose somewhere. You can't be too careful."

"Whew," Geoffrey sighed when the deputy was out of sight. "Hold still while I tie you up again." Cassie flinched with pain when he jerked the rope across her wrists so tightly that it made a raw place on her arm. "Sorry about that."

Geoffrey cranked the car and pulled back onto the road. Tears formed in Cassie's eyes and she finally got up enough nerve to say something. "Why did you kill Kate?" she whimpered. "She never did anything to you or Angie." A tone of defiance began to force its way into her voice.

"She belonged to the Delta Social Club, didn't she?"

Neither Geoffrey nor Cassie said another word until they were inside Geoffrey's house. He walked over to the stereo and nonchalantly turned it on. "I feel like listening to some good old rock'n'roll." With the strains of "Don't Be Cruel" filling the room, Geoffrey leered at his victim and whispered, "Now, Cassie, for the good time I promised you."

To make the experience more pleasurable, Geoffrey dragged Cassie into his bedroom, where Angie could watch the proceedings. Although Cassie and the other girls on campus had been warned by the police not to put up a struggle, she realized that fighting back was her only means of survival. After he had cut the ropes from her wrists, he threw her on the bed and leaned over her. Cassie drew her right hand back and thrust her fingers directly into Geoffrey's eyes.

"Damn!" he yelled, jerking his head back and rubbing his eyes.

Cassie lashed out with her right leg and kicked Geoffrey as hard as she could in the groin. He doubled over in pain, grabbing his crotch.

"You bastard! I'm not going to be your second victim."

Cassie ran out of the bedroom and up the stairs. By this time Geoffrey had enough strength to follow her, although he had to keep blinking his eyes to regain normal vision. His crotch still hurt like hell but he had to finish what he had started. Cassie flung open the first door she found. She slammed the door and turned the lock. Gasping for breath, she willed herself to remain calm. She looked up and saw her only hope. If she could get to the window, she'd leap to the ground. Even a broken leg was better that the alternative Geoffrey had planned for her.

Fear compounded her every move. She heard the door give

way from the weight of Geoffrey's powerful body just after she managed to squeeze the upper part of her torso through the tiny space. Geoffrey ran to the window and grabbed her legs, even though she kicked and screamed. He jerked her back out of the window, smashing her head against the claw-footed tub.

"Had enough, bitch?"

Geoffrey picked up Cassie's limp body and carried it down the stairs and into his bedroom. Although he still hurt, he raped her, smiling with added satisfaction when he realized she was still a virgin. He clicked open his switchblade and angrily jabbed it into her vagina. The blade of the knife easily sliced through the tender flesh. To cause even more pain, he twisted the blade of the knife around inside her body and brought out small pieces of flesh when he withdrew the blade. He calmly wiped his knife blade clean on his slacks and reached around and picked up one of the baby dolls from the shrine. He shoved it up into Cassie's body as far as he could reach. She had regained consciousness by this time and let out a blood-curdling scream as the doll penetrated her already burning tissue. Geoffrey repeated his ritual of carving out a triangle on his victim's forehead, except this time he turned the triangle upside down, and carefully laid the skin on the dressing table next to his bed. A deluge of blood flowed from the wounds as he repeatedly stabbed her in the chest and abdomen. Cassie tried to scream, but the only sounds that came from her mouth were gurgling noises followed by crimson spittle. When she grew still, Geoffrey realized she was dead and finally ceased his carnage.

He picked up the triangular piece of skin and carried it to the refrigerator and put it into the jar, along with his souvenir from Kate. The two trophies floating lazily in the water brought a smile to his face. But he still wasn't satisfied. Angie's real killers remained unpunished.

Although Cassie's blood had seeped into the bedclothes and even dripped onto the carpet, Geoffrey decided to get rid of her body first. He followed the same procedure for transporting her body back to the campus as he had with Kate's.

Disposing of the body was more difficult, though, since campus security had been beefed up. Geoffrey didn't want to arouse suspicion so he waited until the last whistle had blown. This signal indicated that the girls had five minutes to get into their dorms. He watched with envy as the couples kissed good-night or the boys managed one last "feel" in the back of the car. When all the cars had left, the campus was deserted except for the patrols of the "W" cops.

In the darkness, Geoffrey fought to control his ragged breathing and watched the occupant of the car parked nearest the laundry. When the cop's head slumped down on his chest, Geoffrey knew that he must have dozed off. He stealthily opened his car door and unlocked the trunk. His eyes darted furtively from left to right, and he picked up the body and slowly unrolled it from the blanket. With an air of smug satis-faction, he stuffed the blanket back in the trunk and drove off into the night without the dozing guard hearing anything.

Minutes later, one of the myriad of cats that lived near the laundry leapt across the hood of the patrol car of the sleeping cop. He awoke with a start and jumped out to see where the noise had come from. "Oh, my God, not another one!" he yelled when he almost tripped over Cassie's bloody body. He ran back to his car and blew the horn, the prearranged signal that something had happened, and radioed for help. Soon all hell broke loose on the campus. The flashing lights and blaring sirens reminded the old army veteran of a World War II air raid. The girls poured out of their dorms, even though "lights out" had been in effect for twenty minutes.

When Barron and the police chief, Buster Gates, arrived and saw the triangular area of missing skin on the girl's forehead, they knew that the first murder had not been an isolated incident. Gates had curtailed his vacation as soon as he had been notified about Kate Whaley's murder.

"We're going to have a full-scale panic on our hands, Bert. These girls will be leaving here in droves. I can just hear their mammas and daddies when their babies call home to tell them about this murder. We've got to get our asses in gear and catch this maniac before he kills someone else."

Doc Jamieson appeared and began his preliminary investigation. He tugged on his ear and drawled, "Damn, I see our 'Triangle Killer' has struck again. Same M.O. as before. Wonder why he turned the triangle upside down this time? God, he even stabbed her in the vagina. Poor kid, she must have put up quite a struggle. Look at that contusion at the base of her neck and the bruise on her forehead. Let's get out of here, boys," he called to his assistants. "I'll check her more thoroughly at the morgue. God, two more parents now have to be told that their baby has been brutally killed. Do you have a positive ID on her, Buster? I don't want to have to drag some other poor kid down to the morgue again."

"Name's Cassie Franklin and she lived in the Delta house. Same as Kate Whaley."

"Yeah, that's gotta explain why he cut out the triangle on their foreheads. You notice the insignia on the front door of their house? The Greek letter for Delta is shaped like a triangle. Looks like we have our common denominator. Wonder if he left his other calling card? If we can just find a motive…and a suspect."

After the ambulance carrying Cassie's body to the morgue had left, Gates went to the house where the Deltas lived and began to question a group of hysterical girls milling around in front.

One of the girls stopped sobbing long enough to reply. "I was looking out my window and saw this real good-looking guy talking to Cassie earlier tonight. They were facing the house and I remember he was wearing navy blue slacks and a madras shirt. Oh yeah, and a maroon windbreaker. Then the phone rang and I went to answer it. By the time I finished talking, they had disappeared and I didn't think anymore about it until later. We realized after lights out and room check that Cassie hadn't signed her check-in card. That's something we have to do here at the 'W' so they'll know if we've gotten back in the house or not. I always thought it was kinda silly. Now, I don't think so." The distraught girl broke down again and looked wistfully off in the distance.

"Did any of you other girls see anything earlier tonight?" Gates asked.

They all solemnly shook their heads.

"Just take it easy and for God's sake, be careful. We'll catch him before he strikes again. I promise you."

Gates and Barron walked back to their car with Gates muttering to himself, "I hope to hell we do."

Jamieson had returned to the county morgue to begin Cassie's autopsy. He followed the same ritual he had with Kate's body. He sighed and shook his head when he inserted his hand inside her vagina and pulled out a doll exactly like the one he had found in Kate. After he had finished writing the information on Cassie's chart, he slammed it down on the table and struck his palm with his fist.

"Damn! How many more times am I going to have to do this before the monster is stopped?"

7

That afternoon, Deputy Jake Conner was sitting at his desk in the Oktibbeha County Sheriff's office when the phone rang. The voice on the other end announced, "This is Ellis Braxton in Chief Gates's office in Columbus. There's been another murder. We're sending you a photo of the 'Triangle Killer's latest victim. Call us back if you have any information." Conner hung up and stared in disbelief as he looked at the picture coming over the wire.

"Oh, my God! It's the same girl I saw parked on the side of the highway last night. Damn! I felt somethin' was wrong. Why didn't I question them some more? I probably could've saved the poor kid's life."

He closed his eyes and tried to visualize what the car had looked like. Slowly the image of Geoffrey's Chevy formed in his mind. Although it had been dark and he had seen the couple only in the illumination of his flashlight, he distinctly remembered the boy had been a good-looking muscular kid with grayish eyes and a dark blond flattop.

Conner rushed into the sheriff's office and stuck the picture in front of Carl Grayson's face.

"This just came over the wire from Columbus. The killer's struck again. I saw this girl and her boyfriend parked on the side of Highway 82 early last night, 'bout a half mile from the Crossroads. When I questioned them, the boy told me the girl wasn't feeling good. Damn it! I had a gut feeling he wasn't telling the truth. He was drivin' a red and white '57 Chevy Bel Air. Wait a minute, I remember somethin' else, Sheriff. There was a Mississippi State decal on the back window."

Carl Grayson jumped up from behind his desk. "His car would have to be registered if he goes to school there."

After scratching around on the desk for a few minutes, the sheriff spat out a string of curse words and angrily yelled to his secretary who was in the outer office, "Mildred! Find your damn copy of the State directory and look up campus security. I can't find shit on my desk."

"Sure thing, Sheriff. I've got it right here." Mildred Chapman, always the model of efficiency, quickly dialed the number for her boss, stifling a laugh as she did so.

"This is Carl Grayson. Could I please speak to Chief Smith? It's an emergency. Get him to the phone right now."

"Carl, what's up?" Smith asked anxiously. "Is one of our kids in trouble?"

"I'm afraid so, Larry. Do you have a list of all the cars registered to your students?"

"Yeah, but it'll take a little while to look through the card file. What kind of description can you give me?"

We think it was a red and white 1957 Chevy Bel Air. We know it had a State decal on the back window so we figured it must belong to one of your kids. Call me back as soon as you have any information."

"Will do."

Smith's secretary opened her metal file box labeled 'Cars'

and meticulously searched through each section copying the pertinent information whenever she came to a Chevy Bel Air. An hour later, she took the list over to the chief and then dialed the sheriff's office for him.

Carl Grayson picked up the phone on the first ring. "That you, Larry? Got anything?"

"Yeah, 'bout fifty names. We couldn't break it down to the specific color, but it's a start."

"Great! We'll be right over." Grayson hung up and grabbed the keys to his patrol car. "Jake—! Come on," he called as he hurried out the door.

It took the pair about ten minutes to get to the campus security office. Smith was waiting for them. "Tell me what's going on," he said.

"Jake says he saw that Franklin girl, the 'W'-student who got killed, in a car with a boy that, we think, goes to State. He was driving the car we described to you. Let me have a look at the list. Wait a minute. You got a copy of last year's annual so we can find a face to go with the name?"

"Yeah, we keep one to help find delinquent traffic offenders. You know most kids won't pay their fines unless we make 'em. Here you go."

Grayson flipped through the book to the index. "Jake, you call out the names to me and I'll give you the page numbers to write down beside each one."

"Carl, that doesn't always work," Smith interrupted. "Sometimes those page numbers aren't right."

"Well, that's the best way for now. It'd take too long to turn through each class one page at a time."

After Conner had written down the pages beside the fifty names, he began searching through the annual to see if he recognized any of the faces. This task would have seemed menial most of the time, but now Conner's heart was beating with excitement. He had gone through all the A's with no luck when suddenly the face of the boy he had seen in the car stared back at him.

"Sheriff, it's him. His name is Geoffrey Bockker." He pointed to the photo.

Grayson studied the picture. "The listing says his address is 4918 Mockingbird Road. That's out in the county. Come on, Jake. Let's go pay Mr. Bockker a visit. We won't need a search warrant, but if we see anything suspicious, we'll prepare an affidavit and search warrant when we get back and take it to Judge Johnson to sign."

Grayson and Conner jumped into the car. Conner reached over to switch on the siren, but Grayson caught his arm in mid-air. "No sense announcing our arrival, Jake. After all, this is just a social call."

It took a while to finally find Mockingbird Road. "Hey, this is the old Taylor farm," Conner said. "Remember? They got killed in a wreck coming home from a State game last year. Wonder why the kid lives here?"

When they rounded a curve, Conner got a feeling in his stomach of both revulsion and excitement. Just off the road in front of an old two-story farmhouse sat a red and white '57 Chevy. "That's the car, Sheriff," he croaked hoarsely, barely able to get the words out of his mouth.

They pulled up in front of the house, got out of the car, and casually walked toward the front door.

"Let's just play it cool, Jake. I don't want to upset him too much."

After the sheriff had knocked several times, Geoffrey finally came to the door. His heart leapt to his throat when he recognized the deputy who had approached his car the evening before.

"What can I do for y'all?" Geoffrey's voice was steady and polite.

"Son, we just want to talk to you about the girl Deputy Conner saw you with yesterday evening. You two were parked on the side of Highway 82 between here and Columbus."

"Yes, sir. I remember the deputy. My date was sick so I had to stop the car for her to throw up. We were going to the movie in Starkville, but she didn't feel any better after you talked to us, so I took her back to the campus. I haven't heard from her since."

"What time was it when you took her back?"

"I'm not sure, but I believe it was around nine."

"Did anybody see you?"

"No, I let her out at the back door of the Delta house because she was feeling pretty bad. Then I drove straight back here. Why do you want to know?"

"Son, she was murdered last night, and we just wanted to ask you what time you'd last seen her."

"Oh, my God, no! I can't believe it. What happened?"

Grayson eyed Geoffrey suspiciously. "You mean she's your girlfriend and nobody's told you anything about it yet? That's kind of hard to believe."

"She wasn't my girlfriend. Somebody arranged a blind date for us. Last night was the first time I had ever laid eyes on her. I slept in all day so I haven't talked to anybody. Would you like to come in and look around?"

"No, we just wanted to find out when you had last seen the young lady alive. Thanks. We may be back later, though."

After the two men had left, Geoffrey heaved a sigh of relief. *Yeah, bastards, I know you'll be back, but you won't find anything to connect me with any friggin' murders.*

Geoffrey rushed to the refrigerator and grabbed the container of trophies. He couldn't destroy them. He'd have to put them in a safe place for a while.

Rummaging around on the floor of his closet, Geoffrey found an empty Bass Weejuns' shoebox and placed the jar, the knife, the rope, the handcuffs, and the two remaining dolls in it. After walking about fifty yards behind the house into some woods, he began digging with a shovel he had gotten from the barn. The shoebox was small, so the hole didn't have to be very deep. The action brought back the memories of the many times he had buried the helpless animals his voice had ordered him to mutilate during his childhood. But those memories didn't upset him. Instead, he just calmly went about the business of hiding the evidence. To make sure that he could find the burial place when he needed to, Geoffrey chose a towering pine tree and carved a triangle just above eye level. Then, he nonchalantly picked up the shovel and walked back toward the house, stopping only to toss it back inside the barn.

Now let them come back and search all they want to. They won't find a thing.

Geoffrey knelt in front of Angie's shrine like a supplicant seeking the answer to a prayer and slowly began to sob as he talked to her. "Why'd you have to leave me, baby?"

His mood suddenly changed when he glanced over at the picture he had cut out of the "W" annual and he seethed, "I'll get you yet."

He realized the picture of the four girls and the notepad could also incriminate him so he took the two objects and hid them in a duffel bag, which he stashed behind a loose board in the back of his upstairs closet.

Geoffrey stood in the tub letting the warm water from the

showerhead massage his aching muscles and relax his tormented soul. Afterwards, he lay down on the bed and looked at the
local paper to read about his exploits.

For the last few days, the entire front page of the *Columbus
Dispatch* had been devoted to the murders. Until these incidents, the most infamous event in the area had been the alleged
killing of a socialite by her next-door neighbor, a college student. That had been a single, isolated incident, but the murders
of the "W" girls led everyone to believe that a psychopath was
on the loose.

Geoffrey grinned as he read the headline *Search for
'Triangle Killer' Intensifies.* He liked the idea of being given a
nickname. That made him seem important.

*Angie baby, we've got 'em where we want 'em. They won't
forget about us any time soon. Oh, shit. The clothes belonging
to me and the two girls and the bloody bed sheets. Damn, I'll
have to get rid of them too.* He decided he'd take them to the
old garbage dump just outside of town and stuff them in the
incinerator.

As the two law officials were on their way back to the sheriff's office, Conner remarked to Grayson, "That little shit. He
knew we wouldn't go through the house without a warrant. I'll
bet he's gettin' rid of the evidence right now."

"Probably so, but when we get back, I'll prepare the affidavit and search warrant and you run a check on Bockker to see
if he's got any priors."

Grayson walked in the door waving the affidavit and warrant toward Conner's face. "We're all set. What'd you find
out?"

"Nothing turned up. If he had a juvenile record, the courts

probably sealed it."

Grayson frowned. "I guess you're right. Let's go back to Mr. Bockker's house and turn the screws in the little weasel. I'm willing to bet that the punk'll spill his guts if we put enough pressure on him." Grayson called out to Mildred to get Chief Gates on the phone.

"Right away, Sheriff." Mildred looked up the number on her Rolodex and immediately began dialing. "Hello, this is Mildred Chapman at the sheriff's office in Starkville. Sheriff Grayson wants to speak to Chief Gates. It's very important."

As soon as Gates' voice came through, Grayson said, "Buster, we think we've got your 'Triangle Killer' here in Starkville. He's a State student named Geoffrey Bockker. One of my men recognized the girl from the picture you sent out over the wire. We've already been out to his house and asked him a few questions. Acted cool as a cucumber. Even invited us in. Thought you might like to ride with us when we go back out there with a search warrant."

Buster Gates put the phone down and let out a whistle. "Bockker, if you are the 'Triangle Killer,' you're in for a helluva time, 'cause we're gonna nail your ass to the wall and use it for target practice."

The two men in the sheriff's office tapped the soles of their boots on the floor as they awaited the arrival of Gates. Grayson puffed on a cigarette and Conner chewed on a plug of tobacco, grunting something unintelligible every few seconds in response to some statement made by the sheriff. When they heard a car pull up in front and stop abruptly, both men ran out the door to greet their visitor.

"Let's go, guys. I'll get in the car with you since you know the exact location!" Gates shouted.

The three men ran to the squad car and jumped in. Grayson

backed up and headed the vehicle toward Mockingbird Road. When they arrived, the sheriff knocked at the door several times before a sleepy-looking Geoffrey finally opened it.

"Come in, gentlemen." He greeted them with a smirk on his face, as if he knew a dark secret.

"I told you we'd be back, kid," Grayson said as he sauntered into the house. "Now, Bockker, I'm not going to beat around the bush this time. We've got a search warrant and I want you to answer some more questions for me while we take a look around." He then stuck the warrant in Geoffrey's face.

"Look around all you want to. I've got nothing to hide."

"We'll do just that," Grayson countered as they began poking around the house. "Son, Deputy Conner says he remembers that you were wearing navy blue pants and a madras shirt. Why don't you get them for us right now."

"Well, I—I sent 'em to the laundry. They're not back yet."

"Maybe you'd just better get them back as soon as you can. You follow?"

"Yes si—sir, I'll do that this afternoon."

"Son, we'd like you to take us on a little tour of your house if you don't mind."

The three men followed Bockker into his bedroom. Grayson's perceptive eyes honed in on a spot on the carpet, which was just a shade darker than the area around it. He bent down to take a closer look. "Geoffrey, can you explain why this section of carpet looks damp?"

Geoffrey stammered, "I—I spilled a Coke there last night and tried to scrub it up. Guess I didn't do a real good job."

"Don't guess you did, Geoffrey. This doesn't look like Coke to me. Give me your knife, Deputy Conner."

Grayson very carefully cut a wide area around the edge of the stain and removed the piece of carpet, placing it in a paper bag. "We'll just let the boys at the state lab determine what kind of stain this is. For your sake, Geoffrey, it better be Coke."

After the sheriff had cut out the patch of carpet, he noticed Geoffrey's shrine to Angie. "Bockker, what the hell is this?"

"That's my girlfriend, Angie. She was killed in an accident last week in Columbus."

"Oh, yeah," Gates interjected. "She ran off into a ravine. Poor kid. Never had a chance. Her car burst into flames. God, it must have been horrible. Didn't I read in the final report that you were at the scene of the accident, Geoffrey?"

"Yes sir, I was. I talked to one of the firemen and he told me the police might get in touch with me, but they never did." Geoffrey buried his face in his hands so the men couldn't see him cry.

"Okay, son. It's okay." Grayson couldn't help feeling sorry for Geoffrey, even though he suspected somewhere inside the boy there lurked a demonic creature.

"Conner, go upstairs and see if you can find anything. I'll finish searching this area."

After a few minutes, the deputy came down. "Nothing up there, sir."

"I think we've seen enough here. Do you mind if we look at your car, Geoffrey?"

Geoffrey shook his head and handed the sheriff the keys. When they reached the car, Grayson unlocked the passenger door and looked inside, being careful not to touch anything. When he had finished searching the interior of the car, he unlocked the trunk. After scrutinizing it carefully, the sheriff closed the lid. "Let's impound it and have it taken to the lot where the boys'll go over it thoroughly."

Conner spotted the gray, weather-beaten barn and walked toward it. "What's in here, Geoffrey?"

"Nothing much, just some of my grandfather's old tools."

Conner opened the doors and inspected the barn carefully. Just as he was about to the close the doors, he spotted the shovel. "What've you been using this for?"

Instead of answering, Geoffrey grabbed his stomach and almost doubled over.

"Son, what's the matter?"

"I'm okay. It's just, uh, my ulcer."

Conner picked up the shovel carefully with his left hand. Little flakes of dried earth and pine needles fell into the paper bag he was holding in the other hand. "You been doing a little gardening in those woods back there, Geoffrey?"

"No sir, I haven't touched that shovel. Frankly, I'm kinda scared of what might be out there."

"Well, let's just take a look anyway. I think we'll start with the patch right behind the house."

"Let's spread out so we'll cover more area. Geoffrey, you come with me. Buster, you and Jake go toward the right. Give a holler if you find anything. I'll do the same."

Although Geoffrey still had the muscular body of a football player, he knew that he couldn't take on all three men at one time. Now that he and the sheriff were alone, he'd have to wait for just the right opportunity. Since the sheriff still had his car keys, he'd have to get them back if he wanted to escape. Thoughts of his past flashed in Geoffrey's mind. Everything ran together so fast that his brain felt like a spinning top. He knew he had to calm down to be ready when the opportunity arose. He breathed in and out deeply several times, and the panicky feeling subsided.

When he could no longer hear the other men, Geoffrey began a visual search for some sort of object to use on the sheriff. Bingo! He noticed an overhanging limb up ahead. He lunged in front of Grayson and pulled the limb back in one move. He let go and the limb caught the sheriff squarely in the face, knocking him off balance just enough for Geoffrey to attack him. Geoffrey turned around and struck the sheriff flush on the nose with all his strength, feeling the cartilage give way beneath his fist. The lawman fell to the ground with a thud, blood gushing from his broken nose. Geoffrey grabbed his car keys from the sheriff's pocket and took the handcuffs from his belt. Turning the sheriff over on his stomach, he pulled his arms backwards and snapped the handcuffs on them. He took out the sheriff's handkerchief and stuffed it in his mouth.

"This ought to hold you until I can get to my car."

While Geoffrey was attacking the sheriff, Buster Gates and Jake Conner hit pay dirt.

"God almighty, son, the killer's been here and left his mark. Look at that. Sheriff Grayson, come here quick. We've found something. Bockker's carved a triangle on a pine tree."

"That's strange, Chief Gates. He didn't answer you. The woods aren't that deep. Maybe I oughta go look for him. He'll sure as hell want to see this. You stay here. I'll find him."

The sheriff awoke and realized that he was choking on a balled-up rag with blood still pouring from his nose and into his throat. Damn punk, he thought. He'd get him for this. At that moment, though, his main concern was getting the handkerchief out of his mouth before he suffocated. He couldn't breathe through his nose and the blood was gagging him. He turned over on his back and scooted to a nearby tree where he worked his way to a standing position by slowly inching his way up the rough bark. The effort made his head reel and he knew that he would lapse into unconsciousness soon. At that moment, Jake Conner appeared. He grabbed the rag from the sheriff's mouth, enabling Grayson to get a decent breath after he had spit out a mouthful of blood.

"Sheriff, what happened?"

"The little bastard clobbered me with a limb and then punched my lights out. Here, get the cuff key from my ring and unlock these damn things. He's got a head start on us already." With his hands free, the sheriff tried to run, but pain shot through him like an explosion and he lurched forward.

Jake was barely able to break his fall. "Whoa, man. You're not going anywhere in the shape you're in. We'll put out an alert on Geoffrey. He can't get very far. Chief Gates and I found a tree with a triangle carved on it. Bockker must have been in these woods. Gates is by the tree now. I'll radio for backup and seal off the area. Meanwhile we're gonna take you to the hospital. Lean on me and we'll get you to the car."

When they reached the car, Conner radioed for help and called in an alert on Geoffrey. He tried to make the sheriff as comfortable as possible. In a few minutes, three patrol cars came racing up.

"My God, Sheriff, you look like you ran into a sledgehammer!" exclaimed Richard Weston, Grayson's chief deputy.

Conner broke in, "Deputy Weston, the sheriff needs to get to the emergency room. Come with me. I've got something real interesting to show you."

One of the other deputies jumped in the car and turned on his siren as he sped off toward the hospital.

Weston followed Jake Conner to the spot where he had left Chief Gates.

"Sorry, sir, we kinda had an emergency back there to take care of. Geoffrey's escaped."

Weston immediately took charge. "Let's seal off this area. I don't want anyone coming in contact with the tree until the crime boys can get out here." He placed barrier tape around a quadrilateral section surrounding the tree and posted Conner as a guard. "I'll send someone to relieve you after a while, Jake."

Dick Weston had been chief deputy for ten years. He knew whenever Grayson retired, he'd run for sheriff. He sure as hell didn't want to screw up this opportunity. The crackle of the radio interrupted his thoughts.

"We've spotted the suspect headed out of town toward Columbus on Highway 82."

"Great, I'll cut over to 47th Street and try to head him off. Have a roadblock set up at the intersection of Newton and Harvey."

Geoffrey's head pounded, and sweat dripped down his face. *Those four bitches. This is all their fault. Oh, shit. There's a roadblock up ahead. I can't run it. I'll have to give up. If I'm dead, I'll never get even for what they did to Angie.*

Geoffrey slowed down and pulled the car to a stop. He put it in park and raised both hands high in the air so the police would see that he wasn't armed. It seemed as if fifty deputies swarmed on him at once.

"Get out of the car real slow, son," Dick Weston ordered. "We don't want to have to hurt you."

"Yes, sir. I won't give you any trouble."

Relieved that it was all over for now, Geoffrey got out of the car. Weston pulled Geoffrey's arms behind his back and cuffed him. He shoved Geoffrey up against the car with the palm of his hand and frisked him.

"Alright, guys. One of you drive his car to the impound lot. Jake, you take our guest in for questioning. I'm going to let the sheriff know we've caught our man."

Once he had received medical treatment at the emergency room, Grayson was admitted to the hospital for overnight observation. He had an ice pack on his face when Weston came rushing into the room, almost knocking down the surprised duty nurse.

"We got the little bastard. He didn't resist at all. The boys have him down at the station. What do you want us to do?"

"Since it's still daylight, get the photographer out to the woods and have him take pictures of the area, but don't let anyone near that tree. I'll be out tomorrow and we'll see what else Geoffrey left out there besides his 'mark.' " Grayson let out a small groan of pain and readjusted his body in the bed. "When you get back to the station, see what information he'll volunteer. We can keep him for only twenty-four hours unless we charge him with something. Maybe he'll talk, though. Man, I wish I could go out to those woods right now. There's got to be something out there or Geoffrey wouldn't have marked the damn tree."

8

At the sheriff's office, Geoffrey Bockker's mind was playing *Twenty Questions.* He knew the sheriff couldn't arrest him without evidence. But that evidence was buried across from the marked tree in a shoebox, which they might find at any moment. He also remembered he'd forgotten to wipe his prints from the bottle before he put it into the box. Perhaps it would be better to confess and take his chances with a judge instead of a jury, or better yet, he could plead temporary insanity. Yeah, that might be the solution. He remembered hearing about criminals pleading insanity and getting off by going to a mental institution for a little while. That was probably his best chance. When he got out, he'd track down Angie's killers and make them pay. Suddenly a vision of his mama came to him. He remembered that when she had her "spells," his daddy would have to take her off to that awful place. She would be sitting in a chair in some sort of recreation room and all these crazy people were milling around everywhere. He dreaded going to see her because they gave him the willies. Some just sat staring like stone statues, rocking back and forth; others whimpered like babies. A few got so violent that they had to be forcibly removed from the room by orderlies. No, he would never go to a place like that again. Whatever decision he reached, though, he knew he needed some legal advice.

"Hey, Deputy Conner. Come here a minute, please. I want to make my one phone call now. I want to talk to a lawyer."

"I guess I have to let you. Who do you want me to call?"

"I really don't know. Is there a public defender or something like that?"

"Oh, you mean one of those damn do-gooders who're always helping the civil rights people and niggers get out of trouble. Okay, I'll unlock your cell and let you use the phone, but don't you try anything. Kate Whaley was my little sister's roommate. She'd been to our house a bunch of times and was just like one of the family. I'd love an excuse to blow the hell out of you."

Geoffrey hung his head and nodded. Conner dialed the phone and as soon as someone answered, he said, "This is Deputy Jake Conner at the Oktibbeha County jail. One of our 'customers' wants to speak to Josiah Perkins the third." When Perkins came on the line, Connor introduced himself and said, "Listen, we've got a kid here wants to talk to you. He's just the kind you like to defend, a real slime ball, only he's white." He handed the phone to Geoffrey.

"Mr. Perkins, my name is Geoffrey Bockker. I think I'm going to need your advice. Could you come to the jail as soon as possible? It's real important."

Perkins told Geoffrey to "just sit tight and don't say anything until I get there."

Josiah Dement Perkins III, who resembled a young Hal Holbrook, had lived in Columbus all his life. His family, whose ancestors had come from the Tidewater Section of Virginia and still had plenty of "old" money, had been lifelong Democrats and espoused the traditional liberal views of the Democratic

Party. His father and grandfather had both graduated from the University of Virginia law school and had instilled in Josiah a love for his fellow man and a concern for the downtrodden. These feelings had turned a lot of the community against the Perkins family because Columbus was a bastion of conservative beliefs and didn't hold kindly to "do gooders," as people like the Perkinses were referred to. Josiah had broken the family tradition and had graduated from Harvard Law School the year before and chose to return to Columbus to practice with his father and grandfather, although he had received many more lucrative offers. He couldn't wait to see the reaction of his conservative friends if he took this case.

"Hello, Perkins. The kid's in the back. I'll take you to him." Connor spit out the words with disdain. He led him to Geoffrey's cell.

"Bockker, here's your lawyer, Mr. Josiah Dement Perkins the third." Conner turned to Josiah. "Let me introduce you to Geoffrey Bockker. He likes to carve triangles on innocent girls' foreheads in addition to raping and mutilating them. You two ought to hit it off fine."

Josiah started to protest about Bockker being innocent until proven guilty, but he knew he'd be wasting his time. "Hello, Geoffrey."

Josiah looked directly into Geoffrey's eyes and was reminded of a frightened kitten he had once found on the side of the road. He didn't know or care if Geoffrey were innocent or guilty. It would be his job to defend him to the best of his ability, if he took the case.

"Hello, Mr. Perkins. I appreciate you coming over here to see me."

"Call me Josiah, Geoffrey. Sit down and let's talk. So you go to State, do you?"

"Yes, sir. I'm a sophomore majoring in accounting. I'm on a partial scholarship so I have to keep my grades up. Right now I have a 3.8 overall. Mr. Per—Josiah, I'm scared. Sheriff Grayson and Deputy Conner came to my house yesterday. You see, Deputy Conner saw me and this girl pulled off on the side of the highway because she was sick. She's just a friend I was talking to about my girlfriend Angie, but she turned out to be the second victim of the guy they call the 'Triangle Killer.' "

Tears came to Geoffrey's eyes as he told his story. Josiah's heart went out to the boy, and he handed him his handkerchief.

"Okay, son. Just relax and finish your story."

"I'm sorry, Josiah. It's just that I lost someone I loved so much."

Geoffrey's story poured forth like a rampaging river—what had happened to Angie and about finding mysterious blood-stains all over his house and discovering triangular patches of skin in a jar in his refrigerator.

"After the sheriff and Deputy Conner and Chief Gates left my place, I was so scared that I buried a shoebox containing some suspicious items in the woods behind the house and marked a tree so I could find it later. When they came back with a search warrant, they found some sort of stain on the car-pet in my bedroom and cut out a piece of the rug as evidence. I panicked and ran away when they made me go to the woods with them. I didn't mean to hit the sheriff as hard as I did. When I came to the roadblock, I knew it was useless to try to escape, so I gave myself up. After I got to the jail, I realized I had to talk to someone to tell my side of the story. I don't think the sheriff'll believe anything I say. You believe me, don't you?"

"It doesn't matter whether I do or not. It's what the jury will believe. They're the ones we'll have to convince."

"Does that mean you'll take my case? I don't have a whole

lot of money, just some that I inherited from my foster parents after they were killed in a car wreck last year, but most of that is being spent on college to make up the difference in what my scholarship doesn't cover. But when I get out of school, I'll pay you back. I promise."

Josiah shook his head. "Don't worry about the money, Geoffrey. My dad always taught me to take a case based on its merit, not on the amount of money a client has. Yes, Geoffrey, I'll defend you. But remember, don't answer any questions unless I'm here to advise you. Besides, they haven't even charged you with anything yet."

"They probably will when they find the shoebox."

"We'll just wait and see. I've got to go now. Deputy Conner, I'm ready to leave."

Conner came back to let Josiah out. "Thought you might like to know that the sheriff's getting out in the morning. We'll go find whatever it is that's near the tree and then we'll fry your ass, you little piss ant."

Josiah bristled. "That's enough, Conner. I wouldn't make threats if I were you. They might come back to haunt you later. Goodbye, Geoffrey."

When Josiah walked out the front door, Conner went back to Geoffrey's cell and stared him right in the eye. Then he spit out a stream of tobacco juice, which landed at Geoffrey's feet.

"I sure as hell wouldn't want to be in your shoes, boy. When they charge you with murder, those folks in Columbus will want to come over here and tear down the jail. They don't cotton to mutilators, especially of pretty girls."

Although he would have relished cutting out Conner's heart at that moment, Geoffrey just hung his head and sat down on the cot.

9

Early the next morning, the sheriff was dressed and ready to leave with Weston when Dr. Samuel Morrison came to the hospital room to dismiss his patient.

"Now, Carl, I know I can't talk you out of leaving this morning, but you've got to take it easy. You're not a spring chicken. If Bockker had angled his punch a little differently, the blow could have driven your bone structure into your brain. The purplish area around the orbits of your eyes is caused by the blood flowing toward the area of least resistance. Since the tissue around your eye is soft, the blood is more easily dissected into that area. That's why you look like you've gone fifteen rounds with Sonny Liston. I've gotten you an appointment with Dr. Ferrell Hagan in Memphis. He'll examine your nose and tell you what needs to be done. But, and I mean this, don't do anything too strenuous. You're still weak from all the blood you lost."

"Okay," Grayson said automatically. "I'll try to take it easy. I don't know what the hell all that gobbledygook medical shit means, but I'm wasting precious time standing here talking with you. Let's roll, Weston. We've gotta get to the woods to see what y'all found. See ya, Sam."

Morrison shook his head when the sheriff and Weston had left the room and said laughingly, "You old jackass. You're not gonna pay one bit of attention to what I said, are you?"

Grayson beat Weston to the car even though there was a twenty-year age difference. Weston radioed the jail for Jake Conner and Buster Gates to meet them at Geoffrey's farmhouse. When they arrived, Conner and Gates, as well as a police photographer, were already there waiting.

"Well, Carl, you look a helluva lot better than you did yesterday. How's the nose feel?" Conner asked.

"Like hell. But that doesn't matter. Show me the tree."

"Sure thing. Deputy Carson is out there now. We've had someone on duty all night."

Buster Gates felt nauseated when he saw the triangle because he could picture the same mark on the foreheads of the two dead girls. "It's his insignia alright. There's got to be something else around here."

The men meticulously prodded the earth around the tree but found nothing. "Sheriff, look at that patch of ground over there. It looks too packed down," Conner remarked.

"I've found something!" yelled one of the men nearest the area after he had gently cleared away some of the dirt. "It looks like the lid of a shoebox."

Grayson ran over and knelt down. He carefully removed the dirt from around the shoebox and lifted it out of the ground. He could hardly wait for the photographer to take a picture of the box before he removed the lid.

"Well, what have we here? Buried treasure?" Grayson took note of the objects in the box and exclaimed, "Shit, man. We've found the mother lode. We'll send this to Jackson for them to ID fingerprints and to make sure the skins match the two girls' types. We don't want to take any chances. I'll bet a million dollars the prints belong to Mr. Geoffrey Bockker, though. Keep the area sealed off. We sure as hell don't want any curiosity seekers out here disturbin' anything. Let's head on back."

The excited men discussed the case as they rode back to the jail, but when they reached their destination, some reporters were milling around outside.

"Damn," Grayson said, "I guess rumors have been buzzing around town that we've got the 'Triangle Killer' in jail." He got out of the car and made a gesture with his right hand as if to push back the horde rushing toward them. "I don't have anything to tell you boys yet. We haven't charged anybody. I've got some items to send off to Jackson. Then maybe I'll be able to make a statement."

The reporters knew better than to goad the sheriff. He had always been straightforward with them and had never deliberately withheld information. Mumbling to themselves, they walked back to their cars.

Grayson turned to Conner. "Let's get these items packaged up and sent to Jackson for prints and analysis and skin matches. The sooner we get them back, the quicker we can make our case against Bockker. Weston, you and Conner prepare another affidavit and search warrant for Judge Johnson to sign. After he's approved it, go over to Geoffrey's house and turn the place upside down." Grayson called to his secretary, "Mildred, have the results on the carpet come back yet?"

"Yes, sir, Sheriff. They arrived by courier while you all were out searching in the woods. By the way, how are you feeling?"

"I'm okay, but I'll feel a hell of a lot better if the results are what I think they are."

The sheriff hurriedly opened the manila envelope. A smile came over his face and he slapped his hand to his leg. "Blood type A. Hmm, let's see Doc's report on the last victim."

"Here it is."

"Yes, a match. According to his student record, Geoffrey has type O, so it couldn't be his blood. I think we've got enough proof to arrest the kid. Let's book him."

Grayson went to Geoffrey's cell. "Geoffrey, it looks as if we're going to have to charge you with the murder of Cassie Franklin. The stains on your carpet were blood, not Coke, and they matched Cassie's blood type. And as soon as the reports on the objects we found near your 'marked' tree come back, I imagine we'll be able to charge you with Kate Whaley's murder, too."

Geoffrey didn't say a word at first. He just looked straight into Grayson's face and then said calmly, "Please call Josiah Perkins for me."

After the sheriff had left, Geoffrey trudged over to his cot and sat down and stared at the wall. As upset as he was, he knew that he had to stay calm and not make any comments. His head began to throb so hard that he thought his eyes would pop out. However, he could do nothing for the next thirty minutes except to wait for Josiah to drive over from Columbus.

When Josiah arrived, Conner ushered him into the jail. "Come on back. Your client's waiting for you," Conner said with an air of contempt.

Josiah found his client in an extremely agitated state. As soon as Conner had left, Geoffrey blurted out, "Josiah, I'm really scared. The piece of carpet had bloodstains that matched the second girl's blood type and they found the shoebox containing incriminating evidence buried in the woods behind my house. I don't have a snowball's chance in hell, do I? Whatever happens, please don't let them kill me."

"Geoffrey, calm down. Don't talk like that. We've got to be positive. If the grand jury indicts you, I think the first thing we need to do is have you evaluated by a psychiatrist to see if you are even mentally competent to stand trial. You just keep quiet and do what I tell you. First, though, I want to know exactly what you remember." Josiah placed a tape recorder on his lap and set it up. "Okay, now begin with the events leading up to Angie's death and relax and go slowly. Try to remember as many details as you can."

"It all started when Angie called me to come over to Columbus…"

After Geoffrey had finished, Perkins turned off the tape.

"You say the only recollections you have are coming to and finding blood in your house. You don't remember anything about subsequent trips to Columbus?"

"No sir, except for when Deputy Conner approached us when we were parked on the side of the road because Cassie was sick. After that, everything is blurred. I, I have these awful blinding headaches and I sort of lose track of what's happening until they go away. I swear I don't remember killing anybody."

Geoffrey moaned and began to cry softly.

"Okay, son. That's enough for today. Let's see what happens with the grand jury first. If they indict you, then I'll call Dr. Haskins and set you up an appointment. As the old saying goes, we need to hope for the best but prepare for the worst."

On the way back to Columbus, Josiah reflected on Geoffrey's situation. He didn't know whether Geoffrey was insane, but he had a gut instinct that something had to be wrong with the young man. He certainly didn't deserve to be put to death if he were mentally incapacitated. The story of Angie's death, coupled with his episodes of blinding headaches and blackouts, seemed to point to some form of dementia, but Josiah needed to have an expert evaluate his client first. He couldn't begin to prepare Geoffrey's defense properly unless he knew whether or not there were possible grounds for a plea of temporary insanity, and the best person to talk to about that was Dr. Leonard Haskins.

Josiah Perkins and his father had used Dr. Haskins in one of the most widely known cases in Mississippi. Mabel Anderson, a Delta socialite, had brutally murdered her husband and then told the police that voices had warned her that he was planning to kill her that night. She went into the den where he was lying on the couch and calmly blew his brains out. Later, she called the police and reported the crime. In his evaluation, Dr. Haskins discovered that the woman had been subjected to numerous degrading sexual acts by her husband. These attacks resulted in a form of paranoia. Consequently, Mrs. Anderson was found not guilty by reason of temporary insanity. She was sentenced to six months in the state mental hospital and put on medication until she was deemed fit for society. After her release, she lived an exemplary life until her death ten years later.

As soon as he got back to his office, Josiah placed a call to Haskins and asked him to be ready in case the jury indicted Geoffrey.

10

The results of the tests run on the items in the shoebox came back, and a week later, Josiah's worst fears were realized. The Oktibbeha County Grand Jury indicted Geoffrey on two counts of first-degree murder, two counts of rape, and two counts of aggravated assault. The triangles sent to Jackson had matched the skin samples taken from the two young girls, and Geoffrey's fingerprints were found all over the jar, the knife, the handcuffs, and the dolls. Because of such a heavy docket of court cases, arraignment was set for two weeks later. Josiah knew that he had a lot of work to do in that time. He set up an appointment with Leonard Haskins for the next day.

Geoffrey was brought from his cell to the interview room to meet with the psychiatrist, a short, stocky man with a bushy crop of reddish-brown hair. His soft blue eyes gave his face such a gentle demeanor that Geoffrey immediately felt comfortable in his presence.

"Geoffrey," Josiah said, "Dr. Leonard Haskins is here to help us determine your present mental state and to try to find out if you were even capable of committing murder. Just tell

Dr. Haskins exactly what you told me, beginning with when Deputy Conner found you parked on the side of the road."

Geoffrey shook hands with Dr. Haskins before he sat down and then began to relate his version of the story, breaking down several times during the narrative.

The psychiatrist took extensive notes during the course of the interview and questioned Geoffrey closely about the details afterwards. The extent of truth in Geoffrey's story would be a critical determination. There were three distinct possibilities: Geoffrey could be telling the truth and had indeed suffered some form of temporary amnesia and then suddenly "came to" at certain points. Or he could be subconsciously repressing what he had done. A third possibility was that he was simply lying about the whole thing to keep from being convicted. In any case, Geoffrey would have to undergo multiple tests and extensive interviews. Haskins did not take his job lightly and never went to court without being thoroughly prepared.

He leveled a steady gaze at Geoffrey. "Young man, I'm going to determine your mental state after I evaluate you. So I'm telling you now, don't try to con me in any way. My time is too valuable to waste. There are plenty of honest people who need my help, and I refuse to waste it on liars. Do you understand me?"

"Yes, yes sir. I'll be up front about everything. I want to discover the truth, too. I know that I would never have deliberately killed anyone."

As Geoffrey said these words, he looked straight into the psychiatrist's eyes.

Haskins turned to Josiah. "Alright, let's get Geoffrey transferred to the psychiatric ward of the hospital in Columbus where I can evaluate him further."

"Josiah, I don't feel comfortable going to a place full of

crazy people," Geoffrey complained to his lawyer as Deputy Conner put chains attached to manacles around his waist.

"I understand, Geoffrey, but it'll only be for a few days, and you won't come in any direct contact with any of the patients."

"Okay, but do I have to wear these chains? They make me feel like some sort of animal."

Conner glared at him. "As they say, Bockker, 'If the shoe fits...'"

Conner clamped the manacles and leg irons as tightly as he possibly could. Then he looked in Bockker's face and said angrily, "This ought to hold you 'til you get to the crazy ward. They ought to castrate you while they've got a chance. Then maybe you wouldn't have the desire to hurt any more pretty young girls."

"That's enough, Conner. You know you can't harass my client like that. Let him the hell alone."

"Sure, Mr. Do-good Perkins. Just get this sonofabitch out of my sight as fast as you can. He's contaminating my jail."

Geoffrey said nothing. He sure didn't want to antagonize Conner and the others because they would be in charge of protecting him once he returned after his evaluation.

Although Geoffrey had made the drive from Starkville to Columbus many times before, this ride was entirely different. An entourage of cars with flashing lights preceded a dark gray bulletproof armored truck. He was chained to a bench in the rear of the truck. An armed guard kept his rifle pointed at him the whole time, just daring the boy to make a false move. Geoffrey felt like a rabid animal being taken to the pound to be put to death. When they pulled up to the back entrance to Columbus Hospital, a mob of angry people was standing there.

From somewhere in the back of the crowd, a shrill voice called out, "You little bastard! Coming here won't do you any good. You can't get off with an insanity plea. We'll kill you ourselves if we have to!"

Geoffrey shivered as he was hurriedly led into the three-story brick building. After he had been processed into the psychiatric unit, he was taken to a private room where his manacles and leg irons were finally removed. A metal door with heavy mesh wire loomed just down the hall. Geoffrey prayed that he would never have to come anywhere near that area because he knew the real crazies were kept there.

In a few minutes, Josiah walked into the room. His mere presence made the frightened young man feel a lot better. "I'm sorry I wasn't able to ride over here with you. Dr. Haskins will be here shortly. Do you need anything while we wait?"

"No, no thanks, Josiah. I'm all right except my legs and wrists are really raw. Do you think they have anything I could rub on them?"

Josiah could tell by the trembling in his client's voice that Geoffrey was scared to death. He hoped Geoffrey couldn't discern that he was scared, too. If things didn't work out, Geoffrey could lose his life. Josiah pressed the buzzer and asked the old black orderly who came to the door for some lotion.

"I guess the young man's got the manacle rash. That's common for folks who've been brought over from the local jails. They love to put them things on as tight as they can. I think they get some sort of pleasure from causing pain. I've seen 'em with legs and wrists so raw that blood seeped from their wounds. Just a minute. I'll be right back."

When the old man returned with a tube of ointment, Geoffrey rubbed it on his wrists and legs and asked his lawyer, "What exactly are they going to do to me here?"

"First, they'll probably have you write an extensive autobiography. After that, they'll interview you and then they'll run a battery of psychological profiles and physical exams to determine if you have any mental problems. Just go along with them on everything, no matter how silly the tests or the questions may seem. I think our best hope for acquittal is going to hinge on your psychological evaluation. Of course, where the trial takes place is very important. I've moved for a change of venue to Tupelo. The judge should rule in a few days. If he rules in our favor, I'll feel a lot better. The folks over in Tupelo won't be as prejudiced against you as the ones in Starkville or Columbus. If not, we'll just have to play the hand that's dealt us."

11

A short, portly, prematurely-bald man, dressed in starched white clothing, walked into the room where Geoffrey and Josiah sat. He introduced himself as Dr. Adam Lucas, the chief resident of the psychiatric staff.

Dr. Lucas instructed Geoffrey to sit in a large cushioned chair so that he could be more relaxed during the interview.

"Geoffrey, I have some forms for you to fill out, just the usual hospital clap-trap. Then I need for you to write me an autobiography following this outline. Don't leave out anything. No matter how trivial it may seem to you, it may be very significant to us. I'll be back in about thirty minutes. That ought to give you plenty of time." Lucas immediately left the room and Geoffrey looked at his lawyer.

"Josiah, I feel like the first day of school after summer vacation. You know how all the teachers have you write about yourself. It always seemed kind of silly to me. Why couldn't the information be passed on from year to year?"

"Now, Geoffrey, you know how important everything you do here is. Remember, your life could be riding on the outcome."

Geoffrey nodded his head apologetically and began filling out the forms. Then he began his autobiography, making sure that he put in everything about his terrible childhood. He basically said the same thing about the murders that he had told both Josiah and Dr. Haskins. When he had finished, he handed the paper to Josiah to check over.

Josiah glanced quickly at the pages. "Looks pretty thorough to me, Geoffrey. This ought to satisfy Dr. Haskins."

As if on cue, the door opened and Dr. Lucas and Dr. Haskins entered the room.

Lucas spoke first. "Geoffrey, I'm here to observe while Dr. Haskins actually does the interviewing. Some of the questions Dr. Haskins asks you may seem irrelevant or repetitious, but just answer them anyway."

A tape recorder was put in front of Geoffrey and Dr. Lucas pushed the record button.

"I'm Dr. Haskins. Can you tell me who you are?"

"Geoffrey Bockker."

"And how old are you?"

"I'm nineteen years old."

"And when were you born?"

"I was born in 1944."

"Are you married?"

Geoffrey winced. "No, I'm not married, but I have, uh, uh, I had a girlfriend, but she was killed in a car wreck."

"Do you go to church?"

"Sometimes."

"Do you work?"

"Not full time. I'm a student at State—Mississippi State."

"How far along are you in school?"

"I'm a sophomore."

"Do you have any physical problems or handicaps?"

"Well, from the time I was eight years old when my mother

died, I've had these blinding headaches that seem to give me—
that seem to cause me to sort of black out. Sometimes I can't
even remember what happened."

"What's your situation now? What do you think is wrong
with you?"

"I don't know if there's anything wrong with me, but the
police have accused me of killing two girls, and I don't remember doing that."

"And you've talked to them about all of this?"

"I've told them everything I know. I don't remember killing
anybody. I swear it."

"And what did you think when they told you that you did
it?"

"I just didn't think it was possible that I could do something
like that. It's not in my nature to kill an animal, much less a
person."

"Did you know the people that were killed?"

"I had a blind date with one of the girls. And I remember
being in the car with her and having a deputy stop to ask us if
something was wrong because we were parked on the side of
the highway."

"Why did the deputy stop?"

"I guess he wanted to see what was the matter. She was sick
to her stomach, and I had pulled over because she had to throw
up. And the next thing I remember was coming to and finding
blood in my apartment."

"Had you ever had this happen to you before?"

"Yes, that was the second time."

"And you've never been accused of committing a crime
before?"

"Well, when I was younger and living in one of my foster
homes, I was accused of trying to drown my baby brother. But
I was really trying to save him. You see, he had slipped in the

tub and I was trying to get him out of the water before he drowned. That's when my foster mother walked in and jumped to the wrong conclusion. She started screaming and I got scared and ran out of the house."

"Have you ever seen a psychiatrist or a mental health worker before?"

"Not really, but this counselor of some sort came and talked to me about the incident with my little brother, but that's all. Josiah suggested that we talk to you because he, uh—we—want to find out if I have any mental problems."

"Let's get back to your headaches. Is there anything you can do to alleviate them?"

"One of the doctors I went to had me try a form of relaxation therapy. He gave me some tapes to listen to."

"Do they help?"

"Sometimes. But if the headaches are real bad, I have to get in a dark room and lie down."

"Maybe I can give you some medicine for your headaches. There are some new products on the market which seem to work."

"I'd appreciate that, Dr. Haskins."

"Tell me about your childhood with your real parents? Did you have any problems?"

"No, not that I remember. The worst thing that ever happened to me was my mother's death when I was eight. I remember standing there looking at her in the casket and realizing that she was gone. After we buried her, my daddy told me that he couldn't take care of me 'cause he was going to be shipped overseas to Korea in a few weeks. He took me to the county welfare agency 'cause he didn't have any family to take care of me. They told him they'd find a home for me until he got back. But he got shot down and never came home."

"What about your mother's people? Couldn't they have

taken you in?"

"I guess they were dead or something. Whenever I'd ask, she would just turn away and not say anything. Anyway, the welfare department found a foster family for me to stay with. I lived with them about three months until one night the house caught on fire. They were killed, but I managed to escape. After that I was shuffled from first one home to another until finally I was sent to a home where I was happy. The Holleys were like real parents to me, but they were killed in a car accident last year."

"How old were you when you went to live with the Holleys?"

"About thirteen."

"What did your mother die of?"

"I really don't know. Daddy never told me. She just got real sick and died. She used to have some sort of spells and Daddy would take her to this place where all these crazy people were. We would go visit her there, but I didn't like to go 'cause the people there scared me."

"What was wrong with your mother when she would be sent off?"

"I guess she had some sort of mental problems. She'd just close herself up in her room for days at a time. Then Daddy would have to take her to that awful place."

"Did you have any real brothers or sisters?"

"No, just the foster ones."

"How did you do in school? How did you get along with people?"

"I did fine. I made mostly A's and B's. I played on the football team and made all-conference my senior year. I got along well with everybody. Only those headaches would come on."

"How often did they occur?"

"Oh, usually about every three or four months. But sometimes they came more often."

"How long would they last?"

"About three or four hours. And I'd see these flashing lights."

"Did you hear sounds?"

"Yes, I—I would hear a voice."

"What did it say?"

"It told me to do things."

"Like what?"

"It told me to kill people. People who had been hurting me. I've been hearing it lately. Maybe that's what happened with those girls. Maybe the voice told me to kill them."

"What exactly would this voice say?"

"It just said, 'Kill, kill.' "

"Did it tell you how?"

"I don't remember."

"When you were growing up, did you have many friends?"

"Yes, some. But sometimes I liked to be by myself. I was kind of a loner."

"Whom did you most want to be like? Whom did you admire?"

"Nobody really. I moved around so much that I really didn't have a role model. Except for Angie, my girlfriend. We came to college together, or rather I came first and then she came this year. She died last week."

"Was she one of the girls that you were accused of killing?"

"Oh, no, this happened before. The girls who were killed were in the social club that Angie wanted to be in, but they wouldn't ask her to join. When I went over to the 'W' to see her the day bids went out, she was crying and screaming and saying that her mother was going to be upset, and then she ran to her car and jumped in it and ran off and was killed."

"How long had you known her?"

"About five years. We would probably have gotten married after college if something hadn't happened to her."

"Did any of your family have any kind of mental illness that you know of?"

"I guess that's what Mama had. I told you about that before."

"You mean your real mother?"

"Yes, do you think I'm crazy? You're asking me all sorts of weird questions."

"No, I don't think you're crazy. But we have to determine what mental state you're in now. Geoffrey, it's getting late and I think that's enough for today. I'm going to let you go on back to your room now. I'll leave a prescription for some medicine. If you have one of your headaches, just tell one of the nurses and she'll get you something to relieve the pain. Both Dr. Adams and I will be evaluating you further."

"Thank you, Dr. Haskins. I don't think I killed those girls, but if I did, it wasn't deliberate."

"Leonard," Dr. Lucas began. "I don't think that Geoffrey exhibits any evidence of a mental aberration."

"I don't either," Haskins agreed, "but the fact that he focused his revenge on the social club indicates to me that he had a strong fixation on Angie. That could have led him to seek revenge for her death even though they never did anything to Geoffrey himself."

"Another thing, this idea of hearing a voice—that could be something he's making up to convince us he's not normal. If he truly thinks he hears something, then that's certainly abnormal behavior, but it doesn't prove he's got any specific mental disorders."

"In my opinion, Geoffrey needs a lot more testing and observation. We've barely scratched the surface," Haskins said firmly.

"I think you're right."

"Okay, let's get to work and decide what tests he'll need."

The orderly had taken Geoffrey back to his cell and the tired, but upbeat, young man sat on the wooden frame bed. Josiah patted his client on the shoulder.

"I'll be back the first thing tomorrow morning, Geoffrey. Try to get some rest."

After his attorney had left, Geoffrey reflected on the day's proceedings. *I think the interview went over well, but Dr. Haskins asked some really strange questions. By pretending that I suddenly remembered that the voice had told me to kill, I might have convinced them that I wasn't in my right mind, if they decide that I killed the girls. I've got to be careful, though. I sure don't want to make them think I'm crazy because then I could be locked up in a mental institution forever. That wouldn't do me any good. Maybe I ought to admit that I committed the crimes, using my love for Angie as a motive. I could say that her voice told me to kill the girls and that I was just carrying out her instructions. No, that wouldn't work. I'd seem paranoid then. Oh shit, my head's starting to pound. I can't worry about this anymore tonight.*

Geoffrey called out to a passing nurse and requested something to help him sleep.

As he was waiting for the medication to take effect, Geoffrey's past came rushing back to haunt him. Tormenting memories swooped down like a giant eagle. He began remembering in terrible detail specific events that had occurred while he was staying with various foster parents.

Although his first set of foster parents had been fatally burned in the fire, the authorities never questioned him, and the social workers found him another home. There he had tried to drown his foster baby brother because the parents had punished him for an offense he hadn't even committed. Geoffrey winced as he saw himself being beaten by the baby's father. This incident had forced him to be sent to yet another home. The members of that family were religious fanatics who thought he was possessed by the devil, so they had locked him in a closet for days at a time until a welfare worker came in unexpectedly one day and found him covered with body waste. His next family was a strange couple—the husband nearly beat the boy to death while the pathetic wife stood by, too afraid of her husband to do anything. Geoffrey had stolen the man's handcuffs just before he was taken off by the social workers. After two more disastrous experiences with foster parents, he was sent to live with yet another family, the Holleys. They turned out to be a wonderful couple who really loved him. The last vision Geoffrey had before drifting off to sleep was sitting around the dining table eating one of Mrs. Holley's delicious chocolate pound cakes that she would bake just for him.

12

During the course of the next few days, Geoffrey was given a variety of psychological tests, as well as extensive physical evaluations. He had made up his mind not to manipulate the doctors or to try anything foolish when he answered the test questions. He knew from his college psychology courses that it was possible to fake mental illness, but since Dr. Haskins had told him from the outset not to try to con him, Geoffrey calculated that it would be in his best interest to let nature take its course, so to speak. Whatever the tests determined, he would accept. Josiah had reminded him that if a psychiatrist found anything that the client's lawyer didn't want brought out during the trial, then the psychiatrist wouldn't be used as a witness. Josiah was one smart man, and Geoffrey knew that it was best to do exactly what he said.

Dr. Haskins brought Geoffrey and Josiah to his office to give them the results of his findings.

"Geoffrey, you know when I first agreed to evaluate you, I told you that my job was to analyze your intelligence and personality traits to see if you are fit to stand trial. According to our tests and physical examinations, you have no evidence of any form of mental illness."

As the three men were seated around the table, Dr. Haskins began his explanation.

"The first test we gave Geoffrey is called the Wexler Adult Intelligence Scale. The intricacies of the test are here in my report, but I'm sure you're interested in only the results. According to this test, Geoffrey's full scale IQ is 130, which means that he is well above average in intelligence—"

Josiah interrupted. "But, Leonard, just because he scored high on the intelligence test doesn't mean that he can't have some sort of mental illness, does it?"

"Of course not, Josiah. That's why the next phase of our testing involved a thorough physical exam including an EEG to check his brain wave patterns. Nothing severely abnormal showed up here."

"Well, what about the headaches and blackouts I get?" Geoffrey asked. "Isn't there a physical reason for them?"

"In your case, the only thing we found were some abnormal brain waves, which could indicate a possible previous head injury. Do you ever remember falling and hitting your head when you were younger?"

"No, but when I was a kid, I was kind of clumsy and was always having little accidents. But I don't remember any particular incident when I hurt my head except for the time when one of my foster fathers clobbered me with his night stick."

"Tell me about that incident."

"Mr. Karsten, who was a deputy sheriff, came in drunk as usual and began beating my foster mom. I just couldn't stand by and watch it any longer. I jumped on his back and told him to stop, but he threw me off and grabbed for his nightstick. He swung it at my head, but I ducked. It still caught me right here just above my left ear. I fell down, bleeding like a stuck pig.

My foster mom screamed at him to leave me alone. Mr. Karsten ran to the door and yelled that he'd better not find me in the house when he got home or she'd have hell to pay. Then he stormed out. Mrs. Karsten patched me up. She was too scared to call the police because they wouldn't have done anything anyway. They never had before. She told me that she was going to have to call the welfare department to come get me. When they arrived, they tried to convince her to press charges, but she wouldn't. Then they took me off to find another home for me."

"Um. You've really had a tough life, Geoffrey," Haskins said, "but I don't think you exhibit any signs of mental abnormality, although I did find some signs of abnormal personality traits."

Geoffrey became very agitated. "I don't understand the difference between being crazy and having abnormal personality traits. I thought they were the same thing. How can I be normal mentally and have an abnormal personality?"

Josiah reached over and patted Geoffrey's arm. "Just take it easy, son, and let Dr. Haskins explain exactly what he means. He knows what he's talking about. These are the same findings that helped us get one of my clients off with only a few months in the state mental hospital. Her husband had been abusing her for years. One night she walked into the living room where he was asleep on the couch and blew his brains out. We had Dr. Haskins evaluate her and then put him on the stand. He convinced the jury that she was mentally deficient from all the abuse."

"But I don't want to go to a state mental hospital. They might not release me. At least if I went to prison, I might be able to get out."

Josiah's irritation surfaced. "Or you could get the death sentence and rot on death row for fifteen years, going through one appeal after another until they run out. Then they'll finally exact their revenge by strapping you in the gas chamber and letting those cyanide pellets drop into the container of sulfuric acid. You'll try to hold your breath as long as you possibly can. When your lungs feel as if they are about to burst, you'll gasp for air and your eyes will burn from the fumes. Then after several agonizing moments, you'll finally die."

"That's enough, Josiah. I see what you mean. I'm just so damn scared, and I honestly can't remember what happened."

Dr. Haskins nodded. He looked at Geoffrey with sympathy. "I understand, Geoffrey. I think you'll see what I'm talking about when I get through explaining the results to you. The first psychological test we gave you is called the Minnesota Multiphasic Personality Inventory. It's used to determine if a person has neurotic or psychotic symptoms. Geoffrey, do you know what the term 'malingering' means?"

"Not really."

"It means to deceive or trick."

"What does that have to do with my tests?"

"Because certain questions on one section of the test are set up to determine if the person taking the test is faking or being truthful. On that section, some of your answers seemed to indicate that you might not be telling the truth when we cross-referenced them. I told you not to try to con me when we started, Geoffrey."

"I promise you, Dr. Haskins, I was as truthful as I could be on those questions."

"Alright, Geoffrey, I believe you. Now, certain parts of the test were set up to determine if you had any psychological disorder. When we analyzed the results of your scores, we found that you suffer from depression, and that you exhibit anger over things you can't control. Also, you have low self-esteem. These findings correlate with the results of your Rorschach test. In the free association phase of the test, we recorded every word and every sound you made, as well as how long it took you to elicit a response, and we noted what position the card was in when you responded. In the second phase of the test we scored your responses to each figure. This test also indicates, Geoffrey, that you are severely depressed. It also shows that you project blame on others rather than on yourself. The last test that I want to go over with you is the Thematic Apperception Test. It consists of a series of photographs depicting a dramatic or emotional scene, which could have a number of explanations." Haskins turned to the lawyer. "Josiah, we asked Geoffrey to explain the picture and to tell us what he thought went on before and after the scene. In almost all instances, Geoffrey told us that the figure was unhappy because he or she had been deeply hurt by someone or some group. The stories were consistent with the traumas he has suffered in his life: the loss of his mother, being shunted from family to family, and finally, the death of Angie. Geoffrey, you never seem to feel that the individual in the picture is responsible for his or her own problems. They're always blamed on someone else."

Josiah looked anxiously at the doctor. "Leonard, do you think that we have a basis for an insanity plea?"

"Frankly, no."

"I don't understand," Geoffrey said. "Josiah just said that you helped get that woman off for killing her husband. How is my case different?"

"For one thing, Geoffrey, you can't, or rather won't, try to remember if you killed those girls. Secondly, the jury felt sorry for the woman because she had suffered so much abuse at the hands of her husband. I'm afraid a jury won't find much sympathy for your situation."

Geoffrey jumped up from his chair and almost knocked the table over as he screamed out, "Yes, but those bitches did more to me than that man ever did to his wife! They caused the death of my Angie and our unborn baby. They had to pay for what they did."

"Geoffrey, calm down. What are you talking about?" Josiah was shocked.

"Hell, yes, I killed those girls! And I'd do it all over again if I had the chance. They deserved what happened to them. Don't you understand? If they had let Angie into that damn social club, nothing would have happened."

Josiah kept shaking his head. "Geoffrey I, I don't know what to say."

Haskins responded. "I told you I just wanted to know if you were competent to stand trial. This changes things now. Of course, everything you have said here is between us. As I told you before, it's the same as attorney-client confidentiality."

"I know, Dr. Haskins. Josiah, I'm sorry. If you want to quit being my lawyer, you can. I held the truth back as long as I could. It just had to come out. You've been so good to me, and I've been holding out on you."

Geoffrey put his head in his hands and cried.

"Of course, I'm not going to quit being your lawyer," Josiah said. "I can't quit unless you fire me. Do you want to do that?"

"No, no, Josiah. I need you more than ever now."

Josiah sighed and turned to the doctor. "Leonard, what do you think our next move should be? Do we just forget all the tests and start over?"

"I don't think so," Haskins replied and looked at Geoffrey. "Why don't you tell us exactly what you remember, starting with Angie's death."

Once more Geoffrey repeated his story, but this time he told the lawyer and the doctor everything except, of course, that he still planned to murder the four girls he really held responsible for Angie's death.

"Whew, Geoffrey, that's quite interesting," Haskins said

when Geoffrey had finished. He paused, thinking, then finally spoke. "Well, coupled with your life history and our medical findings and the fact that you perceived the social club members to be responsible for Angie's death, we just might be able to get you off with a temporary insanity plea."

Josiah was puzzled. "I thought you just said that the tests didn't show that Geoffrey had any mental problems. How are things different now?"

"I suspected that Geoffrey was holding something back from us because he was afraid of being classified as crazy." He turned to Geoffrey. "I'm sorry, but I was less than truthful about the test results. I just wanted to find out for sure if you had tried to manipulate them and us. Now I know why you did. Okay, let's go over the real results."

An hour later, after Geoffrey had been taken back to his room, the two men who held Geoffrey's fate in their hands began to assess the situation.

"How did you know that Geoffrey wasn't telling the truth, Leonard? I believed him about not remembering anything, even though I knew all the evidence pointed toward the fact that he was guilty. I still don't think that he's some cold-blooded killer, though. I feel sorry for him, even if nobody else does."

"So do I," Haskins acknowledged. "I was bluffing. I just had a gut feeling that Geoffrey was holding something back. With what he's been through, I'm not surprised that he didn't snap before now. By the way, I did find evidence of a skull fracture and other broken bones. I wouldn't be surprised if his foster families hadn't abused him more than that one time. I'm going to do some more tests. Frankly, Josiah, I think we have a good case for incompetency to stand trial or at least an acquittal based on temporary insanity."

Josiah got up and began putting things back into his brief-case. "I appreciate everything you've done for us. I'm going to say goodbye to Geoffrey and then head home. This has been one helluva tiring day. Call me when you have everything worked up, and we'll plan our defense strategy."

Haskins nodded and the two men shook hands.

Josiah trudged down the hall. He was a young man, but the day had drained him of all his energy. When he arrived at Geoffrey's room, he found him stretched out on his bed, fast asleep.

The old black orderly who had brought the ointment to rub on Geoffrey's legs and wrists walked up as Josiah was standing outside Geoffrey's room.

"This is the first time I've seen him sleep like that since he got here," the orderly said.

When Geoffrey awoke the next morning, he felt better than he had since the whole nightmare had first started. Now, all he could do was sit back and wait for Dr. Haskins to finish evaluating him. Maybe a couple of months in a state mental institution wouldn't be so bad after all. Then he could make his move on the evil ones and complete his revenge for the deaths of Angie and their baby.

13

At the district attorney's office, pre-trial procedure was moving along at full speed. Dayton Blankenship had been elected to the office the previous fall and was anxious to make a name for himself. He was a handsome man, with an olive complexion, twinkling blue eyes, coal black hair, and a perfectly chiseled face. In addition to his movie-star good looks, he was a natural politician. This would be the biggest case the office had ever prosecuted, and he wanted to go to court with both barrels blazing. After all, his daddy had once been governor, and he now aspired to the same office.

"Janie," he said to his secretary, "I see Josiah's got the Bockker boy over at the hospital for evaluation. I suppose he's going to try to prove that he's incompetent to stand trial. Well, two can play at that game. Leonard Haskins is a formidable opponent, but I've got an ace in the hole, too. Get Hiram Slaughter on the phone for me, please. He's with the Midtown Psychiatric Group."

As soon as Janie put the call through, Dayton grabbed his phone. "Hiram, this is Dayton. How's it going, man? When are you and Beth coming down for a visit? It's been a long time since the four of us got together. Look, I need a favor. Have you been reading anything in the *Commercial Appeal* about our big murders down here? I figured you had. Josiah is defending the kid who they think might be the killer, and I need some heavy artillery to counter his moves. I know he's going for a dismissal on grounds of incompetency, and if that doesn't work, I'm sure he'll try to get the kid off on temporary insanity. Can you help me?"

"My schedule's pretty full now, but I can clear out some time next week. Do you want a full work-up?"

"Probably so. Josiah's called in his main man, Leonard Haskins, and he's had Geoffrey over there at the psychiatric ward of the hospital for about two weeks. I imagine he's left no stone unturned. You know how thorough he is. Can you be here Monday morning?"

"Sure, that'll work out fine."

"Great. Plan on staying with Joanna and me. She'll be delighted to see you."

Dayton and Hiram had been childhood friends and had roomed together at Ole Miss. They had both pledged Phi Delta Theta and their wives had been Chi Omegas. In fact, the two couples had married the same summer and had served as best men and honor attendants at each other's weddings. While Dayton had remained at Ole Miss to attend law school, Hiram had entered the medical field, completing his work at the University of Tennessee in Memphis. He had decided to remain in Memphis and was working as a staff psychiatrist with one of the most prestigious psychiatric groups in the South. His clients included some of the wealthiest people in Memphis and North Mississippi. In addition, he had developed a reputation as an excellent forensic psychiatrist for both the defense and the prosecution.

Josiah knew that the state would also want to evaluate Geoffrey, so he wasn't surprised when he got a phone call from the district attorney's office informing him that Dr. Hiram Slaughter would be arriving Monday to begin testing Geoffrey. Perkins was familiar with Slaughter's work. In fact, if he had not chosen his friend Leonard Haskins, Slaughter would have been his next choice. Perkins hadn't really thought that he could get Geoffrey declared incompetent; that was merely a formality. His real plan was to get Geoffrey declared not guilty by reason of temporary insanity. He honestly believed that a jury would be convinced of that after hearing all the facts. Now, he had to go to the hospital to break the news to Geoffrey. Fortunately, he had already told Geoffrey to expect the prosecution to have him evaluated by an expert of their choosing. It was a cat and mouse game that he had to win for Geoffrey's sake.

A tall, thin man with wispy blond hair and dark brown eyes walked into the room where Geoffrey Bockker was seated. He put his briefcase down on the floor and held out his right hand. "Geoffrey, I'm Dr. Hiram Slaughter. I'm representing the district attorney's office and I'd like to talk to you and give you some more tests. I know this seems repetitive, but you know the district attorney has the right to have its own psychiatrist evaluate you. I'm not saying what Dr. Haskins found is not valid. He's an extremely competent psychiatrist. But this is the way it's usually done. So, if you're comfortable, let's get started."

"Dr. Slaughter, do you think I need to have my lawyer present?"

"No, Geoffrey. I'm not going to try to trick you or anything like that. I just want to give you the same tests that Dr. Haskins gave, and maybe a few different ones, to see if my findings coincide with his. I'm not trying to dispute anything that Dr. Haskins found. In fact, I don't even know what his results were. I just want to draw my own conclusions based on my findings. Are you ready to begin?"

"Yes, sir. Go right ahead."

Thus began Geoffrey's second encounter with the probing of his mind. He tried to answer the questions as honestly as he could. During the course of the next few days, Hiram Slaughter was every bit as thorough as Leonard Haskins had been. He never crossed the boundary of privileged information, though, and never asked whether Geoffrey was guilty or not. That would have been totally unprofessional. Everything had to be by the book. Hiram knew that Dayton didn't expect him to do anything unethical. He would simply evaluate Geoffrey and then present his findings to the district attorney's office. Dayton could do with them as he pleased.

At the end of the week, Hiram bid goodbye to his patient. "Geoffrey, you've been most cooperative. I hope things work out for you."

"Thank you, Dr. Slaughter. I'll be seeing you later, I guess."

Hiram Slaughter left the hospital and headed toward Dayton's house to write his report. By the time he had finished, Joanna had come in from an exhausting day of volunteer work at Columbus Elementary School. Hiram noticed that, although she still retained the beauty queen features of a college coed, she looked tired and strained.

"Hi, Hiram. Boy, you've been busy. That looks like a book you're working on. We haven't seen much of you this week."

"I know, Jo. I'm afraid this hasn't been much of a social event. I've been so busy with this work-up for Dayton, and he's really been burning the midnight oil down at the office."

"Hiram, this case means so much to Dayton, not only personally but politically as well. You know his dad has been grooming him for governor for years. God, sometimes I wish we could go back to our carefree days at Ole Miss with the frat parties and the football games. Things were so much simpler then."

"Are you okay, Jo? Is everything all right between you and Dayton? Y'all aren't having trouble, are you?"

"Oh no, there's no other woman or anything like that, Hiram. It's just that this damn job takes up all his time. He's seldom at home and when he is, things are so distant between us. It's like we're strangers. I don't know how much longer I can take it."

Hiram put his arm around Joanna. She instinctively laid her head on his shoulder and began to weep.

"Come on, Jo, just let it all out. You'll feel better."

"Damn it, Hiram. Quit treating me like one of your patients. You know it's probably not going to get any better. I wish to God that Dayton had taken that job in North Carolina. Then we'd be out from under his daddy's control. Sometimes I hate him for what he's done to Dayton and me."

"Have you told Dayton how you feel?"

"I've tried to tell him a hundred times. But he just won't listen to me. His daddy's got him wrapped around his little finger and all he has to do is snap his fingers and Dayton jumps. Hiram, can you talk to him? Maybe he'll listen to you."

"I'll try, Jo. Maybe after this case is over, the four of us can get away for a couple of weeks. We've still got that cabin up in the mountains near Pigeon Forge. Remember how beautiful it is this time of year?"

"I sure do. That'd be wonderful. But how long do you think the trial will last? Dayton thinks it could go on for several months."

"I don't think so. Besides, the police have plenty of evidence against Bockker. I don't see how the jury could help but reach a guilty verdict."

Hiram hoped that Joanna hadn't noticed the fact that he hesitated when he told her this. He had not wanted to tell her the truth at that point. No sense upsetting her more than she already was.

"Jo, I'm dead tired, and I'm going to take a shower and lie down awhile before Dayton gets home. Don't worry. Everything's going to be okay. I promise you."

Joanna hugged Hiram. He was like a brother to her and she had complete trust in whatever he said. Maybe it was the fact that he was a psychiatrist, but somehow he could make everything seem better.

"I think I'll take a nap myself," Joanna said, getting up. "I don't have to do much about supper. The steaks are marinating in the fridge and we'll put them on the grill when Dayton gets home. Hiram, thanks for everything. I don't know what we'd do without you."

Dayton Blankenship returned home that evening totally fatigued. Preparing for the trial had consumed his every waking moment. He was positive that Geoffrey had committed the murders, but proving it beyond a reasonable doubt was something else. District attorneys had gone into court with far more evidence than he had and still lost. The outcome depended on which side made the best impression on the jury. Josiah Perkins would be a formidable opponent and knew every trick in the book. They had clashed before in previous trials, but none had the implications that this one did.

The national press had gotten wind of the case and there would be reporters from every part of the country covering the event. He couldn't afford to lose this case. Not with his daddy hounding him to run for governor in 1966. Yeah, this could either make or break him. Right now he was depending on

Hiram to come up with enough facts to first convince the judge that Geoffrey was competent to stand trial. Then he would use him to counter any evidence presented by Josiah's psychiatrist that might convince the jury that Geoffrey was innocent due to temporary insanity.

When Hiram walked through the door, Dayton saw a worried look on his face.

"What's up, Hiram? Things can't be that bad, can they?" Dayton tried to sound cheerful.

"I'm afraid so, Dayton. Let's eat supper first; I'm starving. Besides, I always think better on a full stomach. Go on in and wash up while we cook the steaks."

After supper, Joanna excused herself and Hiram and her husband went into the study to discuss Hiram's report.

Name: Geoffrey Paul Bockker
Age: 20
Sex: M
Referred by: Dayton Blankenship
Test Dates: September 27-30, 1963
Interpret Date: October 1, 1963
Mr. Bockker was referred for psychiatric evaluation in order to determine his competency to stand trial and to further determine if he had any underlying mental disorder that could impair his behavioral controls. In addition to extensive interviews and thorough physical evaluations, the patient was also given a battery of psychological tests. These tests include the Weschler Adult Intelligence Scale, the Rorschach, the Minnesota Multiphasic Personality Inventory, Projective Drawings, and the Thematic Apperception Test.

Dayton was not interested in the specific interpretations of each individual test right now. All he wanted to know were the decisions that Hiram had reached about Geoffrey's competency to stand trial and his probable mental status at the times the murders were committed. He skimmed through the preliminary pages and went straight to the final part of the report.

Certain conclusions have been formed based on the personal interviews, physical evaluations, and psychological tests. First and foremost, Geoffrey Bockker's life history has played an important part in his psychological makeup. His childhood appeared normal until the death of his mother when the boy was eight years old. At that time he was placed in what would be the first of a series of foster homes. There is physical evidence pointing to some form of possible child abuse. Based on X-rays, a fracture of the left temporal bone was present. Also, there was evidence of other healed broken bones. These were the upper part of the radius and ulna of his left arm and the lower part of the femur and fibula of his right leg.

Although the patient does not remember receiving some of these injuries, it is quite possible that he has repressed the events leading up to the injuries. At the age of nine, he was accused of trying to drown his foster sibling, which he denies. He also remembers being locked in a closet for an extended period of time when he lived with yet another family. Immediately afterwards, the boy was sent to a different foster home. When this situation did not work out, he was sent to live with several more foster families. Each time something would happen which precipitated Geoffrey's being placed in a different foster home. Finally, when he was thirteen, he was placed with a very nurturing family, and the situation proved to be successful. He remained with this family until both parents were killed in an automobile accident last year. The patient has suffered periodically from severe headaches and blackouts. These maladies could stem from the previously mentioned head injury. Upon further questioning, the patient revealed that his girlfriend had been killed in a car accident prior to the murders of the two college students. Mr. Bockker blames the girl's death on her reaction to being rejected by the Delta Social Club. He claims to have heard a voice telling him to get even with the members for causing the girl's death. He denies knowledge of actually murdering the girls but admits to finding blood in his house and pieces of skin in a jar after each girl was killed. Based upon the patient's life history and psychological profiles, I have reached the following conclusions:

According to the Wechsler, the patient is of superior intelligence, scoring an aggregate total of 135. The personality inventories, as well as the projective tests, all indicate a depressed young man who is suffering from paranoia. He feels the voice of his dead girlfriend is directing him to commit acts of murder, although he does not actually admit to the killings. Due to the combination of his childhood traumas and the death of the young lady, I feel that the patient snapped and felt compelled to get even with those he perceived to be at fault. He could possibly be projecting the blame of his previous losses on the girls in the social club also. I have reached the conclusion that although the patient is competent to stand trial, according to the American Law Institute Model Penal Code, he was not criminally responsible for the crimes he committed.

Dayton sighed heavily and threw the report down on the coffee table.

"Damn, Hiram, you mean he can get off by pleading not guilty based on insanity?"

"I'm afraid so, Dayton. You knew when you asked me to do the work-up, that things might not turn out in your favor."

"But, Hiram, he killed *two* girls. Doesn't that show that he planned everything? I thought that people who were truly insane couldn't plan two murders, maybe one, but not two."

Hiram shrugged and shook his head. "The penal code just applies to the exact time the murders took place, not prior to them. Geoffrey had so much frustration built up in him that the girl's death served as a catalyst."

Dayton's brows furrowed deeply. "Do you think that Josiah's psychiatrist has come up with the same conclusions?"

"Probably. Geoffrey said that he was given almost the exact same battery of tests by Haskins."

"Damn, I can't take a chance on Geoffrey's going to the state hospital in Whitfield for a couple of months and then getting out. I'd be dead meat. Besides, what assurance do we have that he won't commit other murders when he's released?"

"We don't." Hiram paused. "As a matter of fact, if he doesn't receive psychiatric treatment, he probably will."

Dayton let out a long, resigned sigh. "I think my best bet is to plea bargain down to second degree murder and make sure he stays in prison for a long time. Let's see, two consecutive second-degree murders plus—no, I'll agree to drop the other charges. That would keep him in Parchman for at least twenty years. That's the only choice I have. God, the shit will really hit the fan when the people of Columbus and Starkville find out what I'm going to do. They'll probably crucify me."

"But can you take a chance on the alternative?" Hiram asked his friend.

"No, I can't. I'll call Josiah in the morning."

Joanna entered the study at that moment. "Well, you two look as if you've just lost your last dollar. What's wrong?"

Dayton looked at his wife. His grim expression surprised her. "We may have. I can't tell you now, baby. But you'll find out soon enough. Hiram, I'm bushed. I've got to go to bed. See you in the morning."

"Me, too. Night, y'all."

Dayton tossed and turned all night long. Although Joanna pleaded with him, he refused to tell her what had upset him so. She knew it involved the case, but he wouldn't communicate with her anymore, so she finally gave up and turned over, crying softly into her pillow. Dayton knew that he was hurting Joanna, and he promised himself that things would be different once the trial was over. But in his mind he knew they wouldn't. It was all his fault because he had gotten so wrapped up in his career that everything else had gone to hell.

The next morning Hiram was up at six. He had completed his work, but he wanted to say some things to Dayton before he left for the office. Joanna had gotten up earlier and had gone for her five-mile run, so he knew that he and Dayton would be alone for a while. He found his friend in the kitchen, sitting dejectedly at the table, sipping a mug of coffee.

"God, you look like shit. What happened?" Hiram asked.

Dayton looked exhausted and distracted. "Hiram, I couldn't sleep all night. I played over and over what I was going to say to convince everybody at the office that we should offer Geoffrey the chance to plea bargain. I know how they're going to react, though. At least the public won't find out until the deal is done. Then they'll probably want to tar and feather me, or worse. The really awful part is having to call my dad and tell him. I can kiss my gubernatorial chances goodbye after this."

Hiram had been waiting for such an opportunity to express his feelings. "Damn it, Dayton, is your career all you ever think about? Is pleasing your almighty father the only concern in your life? Don't you see what all this has done to your marriage? Wake up, man, you're throwing away the best thing in your life. To hell with what your father thinks. You've got to grow up sometime. Jo is the best thing that ever happened to you. I'm not going to stand by and see you discard her like an old toy!"

Dayton heaved a sigh of relief and put his head in his hands and began to cry. This was the first time since Dayton's mother had died that Hiram had seen him show any emotion.

"Okay, Dayton, let it all out. I'm sorry I came down on you so hard, but I can't stand to see you ruin your life. Career is important but not half as important as family. I told Jo that after the trial is over, we'll all go up to the cabin at Pigeon Forge. It'd be the first time the four of us have been up there since college. You know, we made a pact to go up there every year, remember? Somehow we got sidetracked with our careers. It'd do all of us a lot of good."

"You're right, Hiram. When this mess is over, whatever happens, we'll go. I promise."

Joanna came bounding through the kitchen door, out of breath from her jog. "What have you guys been up to? You're grinning like a pair of Cheshire cats."

Dayton strode over to Joanna, took her in his arms and kissed her like she hadn't been kissed in years. She pulled back, stunned, not knowing exactly what was going on.

"Joanna, I'm so sorry for the way I've treated you lately. I've put you through hell. If you'll just stick with me through the trial, I promise I'll make it up to you. Things will be different from now on. When this is over, the four of us are going to Pigeon Forge. How does that sound?"

Joanna realized that something must have transpired while she was gone, and she knew that Hiram was behind it. She walked over to him. Kissing him lightly on the cheek, she whispered, "Thank you. You've given me back my husband."

Hiram gave her a satisfied grin. "Well, I've got my things packed, so I'll leave you two lovebirds alone. Call me if you need me for anything else, buddy. Keep me posted on how things are going. I'll be back for the arraignment. After it's over, then it's off to east Tennessee for the four of us."

After Hiram had left, Dayton picked his wife up in his arms and carried her to the bedroom. There, they made real love for the first time in months. Afterwards, although he knew he was divulging privileged information, Dayton told Joanna what he intended to do about Geoffrey Bockker.

"Dayton, you don't really have a choice, do you?" Joanna said gently. "If the defense has the same information, the jury wouldn't have any choice but to find him not guilty on grounds of insanity, and he could be free in a matter of months. Or they could buy into his story and acquit him altogether. But as hostile as this community is, what about the fact that they might convict him and give him the death penalty?"

"I've thought about all those things, Joanna, and to get him to agree to plead guilty to a lesser charge is our best bet for keeping him in prison as long as possible. Besides, while he's in Parchman, he'll receive psychiatric counseling. That way, when he's released in twenty or thirty years, he might be rehabilitated. At least, I pray that he will." Dayton paused and gave his wife a loving kiss on the forehead. "Honey, don't say anything to anybody about this. I don't want the local folks to get wind of what we're doing, or they might storm the Bastille and try to do something foolish. You realize that this isn't going to make us the most popular couple in town, so just be prepared for anything. As long as you're by my side, though, I can handle any situation."

"Dayton, what about your father? He'll think this will ruin your chances for governor."

"To hell with what he thinks. From now on, I do things to please you and me, not him." And with that, Dayton jumped out of bed, hurried into the bathroom, turned on the shower and stepped under the hot, steamy, rushing water. A half-hour later he was on his way to his office to break the news to everyone.

14

Just as Dayton had anticipated, all hell broke loose when he showed his staff Hiram's report on Geoffrey. No two people agreed on the correct course of action. In the end, though, cooler heads prevailed and Dayton convinced everyone that his plan was the best one to implement. Now, if he could only get Josiah to agree. He immediately called the attorney and asked to meet him at three that afternoon at the courthouse. Josiah enthusiastically agreed.

Josiah put down the phone gleefully. "Yes, Mr. District Attorney, I'd be more than happy to discuss the Bockker case with you." Josiah headed down the hall to his father's office. "Dad, hang around if you can. I'm meeting with the D.A. and I may need your advice when I get back."

"Sure thing, son. I love to bring district attorneys to their knees to beg for a plea bargain. I assume that's what Blankenship wants."

"Must be. See you later."

This time the trip to Starkville would pass even faster. Josiah knew that Dr. Haskin's report on Geoffrey had been to their advantage, but now he felt that Hiram Slaughter must have arrived at a similar conclusion. Otherwise, why would Dayton even want a conference? He must have a deal up his sleeve. But just before he left, Josiah spoke to Geoffrey by phone. He was obligated to do what Geoffrey wanted, although he would reserve the right to try to get him to change his mind if he thought that Geoffrey's decision might prove to be detrimental.

"Geoffrey, I think I have good news. The district attorney wants to meet with me this afternoon. Dr. Slaughter must have completed his report on you. Things are looking up. I think the D.A. probably wants to make some kind of deal."

"What do you mean, a deal?" Geoffrey's annoyed voice shot back. "I don't want to be bartered around like some prize animal. I'd rather take my chances with a trial."

Perkins closed his eyes and tried to remain calm. "Geoffrey, you don't understand. If the jury doesn't hear these mental reports and bases its decision strictly on the evidence and facts of the case, you could get the death penalty. Of course, they wouldn't put you to death until after ten or twelve years of appeals, and then, maybe, they'll carry you to the door of the chamber, and at the last minute the governor could grant you a stay. Then you'd have to go through it all over again. No, Geoffrey, you don't want to be sentenced to death, even if you have to make a deal to go to Whitfield for the rest of your life. Don't you see? I'm trying to save your life."

"I understand, Josiah, but you've got to see my point, too. I don't want to die, but neither do I want to rot in some padded cell in Whitfield, surrounded by a bunch of drooling idiots."

"Okay, Geoffrey. I understand. Of course, all this may be moot. We really don't know what the district attorney wants. Let me go see him and find out. Then we'll make up our minds as to your best move."

"That's fair enough."

Josiah hung up the phone and, for the first time, had a moment of misgiving about taking on this client. But he was still determined to put on the best defense he could.

15

Before he entered the Oktibbeha County Courthouse, Josiah stopped to look at it for a moment. He had fond memories of the original building, which had been constructed in 1901. As a boy, he had often gone there with his grandfather. One of the reasons he became a lawyer was the feeling he got whenever he walked into that venerable old building. Like the present edition, it also had two stories, but part of its fascination had come from the towering cupola, which gave it a sort of ambience. He had pretended it was an ancient castle and made up exciting stories about knights and damsels in distress. When the building had been demolished, Perkins felt like he had lost an old friend. Although the architect had tried to retain some of the original charm by placing Greek columns in the front, he never had the same feeling toward this new edifice.

Josiah strode inside and walked toward the district attorney's office. He was greeted by Dayton Blankenship himself. "Come on into my private office where we can talk." Just as he had hoped, the D.A. wanted to strike a deal. Of course he hemmed and hawed around at first before he laid his cards on the table.

"Look here, Josiah. I guess you, uh, have pretty much figured out why I asked you to come to this meeting."

"I've got a fairly good idea that it has something to do with
my client's psychological evaluation. What did your psychiatrist find? Let's just agree that Geoffrey's not competent to
stand trial and let him go to Whitfield until he's deemed fit to
be tried."

"Not on your life, Josiah," Dayton said. "He's as mentally
fit to stand trial as you and I are. Remember, under the Drusky
standard, a client has to be able to understand the trial proceedings and to be able to consult with his attorney with only a reasonable degree of understanding. Geoffrey certainly fits those
criteria."

Josiah nodded at his adversary. "Okay, I concede that point.
But what did Hiram Slaughter find that has you so anxious to
meet with me? It must have been pretty bad—"

"Josiah, if you're going to act that way, just forget it and I'll
see you in court."

"Oh, come on, Dayton, we've been friends since grammar
school. You know I'm just trying to rankle you. Don't be so
damn uptight."

"I'm sorry, Josiah. I've been under so much pressure lately.
You know what this trial could mean to me."

"Well, what about me? At least the people are on your side.
You know, I'm probably the least popular man in these parts for
even daring to defend Geoffrey. I've gotten phone calls in the
middle of the night, even a few threatening letters. Hell, I guess
the next thing they'll do is burn a cross in my yard or bomb my
house. No, Dayton, you don't know what real pressure is."

Dayton stared at Josiah for a long moment. "I figure you're
going to plead not guilty by reason of insanity because I think
you believe that's the only way to save Geoffrey's life. What

exactly did your psychiatrist find?"

"You're the one who called this meeting. You tell me what Hiram found first, then I'll tell you whether or not his findings match what we found."

"No, I tell you what—let's just swap and read each other's report at the same time. That'll save a lot of wrangling." Dayton opened his briefcase and pulled out Hiram's report. He offered it to Josiah. "Now hand me yours."

For the next few minutes, the two men thumbed through the other's psychological evaluation of Geoffrey. Afterwards, they put down the reports, each waiting for the other to make the first move, just like two gunfighters at the O.K. Corral.

Finally, Dayton spoke first. "Okay, you win. We'll just charge Geoffrey with one count of first-degree murder and let the jury decide his fate from the evidence. That's fair."

"I can't agree to that. We want a guarantee that Geoffrey won't get the death penalty. Life in prison, maybe, but not death."

Dayton paused, then nodded. "Alright, you drive a hard bargain. Let him plead guilty to two counts of second-degree murder to be served consecutively. I'll drop the other charges. That'll give him a sentence of twenty years to life. But this is only under the condition that he gets psychiatric treatment in prison. Hiram thinks if he's released without any treatment, he could easily kill again."

"Fair enough. But I have to run this by Geoffrey first. He may nix the whole deal."

Dayton stared at his old school friend. "Josiah, tell me something. Why wouldn't you have been willing to plead not guilty on grounds of insanity? We both know that Geoffrey is mentally disturbed. We couldn't have refuted your findings since Hiram reached the same conclusion as your psychiatrist."

"Geoffrey adamantly refuses to go to Whitfield. He's afraid

they'll keep him there forever and just let him rot. His mother was in and out of mental hospitals until she died. Plus, he got his fill of insane people in the hospital while he was there for his tests. I think being around those crazies and the memory of his mother's illness scared him to death. I'll get back to you later this afternoon with Geoffrey's response."

"Josiah, please don't let a word of this leak out. I don't want anybody to have even a suspicion of what's going on until the arraignment. If this gets out, there'll be hell to pay."

"I can assure you that my lips are sealed. Like I said, I've got just as much at stake as you do."

When Josiah went to the jail and told Geoffrey about the district attorney's deal, the young killer felt a surge of relief. He knew that even with a life sentence, he could be out after serving a minimum of twenty years. Although the prospect of spending twenty or thirty years in the Mississippi State Penitentiary was not the most comforting thought, the alternatives were even worse. Death in the gas chamber would have prevented him from carrying out his sole mission in life, and the thought of being put in Whitfield for any length of time was abhorrent. He could imagine nothing worse than being locked up and constantly examined and tested until he was considered fit for society by a group of asinine doctors who might never choose to find him sane again. No, the idea of a prison term seemed more preferable.

Geoffrey sighed. "I guess I don't have any other choice. What do we have to do?"

"Geoffrey, we're going to handle this a little bit differently from the regular plea bargain. For your safety, as well as that of the district attorney's and mine, we're not going to do or say anything until the day of the arraignment. When the judge asks how you plead, we'll announce that we've reached a plea bargain. Then he'll ask if all sides are in agreement, and we'll affirm that we are. It's up to him to decide whether or not to accept the deal. If he does, he'll set your prison sentence. After that, you'll be transferred to Parchman, where you'll serve out your term."

"Don't we need to sign some papers or something? What's to keep the district attorney from trying some sort of trick?"

"Dayton Blankenship is a man of his word. Besides, he's got to trust us, too."

"I hadn't looked at it that way."

Geoffrey turned around and sat down on his bed. He stared at the floor for a few seconds, then looked up at his lawyer.

"I don't want you to think that I'm not grateful for everything you've done, but..."

Josiah nodded. "I know, Geoffrey. I wish there was some other alternative, but there isn't."

Josiah didn't bother driving back to the courthouse. He called Dayton's office when he got to Columbus and left a message, which simply said, "Everything's okay. I'll be in touch."

16

On the date set for Geoffrey's arraignment, he was led down the hall of the Lowndes County Courthouse wearing the prison-issue orange one-piece jumpsuit. Although Josiah had been unable to get a change of venue, the proceedings had been moved to Columbus because the courtroom in the Oktibbeha County Courthouse wasn't large enough. Geoffrey wore leg irons and manacles on his wrists to prevent any possible escape, although that was the farthest thing from his mind. In the brief, three-week interval since his arrest, he had lost considerable weight and appeared haggard. He suddenly looked older than his twenty years. He held his head down, as if he were studying the pattern of the floor.

There was a mood of anticipation among those fortunate enough to be able to squeeze into the tiny, antiquated courtroom. The group was made up of a cross-section of the inhabitants of both Columbus and Starkville. The level of wealth could be determined by what each person wore and this ranged from overalls and gingham dresses to three-piece suits and Sunday finery. They had all arrived with one thing on their minds—to see for themselves the monster who had dared to profane their simple, innocent way of life by committing such heinous crimes. Those types of atrocities were supposed to be commonplace in other parts of the country, but certainly not here in the peaceful hills of northeast Mississippi. The spectators were packed like sardines on wooden semi-circular benches, which looked more like church pews. However, no one dared to get up, even for a drink of water or to go to the bathroom, for fear of losing his place to one of the many vultures standing in the back of the room and along the walls, just waiting for an empty seat. Even though it was early October, the heat was oppressive and the only air was provided by ceiling fans or by the cardboard hand fans donated by one of the local funeral homes. Paint was peeling off the dingy, cracked walls and the balcony creaked and groaned as if it might collapse at any minute whenever someone so much as shifted his weight. It was into this atmosphere that Geoffrey Bockker was ushered, like the early Christians being led into the arena to face a pack of hungry lions.

As Geoffrey walked through the door, there was a collective murmur from the spectators when they were finally able to get a glimpse of the person they had been eagerly waiting to see. Geoffrey lifted his head and stared momentarily into the angry faces of the multitude before he was led to the defense table located in front of a dark wooden railing. He took his seat alongside Josiah at the plaintiff's table. On the other side of the center aisle, Dayton Blankenship and his assistants were seated.

"Please rise," the bailiff bellowed.

Judge James Stuart Thornell strode into the courtroom with an air of superiority. This was his domain and none dared to infringe on his territory without fear of impunity.

"Well, ladies and gentlemen, are we ready to begin the proceedings? I see the courtroom is decidedly more populated than usual. I don't want to remind any of you more than once that I won't tolerate any undue conversation or responses. Is that clear?"

Almost to the person, everyone nodded. Judge Thornell's reputation was widely known, and the few who had disobeyed him lived to regret what they had done.

"Humph, I see Mr. Geoffrey Bockker's is the only case on the docket this morning," he intoned. "Mr. Bockker, please rise. You have been charged with two counts of murder one, two counts of rape and two counts of aggravated assault. How do you plead?"

"Your Honor," Dayton said quickly.

"Yes, Mr. Blankenship."

"Counsel and I wish to announce that we have reached a plea bargain."

This was the last thing Judge Thornell expected to hear. "Go on, Mr. Blankenship."

"Your Honor, the district attorney's office wishes to lessen the charges to two counts of second degree murder and to drop the other charges. Mr. Bockker has agreed to plead guilty to these charges in exchange for a prison sentence of thirty years to life."

A communal gasp came from the audience, and one person uttered, "My God, he's crazy. They're going to let the sonofabitch off! He'll be eligible for parole in ten years. I'll be damned."

Judge Thornell banged his gavel down as hard as he could.

"I said there would be no reaction in this courtroom whatsoever. Bailiff, remove that man and fine him fifty dollars for contempt of court. Now, let's get on with the business at hand." The judge stared down at Geoffrey. "Mr. Bockker, are these your wishes? Will you plead guilty to two counts of second degree murder?"

"I will, Your Honor."

"This is highly irregular, but I'll take the matter into consideration. Mr. Blankenship and Mr. Perkins, meet me in my chambers when court is dismissed. At two o'clock tomorrow afternoon I'll announce my decision. Court is dismissed until that time."

There was a scurrying from the courtroom, but all the spectators waited until they were out of earshot of Judge Thornell to excitedly express their feelings. Meanwhile, Geoffrey was to be taken to a room in the basement where he would remain until it was time for him to be returned to the jail.

As he walked past Josiah, he said despondently, "Do you still think I did the right thing?"

"Son, under the circumstances, I know you did. Look at the reaction of the crowd. They're in a feeding frenzy."

Afterwards, when Josiah and Dayton found themselves in Judge Thornell's chambers, they both felt like schoolboys standing before the principal, waiting for punishment.

The judge's piercing look was aimed at both men. "Now, what the hell do you think you are up to? I have never heard of anything so outrageous in my life. You both owe me an explanation, and it had better be a damn good one."

"Yes, yes sir," Dayton said, gulping. "Here are the results of our findings on Geoffrey. When you read them, I think you'll concur that what we did was our only recourse."

After he had leafed through the findings, Thornell shook his head and replied, "I'll be a monkey's uncle. I see what you mean. But Josiah, why didn't your client plead not guilty by insanity and ask for a bench trial if you were scared of a jury? Geoffrey would have gotten off with going to Whitfield until the doctors there thought he was fit to come back into society."

"Your Honor, he absolutely refused to take that route. For some reason, he'd rather spend his time in prison."

"Well, I have no choice other than to concur with your findings. Of course, I'll have to give him the maximum sentence, though. Then, he could still be paroled after serving only twenty years. Okay, you two, go on. I'll see you tomorrow at two."

Outside, people shouted and screamed at Geoffrey as he was rushed to the police van.

"You scum!"

"You murdering bastard!"

"I hope you don't think the judge will buy that shit today. Just wait and see. He'll gas your sorry-assed carcass!"

Dayton Blankenship didn't fare any better than Geoffrey as he walked down the steps of the courthouse. Shouts of outrage greeted him.

"You goddamned traitor! What do you think you're doin' letting the little piss ant off like that?"

"We'll remember this come Election Day. You can kiss the governorship goodbye!"

Dayton tried to act as if none of this hurt him, but it did. These were his constituents, and they felt as if he had betrayed their trust in him. Maybe one day he'd get a chance to explain his actions. Right now, though, he couldn't release the results of Geoffrey's examinations. He knew one phone call would be coming that night, the one he dreaded more than any other. Surely by now, someone would have called the "Guvn'r" and told him what a stupid thing his son had done. Dayton clenched his teeth and marched on through the crowd, refusing to say anything. When he reached his car, Hiram and Joanna were waiting for him. They had been in the courtroom, but with all the excitement, he had not seen them.

"Oh, Dayton," Joanna said, giving her husband a hug. "Come on, let's go home."

Hiram let out an ironic chuckle. "Man, you sure stirred up a hornet's nest. You should have seen those reporters rushing to get to a phone to turn in their stories. I'll drive us to your house. You don't need to go to the office just now."

Dayton hesitated a moment, but seeing the angry mob swelling around the car, he nodded to Hiram, got in next to Joanna, and they sped off.

As they walked into the house, the phone was ringing. Dayton knew who it was before he even picked up the receiver.

"Blankenship residence."

"Son, is that you?" The agitated voice came through loud and clear. "What in the hell came over you? I can't believe you're going to let that little bastard off with maybe serving ten years. He belongs in the gas chamber. What possessed you to do such a thing? Damn it, I've worked too hard to get you in this position for you to screw things up with such a stupid move. I'm going to call Judge Thornell right now and tell him to refuse your plea bargain." Dayton winced but said nothing. The 'Guvn'r' went on. "He's an old buddy of mine and owes me some past favors."

"Daddy, don't you dare do anything," Dayton insisted. "We had a legitimate reason for the plea bargain. That's the only guaranteed way that Bockker would even go to jail. I can't tell you the whole story because it's privileged information, but, believe me, we had no other alternative."

"I can't believe you couldn't have done something else. Do you realize what this will do to our campaign for governor? I don't understand why you just flushed all my hard work down the tubes."

"Damn it, Daddy, it's my life. You've always pulled the strings—I'm like your damned puppet. Well, for once I've done something on my own, and you're not going to interfere. I don't give a damn about being governor. I never have. It was always you who pushed me to do what you wanted me to do.

All your pushing and manipulating almost cost me my marriage. Now, butt out and let me live my own life."

There was silence on the other end of the line. The governor was stunned to have Dayton actually talk back to him. "Son, I, I didn't realize how you felt. I only wanted what was best for you. Why didn't you say something sooner? I never meant to run your life. I thought politics was what *you* wanted. Ever since your mother died, my whole life has been devoted to making you successful and happy. I'm so sorry."

Dayton could hear the strain in his father's voice. "It's okay, Dad. It's just that Joanna and I have to live our own lives. Why don't you come up this weekend and we'll sit down and have a long talk about things?"

"Alright, son. I love you."

"I love you too, Dad."

Dayton hung up the phone and for the first time noticed Joanna and Hiram smiling at him. He smiled back. "Whew, I'm glad that's over. Something's strange, though. He never gave up before without an argument. You think he's actually mellowing after all these years? Now, if I can just convince everybody else that I did the right thing."

Hiram's smile disappeared. "That might be a bit harder. Look outside your front window."

A steady stream of vehicles was slowly driving past the Blankenship house. The occupants of the trucks and cars were shouting obscenities and shaking their fists. It was fairly evident that most of them were drunk or well on their way. Some of Dayton and Joanna's neighbors must have been frightened because within a few minutes the wail of sirens was heard. Jake Conner got out of the first car and headed toward the group. An animated conversation took place between the deputy and the leader of the mob. Finally, the rowdies got in their vehicles and angrily drove off. The deputy walked up to Dayton's front door and rang the bell. Although they had not been close friends, Conner had also gone to high school with Dayton and Hiram. He nodded to them when Dayton opened the door.

"Dayton, I'm sorry about that, but you know what you did riled up these folks. I can't say I really blame them for being upset. But then I don't know the reason for your actions. But I hope you knew what you were doing. I don't have any idea if your visitors will be back, but just in case, I'm going to place a twenty-four hour watch on your house. Good to see you again, Hiram, Joanna. Call the station if you need anything, Dayton." Conner turned around and spit a stream of tobacco juice on the grass and headed back toward his vehicle.

"We appreciate your coming over here, Jake."

Conner responded with a wave of his hand.

Joanna looked nervously at her husband. "Dayton, I'm scared. Those people looked mad enough to kill us."

"Don't worry, honey. I know people are upset. But most of them are good, law-abiding citizens. This was just a bunch of peckerwoods looking for any excuse to get drunk and ride around in their pickups brandishing their damn guns. I'm not going to let a bunch of scum-suckers keep me in my house like a prisoner."

Hiram gave Joanna a reassuring nod. "Dayton's right, Jo. Everything's going to be okay. After Judge Thornell rules tomorrow and Geoffrey is sent to Parchman, things will quiet down. Then we'll plan our trip to the Smokies. If there's one thing we all need, it's to kick back and forget about everything."

Nothing else happened that night, and the next morning, a big black limousine pulled up in front of Dayton's house. A burly man, with a shock of graying hair, was helped out of the car by his chauffeur. The driver then went to the trunk to get the occupant's suitcase. By this time, Dayton, Hiram, and Joanna were out the front door to greet their visitor.

"Daddy, we weren't expecting you until later this weekend," Dayton said.

The governor hugged his son, something he hadn't done in a long time. "Dayton, it's so good to see you." He grinned at Joanna. "Come here, Missy, and give your ole father-in-law a kiss. My God, you get prettier every time I see you." He reached out to shake Hiram's hand. "Hiram, it's been a long time. How're your folks?"

"Fine, sir. It's good to see you looking so well."

"Harris," the governor said to his chauffeur, "just take the car over to your brother's house. I'll call you when I'm ready to go back to Jackson."

"Yes, sir," Harris replied and looked at Dayton. "You folks take good care of the "Guvn'r" now. We don't want anything to happen to him."

When they got inside the house, Dayton noticed that his father didn't look well at all.

"Dad, what's wrong? You look awfully tired."

"Oh, it's nothing, boy. I'm worn out from the trip. What time did you say that Judge Thornell is going to make his ruling?"

"At two."

"Good, then I've got time for a short nap. Wake me when it's time for lunch. Afterwards, we'll head on over to the courthouse. I'll see y'all later. Oh, Joanna, do you have anything for indigestion? Something I ate must not be agreeing with me."

"Sure, Dad. I'll get it for you."

After the governor had gone to the guest bedroom, Hiram said to Dayton, "Your dad has really aged since the last time I saw him. Is he okay?"

"He just hasn't been himself since Mom died. I've been kind of worried about him, too. Maybe we can get him to go to the clinic for a good checkup while he's here."

"You don't think he's going to try to influence Judge Thornell, do you?"

"No, he promised he wouldn't interfere with the judge's decision, and Dad has always kept his word to me."

Later, when Dayton went into the bedroom to awaken his father, he noticed that his color was an ashen gray. "Dad, wake up."

Slowly, the governor opened his eyes and looked up at his son. "Boy, I tell you, I swear I'll never eat Cajun sausage again. My gut is killing me. I don't think I want anything to eat just now. Would Joanna mind making me a cup of hot tea? I'll just drink that and eat some crackers. By the way, I found Hiram's report on that Bockker boy on the desk in the bedroom. I see why you took the action you did."

Dayton knew better that to criticize his father for reading private information. He just let it go. His father's health was more important at the moment.

"Dad, would you like me to call the doctor? He'll come over here and check you out. You really don't look well."

"Hell no, boy. I'm not going to waste anybody's time over a damn bellyache. He'd laugh in my face. Just go on. I'll wash up and be out in a few minutes."

Shaking his head, Dayton left the room. He'd never seen his father in that much pain and his ashen color was disturbing. Dayton made up his mind to take him to the doctor right after the judge's ruling, whether he wanted to go or not.

Dayton went to tell Joanna, who was in the kitchen getting lunch ready. "Dad's still not feeling very well. He just wants some hot tea and crackers. I'm going to get him a doctor's appointment this afternoon. We ought to be through at the courthouse by three-thirty."

"It may take all three of us to get him to the doctor," Joanna said, a worried look on her face.

The governor didn't feel much like talking during lunch, and the others were too nervous to say anything that would upset him.

"Dayton, I'm going to call Harris to come pick us up. That way you won't have to drive and if things get too unruly, we'll be able to leave more easily."

"Sure thing, Dad."

Dayton thought this was a good idea because then he could tell Harris to drive to the doctor's office, and the governor wouldn't know he was going to the doctor until they got there.

When Harris pulled up at the courthouse, it seemed as if half the population of the surrounding area was standing out front. There was a rustling among the crowd and whispers of "Governor Blankenship's here. He'll straighten out that son of his."

"Yeah, the 'Guvn'r' will take care of everything."

Harris opened the door and the car's occupants hurried into the courthouse without stopping to acknowledge anyone. The governor was obviously still not feeling well and grimaced as he walked. Once inside, Hiram, Joanna, and the governor were escorted to the first row of seats directly behind the prosecutor's table. Dayton went to the prosecutor's table and sat down. Josiah and Geoffrey were already seated at the plaintiff's table, and Dayton nodded perfunctorily toward them. Geoffrey, in manacles and leg irons and still wearing his orange jail uniform, nodded back at Dayton with a half smile. When Josiah spotted the governor, he immediately stood up and walked toward him with his hand extended, not really knowing what to expect. His family and the governor were not exactly the best of friends.

"Hello, Guvn'r, good to see you again."

Clasping Josiah's hand warmly, the governor replied, "Fine,

son, how are your father and grandfather? Give them my regards."

These remarks and the fact that the governor looked like he had aged twenty years caught Josiah off guard.

"Uh, fine sir. I'm sure they'd be delighted to see you after this hearing is over."

Puzzled, Josiah sat back down. Although his family and Dayton's father had certainly not chosen to follow the same political path, he still had the utmost respect for the governor.

The courtroom was packed, and the crowd overflowed into the street. Finally, Judge Thornell approached the bench, sat down and slowly put on his reading glasses. He cleared his throat and said, "Ladies and gentlemen, after studying all the information and after much soul-searching and prayer, I have reached my decision. Although the crimes committed by this young man were heinous and he deserves to be punished to the fullest extent of the law, due to certain facts, which I cannot make public at this time, I have no choice except to concur with the recommendations of the district attorney. Geoffrey Bockker, stand up. I hereby remand you to the state penitentiary at Parchman for the rest of your natural life. Do you wish to make a statement at this time?"

"No, Your Honor, except to say that I am truly sorry for all the pain I have caused, and I hope to use my time in prison to better myself."

There was a buzz of disapproval among the spectators and the judge was just about to bang his gavel when the governor stood up.

"Judge Thornell, if it is possible after you adjourn, may I please address the courtroom?"

Dayton, panic-stricken, whirled around to face his father.

"Certainly, Governor Blankenship, we'd be delighted to have you address this courtroom. Court adjourned. Sine die.

Those who wish to hear the governor may do so. The others may leave."

No one dared to leave the courtroom. Although Samuel Blankenship had not been governor for ten years, he still commanded respect. He slowly and painfully arose to address his former constituents. From deep within the recesses of his soul, the magnificent voice once again boomed forth, and the people were taken back to the time when he was one of the most powerful men in the South.

"Ladies and gentlemen, it is my pleasure to be able to come before you and ask for a favor. You saw fit to elect me as your governor, and if not for a quirk of fate, I would have been your vice-president. I beg your indulgence for just a moment. Listen to me and then decide for yourself what was the right thing to do. It is true that Geoffrey Bockker committed atrocious crimes, which in themselves seem to merit the most extreme retribution. A few years ago, I would have felt exactly the same way that you do. In fact, I would probably have been at the forefront of the group condemning this young man. I still condemn him for what he did. But I have researched this young man's life, and I have found that unspeakable things were done to him during his childhood. These things all came to a head when he saw his fiancé kill herself for the merciless way she had been treated by a group of selfish unthinking young ladies. He struck out at the one thing that he could blame for her death. The two girls he killed were individually innocent. Yet they bore the stigma of belonging to the group, which Geoffrey, in his tormented mind, held responsible for his beloved's death. It is true that you will not get to exact your revenge by seeing this young man's life snuffed out by the gas chamber. But, I promise you that every day he is in Parchman he will suffer for the despicable acts he committed. He will have a long time to be constantly reminded of what he did. He will never forget his crimes. At the end of Geoffrey's life, God alone will decide if he has suffered enough. Then, he will either receive his eternal punishment or be forgiven if he has truly repented. I ask that you think over what I have said. Now go home to your families and thank God for your many blessings."

The courtroom spontaneously erupted in applause. Many people, including Dayton, had tears in their eyes. As they were rushing to thank him and shake his hand, the governor suddenly slumped forward. Dayton and Hiram caught him before he reached the floor. When he felt no pulse, Hiram yelled for someone to send for an ambulance. Dayton tried in vain to revive his father. By the time the ambulance arrived, it was too late. Everyone stood around in shock, some crying, some trying to say consoling words to Dayton. Joanna put her arms around her husband and held him tightly. Never had Dayton been more proud of his father than in the final moments before his death.

During all the tragic excitement, Geoffrey was escorted back to the van. He would be returned to the jail to await his transfer to Parchman. As he was getting in the van, he turned to Josiah and said, "Please tell Mr. Blankenship that I appreciate what his father just did for me."

"I'll tell Dayton, Geoffrey. We'll be leaving for Parchman the day after tomorrow. Do you need anything before I go?"

"No, but thanks, Josiah. Wait a minute, you can do me a favor. See if you can get Angie's pictures for me. I think the sheriff kept them for evidence. Also, in the top of the closet in the upstairs bedroom, way in the back behind a sliding panel, there's a duffel bag. Could you pack it and the pictures in a box for me. I'll need them if I get out of prison. I really can't find the words to tell you how grateful I am for all you've done for me. I can't even begin to repay you."

"That's alright, Geoffrey. I'll go to your house this afternoon."

Josiah slammed the door of the van and watched it drive off. He stood for several minutes, reflecting on the unexpected irony of the day. He got what he wanted for his client, but the day still had a very unhappy ending. Josiah sighed and his eyes became moist.

17

Thousands of people turned out for Samuel Blankenship's funeral, which was held in the First Baptist Church in Columbus. He would be buried in the nearby cemetery next to his beloved wife. Loudspeakers were placed outside the sanctuary so that the overflow crowd could hear the eulogies and the choir. Flowers were sent from all over Mississippi, as well as from the other forty-nine states. Most of the crowd consisted of ordinary folks who looked on Samuel Blankenship as one of their own. They felt he had never forgotten that he had come from the same humble beginnings as they had. Then, there were dignitaries from all parts of the state and even a contingency of U.S. congressmen. Those who could not attend had sent telegrams of condolence to Dayton and Joanna. It was indeed a service Blankenship would have reveled in. He loved "big-to-do's," as he called such ceremonious occasions.

After everything was over and all the visitors had gone home, Dayton sat reminiscing with Joanna, Hiram, and Beth, who had driven down when Hiram called her with the sad news.

"You know, I think Dad single-handedly saved this town."

Joanna frowned at her husband. "What do you mean, Dayton? You assured me that the crowd that came to the house was just a 'fringe group.' "

"Well, I knew we'd have police protection, but still I wasn't really sure. You know how mob mentality is."

"Dayton's right," Hiram said. "If the 'Guvn'r' hadn't said what he did, things could have really gotten nasty. I believe that's the finest speech I ever heard him make. By the way, did you get an autopsy report yet?"

"No, the preliminary report was a ruptured ulcer as the cause of death. I guess that's why he was in so much pain. Damn. I wish he had let us call the doctor. Then he might still be alive."

"No, Dayton," Joanna said, "he died doing what he loved best, speaking to his people. If you had made him go to the doctor, he couldn't have gone to the courthouse, and things would have certainly turned out differently. I think God had a hand in this. Your daddy was meant to deliver that speech."

"I guess so. But there were so many things I wanted to say to him that I'll never be able to."

"Hon, he knew we loved him and that was enough."

Hiram got up from the living room couch. "I think Beth and I had better head home. Her parents are babysitting, and I'm sure the kids have run them ragged by now. Dayton, after you get everything settled and you feel up to it, we'll talk about the Smokies."

The four hugged each other, said their thank-yous and good-byes and Hiram and Beth left.

"Dayton," Joanna said, embracing her husband, "your father was truly a great man, but right now I think you're just as great."

Dayton buried his face in Joanna's neck and let the tears flow.

18

The day for Geoffrey's transfer didn't come soon enough for him. Although he was going to be transported to "The Farm" at Parchman, where he was scheduled to spend the rest of his life, he was really glad to leave the Oktibbeha County jail. Carl Grayson felt the same way. He was still in pain from the facial surgery he needed after Geoffrey had bashed him while trying to escape.

"You're damned lucky those folks from Columbus didn't come over here in droves and try to lynch you more than that one time," Grayson sneered.

Geoffrey remembered the incident all too well. He had been sound asleep when an awful commotion outside the jail woke him up. He looked out the window and saw three truckloads of men, all of them carrying guns, roar up in front of the jail. They jumped out of the trucks and hollered, "Sheriff, we've come after the little bastard who killed those two girls! Now let us have him and there won't be any trouble."

Geoffrey had been scared to death. He was afraid that the sheriff just might hand him over to the fools.

"Damned right there won't be," Grayson responded

adamantly, " 'cause you fellows are going to get back in your trucks and head back to Columbus. You know I'm not going to let you have my prisoner. As much as I'd personally like to see him hurt," he said, running his hand across the bridge of his tender nose, "we'll just have to let him get a fair trial. I trust the people of Oktibbeha County will have enough sense to do the right thing. We're not going to let you take him, so just go on home."

Geoffrey breathed a sigh of relief. At that moment five deputies ran out the door, each brandishing cocked shotguns. Fortunately, cooler heads prevailed and the leader of the mob responded, "Awright, Sheriff, but he better be found guilty or we'll be back and judge him for ourselves."

They left as abruptly as they had arrived. But Geoffrey didn't get any sleep the rest of that night.

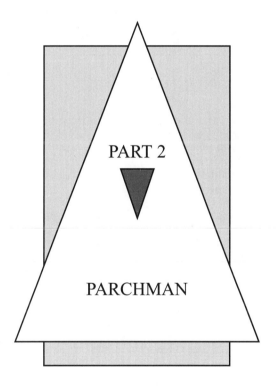

PART 2

PARCHMAN

19

Early the next morning, Grayson placed Geoffrey in the back of a squad car, making sure that his manacles and leg irons were secure, but not too tight to be uncomfortable. Just before Grayson closed the door, Jake Conner leaned over and got right in Geoffrey's face.

"You little shit!" Conner hissed. "I hope to hell those big ole black bucks in Parchman corn-hole you to death. I was prayin' they'd convict you so I could have watched you gasp for your last breath when they dropped those cyanide pellets. Just remember one thing, if you ever do get out of jail and mess up just one time, I'll be on your ass like red beans on rice."

After Conner had walked back toward the jail, Grayson didn't say a word but shook his head and closed the door. Just then Josiah drove up and hurriedly got out of his car.

"Come on, Josiah," Grayson said brusquely. "Let's be on our way. I want to get back home before dark." Josiah jumped into the back seat next to Geoffrey.

Grayson got into the car and revved the engine. They hadn't been driving for more than five minutes when Grayson looked at Geoffrey in his rear-view mirror and said, "Geoffrey, I don't understand why in God's name anyone would choose life in Parchman over a few months in Whitfield. Do you know much about the place?"

"Only what I studied in eighth grade Mississippi history."

"Humph, that book didn't tell you what really goes on. You know, I can't stand you, but I'm going to tell you two things to watch out for. Black Annie and those damn trusties."

"Who's Black Annie?"

"Black Annie's a what, not a who. It's a strap that's six feet long and three inches wide. If you step out of line, they'll beat the hell out of you with it. The trusties are prisoners chosen by the officials to serve as armed guards. They watch over you while you're workin' in the broiling hot sun out in the cotton fields. They can shoot at you if you're not workin' like they think you ought to. I've heard tell they 'allow' someone to try to escape and then shoot the poor bastard in the back while he's runnin' away. That gives them extra points toward an early release."

Geoffrey's eyes were wide with fright.

"Okay, Sheriff. That's enough history for today," Josiah said.

"Damn, Josiah, I was just tryin' to be helpful."

Most of the two-and-a-half-hour ride was uneventful as they made their way up and down the hills along Highway 82. At the top of one of the hills, Geoffrey looked down into what appeared to be the flattest stretch of land he had ever seen in his life. Rows of recently picked cotton fields seemed to reach out in all directions. Incongruously placed within these fields were the mansions of the wealthy Delta planters and the dilapidated houses of their workers.

"Son, you're now in the famous Mississippi Delta," Grayson announced. "Once we turn north here at Highway 49, we'll soon be at your new home. You'll fit right in with the other low life. Maybe you'll even find a girlfriend."

Josiah shot Grayson an irritated glance. "Let him alone, Sheriff. He's got enough problems."

Geoffrey's throat tasted like he had a wad of cotton in it. Jail had not been pleasant, but when they pulled up to the foreboding gate of Parchman Farm, his stomach began to flip flop and one of his headaches compounded his fear. Had he made a mistake in accepting the plea bargain? Could he survive in here at least ten years? He'd heard all sorts of tales about the things that happen to young men in prison. No matter what happened to him, though, he'd be a model prisoner. He could endure anything for his chance to be paroled. And to exact revenge.

"We got a new guest for your hotel, Fred." Grayson tapped his fingers on the steering wheel as the guard checked over Geoffrey's papers to see if they were in order.

"Go right on through, Sheriff. You know the usual procedure. Haven't seen you since you and Chief Gates brought in that college boy last year. Something in the water over there that makes 'em kill girls and women?"

The sheriff grunted an answer and drove down what was referred to as "guard row," a community of frame houses inhabited by the prison employees. About a mile down the road loomed a tall fence with yet another guardhouse. The gate to the fence swung open as if by magic and the sheriff pulled up in front of a one-story red brick building, which served as the prison hospital. It was the first stop in Geoffrey's initiation at Parchman. Grayson and Josiah got out of the car, and when the sheriff opened the door for Geoffrey to get out, he didn't judge the movement of stepping out of the car with the leg irons carefully enough and stumbled forward in Grayson's direction. Suddenly two men with lever action Winchester rifles appeared from the door of the hospital. Cocking their rifles almost simultaneously, they aimed squarely at Geoffrey.

"It's okay, boys," Grayson said quickly. "My prisoner's just a little stiff from the long ride. I assure you he's not trying to escape."

At this point, Josiah and the sheriff had to leave Geoffrey. The lawyer patted Geoffrey on the shoulder and told him that he would stay in touch. Grayson spit out a brown stream of juice and wished Geoffrey good luck.

"If you know what's good for you, keep your nose clean and maybe, just maybe, you'll survive this hell hole, boy," Grayson said.

Geoffrey felt a pang of isolation as the two men pulled away in the squad car.

"Come on in, Bockker," one of the guards said. "We'll 'register' you in the Parchman Hotel."

Once he was in the reception area, Geoffrey's manacles and leg irons were removed, and someone shut and locked the door behind him. Geoffrey now realized he was completely distanced from the outside world, and a feeling of panic set in.

A man just over six feet tall, with the biceps of an NFL lineman, entered the room. "Hello, Geoffrey, I'm J.C. Mixon, and I'll be in charge of admitting you. Awright, boy, I want you to take off all your clothes and place them in a pile in front of you."

Geoffrey was poked and prodded and searched all over to make sure that he had nothing concealed on his body. Mixon then issued Geoffrey the standard prison necessities: underwear, towels, and three pairs of what the prisoners called "ringarounds." Geoffrey's uniform, which had his prison number stenciled on it, consisted of pants and shirts made of heavy duck material with horizontal stripes.

"Awright, boy, let's see how you look in your new clothes."

When Geoffrey had finished dressing, although he knew the situation was very serious, he couldn't help smiling.

"What the hell's so funny?" Mixon asked. "I don't think there's anything to laugh about."

"Yes, sir. I was just reminded of Elvis in *Jailhouse Rock*."

"Well, this ain't no damned movie, and you better get that through your thick skull, or someone will wipe that smile off your face and stick it up your ass."

"Yes, sir. I'm sorry."

By this time, Geoffrey was starving and he was relieved when the sergeant took him to the dining hall located in the rear of the hospital. Here he was given a much better meal than he had expected. Since Parchman was still a somewhat self-supporting farm at the time, Geoffrey greedily ate his first of many prison meals, this one consisting of fresh vegetables, milk, meat, and bread. He hadn't tasted food this good since he left Mississippi State.

After supper Geoffrey was brought back into the hospital and given a physical examination to determine if he was healthy enough to be assigned to work detail. He also was fingerprinted and photographed. Afterwards, Geoffrey was driven to the Maximum Security Unit, where he was placed on death row. Because of his notoriety, the prison officials felt he would be safer there.

The Maximum Security Unit, or "Little Alcatraz" as it was called by its inhabitants, was a one-story building made of concrete, brick, and steel. A twelve-foot high fence, topped with barbed wire, surrounded the sinister- looking structure. Guard towers stood like sentinels at each corner. Standing directly in front of the building, Geoffrey could see a row of windows extending along its entire length. When he and the guards entered the building, Geoffrey was taken to a receiving area, where he was once again ordered to strip naked. He was given another body search, this one even more thorough than before. Afterwards, the clerk gave Geoffrey a blanket and some long underwear instead of his prison uniform. Two armed guards escorted him from the receiving area to the cellblock. As Geoffrey walked down the long corridor, he was overwhelmed by the stench of urine and disinfectant, and he could feel the eyes of the other prisoners staring at him. They seemed to know all about him.

"Hey, pretty boy, welcome to 'Little Alcatraz,' "one prisoner said, his hand reaching through his cell bars toward Geoffrey. "I sure want a piece of you. You want to stick a baby doll up my ass?"

"Look at the little shit. He don't look so hot to me. I could take him down with one hand behind my back," another prisoner sneered.

"Shut up, you bastards, unless you want your rear ends put in solitary," the guard warned.

The very mention of solitary was enough to quiet the inmates. Some had already experienced the punishment. Their heads had been shaved with mule clippers, and they were placed naked in a 6´ x 6´ cell, which had no windows or sink, a bare bed, and no soap or toilet paper. No food or water was provided and the stay was usually seventy-two hours.

When Geoffrey arrived at his cell, the door rolled open and he walked in. It shut behind him with a solid clank. For the first time, Geoffrey knew the meaning of true confinement. As awful as the jail at Starkville had been, it could not compare with Parchman. Fear overtook him as he stared around the eerie place. The corridor of the cellblock was ten feet wide and about one hundred feet long with thirteen cells and a double shower stall along the corridor. His concrete cell was about 6´ x 9´ with steel bars across the front and a sliding door controlled by a panel located at the entrance to the cellblock. The windows, which he had noticed from the outside, ran along the top of the corridor across from the cells. Along the ceiling, seven or eight light bulbs were evenly spaced.

As soon as the guards had left, once again Geoffrey's harassment began, this time in earnest. The prisoners kept their voices loud enough for Geoffrey to hear, but not loud enough to be heard by the guards. When he had endured all he could, Geoffrey, exhausted and depressed, lay down on his cot.

"Don't worry, Geoffrey. I'll help you get even with these bastards."

"Just shut the hell up and let me alone. It's all your fault I'm in this mess," he said just loud enough for several inmates to overhear.

"Oh, now he's talking to himself," one prisoner cackled. "Poor little baby. He hasn't got his mommy to tuck him in."

Geoffrey turned over and faced the wall. Although he covered his ears with his hands to block out the chatter, he could still hear the taunts of the men he'd be spending the next two decades with. As tired as he was, Geoffrey couldn't fall asleep.

The arrival of a new day brought some relief to Geoffrey's torment. The other inmates finally grew tired of their little game and left Geoffrey alone. One of the men actually started a conversation.

"Hey, Bockker—you're okay. My name's Pete Mitchner. I've been here for two years 'cause I killed some dude over a woman. This guy next to me is Johnny Deal. He kidnapped a little eight-year-old girl and murdered her. That fellow across from you is Brad Rule. He killed his wife and stepson while he was drunk. The ugly guy at the end is Jack William Thomas. We all call him the Gris Gris Man since he's from Louisiana and practices voodoo."

"What's he in for, Mr. Mitchner?" Geoffrey asked politely.

"Hey, call me Pete," Mitchner said with a laugh. "He killed a teenager who was parked on the levee with his girlfriend. Shot and raped the girl, but she lived to testify against him.

Poor kid, she'll be crippled and blind for the rest of her life. You don't mess with that mean sonofabitch. The other people here are like you, I guess. They must be temporary. None of them have been sentenced to death."

After that first night, Geoffrey was given back his "ring-arounds." He grew to hate the routine of life on death row, but he knew he had to endure it without complaint. After all, prison had been his choice. He and the other men housed in "Little Alcatraz" were allowed to leave their cells only twice a week to take a shower and shave. They were fed twice a day, at six in the morning and three in the afternoon. Their only other means of recreation was reading or listening to a portable radio or talking to each other. Geoffrey joined in the conversations because the other prisoners had all accepted him after his first night's initiation. The rest of their time was spent in idle boredom, which sometimes led to insurrection among the inmates.

20

The First Decade: 1963-1973

Early one morning, Geoffrey awoke to the pungent smell of burning cloth. "Pete, what the hell's going on?"

"Some fools must have set their mattresses on fire. They're protesting the crap we have to eat. Don't worry. The guards'll be here pretty soon. Just lay low. You don't need to get involved."

In a few minutes, ten guards came running down the hall dragging a fire hose and blasted the burning mattresses, along with the occupants of each cell, except for Geoffrey's and Mitchner's. After the fires had been put out, a group of armed guards came to the cellblock.

"Bockker, get your stuff and come with us," one of the guards ordered.

"Wh—where are you taking me?" Geoffrey was as scared as he was confused.

"Just shut your mouth. You'll know soon enough."

When they arrived at the front entrance of the prison hospital, one of the guards rang the buzzer and a tall, dark-skinned man let them in.

"I see you've brought me my new worker. Hello, Geoffrey.

I'm Dr. McBride. Your friend, Josiah Perkins, pulled some strings and got you transferred here. I do hope that you won't be a disappointment."

Geoffrey managed to stammer out a grateful reply. "Oh, no, sir. I'll do the best I can."

"Good. I'll show you around."

McBride led Geoffrey to a large, rectangular room. Some of the inmates were sitting around playing cards. Others were huddled around a television set located at one end of the room.

"Listen up, guys," McBride announced. "This is Geoffrey Bockker. He's going to be working with us."

The prisoners looked up from their activities and nodded at Geoffrey.

"Bockker, you can have the third cot from the end. Oh, there's a bathroom down the other end of the hall. If you behave yourself, you can be here as long as you like. I've got to get back to work. I'll give you a little while to settle in, then I'll explain what your duties are."

Geoffrey placed his few belongings on the cot. He hoped he wouldn't have to go through another initiation.

One of the men in front of the television turned toward him. "Bockker, come on over and watch this movie with us. This place's a helluva lot better than where you were."

Geoffrey sighed with relief as he walked toward the group.

A few days later, several guards rushed into the emergency room carrying three prisoners on stretchers.

"My God, what happened?" Geoffrey asked.

One of the guards pointed to the most seriously wounded inmate, whose entrails oozed out through a gaping hole in his stomach. "Joe here sat on Porkchop's bed without permission. That really pissed off Porkchop, so he stabbed Joe in the belly with a knife he stole from the kitchen."

"What happened to the other guy?" Geoffrey asked, wide-eyed.

"Hell, he tried to break up the damn fight and got his throat cut. The guards came and busted Porkchop upside the head with their rifle butts."

Geoffrey stood there momentarily frozen, watching the blood spurt out all over the concrete floor.

"Bockker, snap to!" McBride shouted. "Help hold this guy down while I sew him up. We haven't got time to put him to sleep."

Geoffrey did as ordered, staring in horror while the doctor stitched the inmate's gaping stomach. Eventually, they patched up the two remaining prisoners. All three recovered but were sent to the Maximum Security Unit as punishment. Geoffrey hoped his indoctrination into the brutality of prison life was over.

Geoffrey gradually fell into the penal routine, and before he knew it, a whole year had passed. On Christmas Eve 1966, the convicts were given a real present: they were allowed to swap their hated "ring-arounds" for new outfits consisting of trousers with white stripes and blue denim shirts. Although life was bearable for Geoffrey and his fellow workers, many of the prisoners in the mainstream had much to endure. Geoffrey often saw the fruits of their frustrations in the emergency room and wondered why things couldn't be improved. By 1970, though, he came to realize that Parchman's reputation extended beyond its walls and heard talk among the inmates that "something big" was up.

One of the hospital employees had a knack for finding out everything that went on in Parchman. One day Geoffrey sat down next to him in the cafeteria. "What's going on, Fred? I've been hearing some really wild rumors."

"Some Yankee dude from New York is down here interviewing a bunch of prisoners. I guess he's tryin' to start some shit. Won't do any good, though. It'll be a cold day in hell 'fore they make any real changes around here."

Geoffrey just smiled and said, "You never know, man. If the federal government's sticking their nose in it, something might come of it."

21

The Second Decade: 1974-1984

By 1975, Geoffrey had become bored with the routine of working in the hospital. He requested a transfer to the library. There, a whole new world opened up for him when he discovered the myriad of books housed in the building. During the next few years, Geoffrey was allowed to earn enough credits from correspondence courses and from the classes taught by professors who had come over from local colleges to complete his college education. His happiest moment in prison occurred when he was awarded his college diploma in June of 1980.

"Geoffrey, I'm so proud of you," Josiah said. He had been a faithful visitor to his client and now shed real tears of joy when his young protégé was handed his diploma.

"I'd never have done it without your support and encouragement, Josiah. I'm just glad that the federal government saw fit to intervene after that group of prisoners filed their lawsuit. It's made a big difference here. I've got to admit, though, there were times when I wanted to quit, but I knew that I'd disappoint you as well as myself." Geoffrey, too, had tears in his eyes as he hugged his former lawyer and now his friend.

Although Geoffrey appeared normal to everyone else, he was still consumed with hatred for the four women who had taken away Angie and their unborn baby. Psychologists from a local college were finally allowed to come to Parchman in the late 1970s, and Geoffrey was given the testing stipulated in his plea bargain. Geoffrey felt that he was perfectly sane and had gleaned so much information about psychology from the hospital's medical books that he was able to con the psychologists into thinking there was nothing wrong with him. After several sessions, they dismissed him and concentrated on those patients they deemed more needy. He laughed to himself as he left the doctor's office for the last time. *Now, I can get on with my plans. I won't have to waste any more of my precious time having my mind probed by some dumb-ass doctor.*

One day in November of 1980, Liz Anderson, a free-lance reporter for the *New York Times*, appeared at the prison library to interview Geoffrey for an article she was doing on serial killers. The woman was almost a dead-ringer for Angie, and Geoffrey couldn't take his eyes off her during the entire interview.

After she had placed her tape recorder and notebook back into her briefcase, she reached out and gently stroked Geoffrey's face. Feelings that had been repressed for years overpowered him and he grabbed Liz's face with his hands and kissed her hard. His breath came in gulps but he pushed her away.

"I, I can't do this. It's not right."

"Yes, it is. You deserve to be a normal man after all these years."

Geoffrey could tell by the huskiness of her voice that Liz had also become aroused.

"Okay, but we can't do anything here. I've got a key to a private study area. Nobody'll bother us there."

As soon as the couple was in the room, both of them gave in to their sexual urges and began stripping off each other's clothes.

During one heated moment, Geoffrey forgot who he was with. "Oh, Angie," he cried out. Realizing what he had done, he immediately tried to apologize.

"I'm so sorry, Liz."

Liz put her finger to his lips and whispered. "Shh, don't worry. I understand. She's the only girl you ever loved."

That night Liz listened to the tapes she had made that day. Tears of empathy rolled down her cheeks. She understood the pain of a tormented childhood. Liz's mother had died when she was two, and her father, a colonel in the army, had physically abused her from the time she was five years old. His rigid military background made it impossible for him to accept disobedience of any kind. Liz had been rebellious by nature and took delight in arousing her father's anger. She never showed any remorse, even after a severe beating. She'd just laugh and run off to do more mischief. When she was fifteen, she'd fallen in love with Greg, an eighteen-year-old boy her father vehemently disapproved of. Greg had long, greasy hair, smoked marijuana and drank heavily. One of these transgressions would have been enough to send Liz's father into a rage; all three constituted the wrath of God. Liz vividly recalled the night she began to really hate her father.

She had sneaked out of her room to run off with Greg on his motorcycle. She loved the feeling of the wind as it caressed her face and blew through her hair. When they got to the lake, they headed toward the local "make-out" shack. Greg lit a joint and handed it to her. At first Liz refused, but his wily charm soon convinced her that it wouldn't hurt her. When she inhaled, her inhibitions seemed to disappear and she eagerly took the cup of wine he had poured for her. She giggled with pleasure and at first didn't notice that Greg was slowly removing her clothes.

"No, Greg. I've never done this before. I'm scared. What if we get caught?"

"Come on, baby. You said you really loved me. Now prove it. Besides, there's no one for miles around. Remember, there's a big football game tonight."

"I guess so. I love you so much."

At that moment, Liz's father burst through the door. He had seen her sneaking out and had secretly followed the pair. "Get your clothes on, you little slut! I'll deal with you when we get home."

Greg ran out the back door and roared off on his motorcycle.

Liz dressed hurriedly and her father jerked her out the door and shoved her into the car. He never said a word but sat stone-faced with his jaw clenched tightly. When they got home, he yanked off his belt and beat Liz until he was exhausted.

"If you ever so much as look at that boy again, I'll call the cops. Do you understand?"

Liz glared at her father and nodded. Then she ran upstairs to her bedroom and slammed the door shut.

Her father refused to let her out of the house except to go to school or church. Greg never tried to contact her again because he was already on probation for possession of drugs.

Oh, Geoffrey, you and Greg are so much alike, just two misunderstood boys who desperately needed someone to love you.

Liz cried herself to sleep that night.

The next day, Geoffrey continued telling Liz about his past. When he had finished, she looked at him with pity in her eyes.

"It must be terrible for you in here," Liz said, touching his hand.

"I've gotten used to it. I'm pretty isolated here in the library, and I don't have to associate with the really bad inmates."

He kissed her gently and once again they went to their lovers' retreat.

As Liz listened to the tapes of that day's interview, she cried over Geoffrey's plight. She didn't understand that she was falling prey to Geoffrey Bockker. His charming personality had caught her off guard and had opened up old wounds, making her vulnerable to him, emotionally and physically. She never realized that she, like so many other women who had suffered childhood abuse and lacked self-esteem, were kindred spirits. They were ideal victims for the jailhouse predator. These were women very easily manipulated into thinking that the killer didn't deserve the punishment he had received. They often felt that a normal man could never love them, but that *their* love of a criminal would be enough to rehabilitate the man.

The next day Liz and Geoffrey held each other tightly and said a tearful goodbye. Both knew that nothing could come of the affair because she was a married woman and he had no expectations of getting out of prison anytime soon.

Liz drove back to the Memphis airport in a state of confusion and distress and yet ready to make momentous changes in her life.

On the plane, as she sat staring out the window at the approaching night from 30,000 feet, she realized that her marriage certainly hadn't been perfect, but she and Harry had tried to make it work. It was just that now, after falling in love with Geoffrey, she'd never be able to go on living with Harry. She'd have to get a divorce. And then do whatever she could to help Geoffrey get out of jail.

22

The Final Years: 1985-1993

Thanks to a federal judge's orders, a whole section of the library was now filled with law books. Law became Geoffrey's obsession, and he spent most of his time doing research and helping his fellow inmates file briefs for their appeals. He believed that many of the convicts had received unfair trials and he worked painstakingly to have their sentences overturned. By this time, Geoffrey was convinced that he would have to spend the rest of his life in prison. He had applied for parole as soon as he was eligible, but for one reason or another had been turned down each time, even though he thought he had presented his case eloquently.

All this changed in January 1992. He was called to the administration office and, to his surprise, was greeted by Josiah Perkins and a stranger in the reception room.

"Geoffrey," Josiah said, "this is Larry Collier, an FBI agent. He wants to talk to you about helping the FBI solve a serious problem here at Parchman."

When Collier stood up, he towered over Geoffrey. His muscular legs strained his tan woolen suit. He encased Geoffrey's hand in his bear paw and smiled disarmingly. Geoffrey could see the bulge of a pistol holster underneath Collier's jacket.

"Geoffrey, according to your plea bargain, you could spend the rest of your life here." Geoffrey nodded. " Well," Collier said, "how would you like to get out of prison next year?"

Geoffrey stared at Collier suspiciously. "What's the catch? I've been a model prisoner, but every time I've applied for parole, I've been routinely turned down. That sonofabitch Jake Conner comes over whenever I have a hearing and reminds the board about my 'sadistic' crimes. They buy the crap and I have to wait another year before I can apply again. Conner's determined for me to spend the rest of my life in this hellhole. So what can you possibly do to help?"

"Take it easy, Geoffrey," Josiah said.

"I'm sure you're aware there's a huge drug smuggling ring right here in Mississippi," Collier continued, "and it's a damn embarrassment to the U.S. Justice Department. Johnny Garofoli is the drug kingpin here in the South, and even from Parchman he controls the supply of drugs coming into this area from the Mississippi coast. If you could help us put a stop to his operation, I can promise you an early release."

"Yeah, and an early grave," Geoffrey said with a snicker. "I'd wind up at the bottom of the Mississippi River with cement blocks attached to my feet."

"Just listen to my deal first," Collier responded. "We'll put you in the Federal Witness Protection Program and change your identity. Since you don't have any family, no one will even miss you."

Before Geoffrey could say anything, Josiah spoke up. "The U.S. Marshal Service and I have arranged with a friend of mine who's the dean of the Samuel Pipher School of Law at Carter University in North Carolina to admit you to law school where you'll be able to realize your dream of becoming a lawyer. He's someone I can trust completely. You'd first have to take a year of pre-law, though. I think that Jupiter Mountain College would be a good choice. It's near Asheville, in the Blue Ridge Mountains. Both schools are in remote areas, so there's little likelihood of your running into anyone who knows you. I think it's a good idea, but it's entirely up to you."

"Josiah, won't somebody be suspicious if I just disappear one day?" Geoffrey asked anxiously. "You know how long the arm of the Mafia is."

Collier answered for Josiah. "We've thought of that, too. All you have to do is make friends with Garofoli and we'll take care of the rest. We can record all your conversations with him. Once we connect him directly with the drug smuggling, he'll end up in federal prison. We only got him here in Parchman on some trumped up charge of state tax evasion. Will you help us?"

Geoffrey hesitated before giving his reply. "Okay. I guess it's the only way I'll get out of here alive. What do I have to do?"

As soon as Collier explained the plan and left, Geoffrey and Josiah had a long talk. Geoffrey still had some reservations, but he also realized it was the only way he would get out in time to finish what he had started nearly thirty years ago in Columbus. First, though, he had to go to the prison hospital, where he still had complete run of the building, and then he had to have a meeting with one of his "clients" to collect a very important book that the man had obtained for him.

Geoffrey had heard all about Johnny Garofoli from the other prisoners. He was a strikingly handsome, very articulate, and polished man. He had grown up in the Mississippi Delta and graduated from Ole Miss. He won a scholarship to Harvard, where he had received his MBA. Garofoli possessed a brilliant business mind and could have amassed a fortune in an honest profession. Except for a terrible mistake his father had made. The old man had gotten involved with some heavy-handed loan sharks and had not been able to pay back the considerable sum of money he owed them. They agreed to forgive the debt if Johnny would bring in some drugs the next time he flew back from Mexico in his private plane. The success of this venture led to another job and, before he realized it, he was too deeply involved to get out. Besides, he liked the excitement, the feeling of power he derived from the daring missions. Over the years, Johnny had climbed up through the ranks until he was *the* drug smuggler in the entire South. And nobody dared encroach on his territory. For years, the government had tried to get enough evidence to convict him, but he covered his trail too thoroughly. Now, it was up to Geoffrey to gain Garofoli's trust.

A week after Geoffrey had met with the FBI agent, the plan went into operation. For a long time, Garofoli had been trying to arrange a meeting with Geoffrey to discuss setting up a possible appeal. Because he knew that beneath Garofoli's suave exterior beat the heart of a cold-blooded killer, Geoffrey didn't want to help Garofoli get out under any circumstances. But he realized the only way to execute the plan successfully was to gain Garofoli's confidence. He had sent word through the system that he would now have time to talk.

"Hello, Bockker. Thanks for meeting with me," Garofoli said, as they sat in a conference room. "I know your schedule's busy, so I won't take too much of your time. Listen, I've got to get out of this place. I can't run my business operations from here because my partners are getting antsy. Personally, I think they wouldn't mind replacing me, if you know what I mean."

Garofoli had thoroughly checked out Geoffrey before their first meeting and felt comfortable talking with him. Agent

Collier had issued Geoffrey a surveillance device thin enough to be worn inconspicuously. The device recorded every word of their conversations. After three visits, Garofoli opened up to Geoffrey and gave him enough evidence for the government to finally bring federal charges against him, so that if he were convicted, he'd be sent to federal prison.

By September 1992, the FBI had enough evidence for a grand jury to indict Garofoli. Five months later he went on trial. Geoffrey was allowed to give his testimony via a video camera. To protect his identity, he had been put in a room adjoining the courtroom. His features and voice were disguised. Garofoli had bragged to so many fellow inmates about his exploits that he never suspected Geoffrey was the one who had brought him down. After his conviction, the once untouchable drug lord was sent to federal prison in Marion, Illinois, for the rest of his life and without the possibility of parole.

Geoffrey continued helping his fellow convicts until enough time had passed for him to be "released."

He was sitting in the library one afternoon giving advice to another inmate. "George, I think you've got a strong enough case to appeal for a new trial. Look at this article in the law book. According to section twelve—"

Geoffrey clutched his chest and slumped over on the table.

George Mahoney panicked and didn't know what to do at first. Then he reached for the phone and rang for the guard on duty.

"Come in here quick! Something's happened to Mr. Bockker."

The guard rushed in and tried to find a pulse. He found only a faint beat and immediately called for the prison paramedics. They started an IV, placed Geoffrey on the stretcher and wheeled him to a waiting ambulance.

He was then transferred to the prison hospital. Shortly there-after the Air Ambulance from St. Frederick's Hospital in Jackson buzzed over the prison and landed in front of the hospital unit. Geoffrey was supposedly carried to the coronary care unit at that facility. The tragic news that Geoffrey Bockker had succumbed to a fatal heart attack reached the prison in late July of 1993.

In reality, Geoffrey had been taken to a secret government facility in Jackson, where he had met with officials from the U.S. Marshal's office. He remained in the facility until his new identity was processed and all the paperwork for his admission to the colleges in North Carolina was completed.

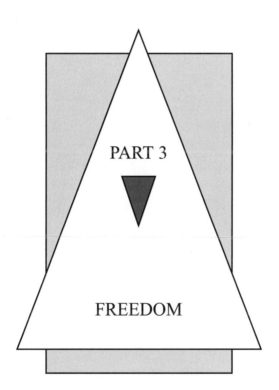

PART 3

FREEDOM

23

On August 20, 1993, after thirty years of confinement in Parchman and several lonely weeks in the secret government facility, Geoffrey Bockker walked out a free man. Josiah Perkins came to pick him up. Even though he knew that Geoffrey had never told him the complete truth about the murders in Columbus, he never felt compelled to confront him and ask any questions. He had a gut instinct, however, that Geoffrey would be able to live in the outside world without committing any further crimes.

"Hello, Josiah. Thanks for coming for me."

"You're welcome. Hey, you look pretty good for a dead man."

Prison had taken its toll on Geoffrey, though. His hair had turned partially gray, he no longer had the physique of a former football player, and his skin was pasty white because he had chosen to spend his free time in the library studying and helping his clients instead of exercising.

"Thanks for everything, Josiah. You've been my only friend all these years. I'll repay you somehow. By the way, have you still got that box of my stuff?"

"I know you will, Geoffrey. Yes, it's up in my attic. Just let me know when you want it. Now let's get on the road. It's eight and we're to meet the U.S. Marshals at four. Your plane doesn't leave for Atlanta until six. That'll give us plenty of time to eat and get you some clothes."

Normally, the marshals would have taken Geoffrey to Memphis themselves, but Josiah had enough influence and such an impeccable reputation that he was allowed to transport Geoffrey. The drive from the secret government facility to Memphis carried the pair through the fertile land of the Mississippi Delta.

"Have you ever been through this part of the state before?" Josiah asked. "Tennessee Williams made it famous in his plays. When I was in undergraduate school at Ole Miss, we used to come over here to some of the famous Delta plantation dances."

"Josiah, I've never been anywhere except around Poplar Ridge or the area around Starkville and Columbus—and, of course, my residence at Parchman the past thirty years. The only thing I know about Memphis is that Elvis lived there."

"You'd love Memphis. I wish you could stay there, but it's just too close to this area."

"Josiah, if you don't mind, I think I'll take a nap. I was so excited about today I couldn't sleep last night."

Josiah nodded.

Geoffrey relaxed a little. He really wasn't sleepy. He just wanted to think. His mind wandered back to that day he had received a very important package from one of his "clients." He had talked the prisoner into getting his wife to come up with a copy of an MSCW Alumnae Directory. Almost everyone who had graduated from the "W" was in the book. His fellow inmate asked why he wanted the book as he handed it to Geoffrey.

"Oh, I'm just going to look up some old friends and pay a surprise visit to them if I ever get out," Geoffrey had replied.

When he was alone that night, Geoffrey thumbed through the pages to find the four names he was looking for. As he read, he said aloud to himself, "Thank goodness they're listed under their maiden names. Let's see. Flowers, Barbara. Here it is. Hmm. Her married name is Barbara Atkins, and she lives at 3456 Sunset Drive in Center City, Mississippi. That's not too far away. Harris, Arlene. She's married to someone whose last name is Holcomb. Shit, she lives in Tampa, Florida. That's gonna present a problem. Walton, Janine. Bingo. She's Mrs. Lamar Beauregard now. Damn, she lives in Rich, Mississippi. All this time I haven't been more than two hours away from her, and I couldn't touch the bitch. Well, that's okay. I've got plenty of time. Now, the last name on my list. Here it is. Yates, Suzanne. Hmn, she's listed only as Suzanne Carter. That probably means she's divorced. Good. Maybe that'll make her more vulnerable. She lives in Memphis. I think if I ever get out of here, Memphis will be my destination. At least I'll have easy access to three out of the four. Those are pretty good odds." Geoffrey smiled smugly.

"Geoffrey, wake up! We're in Memphis," Josiah said, taking one hand off the steering wheel and gently nudging Geoffrey.

"Um! That was a good nap." Geoffrey stretched and shook his head, pretending to remove the cobwebs of sleep.

"First thing we're going to do is get you some new clothes. The Witness Protection Program isn't too generous when they outfit someone for a new identity. Are you hungry? After we get your clothes, we'll go to the Rendezvous for some ribs."

"Sounds great. After thirty years of prison food, anything will taste good."

For thirty years the only civilian clothes Geoffrey had seen were on visitors and instructors and the ill-fitting outfits he had worn at the government facility. He knew very little about clothes and even less about style. Malls were even a novelty to him and he stared in amazement at the throngs of people crowding the Oak Court Mall. How could so many stores be under one roof?

"Come on, Geoffrey," said Josiah. "Let's get you a suit and some slacks and shirts for classes. You're just about my size. Try this one on," he said, selecting a dark blue suit and a white cotton shirt to go with it.

Everything fit perfectly. Then Josiah picked up the essential items, including shoes, socks, and underwear.

"Now that we know your size, we'll get the rest of your clothes," Josiah told a very grateful Geoffrey. "Oh, by the way, I had an extra set of luggage at home, so I brought it for you to use. We can pack everything when we get you to the place where we're meeting the marshals. You can change into some of your new clothes there, too."

The drive to downtown Memphis took about fifteen minutes. Josiah turned left onto Second Street and then eased onto Union and pulled into the parking lot of the "Grand Old Lady of the South," the name given to the Peabody Hotel. The pair then walked up Second Street to the Rendezvous, where the aroma of barbecue permeated the air.

"I remember hearing kids talk about coming here," Geoffrey said quietly as he realized his youth had passed him by during the thirty years in Parchman.

"Hi, Mr. Perkins, your regular table, sir?" greeted Cal, the old waiter who had toiled at this restaurant for the last thirty-five years.

"Sure thing, Cal."

When they were seated, Josiah ordered for both of them. After they had finished eating, Geoffrey leaned back in his chair and licked the rib remains from his fingers.

"I can honestly say that's the best food I've had in over thirty years."

During the half-hour drive to the meeting point, Geoffrey seemed in a pensive mood so Josiah didn't say anything until he pulled up in front of a nondescript brick building. It was located directly across from the Memphis Airport. Josiah popped the trunk and he and Geoffrey got out their purchases and the luggage.

"Geoffrey, I want to say this to you right now and you remember it. If you ever need me for anything, call me collect at home and say the call is from Mason Dixon. That's a silly name, but it's easy to remember. Now don't forget what I just said."

Geoffrey nodded but didn't say anything. He was too overcome with emotion because he realized that he might never see Josiah again.

They walked into the lobby of the federal building, their arms loaded with suitcases and packages. Josiah told the receptionist to let the U.S. Marshals know that he and Geoffrey had arrived.

In a few minutes, two dark haired, muscular men wearing dark blue business suits came into the room. After the introductions, the taller of the two men, Marvin Collins, spoke up. "I suppose those are Geoffrey's new clothes. Come on, we'll go into this room and inspect everything and then let you pack them."

The two marshals studied every item carefully and X-rayed Josiah's suitcases to make sure that nothing was hidden anywhere. They ordered Geoffrey to disrobe and checked him thoroughly. When they were satisfied that he wasn't concealing anything, they told him to dress and allowed Josiah and Geoffrey to pack Geoffrey's bags for the trip to North Carolina.

"What do you want us to do with your old clothes, Geoffrey?" Collins asked.

"You can burn them as far as I'm concerned. They're a reminder of the old life I'm leaving behind."

Deputy Harvey Gomez said in a somewhat raspy voice, "Okay, let me explain your new identity, Geoffrey. From now on, you're William Caldwell, and you grew up in a remote part of Mississippi in a very small town named Oak Vale. The U.S. Marshal's Service has written out an autobiography for you to study. All your paperwork is in order. Here's your new driver's license and social security card. Your college transcripts have been taken care of. You're registered at Jupiter Mountain College in North Carolina. We've rented you a house near the campus. At the end of the first year, you will transfer to Carter University. Someone from our office will be there when it's time to make that move. We'll be in contact with you from time to time. We want to get all these things out of the way before we board the flight. As far as the other passengers are concerned, we will be three men on a business trip. I don't think we have to tell you not to try anything foolish because both of us are armed, and we won't hesitate to use our weapons if we have to. Now, is everything clear?"

"Yes, sir, it is. But you won't have any trouble from me, I can assure you."

"Mr. Perkins, I think it's time for you to leave. We have to escort Mr. Caldwell to the terminal, and that takes a little while. By the way, Caldwell, Mr. Perkins, I believe, has taken care of your money for you."

"Geoffrey, uh, William," Josiah stumbled, "I've been keeping the money your parents left you in mutual funds. They're worth a good deal of money now. I opened a checking account for you in the First National Bank in Jupiter Mountain. Here's some draft checks. You can have some new ones printed with your new address. Your tuition for the whole year has been pre-paid. Just watch your money and don't spend it foolishly. Good luck. The only way I can contact you is through the U.S. Marshal's office, but I promise I'll be in touch."

Josiah extended his hand, and Geoffrey shook it warmly, thanking him profusely.

"I just don't know what I'd have done without you, Josiah. I don't think I could have survived the thirty years without your friendship. Oh, why don't you send that package you've been keeping for me to my new address. That way I know I'll get some mail."

Josiah nodded with a smile. "I'll get it off first thing tomor-row."

Geoffrey felt kind of guilty. He truly appreciated everything that Josiah had done for him, but he still had an even greater obligation to Angie.

Josiah walked out the door of the room into the outer office, stopping long enough to have a lengthy chat with Agnes Claypool, the attractive receptionist.

The two marshals led Geoffrey into another room. They loaded his clothes onto an airport baggage cart and walked down a small corridor until they came to an elevator.

"Okay, Caldwell, now begins the first part of your journey to a new life," Collins said.

The elevator descended several floors. When the door opened, they boarded a tram, which took them down a long corridor to another elevator. This time Collins punched "2." When the elevator came to a stop, the door opened into a room filled with official-looking people manning computers or milling around.

One man came over to greet the marshals. "Hi, Collins, Gomez. I assume this is William Caldwell." He handed Collins a packet. "Here are your tickets to Atlanta and Asheville. Just show them to security and you'll be allowed to go beside the detector, while William gets X-rayed. They know you're on your way. Oh, William, here's a briefcase for you to carry. We've put some maps of the town and the campus in it for you to look at when you get to Jupiter Mountain. The briefcase will make you look more like a businessman."

"Great, thanks," Geoffrey said with an appreciative nod.

"Come on, Caldwell," Gomez said as he opened the door leading out into the main area of the terminal. "We don't want to miss our plane."

After they had checked Geoffrey's luggage, they headed toward the concourse. When the trio reached the entrance to the concourse, the two marshals stood to the side, waiting for Geoffrey to walk through the metal detector while his briefcase slid along the conveyor belt.

At the waiting area for their flight, Gomez said, "Caldwell, if you have to go to the restroom, let's go now, because we can't let you go once we board the plane."

Geoffrey took up their offer, and the three men filed into the restroom. Geoffrey was thankful that, at least, the marshals didn't have to go into the stall with him.

As they boarded their plane, Geoffrey swallowed hard. He had never even been on a plane before, and now one was taking him to a brand new life.

"It's okay, William," Collins said reassuringly. "We've flown hundreds of times. Actually, flying is statistically safer than driving."

This was the first time either marshal had referred to him by his first name. Geoffrey wondered if perhaps they were warming up to him a little. He certainly hoped so.

On the plane the marshals were seated, one on either side of Geoffrey. He felt sandwiched in because each weighed about 250 pounds. But Geoffrey decided not to complain—their size was so intimidating.

After the flight attendant made her routine announcements, the plane picked up speed as the pilot accelerated down the runway. Geoffrey gripped the arms of his seat and leaned over a little to look out the window. He watched in amazement as the ground whizzed by. Then, the plane tilted its nose upward, the ground grew farther and farther away, and they were airborne.

"You okay, William?" Gomez asked. "You're as white as a ghost. Don't get sick on us."

"I think I'm okay, Deputy Gomez. Everything just sort of took me by surprise."

Geoffrey stiffened when he felt a clunk coming from beneath the plane.

"Just relax," Gomez said. "That's only the landing gear being locked into position."

Once they were at cruising altitude, Geoffrey was finally able to relax. But, by this time he was getting really hungry and groaned when he was handed a Coke and a package of peanuts.

"Don't worry, William," Collins said. "We'll have enough time to get a bite in the airport before we catch the flight to Asheville. Why don't you get out your autobiography and study it for a while?"

Geoffrey barely had time to read about his new identity before the plane began its descent into Hartsfield Airport. When he felt the bump of the plane on the ground, Geoffrey was thankful that he had survived his first flight.

"What do you want to eat, William?" Collins asked as they were walking down the concourse.

"A hamburger and fries is fine with me. Look, I've got some money. Let me treat you guys."

This was the first time that either of the agents had been given anything but grief by someone they were escorting.

"Thanks, William, but it's against federal policy."

The three men ate hungrily. The agents were well aware of Geoffrey's past, but they didn't question him about it. Instead, they talked to him about his future plans.

"When I get out of law school," Geoffrey said, "I plan to set up a practice where I can help indigent people, you know, those that can't get a good defense. I know that most prisoners in Parchman were guilty, but a lot of them didn't receive fair trials. They didn't have enough money to hire a really good lawyer. You know, you don't see many rich people in jail. Also, I'd like to work with young, abused kids to maybe keep them from making the same mistakes I made. I think a good prevention program in schools can keep a lot of kids from becoming criminals."

"Yeah, maybe it'd cut down on our jobs. Well, Bill—you don't mind if I shorten William to Bill—do you? I hope you can accomplish your dreams. We need more people in the world with ideas like yours."

"That's true, Harvey," Collins said with a nod.

After their flight for Asheville had been called and the three were boarding the plane, Geoffrey was much less nervous than he'd been when they left Memphis. He chuckled to himself.

They bought that shit about helping others. Hell, I'm just going to bide my time until I can get back to Memphis and punish the four bitches who destroyed my life.

During the flight, Geoffrey was so relaxed that he actually went to sleep and didn't wake up until he felt Deputy Gomez shake his arm and tell him they had arrived in Asheville.

The ride from the airport to Jupiter Mountain took about thirty minutes. Geoffrey's rental house was on Cascade Street, just a block down from the college.

"Okay, Bill, here we are. Let's go in and see how everything looks," Deputy Collins said. He handed Geoffrey the keys to his new place, and Geoffrey eagerly unlocked the door. After the three men had carried Geoffrey's belongings inside, the two deputies walked to the door to leave.

Collins spoke first as he shook hands with Geoffrey. "Bill, I wish you the best of luck. I'll be honest with you. Not too many people make it in the program. They screw up somewhere along the way. But I think you're different."

Gomez gave Geoffrey a warning glance. "Yeah, but just remember your prints are on file at headquarters. Even though you have a new identity, if you commit a crime, you'll be caught and then you'll rot in prison sure enough. But, I can honestly say that this has been the most pleasant experience we've had with someone in the Witness Protection Program. Somebody'll check on you from time to time. Here's our card in case you need anything. Don't hesitate to call. Good luck."

Geoffrey thanked them and closed the door of his new home. He kicked off his loafers and began dancing around the room. He pumped his fist in the air several times, shouting, "I'm free! I'm free!"

24

The next morning Geoffrey got out the campus map. Josiah and the U.S. Marshal Service had already registered him, but he needed to see the dean to let him know that he had arrived on campus.

The door to the dean's outer office was open and Geoffrey looked intently at the man seated at the cluttered mahogany desk. When Geoffrey cleared his throat, the dean looked up from his work and pushed his horn-rimmed glasses farther up on his thin, beak-like nose. Then, after brushing his few strands of black hair away from his forehead, he stood up and walked toward Geoffrey.

"May I help you, young man?"

"Dean Spangler, my name is William Caldwell."

"Of, course, William, we've been expecting you. I see from your transcript that you've made excellent grades. We are certainly looking forward to having you as a student here at Jupiter Mountain. I just wish that you could stay for more than one year, but I understand why you want to go on and finish your law degree as soon as possible. How is Josiah doing?"

"He's fine, sir. I'm certainly impressed with what I've seen of your campus so far. Josiah has told me how beautiful the mountains are in the fall."

"Well, we like to think that we have the perfect location. Our campus is surrounded by rivers, mountains, and woods, and yet we're close enough to Asheville to offer the most sophisticated person every advantage. I know that you'll be doing a lot of studying, but in your free time there are so many attractions around here, like the Biltmore House and Mt. Mitchell. Do you like to hike?"

"I haven't had the opportunity before, but I think I'd enjoy it."

"Good. Well, you didn't come here to listen to my tourism spiel about our state. Here's you schedule. Look it over a minute and see if you have any questions."

Geoffrey noticed that there was a wide variety of courses. The dean had registered him in American Government, Social Psychology, Calculus I, Business Law I, and Problems in Philosophy. He would be taking fifteen hours, which would keep him busy but would still allow him enough time to relax and to make plans for eventually returning to Memphis to carry out his project.

"This looks fine to me, sir," Geoffrey said. "I think I'll just walk around the campus and then maybe check out the town. I'll be seeing you again. Thanks for everything."

The dean smiled and said, "If you need anything, just let me know. Oh, the names of the books you'll need for the courses are listed at the bottom of your class schedule. You'll find everything at the campus bookstore. Good luck, and welcome to Jupiter Mountain College."

Geoffrey couldn't wait to get away from the dean. He reminded him of the mortician who had prepared his beloved mother for her burial. Besides, Geoffrey was beginning to get one of his headaches. He walked quickly back to his house to get his Imitrex. After lying down for a while, he felt better and decided to take a walk and check out the area. The fresh air invigorated Geoffrey and the mountains were so majestic that soon his hostility toward the dean lessened. After all, the poor man was only trying to be helpful.

Each afternoon when Geoffrey returned from class, he checked his mail to see if his package was there. On the third day it finally arrived. His hands shook as he tore the tape off the box. Inside he found a package covered with bubble wrap and a duffel bag. His eyes teared up as he removed the bubble wrap. His trembling hands held the pictures he hadn't seen in over thirty years.

As he gazed at the photographs of Angie, he whispered, "Oh baby, it seems like forever since I've looked at your beautiful face. I couldn't take your pictures to prison and have those monsters leering at you. I still love you so much. I promise you I'll kill those bitches. Then I don't care what happens to me."

Geoffrey unzipped the duffel bag and his gray eyes flashed with hatred when he saw the triangular photograph. Rage seized him and he roared, "Your days are numbered!"

He pulled out the spiral notepad and leafed through the pages filled with his exploits. As he was reading, an old friend made its presence known. "Geoffrey, I've been so lonely. It's time to come out and play. Surely we can find someone here to kill. I've missed your company so much. Please set me free."

Geoffrey salivated at the thought of murder, but after thirty years, he couldn't kill just for the sake of killing. The victim would have to be someone who had harmed him in some way. This time he chose to ignore his voice and returned to his spiral notepad.

25

At the end of the first week of classes, Geoffrey realized that Josiah had done a good job of choosing his school. The professors were excellent and the students went out of their way to be nice to him, even if he were old enough to be their father. He bought a computer and hooked up to the Internet. This made it easier to do some of the assignments because many professors posted them on the Web.

Sometime during the first month of classes, a group of his friends invited him to tour Biltmore House, the palatial turn-of-the-century Vanderbilt mansion. He had really enjoyed the trip until something terrible happened. While everyone else was inside the building, Geoffrey was wandering alone on one of the trails around the perimeter of the estate, when he almost collided with a young woman. While she was apologizing to him quite profusely, she suddenly stopped and looked him squarely in the eyes. She had a puzzled look on her face.

"You, you're supposed to be dead. They said you had a heart attack and died."

"I'm sorry, but I don't know what you are talking about. Look I'm alive and well, or you wouldn't be standing here talking to me."

"I *know* you're Geoffrey Bockker," she insisted. "You were in Parchman with my father. Then we heard that you had a heart attack and died in Jackson."

"Look, I'm not Geoffrey Bockker or whoever you claim I am. Here, look at my driver's license and here's my social security card. See, I'm William Caldwell, and I go to college near here."

Geoffrey's steel gray eyes turned almost black as he vehemently denied the girl's accusations. She was so mesmerized by his stare that she seemed to waver in her certainty. Finally, she shook her head.

"I'm so sorry, Mr. Caldwell. It's just that you look so much like Geoffrey Bockker. I guess it was wishful thinking. He helped to get my father out of prison several years ago. Dad was serving time for a crime he didn't commit. Geoffrey spent three years working on his case, but he finally managed to get my father a new trial. Miraculously, someone came forward and confessed to the killing. I'll be eternally grateful to Mr. Bockker."

"I can understand how you feel about him, and I'm truly sorry that I'm not the recipient of your gratitude."

"William, come on," called one of Geoffrey's classmates when he found him talking to the young woman.

Geoffrey gave her an apologetic look. "Sorry, I'd like to stay and talk, but I've got to catch up with my group."

"Oh, sure. Sorry for the confusion."

A female tour guide, who had been standing close enough to overhear the entire conversation, turned away quickly as Geoffrey headed back to his group. When she got home that night, she placed a long distance call to a relative in Mississippi to report what had transpired.

"Jake, this is Marjorie. You'll never believe what happened

today…"

Jake Connor stalked into his office the next morning.

"What's wrong, Sheriff? You look mad as a wet hen," his secretary, Nancy, said.

"My cousin Marjorie, the one who works as a tour guide at the Biltmore House Estate in North Carolina, called me last night. It seems that our old friend Geoffrey Bockker was in a group of tourists yesterday."

"But didn't he die in Jackson?"

"That's what the damned government must have wanted us to think. I'm going to get on the phone right now and get some answers. Nobody's going to screw around with me."

Several minutes later, Conner slammed down the phone.

"More government crap! They say Marjorie couldn't have seen Conner because he's buried somewhere in Jackson. I don't believe their shit for one minute. Nancy, call the airport, get me a ticket on tomorrow afternoon's flight to Atlanta and a connecting flight to Asheville. I'm going to see what the hell's going on. If Bockker's there, I'll find him."

As soon as the tour was over, Geoffrey rushed back to his house. *I guess I'm not even safe here in North Carolina. I can't afford for anyone else to recognize me. I may not be so lucky next time.*

The next morning, Geoffrey walked into Hair World, where he'd been going for haircuts. "Joseph, I need to change my hairstyle. I look too much like an old man. What can you do to make me look different?"

"Umm, have we spotted a cute coed we want to impress? Just leave it to Joseph. I'll turn you into such a stud the girls will fall all over you."

When Joseph had finished, Geoffrey was really astonished.

The image that stared back at him from the mirror had dark brown hair instead of blond, and the new hairstyle make him look twenty years younger.

"This looks great, man. Thanks."

"Just keep me posted on your success. If you have too many girls hanging around, send a few my way."

Geoffrey headed to the nearest Eye Masters. He knew he probably needed glasses anyway. After the eye exam, he selected a pair of very youthful-looking glasses and spent a few hours shopping before he returned to pick them up.

Jake Conner had arrived in Asheville. He was dialing his cousin's house on his cell phone when two men approached him. The taller of the two flashed a U.S. Marshal's badge and said, "Mr. Conner, we'd like you to come with us, please."

The men led Conner to a private office just off the concourse. "We hear you've been making some pretty ridiculous statements about Geoffrey Bockker. Mind telling us why?"

Conner twitched in his chair and nervously replied, "My cousin swears she saw Bockker at the Biltmore Estate in Asheville and I thought I'd do a little investigating on my own, since the damn government won't help."

One of the marshals leaned over and stared directly into Conner's face. "Geoffrey Bockker's dead. Period. End of case. Nobody needs some half-cocked hotshot Mississippi sheriff going off on a wild goose chase. Your cousin was wrong. We've arranged a flight for you back to Mississippi. Don't go snooping around anymore or you might get in trouble. Comprendé?"

Conner, fuming inside, chewed on his lip and looked back at the man. "Yeah, I understand."

"Good, now let's get you on your way. We wouldn't want you to miss your flight."

Thirty minutes later, Jake Conner slouched down in his seat. He jammed the seat belt together and stared straight ahead. He didn't care what the federal marshals said, he was going to keep searching for that sonofabitch until he found him. But he'd have to be very careful about it. Then he wondered why in hell the federal government was protecting such a vicious murderer.

26

Geoffrey was so pleased with his new appearance that he relaxed and began to enjoy his surroundings. During the fall, he learned to love the outdoors and often went hiking in the mountains with his fellow students or with some of the professors closer to his own age. He began to feel comfortable even when he hiked by himself. In fact, he preferred the solitude of the environment. From the top of Mt. Mitchell, he felt at peace as he looked down through the mists that floated beneath him. The panoramic view of the explosion of fall colors on the slopes below almost took his breath away. The rhododendron and other fauna that grew along the mountain trails even inspired him to write poetry. After a while, Geoffrey realized that he knew the mountains like the back of his hand. They were truly his comfort zone and his protector—they nurtured him.

Since he had nowhere to go, Geoffrey spent the Thanksgiving break at the Wolf Laurel ski resort located just outside Jupiter Mountain. He took skiing lessons and by the end of the week had graduated to the expert slopes. For Geoffrey the first semester seemed to rush by. He had studied hard and finished with a perfect 4.0 average. When Christmas break arrived, Geoffrey rented a car and drove to Beech Mountain, where the skiing was more challenging. He felt a rush of excitement as he sped down the icy terrain of White Lightning, considered by many to be the best of the black diamond trails. Whenever he tired of Alpine skiing, Geoffrey simply put on his cross-country skis and glided along the Cherry Gap Trail. After three weeks, a tired but invigorated Geoffrey packed his car and returned to Jupiter Mountain, ready for the next phase of his education.

During the second semester he again took fifteen hours, including Advanced Composition, History of the U.S. to 1877, Criminal Law, Social Problems, and Advanced Philosophy. Because of his excellent grades, he was elected to the Pre-Law Society, as well as to membership in several other honorary societies. Geoffrey had adapted well to his new academic life and was genuinely happy for the first time in many years.

All too soon, the year came to a close and just as everything seemed to be going perfectly for Geoffrey, a horrible event occurred. He went into his exams with a 3.8 grade point average. He had straight A's in all his classes except for Advanced Philosophy. Geoffrey, outspoken and opinionated, often clashed with his professor over ideologies. On the day before the exam, he and Professor Erickson became embroiled in such a heated discussion that the rest of the students feared a fight might erupt. When class was over, Geoffrey and the professor were still going at it. One of his fellow students, Peter Morris, a thin boy who wore wire-rimmed glasses, was afraid Geoffrey would jeopardize his grade average if the fiery exchange continued so he tried to pull Geoffrey away. Forgetting where he was, Geoffrey whirled around and pulled a switchblade out of his jacket pocket and jerked the student toward him until the blade of the knife was flush against the boy's throat.

"Peter, don't you ever grab me again, you goddamn sonofabitch, or I'll slice you to ribbons!"

The campus police, who had been notified by one of the students in the class, burst into the room and managed to subdue Geoffrey and to wrest the knife from his hand. Geoffrey was immediately escorted to the Security Office where the campus police questioned him extensively. The chief of police, David Post, had often gone hiking with Geoffrey and knew him as well as anybody.

"William, what came over you? I've never seen you like this before. You know it's against the law for any unauthorized person to carry a switchblade knife. What possessed you to attack Peter like that? The poor kid couldn't hurt a fly. The other students say that you and Professor Erickson were jawing at each other pretty hot and heavy, and he was just trying to keep you from getting in trouble."

"I don't know why I did it, David. I guess I just snapped. Erickson's harassed me all semester and I couldn't take it anymore. What's going to happen to me? Please don't let them arrest me. I'll do anything to make things right."

"The main thing you have going for you is that this is your first offense. I'll see what I can do."

After the campus police had left with Geoffrey, Erickson and Peter stood there momentarily, neither saying anything. Finally, Erickson spoke up. "Let's go to my office so we can have some privacy."

Once inside the confines of the office, Erickson embraced the boy tenderly.

"My God, Peter, what were you thinking? The bastard could have killed you."

"I don't know. I just didn't want Geoffrey to jeopardize his grade. You've been awfully tough on him this semester." Peter's head rested on Erickson's shoulder.

"What the hell difference should that make to you?" Erickson said, breaking their embrace. "Oh, God, you've fallen in love with him, haven't you? I've seen the way you stare at him in class. You can't keep your eyes off him." His eyes bore into Peter's.

"Daniel, you know I could never love anyone but you. How could you suggest such a thing?" Peter asked, his voice rising to a crescendo.

The phone rang and Erickson turned around to answer it. "We'll continue this conversation later. I'll call you when I get through with my classes," he said angrily.

Peter walked dejectedly out of the office. In his haste, he almost ran into Erickson's student assistant, who had been standing just outside the door.

"Sorry," Peter mumbled. He kept his head down so that the boy wouldn't see the tears forming in his eyes.

When Geoffrey arrived home that night, completely confused and angry with himself, he went to his bedroom and looked at Angie's pictures. *What could have made me do something that stupid? If they call the police in on this, I won't have any prior records as William Caldwell, but if they get the fingerprints from my knife—Jesus, why didn't I keep my mouth shut? Oh, God, what am I going to do?*

"Hello, this is the long distance operator. We have a collect call from Mason Dixon. Will you accept the charges?" Geoffrey waited nervously in the phone booth as the call went through.

"Geo—William, what's wrong? Has something happened?" Josiah sounded very worried.

After Geoffrey told Josiah about the incident with Peter, his lawyer tried to reassure him.

"William, just don't worry right now. I'll talk to the dean

and see if we can't work something out. The main thing is that the police don't get involved. We can't have them sending your prints to the FBI. Even with your new identity, your prints on file will belong to Geoffrey Bockker. That'll be the beginning of the end—you'll be kicked out of the protection program and sent back to prison. Just keep a low profile until I can check things out. If you don't hear something from the dean by tomorrow afternoon, then call me back collect."

"Josiah, I'm so sorry I screwed up after everything you've done for me."

The two men said goodbye, and as Geoffrey hung up the phone and walked back to his house, Josiah placed a call to Dean Spangler.

"Fritz, this is Josiah Perkins. How are you? I just spoke to William Caldwell, and he told me what happened. How do you assess his situation?"

"Well, Josiah, it's his first offense and he's been an exemplary student up to this point. One thing is in his favor, though. I handle all disciplinary matters during the last ten days of school. Do you have any idea why William might have attacked the young man? Peter's only reason for pulling him away was to keep him from getting in trouble with Professor Erickson."

"Fritz, I don't want what I'm about to tell you to become public knowledge, and it doesn't really justify what William did. But let me fill you in on his background; it may help to see him in a different light. When he was a child, his mother suffered from severe depression and had to be sent off periodically to a mental hospital. When William and his father visited, some of the patients scared the child to death. His mother died when he was eight and his father sent him to live with a foster family because he was about to be shipped off to Korea. As it turns out, his father was killed over there. William must have been abused in one of the homes because X-rays taken when he got hurt in college revealed an old skull fracture and several broken bones. From what he intimated to me, he may have even been sexually molested. When he was thirteen, he finally went to live with a family who loved him. When he was a freshman in college, they were both killed in a car crash. William has terrible migraines and periodic blackouts. Mind you, Fritz, I'm not excusing him, but he has had some tough breaks in his life. My guess is that when the young man pulled him by the arm, it brought back memories of William's abusive past and that triggered the attack."

"Well, that could help explain his actions," Spangler responded. "I'll tell you what I'll do, Josiah. I'll convince Peter not to press charges, so the police won't be involved, but we'll have to suspend William for the summer term. It won't affect his getting into Carter University, though. This incident will stay sealed at Jupiter Mountain unless he commits another illegal act here. I'll call William in tomorrow after I talk to Professor Erickson and Peter."

"Thanks, Fritz. I promise you he won't cause any more problems."

After he had hung up, Josiah clasped his head in his hands and sighed. *Did I make a mistake sending Geoffrey to prison for thirty years? Something must still be wrong with him if he reacted like that. Oh, God, have I helped release a monster back into society? I think I'll give Leonard Haskins a call.*

The next morning Dean Spangler called Geoffrey to his office. "William, I've talked to Josiah and to Peter. Peter's agreed not to press charges. In light of your excellent record, we're only going to suspend you from college this summer. You'll still be able to attend law school this fall, though. You'll have more than enough credits. We'll just put a withdrawal with passing grade on the philosophy course so you won't have an F for missing the exam. Will you agree to these conditions?"

"Yes sir, Dean Spangler. I don't know what came over me. I'd like to apologize to Peter and to Professor Erickson if that's possible."

"I think we can work that out."

Geoffrey left the dean's office, went back to his house and into the bedroom to "talk" to Angie.

"Baby, I almost screwed up but good. Thank God for Josiah. Once again, he got my tail out of a crack. That weasel of a dean. I'd like to carve a triangle on his little pointed head. The no-good bastard. And Professor Erickson and that friggin' Peter. They had better thank their lucky stars I'm out of here after the summer. Witness Protection or not, I've waited long enough to collect what those bitches owe us. I'm going to be in Memphis this fall, I promise you that, baby."

The next day Geoffrey was back in the dean's office, this time to profusely apologize to Peter Morris and Professor Erickson. They both accepted his apology. Erickson even offered to let him skip the exam and take a grade of B. Geoffrey took the offer and walked out of the dean's office feeling great relief.

When he got back to his house, he sat down in front of Angie's pictures, hoping for inspiration. He needed to convince Josiah that going to law school near Memphis would be in his best interest. After he had decided what to tell Josiah, he got out his spiral notebook and devised his plan for revenge. He had been fascinated with the surveillance equipment used to record his conversations with Johnny Garofoli and with the FBI's equipment that disguised his identity during Garofoli's trial. He decided to purchase some of the equipment for himself. He turned on his computer and began to search the Internet for companies that sold similar equipment. One company had everything he needed: a Caller-ID Buster, a Portable Voice Changer, a bug for eavesdropping on conversations, and, for later use, three pairs of special handcuffs, and a disguise kit.

That night Geoffrey went to sleep, expecting to have pleasant dreams of what it would be like to torture and kill the four women he reviled so much. But instead, something else happened. In the middle of the night, he awoke in a cold sweat and saw a figure standing before him.

"Geoffrey, have you forgotten about me? Don't you remember the promise you made so long ago? I'll never leave you alone until you keep your promise. I love you."

He reached out to touch Angie but could feel only the cool stillness of the room as he groped blindly in the dark. Had he gone crazy? He must have just had a nightmare, he thought. But it shook him so terribly that the next day, he placed an urgent call to Josiah Perkins.

"William, what's the matter?" Josiah asked anxiously. "Didn't you get everything worked out at school?"

"Everything went fine, Josiah. It's just that I can't take the courses I planned to take this summer. But I called you for another reason." Geoffrey hesitated for a moment, then plunged forward. "I can't stay up here any longer. I don't want to go to Carter University. I want to go to a law school near Memphis. I love it here, but I'm homesick for that area. Do you understand?"

"Yeah, but I don't know if the U.S. Marshals will let you come back here and remain in the Witness Protection Program."

"I don't care. I want to be near Memphis. What's available in the area?"

"I still don't think it's such a good idea," Josiah said with disappointment in his voice. "But if you insist. You'd have two choices, the Ole Miss Law School at Oxford or the law school at Southwestern Tennessee State University in Memphis. I'll send you their catalogues and you can make up your mind. By the way, I'm getting married next week to the receptionist who worked at the U.S. Marshal's Building."

"You old sly fox. I noticed that you were falling all over yourself when we met her."

"And after you left with the two marshals, I got her phone number and called her several days later. We started dating and one thing led to another. And now we're getting married. I know this sounds funny for a sixty-year-old to be getting married for the first time, but I realized that life was passing me by."

"It's never too late for love, Josiah. By the way, where's the wedding going to be?"

"Since neither one of us is a spring chicken, we decided to let Judge Thornell perform the ceremony in his office. I wish you could come, but under the circumstances, it would be too dangerous."

"Oh, I understand, Josiah. After I decide where I want to go, please see what you can do about getting me into a school down there. When you find out, send me an e-mail to bc@gmi.com that says 'All is well.' Then I'll call you in a few weeks. I'm really happy for you, Josiah."

When Geoffrey came back to his house, he looked at Angie's pictures and said, "Baby, you and I should be celebrating thirty years of marriage. Instead, you're dead, and all I have to look forward to is plotting how to get rid of four people. I'm so sick and tired of having nothing to anticipate except murder."

A week later, Geoffrey received the two catalogues from Josiah and eagerly began poring over them. As he was reading about Southwestern Tennessee University Law School, he came to a picture of the Assistant Dean and his secretary, and his heart skipped a beat. She was the spitting image of Suzanne Carter. He immediately dialed the number of the dean's office and held his breath while he waited for someone to answer.

"Dean Simpson's office. Alicia Carter speaking. How can I help you?"

"Uh, I'm so sorry," Geoffrey stammered. "I must have dialed the wrong number."

Fate had made the choice where Geoffrey would attend law school. He immediately e-mailed Josiah and prayed that his friend could get him admitted.

Two weeks later, Geoffrey got the answer he wanted. When he called Josiah, a woman answered the phone. He was afraid at first that she wouldn't accept a call from Mason Dixon but felt relieved when she did.

"William, this is Agnes Perkins. Just a minute. I'll get Josiah."

Josiah came on the line almost immediately. "Geo—, damn, I've got to remember to call you William. I managed to pull some strings with the dean of the law school. They'll accept you for the fall term, but you'll have to get Jupiter Mountain to send your transcript. I don't think that'll be a problem."

"That's great, Josiah. What about the other problem, you know, with the Federal Witness Protection Program?"

"Agnes contacted the U.S. Marshal's regional office in Oxford, and they said that since you were coming back of your own volition, you'll be on your own, but you can keep the identity of William Caldwell as long as you don't get into any trouble."

"I can handle that part. Do you know of any houses near the campus that I could rent?"

"I have a friend who has some rental property. I did some work for him several years ago. I'll see what I can do. When do you plan on coming down here?"

"My lease on the house doesn't run out until the end of the month, so I'll stay here until then, relax, do some hiking. Just e-mail me about the house. I'll let you know exactly when I'll be coming home. I'll rent a car 'cause I have too much stuff to carry on a plane. See you around the first or second week of August."

Man, that was pretty slick of me to think about renting a car. There's no way in hell I could get through airport security with all my surveillance equipment.

Kneeling in front of Angie's pictures, Geoffrey told her of his immediate plans. "I have a mission to accomplish before I leave North Carolina. My voice has convinced me to get even with the two people who almost ruined my life here. I'm going to get Peter Morris first. I know deep down he wasn't trying to help me, the little prick. I'll lure him into the mountains on some pretense and then kill him. Then I'll do the same thing with Erickson. None of this would have happened if he hadn't been such a smart ass and always tried to humiliate me in front of the class just because I didn't agree with him. I'll make both their deaths look like accidents."

Geoffrey then decided to try out his Caller ID Buster and Portable Voice Changer "just to see if they work."

"Peter, this is Daniel. Are you busy right now? Could you help me with a little problem I'm having with my car?"

"Daniel, I can barely hear you. Is something wrong with your phone or mine?"

"I don't know. Maybe there's a bad connection. Could you come out to the old cemetery? I'm researching some of the graves out here and my car battery's gone dead."

"Sure, I'll be there in a few minutes."

Pretending to be Peter, Geoffrey then proceeded to enact the same scenario with Erickson.

Both men arrived at the cemetery at the same time. "Peter, I thought your car broke down. You just called me a few minutes ago, didn't you?"

"No, I just got a call from someone saying he was you. Did your phone sound kind of weird, Daniel?"

"Yeah, the voice was muffled."

"Someone has played a trick on us."

"Well, gentlemen, I see you both fell for my little joke."

The two men turned in the direction of the voice and found themselves staring down the barrel of a 30.06 rifle.

"William, this isn't very funny," Erickson said." What are you doing with that rifle?"

"Why are you wearing gloves?" Peter asked nervously.

"Oh, I thought I'd do a little hunting this afternoon, and I don't want to get blood all over my hands. Let's go over toward those woods where we can have some privacy."

The three men walked deep into the woods. The scent of pine trees hung heavy in the air. Their feet padded on the soft vegetation. Two gray squirrels scampered to get out of their way, barking a warning to others nearby. Geoffrey followed close behind the men, pointing his rifle at their backs.

They came to a stream bank thick with rhododendron. "Okay, this is far enough," Geoffrey ordered. "Now, kneel down at the edge of that stream."

"William, why are you doing this to us?" the professor pleaded. "We never deliberately hurt you. In fact, if Peter hadn't dropped the charges, you'd be in jail now awaiting trial."

"Shut up, you bastard! Wait, I've got a better idea. Both of you stand up and take off your clothes. I'm going to make this look like some mountain man came out here and attacked and killed you."

Peter lunged toward Geoffrey, who instinctively pulled his hunting knife from its sheath and flipped it directly toward Peter's heart. Peter screamed out and fell to the ground. Geoffrey bent over and pulled the knife from his chest, keeping the rifle pointed toward Erickson the whole time.

"That wasn't exactly what I intended to do with him. Now, Professor, you finish taking off your clothes."

When Erickson had almost finished undressing and was leaning over to untie his shoes, Geoffrey grabbed him around the neck with his left arm and stabbed him in the chest with his right hand. He kept on hacking Erickson until the man's body became limp. Geoffrey let the body crumple to the ground next to Peter's. He took Peter's hand and placed it around the handle of the knife and then pried Peter's fingers loose. He repeated the action with Erickson's hand. After he had loosened the professor's fingers, he let the knife fall to the ground.

Now, this will look like some sort of attempted rape and murder.

Geoffrey's plan worked even better than he had expected. That afternoon some hunters found the two bodies and immediately notified the local police. The investigation rocked both the town and the campus. Of course, as soon as the news broke, everyone began to whisper and make innuendoes that they had known all along that something had been going on between the bachelor professor and the effeminate student. Erickson's student assistant came forward and related the conversation he had heard between Erickson and Peter. The official investigation reached the conclusion that the pair had a violent lover's quarrel and had killed each other. Only Dean Spangler suspected that Geoffrey was the least bit involved, but he never said a word.

27

Jake Conner was obsessed with capturing Geoffrey and assumed that he would remain in the Asheville area. It was too dangerous to go there himself, so he kept up with the local newspapers through the Internet. One day as he was scanning some articles from the *Asheville Citizen-Times*, a story about a double murder in Jupiter Mountain caught his eye.

Bockker just might have screwed up big time, he thought. He picked up the phone and quickly got himself through to Dean Spangler.

"This is Jake Conner. I'm the sheriff of Lowndes County, Mississippi, and I'd like to ask you a few questions about the double homicide that occurred recently in Jupiter Mountain. You mind talking with me?"

"Uh, of course not, Sheriff, but you did read that the authorities came to the conclusion that the two men had killed each other."

"Yeah, but something smells fishy to me. I think the real killer could be someone who committed several murders in this area thirty years ago. I believe he goes by the name of William

Caldwell now. Would you hold on while I fax you a photograph?"

"Sure."

Dean Spangler swallowed hard and nervously awaited the picture. When it arrived, his heart fluttered. There was a definite resemblance between the teenage killer and the man he knew as William Caldwell. But he really didn't want to get involved. If he was the killer, he sure didn't want Caldwell coming after him.

"I'm sorry, Sheriff Conner, but the man in this picture doesn't look like anyone who goes to school here."

"Are you sure? Look real good."

"I'm sure. Uh, I've got to hang up. I've got a call on another line. I'm really sorry I wasn't able to help you."

When Conner hung up the phone, he slammed his hand down on the desk so hard he winced in pain. Frustration overwhelmed him. He knew he couldn't go up to Jupiter Mountain and start nosing around or the Feds would give him a bunch of grief. He'd have to just keep trying. Bockker was bound to slip up somewhere, then he'd nail him. He prayed it would be before Geoffrey killed someone else.

28

After three weeks, the scandal had died down somewhat and Geoffrey went to Dean Spangler's office early one afternoon.

"William, what can I do for you?" the dean asked, barely able to look at Geoffrey.

"Dean Spangler, I've talked things over with Josiah Perkins, and he agrees that I need to attend a law school closer to home. I've decided to go to Southwestern Tennessee University in Memphis instead of Carter University. I need for you to send a copy of my transcript there, if you don't mind." Geoffrey's voice was all politeness.

A very relieved Dean Spangler replied, "Of course, William, if you and Josiah think that's for the best. I'll get the transcript off today. I'm sorry things didn't work out for you here. I hope you find what you're looking for in Memphis."

Geoffrey replied, "Thank you, Dean Spangler, I do, too. Since I'll be leaving shortly, I'll just say goodbye now."

After Geoffrey had left, Dean Spangler heaved the largest sigh of relief in his life. He suspected that William had killed the two men. However, he had said nothing to anyone because he had no proof and, frankly, he was scared to death of Caldwell. Now, at least the man would be gone from the area forever.

As he was walking away from the dean's office, Geoffrey seethed with anger. *You sonofabitch. If there had been any possible way, you'd be dead, too, but I just couldn't take a chance on another murder.* He decided he would now concentrate on his big assignment. The last two murders were just practice.

Geoffrey hurried back to his house and packed all his belongings. He called the Enterprise Car Rental Agency and had them deliver a car. The further he drove away from Jupiter Mountain, the more relieved he became.

The trip to Memphis, however, was a sentimental one. He had come to know and love the Blue Ridge Mountains. He followed the route along the Blue Ridge Parkway from Asheville to the Great Smoky Mountains National Park. He took leisurely hikes and camped out in the park among the plants and wildflowers. At dusk, he was often greeted by black bears and white-tailed deer. He took refreshing dips in the nearby mountain streams and lakes. As he drove, he felt a tremendous ambivalence. Part of him was eager to get to Memphis, yet another part wanted to stay in these bucolic mountains, where his soul had found some measure of peace. If Geoffrey had not allowed his demons to compel him to kill, he might not have left the inspirational hills that had offered him the beauty and compassion he had sought all his life. Several times he almost turned around and headed back, but the psychopath that dwelled inside him took control, and he continued on his journey.

Finally, after three weeks of leisurely travel, he drove into Memphis. Along the way, he had called Josiah and told him when he would arrive. Josiah gave Geoffrey the directions to his new house and agreed to meet him there to give him the keys. It was August 13, Geoffrey Bockker's fiftieth birthday.

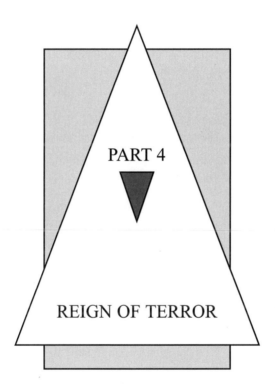

PART 4

REIGN OF TERROR

29

August 1994

Josiah Perkins couldn't get over how good Geoffrey looked. "I swear you look at least twenty years younger," he said, then added, "I don't think anyone who knew Geoffrey Bockker could even recognize you. You're not the same person who left here."

"Josiah, I'm not. I feel better than I have in years. North Carolina did me a lot of good. Thank you for picking that area. As much as I loved it, though, I realized it was time to come home."

Josiah helped Geoffrey with his luggage and cartons. "Oh, by the way, I had the gas and electricity turned on, and you also have telephone service."

"Josiah, I can't thank you enough. You're always going out of your way for me."

Josiah shrugged off the compliments. "I guess it's safe to call normally now. Just as a preliminary precaution, I had to tell the U.S. Marshal's office where you're living, but I don't think they've bugged your phone or anything like that. Be careful and let me hear from you, William." Josiah emphasized Geoffrey's name.

"I will, Josiah. And thanks again."

As Josiah was turning to leave, he suddenly remembered something.

"Oh, by the way, I got a call from someone wanting your telephone number. It was Liz Anderson, that reporter who interviewed you in prison. I told her that you had died, but she sort of laughed and gave me her phone number in case you ever 'came back from the dead.' "

Geoffrey swallowed hard. He had never expected to hear from Liz again. He wondered what she could want after all these years.

"Thanks, Josiah. I'll just keep the number as a sort of souvenir."

After Josiah had left, Geoffrey twirled the card with Liz's phone number around and around between his fingers and then tossed it on the coffee table.

The next morning, Geoffrey set his plan into action. He attached the Caller-ID Buster and the Portable Voice Changer to his phone and was ready to begin the initial torture of his victims. He looked in the "W" directory and easily found Suzanne's address and phone number. Just to be on the safe side, though, he checked the Memphis phone book to see if the numbers corresponded. The name and the address were a perfect match.

"Well, Mrs. Carter. You're about to receive a phone call from hell."

Geoffrey had waited so long for this moment that his hands perspired and his throat felt parched.

"Hello?"

"Is this the residence of Suzanne Carter?"

"Yes, it is. Who is this?"

"Suzanne, I'm going to kill you. You have to die for what you did, you damn bitch!"

Before she could respond, Suzanne heard the phone click on the other end. The voice had sounded muffled and monotone. But she heard every word. Visibly shaken, she went into the kitchen for a glass of water. Over the years, she had received prank calls but none as terrifying as this.

"Okay, just calm down and see if he calls back in a few minutes. Maybe he just picked my name at random," she said to reassure herself that she really wasn't in danger.

When the phone rang again, Suzanne hesitated; then she picked up the receiver, fully expecting to hear the same foreboding voice.

"Hel—Hello," she said meekly.

"Suzanne, is that you?" her sister asked.

"Oh, Julie, thank God. The most awful thing just happened. Some man called and threatened to kill me."

"Slow down, Suzanne. Now tell me exactly what happened."

"Well, he wasn't on the phone even a minute. He told me he was going to kill me and then he hung up. I'm scared. He meant the call for me because he asked if this was my residence."

"Now, Suzanne, you know you're safe in the apartment building. There's security at the front gate and someone inside has to let any visitors in."

"Yeah, but what about on the outside?"

"Get the security guard to walk you to your car. You've got a car phone. Just call me when you leave and again when you get to work. By the way, I called to invite you down this weekend. I'm keeping Carla's baby, and I thought you and Mom and I could babysit Saturday afternoon."

"That sounds great. Look, I'm leaving now. I should be at work in thirty minutes. I'll call you then."

Suzanne buzzed the desk.

"Mrs. Bridges, I just received a frightening phone call.

Could you have George walk with me to my car."

"Sure, Mrs. Carter. He'll be here when you get down. Do you want me to call the police?"

"No, there's nothing they can do."

The security guard, George Haynes, walked Suzanne to her car. On the way he suggested she get Caller I.D. "That way you'll know who's calling before you answer the phone." Once she was safely out of the parking lot and onto the street, he turned and walked back into the apartment building. Suzanne didn't realize it, but George would have laid down his life for her. From the moment she had moved into the building, he had been in love with her.

30

Geoffrey wished he'd said more to Suzanne Carter. The second he had heard her voice, he'd gotten a sick feeling in the pit of his stomach. He had to call her again, scare her some more.

When he dialed her number the second time, a recording answered. "This is the Carter residence. No one can come to the phone right now, but if you'll leave your name and number, we'll get back to you as soon as possible."

After the beep, Geoffrey spoke. "Mrs. Carter, we didn't get to finish our phone conversation a while ago. I had so much more to tell you. I'll call you again soon, bitch."

After eating a light breakfast, Geoffrey got out the maps and bus schedules that Josiah had marked. Geoffrey made his plans for the day. He could catch the bus directly across the street at eight o'clock. The one to the law school stopped directly in front of the law complex on Central. He picked up his briefcase and hesitated only long enough to go into his bedroom to cast a farewell glance at Angie.

"Bye, baby. I'll see you tonight. Then I'll really scare the hell out of that bitch for you."

31

At precisely eight the next morning, the big MATA bus pulled to a stop and the doors popped open. Geoffrey climbed on board.

"This bus stops at the Southwestern Tennessee University Law School, doesn't it?"

"Every day, man," the bus driver replied, his shiny white teeth flashing against the backdrop of his black face. "You a new student? You look kind of old to be going to college, even law school."

"Well, I had another profession for about thirty years," Geoffrey said with a grin. "Then I decided I wanted to be a lawyer. So, here I am."

"That's cool, man."

Geoffrey took a seat near the exit door and drummed his fingers nervously on the top of his briefcase perched on his lap. Thirty minutes later, the driver called out to him, "Okay, Mister, this is the law school. Have a good day."

"Yeah, same to you."

Geoffrey Bockker could have been a top-notch law student and would have made a damn fine lawyer if only that had been

his primary goal. He had a razor-sharp mind and a genuine concern for people. He had scored well above average on the
LSAT, in addition to the grades he had made at Jupiter
Mountain. But, sadly, his love of law was merely a means to a
tragic goal.

Swallowing hard and blinking back tears, he entered the
building with an air of trepidation and determination. He asked
the receptionist for directions to Dean Frazier's office and was
soon knocking on the dean's door. A booming voice called out,
"Come in. Come in."

Geoffrey entered the office. "Dean Frazier, I'm William
Caldwell. Josiah Perkins is a friend of mine. I believe you're
expecting me."

Frazier, a heavy-set man with wavy gray hair and a full
beard, got up from behind his desk. "Yes, William. Let me get
your file." He rifled through a pile of folders. "Here it is. You
did your undergraduate work at Central Mississippi University
and then completed a year of Pre-Law at Jupiter Mountain
College in North Carolina. Your credentials are excellent. Your
LSAT score puts you in the 90th percentile. That's terrific.
From what I see here, you have the makings of an excellent
attorney."

"Thank you, sir. Josiah is counting on me and I don't want
to let him down."

"Great, here's your class schedule. I didn't want you to have
to go through all the hassle of registration. All of your classes
are in this building. The law library is that tall building behind
us. I imagine you'll be spending a lot of time there. Is there
anything else I can do for you, William?"

"Yes sir, there is. Could you tell me if Alicia Carter still
works in one of the offices here? She's an old family friend and
I'd like to say hello to her."

"Just go down the hall to the left. She's in the first office on your right."

Frazier walked over and shook hands with his new law student. Afterwards, Geoffrey walked out the door into his new life.

As he stood outside Alicia's office, he clenched his teeth and cursed under his breath when he felt the onset of one of his blinding headaches. Geoffrey headed quickly to a nearby water fountain just down the hall. He gulped down an Imitrex and began slowly breathing in and out as the therapists had taught him to do. The headache subsided a little, and he knocked on the door with a trembling hand.

"Come in."

Geoffrey turned the knob and entered the room.

A beautiful red-haired woman in her early 30's looked up at him. "Can I help you?"

Geoffrey was caught off guard.

"Uh, yes. I'm looking for Dean Frazier. His secretary said he might be in this office."

"No, he's not here. Try the law library."

"Thanks, I'll try to find him later. I'm going to be late for class. This is my first day of law school. Oh, sorry, I'm William Caldwell," he said, reaching out to shake Alicia's hand.

"Hi, I'm Alicia Carter. This'll be my first day, too. I just enrolled in law school."

Geoffrey glanced at his watch. "I hate to run, but I don't want to be late. It's bad enough being twice as old as everyone else. Do you happen to know where Room 310 is?"

"What a coincidence! That's my first class. Come on, we'll go together."

As they walked up the stairs to their class, Alicia couldn't help but notice how handsome Geoffrey was. She thought of how lonely her mother had been after the divorce. Alicia had been praying for her mother to meet someone, maybe to get married again.

Once Geoffrey and Alicia had taken their seats, the professor intoned, "Good morning, ladies and gentlemen, welcome to Contracts I. This is your first year of law school, and, frankly, some of you are not going to make it through the year. Those who do will find the next two years much less difficult. They won't be easy, but at least you will have some idea of what is expected of you."

After a grueling fifty minutes, the class was over.

"Man, if the other classes are like this, he's right," Geoffrey said to Alicia as they headed to their next class, again a class together.

When the class was over, Geoffrey and Alicia were the first ones out of the room.

"Alicia, why don't we get a bite to eat before our afternoon class? I don't know about you, but I'm starving."

"Okay, the Student Union has pretty good food and it's fairly cheap, too. We have plenty of time before Torts class tortures us."

Geoffrey laughed at her little joke.

When Alicia wasn't looking, Geoffrey stared at her. Although her features were nothing like Angie's, something about her brought back memories of long ago.

"William, hello?" Alicia nudged Geoffrey. "We have to go to the counter to get our food."

"Oh, sorry, An—uh, Alicia. I was daydreaming."

"It must have been really terrible. You had this awful look on your face."

Geoffrey shook his head. "Naw, just an unpleasant reminder from the past that sneaks up on me every once in a while."

Alicia found them a table in a quiet corner where they sat down with their food trays and hungrily began eating their hamburgers and french fries.

"Speaking of the past, tell me all about yourself," Alicia said, swallowing a mouthful. "Is yours a fascinating life?"

"Not exactly. I'm from a small town in Alabama. I went to college for two years. Then my parents were killed in a car accident, and I had to quit college and get a job to take care of my younger brother. After he was grown, I just kept on working. A couple a years ago, I decided I wanted to be a lawyer, so I went back to school and got my degree. And here I am. Okay, your turn." Geoffrey took a swig of his Coke and a huge bite out of his hamburger.

"Well, let's see," Alicia began. "My daddy's Johnny Carter. You know the ex-pro football player. He and my mom are divorced. If you really want to hear it, I'll tell you the whole sordid story."

"Sure. Go ahead. I'm all ears."

"After Mom graduated from MSCW, she moved to Gainesville to go to graduate school. She met Daddy in 1966, they got married the next year, and I came along six months after the wedding. Mom thinks Dad always resented her because her folks forced them to get married. He had always been the kind of guy all the girls loved. Marriage didn't change that. After graduation, he was drafted by the Miami Dolphins, and then he had women stashed away in every city the team played in. My mom pretended they didn't exist, but there were plenty of telltale signs, like little pieces of paper with unfamiliar phone numbers, motel receipts, all sorts of things. The heavy drinking and drugs started, too, once he turned pro. When he blew out up his knee in '85 and couldn't play at full speed, his local junkie provided him with enough painkillers to get through the season. The older and more crippled he got, the more painkillers it took. Toward the end of his career, he could hardly exist without his two crutches, booze and drugs. In 1987 my father was forced to give up the only thing he really loved.

He used the money Mom had carefully invested to open a sports bar and restaurant and spent every minute at the place. My mom got so lonely and depressed that she wouldn't even leave the house. I came home one weekend and found them screaming at each other. She was calling him a drunken bastard who only cared about his booze and whores and he was calling her a damn zombie who lived in a million-dollar house and had a membership in the most exclusive country club and didn't appreciate any of it. She cried and said all she really wanted was for us to be a family. Then he said he was leaving—for good." Alicia had tears in her eyes. "I really hated my mom for a while—I always thought she drove him away." Alicia paused. "After that, things got even worse. Mom stopped eating and lost a lot of weight. Finally, in desperation, she moved to Memphis to be closer to my grandmother and aunt. They convinced her to get professional help. She spent several months in a clinic that treats people for severe depression. I moved to Memphis last year and got my job here at Dean Thompson's office. My mother's better now, but I know she's lonely." Alicia stopped, suddenly embarrassed. "Oh, my God, I can't believe I just told you all this. I'm sorry."

"Hey, it's okay. I'm a good listener." Geoffrey flashed his most appealing smile at Alicia.

At first, Geoffrey actually felt a twinge of sadness upon hearing about Suzanne's problems, but then he pictured Angie lying on the autopsy table, and all thoughts of compassion were driven from his mind.

At the end of their third class together, Alicia exclaimed to Geoffrey, "Wow! We've made it through out first day of law school. Uh, William, can I call you Bill?" Geoffrey nodded and Alicia continued. "Would you like to come over one night? I think you and my mom would hit it off. Just as friends. I'm not trying to promote anything. Oh, I'm sorry, I never even thought about whether you're married or have a girlfriend."

"As a matter of fact, I'm not married, and no girlfriend. There was someone a long time ago in college, but she's uh— dead now."

His response was barely audible.

"Oh, Bill, I'm so sorry."

"No, it's okay. As a matter of fact, I'd love to come to your house if you'll give me a couple of days' notice."

"Well, I'll see you tomorrow," Alicia said. "We both have Contracts I again and Civil Procedure. Do you want to meet here in front of the building?"

"Yeah, that'll be great."

Geoffrey headed across the street to the bus stop. As soon as he got on the bus and took a seat, he realized how tired he was. He leaned back and closed his eyes.

Oh, Angie girl, I miss you so much, but my plan's working out even better than I could have ever dreamed. It won't be long now.

He snapped to when he heard the driver call out the name of his street. He picked up his briefcase and got off as soon as the door opened. In a few minutes, he was standing in front of his house. Once inside, he headed to Angie's shrine.

"Oh, baby, it's so hard to be nice to Alicia, knowing that she's Suzanne's daughter. I ought to kill her just to punish Suzanne. But I won't. Alicia's a nice person, and she never hurt you. I think killing her mother and the other three will be enough. But listen to this—Alicia wants to set me up with Suzanne. That'll make it easy to do what I have to do. Of course, I'll have to pretend to like her. But you know there's no one for me but you."

The phone ringing broke Geoffrey's communication with Angie. Geoffrey let the answering machine pick up. He heard Josiah's voice saying, "William, just thought I'd give you a call to see how everything's going. I'll call back later."

"Josiah, old man, things couldn't be better. Everything's going just fine."

Geoffrey picked up the receiver and smiled.

"I think it's time for another phone call." Geoffrey had spent quite a bit of money on the Voice Changer. It was time to try it out again. If Alicia answered the phone, he knew she wouldn't recognize his voice.

When the phone rang, Alicia picked it up. Suzanne could tell that something was wrong by the horror-stricken look on her daughter's face.

Alicia slammed down the phone.

"Oh, Mom, some awful creep just kept repeating, 'You're going to die. You're going to die.' Then he hung up before I could say anything."

"My God," Suzanne cried. "That's the third time today. He called this morning after you left for school. It scared me to death. Then when I got home, I found a message from him on the answering machine. I'm going to report this to the police right now."

Suzanne spoke to a sympathetic cop who suggested she keep a record of exactly when the calls were received. But he hastened to add that this may have been a one-day thing. Then he asked, "Did you recognize the voice at all?"

"No, it was muffled sounding and he spoke in a monotone voice," Suzanne replied.

"He must have used some sort of voice disguiser. I'd call the phone company and have them add Caller ID. You can buy an inexpensive ID box at Radio Shack. When he phones the next time, the number and name of the caller will automatically appear."

After she had hung up, Suzanne recounted the conversation with the officer to her daughter. Alicia said she'd pick up the

ID box. Then, she brightened. "Mom, I met the nicest man today at law school. We have almost the same schedule. I think you'd really like him. His name is Bill Caldwell, and he's about your age."

"Alicia, you're not playing matchmaker again, are you? Honey, my life is busy enough. Besides, I don't feel like going through the dating routine again."

"But, Mom, he's so sweet and he's really good-looking. I think you two would hit it off."

32

Geoffrey was disturbed after the phone call. He really hadn't wanted Alicia to answer the phone, and it upset him to imagine her reaction. His hatred was for Suzanne, not her daughter. Next time, if Alicia answered, he'd just hang up. As he walked through the living room, he noticed the card with Liz Anderson's number on it lying on the coffee table. His life was complicated enough without bringing her back on the scene, but he just had to talk to her. He turned off his voice disguiser and caller ID blocker and nervously dialed Liz's number. A young man's voice surprised him.

"Uh, yes, is Liz Anderson there?" Geoffrey asked hesitantly.

"She's busy right now. Who's calling, please?" the young man asked.

"Just tell her it's an old friend from the—uh, library in Mississippi." There was a short pause and then an excited Liz Anderson came on the line.

"Geoffrey, is it really you? Josiah Perkins told me you had died, but I knew it wasn't true. Hold on a sec." Liz called to the young man who had answered the phone, "Rex, have a good time, and don't stay out too late." She spoke into the phone again. "Sorry, but I guess you know how kids are."

"No," Geoffrey said sadly, "I'm afraid I can't relate to that."

"I'm so glad you called. I just had to talk to you. When I left Parchman after our interview sessions, I intended to divorce Harry and come back to Mississippi to work for your release. Then something happened that changed my plans." She took a deep breath and went on. "When I got back, Harry was so sweet and seemed to have missed me so much, that I decided to postpone asking for a divorce. I'd been home about a month after our interview when I discovered I was pregnant. Harry and I had sex right after I got back, so I didn't dream that Rex wasn't his child. A month ago, Harry's kidneys failed and he needed a transplant. Rex volunteered, but it turned out that he wasn't a compatible donor. I made up the story that his blood contained too many enzymes, and he never suspected a thing. But I knew something was weird so I had them run a DNA test. The results proved that Harry wasn't Rex's father. Geoffrey, that means that he's *your* child. I don't want anything from you, but I thought you should know that you have a son. I haven't said anything to Rex or Harry. They love each other so much." Geoffrey heard the sound of a door slamming shut. "Geoffrey, I've got to go. Harry just came home. But you can call me whenever you want to. 'Bye."

Geoffrey stared in shock at the phone still in his hand. He was utterly speechless. He felt weak all over. *A son. I have a son.* He sat down on the couch to compose himself. Soon, an unwelcome visitor made his presence known. "Geoffrey, just forget about the kid. We have more important work to do. He'll just get in the way of our plans."

Geoffrey pounded his head. "Shut up and let me think! I'll decide what to do."

Geoffrey struggled to overcome the power of this monster, but his battle was in vain. Exhausted, he tried to sleep, but visions of his unborn child and his son haunted him all night long.

Geoffrey got up before dawn. He had to return the car to the rental agency, and he needed to get to school early. Knowing that Alicia would be upset about the call, he planned on being there to console her. When he got to school, she was waiting for him in front of the law building. She looked so tired and nervous. Feigning sympathy, he asked what was wrong.

"Oh, Bill, some creep called our house three times yesterday and told my mom he was going to kill her. Actually, I answered the phone the third time. She's scared to death. So am I."

"Now, Alicia, it's probably just some crackpot who gets his jollies by making these kinds of calls. I'll bet he won't bother y'all again."

"I hope not. But just in case, Mom's having caller ID put on her phone and I'm picking up the box today between classes."

Geoffrey nodded. "That's, that's a good idea. Then your mother can at least screen her calls."

"Bill, you said for me to give you a couple of days' notice about dinner. Could you come over tomorrow night?"

"I don't see why not. I don't have any plans for the weekend. What time should I be there?"

"About 6:30. We live in the Tanglewood Apartments, 3-D on Sycamore Lane. Tell me where you live and I'll give you directions from your house."

"No," Geoffrey said quickly. "I've got some errands to run first. Just tell me how to get there from Oak Court Mall. By the way, what can I bring?"

"Just bring yourself," Alicia said with a warm smile.

Geoffrey glanced at his watch and exclaimed, "We've got

exactly two minutes to get to class. We'd better hurry."

That night Geoffrey could hardly sleep. He felt just like he had on Christmas Eve when he was a child and still believed in Santa Claus. He was always too excited to close his eyes.

Finally, the first light broke through and he could barely control his emotions. He bounded out of bed and took a quick shower. Every fiber in his body bristled with anticipation. The adrenalin was coursing through his body so fast that at first he thought he might be having a heart attack. Then he laughed out loud. *I've got to calm down. Okay, now just lay out a plan for tonight. I'm going to take a cab over there. If I time it just right, I can catch a bus home, though. Everything's got to be perfect. I think I'll give Suzanne a call just to unnerve her a little more. Then she'll be more receptive to my offer of help. I'll have the bitch playing into my hands before the night's over. Oh, Angie, after all these years, we're finally going to get our revenge. I'll make them cry out for mercy before I kill them, one by one. I wish I knew how to get them all together, though. Too bad.*

He smiled as he dialed the first three digits of the number. *Suzanne, that damn caller ID won't do you any good with my trusty little device.*

He patted his caller ID blocker and voice changer as he dialed the other numbers, which he had now learned by heart. When Suzanne answered, he began his routine spiel. She cried out and slammed down the phone before she realized what she was doing. The police had instructed her to be sure to listen for any sounds she might hear in the background. But she was so upset, she hung up much too quickly.

Seeing the frightened look on her mother's face, Alicia rushed to her side. "Oh, Mom, it was that bastard again, wasn't it?"

"Yes, honey. It makes me so mad. Each time before he calls

I tell myself, 'Just stay calm and keep him on the phone.' But I forget that as soon as I hear his horrible voice. At least we can tell where the call came from."

When Suzanne and Alicia checked the phone that was connected to the caller ID, they both groaned when they saw the words: *Unable to identify caller.*

"Damn! I thought this thing would work no matter where the call came from," Suzanne said in angry frustration.

"Mom, I forgot to tell you, they aren't sophisticated enough to pick up cell phones or pay phones," Alicia explained. "Why don't we change our number? At least it would give us some respite from his calls."

"I guess that's a good idea. I just hate to let him control our lives, though. Oh well, he's not going to spoil our evening. What time did you say Bill was coming? And what should I wear?"

"Six-thirty, and your new blue pants suit will be perfect. Come on, let's work on your hair and makeup. I want you to knock Bill off his feet."

Geoffrey was agonizing over what to wear, too. He wanted to impress Suzanne as much as Alicia wanted her mother to impress Bill. He finally selected a beige sports coat and brown slacks with a cream-colored turtleneck. He had to admit, as he stared at himself in the full-length mirror, that he cut a dashing figure.

He took a cab to the Tanglewood Apartments and then walked to the locked gate, pressed the intercom button and told the security guard his name and whom he was coming to visit. George Haynes found "William Caldwell" on his list, opened the gate and unlocked the front door. Geoffrey nodded to the receptionist at the desk who waved him on by. He got on the elevator and punched 3, his nervousness mounting with each moment. He didn't know how he was going to react when he saw Suzanne for the first time, but he sure didn't want her to suspect anything. The elevator door opened and he walked down the corridor, taking measured breaths so that he wouldn't hyperventilate. When Geoffrey came to apartment 3-D, his hands were sweating and he could barely catch his breath.

"God, don't let me faint right now, please."

Geoffrey rang the doorbell and was actually relieved when Alicia answered it. She greeted him with the warmest of smiles.

"Hi, come on in. Mom'll be ready in a minute. Why don't we sit here in the den, okay?"

"Okay," said Geoffrey and headed toward the nearest chair.

"Would you like some iced tea?" Alicia asked, still smiling.

"Fine," Geoffrey said, and Alicia disappeared into the kitchen.

Geoffrey spotted a vase on the table next to him and quickly picked it up. He inserted an object far up in the hollow bottom and carefully set it back down.

Alicia returned with two glasses of iced tea. Geoffrey had taken only a few sips when Suzanne entered the den.

"Mom, I'd like you to meet Bill Caldwell."

Remembering his manners, Geoffrey stood up and found himself gazing at the most beautiful face he had ever seen.

"Hel—hello, Mrs. Carter," Geoffrey stammered like a love-starved teenager, which he really was socially. It had been over thirty years since he had gone out with a woman, not counting the brief affair with Liz Anderson.

"Please call me Suzanne," she said with a smile as she extended her hand.

Geoffrey was fascinated by Suzanne's beauty, yet at the same time repulsed by her. When he looked into her eyes, he saw those of a poisonous snake. A shudder rippled through Geoffrey's body and he let out a gasp, barely audible, but still discernible.

Trying to cover up his reaction, he stammered, "I'm so sorry for staring, but you look so much like someone I used to know many years ago."

"Oh, you're forgiven," Suzanne cooed, turning on the charm she had once used to make crew-cut high school boys weak-kneed at the mere sight of her.

"Sit down, Bill, tell me all about yourself," Suzanne said with genuine interest in her dinner guest. "Alicia hasn't stopped talking about you."

Geoffrey told Suzanne basically the same story he had told Alicia, hoping that he got all the details right.

At that moment, Alicia, who had eased out of the room to the kitchen, announced that dinner was ready. The three made casual conversation during the meal. Geoffrey and Suzanne realized that they had many of the same likes and dislikes. Geoffrey felt so comfortable talking to these two women that he almost forgot his purpose for getting to know them. He glanced at his watch and felt like Cinderella when he announced that he had to get home. In reality, he knew that he had to be at the bus stop in five minutes, or he'd miss the last bus and he probably wouldn't be able to get a cab this late.

"Thanks again for a great evening, Suzanne. We'll have to get together again, maybe for a concert?"

"I'd like that, Bill," Suzanne said.

He leaned over and kissed Suzanne tenderly on the cheek and then told Alicia he'd see her Monday. He was out the door quickly and hurried down the street. A wave of relief swept over him. Things couldn't have gone any better. The only thing he hadn't planned on was the way he would feel toward

Suzanne by the end of the evening. He had spent all those years hating a person he had never met and now that they had finally come face to face, his hatred toward her had actually lessened. She was so captivating, and yet vulnerable, that a whole new wave of emotions washed over him. Then, suddenly the image of Angie filled his head and, once again, hatred and revulsion dominated his thoughts.

Geoffrey barely managed to catch his bus. He ran so hard that he was gasping for breath when he took the first empty seat he saw. The trip home seemed like an eternity. His head had begun to pound and nothing seemed to help, no matter how hard he tried to control it with his exercises. Fortunately, he arrived at his stop just when he thought he couldn't take any more.

"Goodnight, man," the bus driver said, "Say, are you okay?"

"Huh? Oh, uh, yeah. I've just had a rough day. Goodnight."

Geoffrey ran from the bus stop to his door. Once inside, he went straight to the bathroom and gulped down two Imitrex. As soon as he entered his bedroom, he began talking to Angie.

"Our plan's going great, baby. I've got the bitch eating out of my hand. I'll take her out a few times and pump her for information about the other three. I think I'll buy a video camera so that we can preserve each murder and relive it step by step. Don't you think that's a great idea? By the way, I put the listening device in a vase in their den. I'll turn on the tape recorder so that we can hear everything that bitch and her daughter say."

Later, after his headache had subsided, Geoffrey felt well enough to go to bed.

Over at the Tanglewood Apartments, Suzanne and Alicia were less like mother and daughter and more like two giddy teenagers who had just met the handsomest boy at school and he had asked one of them for a date.

"Isn't he neat?" Alicia said, hugging her mother.

"Oh, Alicia," Suzanne replied, "he's everything you said and more. I'm so excited. Did he really mean what he said about going out with him?"

"Of course, Mom. Bill is the most sincere person I've ever met."

"Well, don't forget to tell me if he says anything about me when you see him in class on Monday."

"I'll take notes, I promise."

Suzanne practically waltzed up the stairs and into her bedroom. Alicia hadn't seen her mother this happy in years.

33

The next few weeks passed uneventfully. Geoffrey purchased a small Panasonic Palmcorder because it wouldn't take up too much room and was easy to use. He also bought a tripod and a remote so that he could direct the filming of his handiwork. He continued the threatening calls, each time feeling more and more in control. He also thought that going out with Suzanne wouldn't be too bad. He was certainly attracted to her, and after so many years, it was nice to be around a beautiful woman. He had made friends with a few women in North Carolina, but had never allowed himself to actually go out on dates.

A few days after Geoffrey purchased the camcorder, he had come to the conclusion that he needed a car. He couldn't rely on buses and cabs to get everywhere he needed to go. He calculated that with his college tuition and the amount he was paying Josiah each month, he'd still have plenty of money to buy a car, thanks to those CD and mutual fund investments that Josiah had made for him. He didn't need a real luxury car, but if he was going to start dating again, he didn't want a heap either. After some quick but careful research, Geoffrey settled on a Ford Taurus. It was practical, but not fancy. Now he would be more independent, could come and go as he pleased, he thought with great satisfaction. The same day that he picked up his new car, he also splurged and bought a cell phone. This device would allow him to make his menacing calls from anywhere.

Early one night, while reading the newspaper, Geoffrey noticed an ad for a Bob Dylan concert. This would be the perfect opportunity for their first real "date." Before he dialed Suzanne's number, he remembered that this would be the first time he called her house as Bill, not Geoffrey, so he disconnected his caller ID blocker and the voice disguiser first.

"Hi, Suzanne, this is Bill." He could tell by the way she said hello and his name that she was thrilled to hear from him. "I just noticed in the paper that Bob Dylan's going to be at the Orpheum next weekend. If I can get tickets, would you like to go?"

"I'd love to. I guess the last time I saw Dylan was when he put on a show at State, my freshman year in college."

The word "college" brought back memories of Angie, and Geoffrey had to pause to control his emotions.

"I'll call right now and order the tickets. I know this is sort of sudden, but would you like to have dinner tonight? I've got a craving for some Rendezvous ribs."

"That sounds great. What time?"

"Seven okay?"

"Sure, see you then."

34

Geoffrey pulled up to the gate in front of Suzanne's apartment building in his new car. He was really nervous this time. This was a real date, the first one he had been on since college. He told himself to just relax, praying that he wouldn't get one of his headaches. At the security desk in the lobby he gave his name to the guard on duty. "Oh, hi, Mr. Caldwell. Just go on up. Mrs. Carter's expecting you," George Haynes said pleasantly.

Geoffrey waited impatiently for the elevator to arrive. On the ride to the third floor, he grew more nervous. *Oh, hell, why didn't I think to bring her some flowers? All women like flowers. Well, it's too late now.*

When the elevator door opened, he took a deep breath and walked to Suzanne's apartment and rang the bell. He was surprised to see a young man open the door.

"Hi, I'm Max Quinn, Alicia's boyfriend. You must be Bill."

"Max. Glad to meet you." The two men shook hands just as Suzanne came to the door.

"Bill, I'm ready to go unless you want to sit and visit a while," she said, flashing the most beautiful smile Geoffrey had ever seen.

"Uh, no, I think we had better leave," he said, unable to take his eyes off her. "They don't take reservations."

On the drive to the restaurant, Geoffrey and Suzanne talked about her job at Federal Express and how law school was going for him. Since the only thing Geoffrey had eaten at the restaurant had been ribs, he ordered Suzanne and himself a slab with baked beans. They ate leisurely, laughing and talking the entire time. Both gazed at each other frequently during the meal.

When they had finally left the Rendezvous and were back in Geoffrey's car, before he put the key in the ignition, he turned to Suzanne and said, "Suzanne, I, I don't know how you feel, but I, I really enjoy being with you. I hope you'll go out with me on a regular basis. I know this is sudden, but I'm the kind of person who believes in being honest and straightforward. You're the first woman I've felt this way about in years. How do you feel about me?"

"Bill, I've been through some terrible times, and I was resigned to the fact that I'd never allow myself to get close to any man again, but now you've come along and changed my mind. I like you a lot."

After Geoffrey had cranked the car and they had left the parking lot, he put his arm around Suzanne's shoulder, and she laid her head gently against his shoulder.

"Bill, I want to move slowly with this, though. I know that today most couples jump into bed on the first date. I'm not like that. I need to be secure in a relationship before I—"

"Suzanne," Geoffrey interrupted, "I wasn't telling you I liked you so much just to get you to sleep with me. I've been hurt before, too, and, to me, sex is something very special."

As they drove through the front gate, George waved nonchalantly at them.

When they arrived in front of her apartment building,

Geoffrey gently pulled Suzanne's face to his and gave her a tender kiss. He drew away and they got out of the car and walked to the entrance.

Suzanne's velvety brown eyes gazed at Geoffrey. "I'm not going to ask you to come up because I don't want to do something I might regret. Good night, Bill. I had a wonderful time."

Suzanne punched the combination on her remote and the night clerk let her in. She couldn't wait to tell Alicia what had happened.

On the way home, Geoffrey was totally confused. He found himself truly attracted to Suzanne, not only physically but also emotionally. He knew that he couldn't allow himself to get really serious about her. That would complicate things too much. He had been aroused physically by a beautiful woman for the first time since he and Liz Anderson had the torrid affair at Parchman. He could handle the physical urge, but the emotional attachment was really a concern. In the past, he had even visualized cutting out Suzanne's heart with his knife. At this moment, though, he couldn't imagine harming her.

When Geoffrey got home, he was still confused about his feelings, until he walked into his bedroom and saw Angie's shrine and the pictures of his enemies. It was then he knew that he could never truly care about Suzanne. He reconnected the caller ID blocker and voice disguiser and angrily picked up his phone and dialed her number.

When Suzanne first came into her apartment, Alicia was waiting in the den for her mother.

"Okay, tell me everything. Don't spare any details."

"Alicia, I had a fantastic time. I never thought I could ever feel like a normal woman again. We had a great dinner, and then we just sat and talked. Bill told me he really cared about me a lot. I said I felt the same way about him, but that I didn't want to rush into a physical relationship right now." Suzanne blushed as she said this to her daughter.

"Oh, Mom, you don't have to be embarrassed to talk about sex with me."

"I know, Alicia, but I feel like I'm the daughter and you're the mother. Remember, I haven't been to bed with anyone since your father and I broke up. Anyway, Bill and I agreed to take things slowly. He doesn't want to rush into anything either."

At that precise moment, the phone rang.

"Hello, bitch. Did you have a nice time on your date? I hope the ribs were good. I see you and lover boy didn't get it on tonight. What's the matter? Was he queer or something? I sure wouldn't have let this night go to waste. By the way, I still plan to kill you. Good night. Pleasant dreams."

"Oh my God!" Suzanne screamed. "He's watching me."

She hurriedly checked the caller ID box, but to no avail. Geoffrey's caller ID blocker had done its job.

The phone rang, and Alicia snatched it up shouting, "You bastard, leave my mother alone!"

Just before she slammed the phone down, Geoffrey yelled, "Alicia, it's me, Bill. Don't hang up. I just called to tell your mom goodnight and that I was thinking about her. Don't tell me you just got another one of those awful calls. Do you want me to come over? I'll be glad to."

Alicia handed the phone to her mother, mouthing the word "Bill."

Suzanne's distraught voice said, "Oh, God, Bill. I'm at my wit's end. I had a wonderful time tonight, and then that creep— my only salvation is that I'm going out of town this weekend."

"At least he can't call you if he can't find you. I'll come on over."

"No, Bill, I'm not going to let him ruin my life. Thanks for offering. Goodnight."

"Wait—you didn't tell me you were going out of town.

Where to?"

"Oh, we're having a reunion at the 'W.' My three best friends from college are meeting here and then we're all going to drive on over to Columbus.

Why don't you come over tomorrow afternoon and meet them? I know y'all would really hit it off."

Geoffrey knew all about the plans from listening to the tape recordings, but he had to feign ignorance and a little bit of anger.

"Uh, no, thanks. I have something important to do tomorrow afternoon. When are you coming back?"

"Monday night. Are you okay? You sound kind of funny," Suzanne said.

"It's nothing. I, uh, sort of had plans for us this weekend. I should have said something to you first, though. Don't worry. Everything's okay. But I think I'm getting one of my migraines, so I've got to hang up. Have a great time and call me when you get back."

"Goodnight, Bill. I'll talk to you Monday night."

"Is anything wrong, Mom?" Alicia asked, noticing her mother's puzzled look.

"I don't know. When I told Bill about this weekend, he acted kind of funny. He said it was because he had plans for us. Maybe it's just my imagination, but I think he got upset when I told him about our reunion. I don't know why that should bother him. He doesn't even know the other three."

"He's probably jealous that he's not getting to do anything with you this weekend. You know how guys are. They get rather possessive. Since we're both leaving tomorrow, we'd better finish packing. See you in the morning."

"Maybe you're right. Goodnight, sweetheart."

Suzanne was still unsettled. The phone call had unnerved her, but Bill's response was really puzzling. She knew that she had not imagined the change in his voice just when she had mentioned the trip to the "W."

Geoffrey hung up the phone and walked over to Angie's shrine. He picked up one of her pictures, caressing it over his heart.

"Guess what, Angie? Our prayers are answered. The four bitches are definitely going to be together this weekend. They'll all gather in Memphis tomorrow and then go on to Columbus. Things couldn't have been planned any better."

35

The next morning Geoffrey placed several phone calls to Suzanne's house and then replayed the last part of Suzanne and Alicia's conversation. He wanted to make sure that he knew exactly what Suzanne's plans were. One of the group, Janine Beauregard, was going to the airport to pick up Arlene Holcomb, who was arriving that morning from Tampa on Northwest Airlines. He drove to the airport and headed straight to the Northwest Airlines terminal to await her flight. Since he wanted to be as inconspicuous as possible, he chose a seat where he could observe the action without being noticed. He sat down and pulled the triangular-shaped picture from his jacket pocket and fidgeted with it as he stared across the concourse. A very important reunion would soon be taking place, and he certainly didn't want to miss the joyous event. As he shifted his steel gray eyes from the tattered photograph to the various women seated in the rows of red-cushioned chairs, he tried to imagine what Janine would look like after thirty years. Like an eagle spotting his prey, his eyes honed in on a middle-aged woman wearing a beige pantsuit. His breath began to come in gulps and his heart raced. She had to be the same person in the picture, although she had gained at least a hundred pounds and had graying hair instead of the light brown of her youthful self. He sat and stared at the picture as tears of pain and rage welled up in his eyes.

Janine Walton Beauregard, totally unaware that she was being observed, turned around in her chair and searched the hazy skies for the plane that would reunite her with her former college roommate. An ominous feeling made the hair on the back of her neck prickle, but she shook it off.

Although Janine and the other three had kept in contact over the years by phone calls and letters, this would be the first time all four were together since graduation. She wondered if the others had changed as much as she had. She knew that through the years all four had undergone more than their share of misfortune.

Janine Beauregard typified a matronly schoolteacher. Except for the fact that her body was enveloped in several layers of fat, she was quite attractive. Her sparkling blue eyes, which seemed to dance when the light hit them, grew heavy as she continued to await Arlene's arrival. She shut them for a moment and her thoughts drifted back to those days in the fall of 1960 when she had begun college as a self-conscious, timid freshman.

One of the unique aspects of life in the South was its desire to retain its status quo. For generations the importance of joining a fraternity or sorority had been impressed upon its sons and daughters. The founding mothers of MSCW thought that sororities would interfere with their finishing-school mentality and might foster unladylike competition among their "delicate flowers," so they opted instead for social clubs. Their original intention had been to provide enough clubs so that anyone who wanted to become a member could join. Through the years, though, the number of eligible girls far outweighed the number of clubs and membership became a premium. Janine Walton was thrust into this environment and knew that if she were to be accepted by the other girls, she would have to be invited to join one of the clubs. All her hometown girlfriends were members of Delta and Janine's goal was to get a bid from that group.

At the first rush party, Jane became reacquainted with Suzanne Yates, a striking, sophisticated beauty coveted by every social club on campus. Suzanne lived in Friar's Point and often went to the annual Christmas dance given by Janine's high school sorority. Since Barbara and Arlene were also being rushed by the Deltas, the four girls were thrown together at the parties and developed a friendship, even though they all had vastly different personalities.

On the morning that bids were being issued, Janine, who wasn't even sure she was going to receive one, could hear doors opening up and down her hall, indicating that the members were coming to get their chosen rushees. She prayed she'd be one of them.

When her door burst open and a group of Deltas shouted, "Get dressed, Janine, we want you to be one of our pledges!" she almost fainted with excitement and relief. It was a particular triumph for Janine because her roommate, who was also hoping to be invited to join Delta, didn't get a bid. Janine was grateful that her roommate's hostility and sarcasm would not follow her into the Delta club.

"Oh, Janine, we made it!" gushed Suzanne, Barbara, and Arlene as they hugged each other at the pledging ceremony, where they received their wooden triangles attached to blue ribbons. At the end of the ceremony, the pledges and members joined hands and promised eternal sisterhood.

36

The announcement on the loudspeaker brought Janine back to reality. "Flight 881 will be arriving approximately thirty minutes late."

Janine was clearly annoyed. She tried reading a magazine but couldn't concentrate. A drink in the bar was out of the question since she'd be the one driving that afternoon. In desperation, she adjusted her plus-size body in the chair and leaned her head back against the wall opting for a quick nap. Just before her lids closed, she noticed that a man across the concourse was staring at her. The next thing she was aware of was the loudspeaker announcing the arrival of Arlene's plane. Nervous anticipation coursed through Janine's body. Arlene had always intimidated her, even though they had been friends for over thirty years. The door leading to the plane opened and passengers hurried into the waiting area. When Janine spotted a tall, middle-aged woman with a silver streak in the front of her hair, she frantically waved to get Arlene's attention. The two hugged and both tried to talk at the same time.

"You look great!" they shouted to each other in unison.

Both lied. Time had certainly taken its toll on each of them, but that didn't matter. This reunion was far more important.

When they turned to walk down the concourse, Janine caught sight once more of the man who had been staring at her. They made eye contact and the man dropped his head and looked at a picture he was holding in his trembling hands. As the two women continued on their way, he slipped the photograph into his jacket pocket and followed their movements with his eyes. He watched them walk down the concourse as his head throbbed and the voice within once again ordered him to kill. But he knew that he would have to be patient a little longer. He controlled his urges and remained where he was until the two women were out of sight.

After the women had gathered up Arlene's luggage from the baggage carousel, they headed toward Janine's car.

"We'll pick up Suzanne and Barbara and then go on to Columbus," Janine told her friend. They drove out of the airport and within a half-hour were going through the security gate at Tanglewood Apartments.

"Well, let's see how time's treated Suzanne and Barbara. I'm dying to see how much they've changed," Janine said with a bit of trepidation as she rang the bell of Suzanne's apartment.

When the door opened, Janine and Arlene gasped in amazement at their two friends. They looked so incredibly good—had hardly aged in thirty years. Suzanne had retained the perfect features of a beauty queen and Barbara, round faced and curly headed, still reminded them of a cherub in a Botticelli painting. But from the expressions on their faces, something was terribly wrong.

"What on earth's the matter?" Janine asked.

"Come on in and we'll tell you all about it. Gosh, I can't believe it's been thirty years since we've been together."

Once inside the apartment, Suzanne explained, "We've been getting these awful phone calls."

"Yeah, some creep has called us repeatedly ever since I got here this morning," Barbara said. "As soon as anyone answers the phone, he talks in this monotone voice and says, 'You know you've got to die, bitch. I'm going to make you pay for what you did to us.' I don't think it's just a prank."

"Actually, it's been going on for several weeks," Suzanne said. "Alicia and I started getting the calls soon after she began law school. I've called the police and had caller ID put on the phone, but somehow, whoever is calling is able to block it out. The police want us to put on a phone trace. I think when we get back I'm going to let them do it."

At that precise moment, the phone rang. When Suzanne recognized the now familiar voice, she punched the speakerphone button so that everyone could hear the caller's words.

"I see your two friends have arrived. Nothing can save you now. I'm going to kill all four of you for what you did to us."

An evil laugh pierced the room, followed by a clicking sound, and then the hum of the dial tone permeated the silence. At that moment, Alicia came downstairs and noticed the concern on the faces of the four women.

"He called again, didn't he, Mom? God, why won't he let us alone?" Then she noticed the two new guests. "I'm sorry. You must be Janine and Arlene. Forgive my manners. It's just that this guy has almost driven us crazy with his damn threats. Frankly, I'm glad we're all going out of town. I've got to run a couple of errands and then I'm going to pick up Max. Y'all have a wonderful time at your reunion."

"We will, sweetheart," Suzanne said, giving her daughter a hug. "Be careful. Don't forget to call when you leave Gatlinburg."

"Oh, Mom."

"I know, I know. But you're still my baby."

Suzanne didn't mention the fact that their caller knew that

her two friends had arrived. She decided there was no point in spoiling Alicia and Max's trip. After Alicia left, Arlene turned to the other women and said, "Well, whoever it is knows we're all here. He must be watching our every move. I don't understand why the police can't do more."

"I told you he has some way to block caller ID," Suzanne said.

"You two get your clothes together. The sooner we get out of here the better," Janine said. "Surely he won't follow us to Columbus. The only men at homecoming are the hen-pecked husbands whose wives make them go."

"Have you forgotten? The 'W' has male students now. They'll probably be there," said Arlene with concern in her voice.

"Oh, that's right. They made us let them in, didn't they?"

The four women loaded the car for what had promised to be one of the best times of their lives. But now the memory of the phone calls hung like a pall over each one.

"We'll be in Columbus in a few hours and then we'll be safe." Suzanne tried to sound reassuring, but she really didn't believe her own words. At least she didn't have to worry about her daughter. She and Max were on their way to Gatlinburg by now.

They had just pulled out of Suzanne's parking lot when Barbara blurted out, "Oh, damn! I forgot to bring pantyhose. Is there a mall near here?" Barbara said in a pleading voice.

"That'll take us an extra hour. Barbara, just wear some of mine," Suzanne said.

"Oh, Suzanne, y'all know I have elephant feet. I can't wear anyone else's. Just take us to the nearest mall. I'll hurry. I promise."

"Okay. What's the closest place?" Janine asked.

"Oak Court, I guess," Suzanne replied. "Just turn left at the next red light and that'll get us to the back entrance."

37

Alicia and Max planned on spending a week with friends in Gatlinburg. It would be the first real vacation she had taken in years. She was not only looking forward to her trip, but was thrilled that her mother was getting together with her old college friends—she knew how much this meant to Suzanne. And she knew her mother was truly happy for the first time since the divorce because there was a new man in her life. Alicia pulled out of the driveway, but she decided to pay a visit to Bill before she picked up Max. She just wanted him to know how happy he had made her mother. She hoped she wouldn't embarrass him by telling him this.

Geoffrey had returned from the airport and was busy preparing for his upcoming trip. With his back to Angie's pictures, he carefully laid on the bed all the items he thought he might need, like a doctor laying out his surgical instruments before an operation. As Geoffrey "worked," he spoke aloud to Angie.

"I have to pack my switchblade. I'm going to make sure they suffer just like you did, Angie. Then I'll put them out of their misery after I collect my souvenirs from each one." He held up several objects and turned to show them to Angie.

"Here are the two bottles of Ketamine and some syringes I stole just before I left Parchman. The Ketamine will knock them out. That's the only way I can handle four prisoners at one time. Ah, the bottle of formaldehyde to keep the souvenirs in. That works a helluva lot better than water. I'm going to need something to restrain them with. Handcuffs and several pieces of rope ought to do. Now, in case they decide to scream, I'll put this duct tape on their mouths. Let's see. Have I got everything? I almost forgot that I was going to film our masterpiece, my love. Here's the video camera and its accessories. That should just about do it. Now let's put everything in the duffel bag."

Geoffrey's actions were interrupted by the doorbell.

"Oh, shit. Who on earth can that be?"

Looking out the side window, Geoffrey froze when he saw Alicia. He called out toward the closed door. "Just a minute. I've got to finish dressing."

He hurriedly put everything except one of the bottles of Ketamine and a syringe and two pieces of rope in his duffel bag and shoved it under the bed. He withdrew some Ketamine from the bottle and stuffed the syringe into his jacket pocket and laid the rope on the nightstand by his bed. He walked to the door, trying to regain his composure.

"Alicia, what are you doing here?" Geoffrey asked nonchalantly. "I thought you and Max were on your way to Gatlinburg. How on earth did you find my house?"

"Oh, you know women have their special ways of finding out things," Alicia teased. "I just had to run by and thank you. Mom's a different person since you came into her life."

Alicia hugged Geoffrey tightly. He stiffened but hugged her back.

"Alicia, I really like your mother a lot. She's given me a new lease on life, too."

Just then the phone rang. Geoffrey picked it up and instant-ly recognized Josiah's voice.

"Alicia, excuse me just a minute. I need to talk in the other room. I won't be long. Why don't you go to the kitchen and get a Coke or something out of the fridge. It's right down the hall and to the left."

Alicia said thanks and walked toward the kitchen. She had to pass Geoffrey's bedroom on the way. A flicker of light caught her eye and she hesitated momentarily to see where it was coming from. Her eyes were drawn to a group of framed pictures surrounded by candles. The whole thing reminded her of a shrine in a Catholic church. Curiosity got the best of her and she walked into the room to get a closer look. Although most of the photographs were of a beautiful young girl, Alicia gasped when she realized that one of the photographs was of her mother, Arlene, Barbara, and Janine. The picture looked like it had been cut out of an old annual. Across the photograph was written the phrase "Killer Bitches" in a faded red sub-stance. Beside the pictures were newspaper articles about sev-eral murders that had occurred in September 1963, while her mother and the others were attending the "W." Alicia studied the pictures of the killer and shuddered when she realized that he had the same mesmerizing eyes as Bill. A tape recorder sat next to the pictures. When Alicia punched *Play*, a feeling of terror and anger came over her. The voices on the tape belonged to her and her mother. She quickly punched *Stop*, fearing that Bill might hear the tape, but she was too late. Sensing that she was no longer alone in the room, Alicia turned around just in time to see Bill lunging toward her. Before she could defend herself, he threw her to the floor and knelt on top of her, pinning her down. Alicia struggled, but was no match for the man who was looking at her and shaking his head.

"Bill, what in God's name are you doing! Is this some kind

of sick joke?"

"Alicia, why did you come over here? I never meant for you to be hurt. It's your mother I'm after."

"But why, Bill? She never did anything to you."

"Oh yes, she did. It started one September day over thirty years ago." After Geoffrey had finished his story, he looked at Alicia with tears in his eyes and said softly, "Now you see why I have to kill her, don't you? She and the other Deltas took away the dearest thing in my life when they denied Angie admittance to their precious social club."

"Bill, you can't kill Mom. You're, you're in love with her."

"I know, Alicia, but I promised Angie that I'd get even for what happened to her and our baby and I have to keep my promise. It's what kept me alive while I was in prison. Don't try to argue with me. My mind's made up. The only thing I regret is having to kill you, too. But I'll make it painless. It won't be anything like what I have to do to your mother and the others. They're going to beg me to kill them before it's over."

Geoffrey reached into his pocket to get the syringe. Alicia suddenly flipped over, knocking Geoffrey off balance. He stuck out his arm to break his fall and the syringe fell to the carpet. Alicia reached out and grabbed it. She jabbed the syringe toward Geoffrey's arm. He jerked his arm back and only a small amount of the drug got into his system. But that minute dose had an effect. Geoffrey lurched forward and then backward, finally crumpling on the carpet. Alicia tossed the syringe on the floor and stood up. She had to step over Geoffrey's body to get out of the room. Suddenly, his hand shot out and grabbed her, pulling her down on top of him. He shook his head to clear his senses and picked up the syringe, which still had enough Ketamine to render a person unconscious. This time the needle found its mark, and Alicia collapsed on top of him. He pushed her body aside and stood up. While she was still unconscious, he placed the rope around her neck and jerked it tightly.

Alicia's death was instant and painless. Afterwards, Geoffrey began to cry. "I'm so sorry. I really liked you, Alicia."

From deep within, his demonic voice cried out. "Don't be such a baby. It was all Alicia's fault anyway. If she hadn't been so nosey, this would have never happened. You can't let your feelings for the dead girl cloud your mind. You've still got to finish the job. I'll be with you every step of the way."

Geoffrey clamped his hands over his ears, but he knew the voice was right. It had been necessary to kill Alicia. But now he had to dispose of her body before he could begin the next phase of his revenge. Burying the corpse in the isolated field behind his house would take the least amount of time.

The shovel made a thunking sound when it struck the iron-hard dirt. After several frustrating minutes, Geoffrey gave up and went back into the house, completely exhausted from his futile labors.

I've got to do something fast. Max'll be calling Suzanne if Alicia doesn't show up. Then they'll start a search. I want Suzanne and the others to go on and leave town so that I can finish my job. The retribution has to take place in Columbus or Angie will never be fully satisfied. She'll come back and haunt me like she's done so many times before. God, why did Alicia have to screw everything up?

Suddenly, he thought of a solution to his problem. There was an old rug in the storeroom. He could wrap Alicia's body in it and carry it to one of the dumpsters out in the country. There was a secluded one just off Old Fleming Road leading into Collierville. Underneath the kitchen sink, Geoffrey kept a box of latex gloves. He put on a pair and rolled Alicia in the rug and carried her to his car. He had already opened the trunk. Luckily, Alicia wasn't very tall and easily fit inside. Before closing the trunk, he went back into his house and got his duffel bag. He felt pretty confident since no one was anywhere in sight. The next step would be to get Alicia's car away from his house. He opened the door and spotted the keys in the ignition, where he knew they would be. He drove to the parking lot of Oak Court Mall and left the car. He peeled off the latex gloves he had been wearing and stuffed them in his pocket. He knew the car wouldn't arouse anyone's suspicions until he had time to get away. By the time Alicia was reported missing, he would probably be in Columbus. He caught the next MATA bus back to his house. When Geoffrey got home, he jumped into his car and dialed Suzanne's house just to make sure the four women had left before Max could have called. When the answering machine picked up, Geoffrey hung up the phone with a smile. Now all he had to do was to dispose of Alicia's body and he'd be on his way to complete his mission. When he reached the dumpster, he put the gloves back on. No one was anywhere around and he quickly lifted the lid and slid the rug in. He went back to his car and got a sack containing the rope, the used syringe, and the empty bottle of Ketamine. He opened the sack and shook the items into the dumpster. With a sigh of relief, he got back into the car and headed toward Highway 78.

38

When Janine pulled up at the rear entrance of Oak Court Mall, each of the four women thought of something she needed. Two hours later, they were finally on their way again. Just outside Tupelo, Suzanne noticed something familiar and started to tell Janine to stop but reconsidered and kept quiet.

"I still can't believe it's taken us thirty years to get together," Arlene said. "Remember at graduation we made a pact that no matter what happened we'd see each other at least once a year?"

"I guess the best laid plans..." Barbara started to say but was interrupted by the ringing of Suzanne's cell phone. None of the four were very surprised when the muffled voice began its familiar intonations. "You can't get away from me no matter where you go. I'm going to kill you bitches. See you in Columbus."

"Damn that bastard!" Arlene cried out. "Can y'all think of anyone who hates us enough to threaten us like this?"

They all solemnly shook their heads.

At a nearby Double Quick, Geoffrey Bockker laughed as he

hung up the phone. "Now, I've got you just where I want you." After a few minutes, he pulled out onto the highway and set the cruise control. After all, he didn't want to break the speed limit.

39

When Alicia hadn't arrived by noon, Max became concerned. He tried to call her, but no one answered. He wrote a note and stuck it to his front door so that if Alicia came for him while he was gone, she would know to wait for him. He figured that Suzanne and the others had already left for their reunion. Then he reasoned that perhaps Alicia had some last minute shopping to do, so he decided to wait for her. The few minutes turned into an hour and Max became frantic. He dialed her car phone but received the response that the customer was either out of range or was unavailable to answer the phone. He wanted to call Suzanne, but realized he didn't know the number of the bed and breakfast where she was supposed to be staying. He decided to go over to Suzanne's apartment to try to find it.

When Max reached the gate, he was relieved to see that George Haynes was on duty.

"George, I'm worried that something's happened to Alicia. She was supposed to pick me up over two hours ago."

"Mr. Quinn, Alicia left about two hours ago. I don't know where she was headed, though. Mrs. Carter and her friends

have left, too. They went to Columbus to their college reunion."

"I've got a key to the apartment. Do you think it'd be okay
for me to go up there to see if I can find the number of the place
they're staying? You can come with me if you want to."

"That's okay, Mr. Quinn. I can't leave my post here. But it's
okay for you to go in. I'll tell Mrs. Bridges that you've got permission."

George suddenly had a sick feeling in the pit of his stomach.

Max waited impatiently for the elevator to reach the third
floor. He got off and almost ran to the apartment. Shuffling
through some papers on Suzanne's desk, he found a brochure
for the *Four Seasons Bed & Breakfast* and dialed the number.

"Hello, this is Max Quinn in Memphis. My fiancé's mother,
Suzanne Carter, is supposed to be staying there this weekend.
Has she checked in yet?"

The bed and breakfast owner said the women hadn't arrived
yet and asked Max if he'd like to leave a message.

Not wanting to unduly upset Suzanne, Max decided to leave
a phony message. "Just tell her that Alicia and I have had a
change in plans and aren't going out of town after all. Ask her
to call us at home when she checks in."

Max Quinn had always prided himself on being in control of
his emotions. He had served in the Gulf War and had known
firsthand what it felt like for friends to die. But this was a different feeling. He never expected anything to happen to Alicia.
He reached into his coat pocket and felt for the box he had
placed there earlier. Opening it, he looked at the engagement
ring, which he had planned to surprise her with on their trip. He
quickly flipped the lid shut and sat down. He remembered the
first time he had met her. It had been at a cocktail party given
for one of their mutual friends. Max had turned around and
bumped into a gorgeous, red-haired girl, sloshing his drink on

her dress.

"Gosh, I'm so sorry. Here let me wipe that off for you. Oh, I'm Max Quinn."

A smile came over Alicia's face. "Don't worry about it. When it dries, you won't even be able to see the stain. I'm Alicia Carter."

Max grinned, too. "You're the one our mutual friends have been trying to fix me up with. I guess I've saved them the trouble."

In a few short months, love had blossomed between the two, and this trip was to have been the beginning of their more committed relationship. Now, something or someone was trying to ruin everything. It wasn't like Alicia to be late, so Max had a premonition that something terrible must have happened.

He frantically called all the hospital emergency rooms in Memphis, but Alicia wasn't in any of them.

The phone rang. Max picked it up, praying that Alicia would be on the other end and explain everything.

"Max, this is Suzanne. What happened to change your plans? Is Alicia okay?"

"Mrs. Carter, I don't have any idea where Alicia is. I got here about three hours ago. George Haynes said that she had left about two hours before I arrived. I'm frantic. She's not at any of the emergency rooms. I guess I should notify the police."

"Max, I'll get the first flight out. Stay there and I'll take a taxi from the airport. Don't leave the apartment. Alicia might try to call."

As Suzanne hung up the phone, Barbara asked nervously, "Suzanne, what's the matter?"

"It's Alicia. She's disappeared. She left the apartment and never arrived at Max's. I've got to get a reservation on the next flight to Memphis. Oh, God, something's happened to my baby.

I just know it."

After she told Janine and Arlene the bad news, Suzanne collapsed into her friends' arms. A wave of nausea swept over her and for a minute she was afraid she was going to be sick.

Janine said, "I'll make the reservations and go with you, Suzanne." She realized that, at last, Suzanne truly needed her friendship and support. "You don't need to go through this alone."

"Okay, Janine, I really could use some company, but, Barbara, you and Arlene stay here. Max might call back with some information while we're on the way. Besides, it could be nothing, and I don't want to spoil our reunion."

Just as Suzanne and Janine were walking out the door, the phone rang. Barbara grabbed it, thinking it was Max with news about Alicia.

"Hello, bitches, having a good time here in Columbus? I just wanted to let you know I'm here too, and I'm going to enjoy this reunion even more than you will. I'll be calling you later. Just remember, these are your last days on earth. Enjoy them!"

Barbara stared in stunned silence at her friends.

Suzanne cried, "What? Tell us. Was that Max? Has he found out something about Alicia?"

"No, it was that bastard again! He's here in Columbus. My God, do you think he's connected with Alicia's disappearance?"

"No, no, I can't, I don't," Suzanne stammered as she and Janine left the room.

After the two had walked out the door, Arlene and Barbara just stared at each other in shock and silence.

40

Geoffrey Bockker hung up his car phone. He headed toward Josiah's country retreat several miles outside of Columbus. Josiah had called him earlier to say that he and Agnes were flying to Cancun and he just wanted to touch base before they left. Geoffrey knew that he would have the place to himself. Years earlier Josiah had told Geoffrey where he kept the key to the cabin. The location was perfect—deeply secluded in the woods and no neighbors for miles around. He could finally carry out his promise to Angie, and then he could rest. The one obstacle was that he had to figure out a way to get rid of all four women at one time. Then a diabolical solution popped into his head. Once inside the cabin, he dialed the number of the bed and breakfast where the four women were staying.

"Suzanne Carter's room, please."

"Just a moment, I'll ring it for you," the woman at the other end said. Then a voice said, "Hello."

"Is Suzanne there? This is her friend Bill Caldwell."

"Oh, Bill, this is Barbara Atkins. Where are you? Something's happened and Suzanne had to fly back to

Memphis with one of our other friends. Alicia's disappeared."

Geoffrey felt like he had been kicked in the stomach. His plans were thwarted because of Alicia's screw-up. If only she hadn't come over to the house. She had ruined everything.

"What, what do you mean? Alicia and Max were supposed to go out of town. Oh, God, poor Suzanne. I drove down to check on my sick aunt who lives here in Columbus. If it's okay, can I come over there and wait with y'all until you hear from Suzanne?"

"Sure, Bill. We're at 1809 Old Dominion Drive. You can't miss it. We're in the second cottage, so you don't even have to go to the front desk."

On the way there, Geoffrey mulled over what he could do. He had to get the two women away from the bed and breakfast in order to kill them. Afterwards, he'd still have to kill Suzanne and Janine. His plans were messed up, and now his head started hurting. Spots flashed in front of his eyes, and the pain wouldn't go away. He screamed out loud and slammed his clenched fist on the steering wheel.

Okay, Geoffrey, it's not the end of the world. You've just hit a minor glitch. It's nothing that can't be rectified. Just calm down and think. You've come too far to give up now.

A brilliant idea came to him and he pressed down on the accelerator as he headed in the direction of Old Dominion Drive.

"Oh, Angie, two of the bitches will die tonight. I promise."

Barbara and Arlene greeted Geoffrey at the door to the cottage. "Bill, come on in. I'm Barbara Atkins and this is Arlene Holcomb. We've heard so many nice things about you from Suzanne."

Geoffrey swallowed hard when he came face to face with his intended victims. He had to fight off the urge to strangle them both right then and there. All the memories of those last moments with Angie came flooding back to him. If there had ever been any doubts about killing the four, they disappeared. He did care deeply for Suzanne, but had only feelings of utter hatred for these two. They had helped destroy the most precious thing in his life.

"I feel the same way about y'all," he said, forcing the words out through clenched teeth. "You two can't do any good sitting around here. Why don't we go get something to eat? Call the desk and leave word that you'll be back in about an hour."

Arlene answered first. "I guess it'll be okay. The plane doesn't leave for half an hour and then the flight to Memphis will take another hour. Plus, they've got to get from the airport to Suzanne's apartment."

Barbara agreed. "Yes, let's go."

Arlene called the front desk and asked them to take a message if there were any calls.

Geoffrey nonchalantly escorted the two women to his car. He certainly didn't want to arouse their suspicions.

"Listen, I'm staying at a neat resort cabin out near the lake. There's plenty of food in the fridge. Why don't we go out there instead of to some crowded restaurant?"

Geoffrey's charming smile and all the wonderful things Suzanne had said about "Bill" made both women feel perfectly safe with him.

As they drove to the cabin, Geoffrey tried to make polite conversation.

"Suzanne said it's been over thirty years since the four of you have gotten together. I know how much this weekend was going to mean to her. It's all she's talked about for the last three weeks. Y'all must have been really close in college. She's got pictures and scrapbooks of your 'W' days. I guess she's shown them to me a dozen times. I think those days help her forget the rough times she's been through."

Arlene responded nostalgically, "You know, I suppose that's all any of us have to hang onto. Those were the last carefree days we had."

At that moment, if Geoffrey hadn't hated the two women so much for what they had done to Angie and their unborn baby, he might have felt sorry for them. But weren't they to blame for his going to prison for thirty years? He had been robbed first of his great love and then of his youth. Hell, yes, they deserved to die.

As they entered the cabin, Arlene sighed. "This place reminds me so much of Carrier Lodge," she said to Barbara. "Do you remember the great times we had there during rush week?"

Barbara emitted the little laugh she gave whenever she was really happy.

"Yeah, everybody was so excited because we thought we were going to get the top pledges on campus."

With the mention of rush week, Geoffrey bristled. "What's rush week?"

"It's when all the freshmen are matched up with the social clubs they want to join," Arlene explained. "At least it works that way unless somebody's a real slut or geek. Then they get cut and have to join one of the inferior clubs. The really terrible ones don't get invited to join any club."

Geoffrey frowned. "That sounds so unfair. What if somebody really wanted in a club badly? And then were so hurt they might, well, uh, do something foolish."

Barbara shrugged. "Well, Bill, that's life. You know, I just thought about something. Arlene, do you remember when we had all left for practice teaching our senior year and that poor little freshman killed herself because she didn't get in Delta? Her creepy boyfriend blamed the club and murdered two of our members."

"Yeah, didn't they call him the 'Triangle Killer'?" Arlene shivered. "God, I haven't thought about that for ages."

Barbara suddenly noticed that Geoffrey had started crying. "Bill, what's wrong? Have we said something to upset you? What's the matter?"

Geoffrey edged toward the nightstand by the bed. "There sure is something wrong. That girl you so carelessly tossed away was my girlfriend, my precious Angie. I'm the creep, the so-called 'Triangle Killer.' Now you're going to have to suffer just like those other girls for what you did to my Angie and our unborn child."

Cold chills of horror and fear ran up the backs of both women, but before either could utter a sound, Geoffrey, with cat-like reflexes, grabbed his pistol from the nightstand and whirled around. His steel-gray eyes flashed with pent-up hatred and literally mesmerized the women.

"Bill—" Barbara said, her eyes wide with terror.

"The name's Geoffrey, you bitch! Now shut up and don't say a word, or I'll blow your brains out right this minute. Those aren't my plans, though. You're going to have to suffer just like I've suffered for the last thirty years. First of all, I'm going to turn on my video camera so that Angie and I'll have a memento of our special evening." He gave each woman a pair of handcuffs. "Both of you, sit down and handcuff yourselves to each other and then to those chairs."

"What, what are you going to do to us? We didn't do anything to that poor girl. We weren't even on campus when the bids went out," Barbara stammered.

"But you still had the final say-so, didn't you? You four had the authority to override anyone's blackball. Answer me!" Geoffrey spat out the words.

"Yes, but we went along with everyone else," Arlene cried.

"As I recall, they said she wasn't quite attractive enough. For some stupid reason we were supposed to go for looks that year, not personality. I'm truly sorry, Bill, uh, Geoffrey. We shouldn't have listened to that dumb directive, but we really didn't know any better. Honestly, we had no idea—"

"No! You didn't give a damn who you hurt. Just because she didn't live up to your phony standards, you drove her to suicide. You call me a monster. I was just getting even with you Deltas. Giving you a little taste of your own medicine."

"But it's not too late, Geoffrey. You've paid your debt to society. Just let Barbara and me go and we won't say anything. We promise."

"I'm afraid it is too late. You see, I had to kill Alicia because she accidentally found out who I was."

"My God," Barbara cried. "Poor Suzanne. You are a monster. This was all part of your diabolical scheme to get even. You won't get away with this!"

Barbara lunged forward, pulling Arlene with her. Geoffrey aimed the pistol just above her knee and fired three shots. She screamed and both women fell backwards, knocking the chairs over. The two women lay in a pool of blood and broken chairs. Geoffrey dragged them to a sitting position and looked directly at Arlene.

"Don't you try anything or you'll be next."

"Go ahead," Arlene screamed. "I don't care. Just shoot me and get it over with."

"You'll beg me to shoot you before I'm through with you two. Now damnit! Just shut the hell up!"

Geoffrey balled up a soft cloth and stuffed it in Barbara's mouth and covered it with duct tape. She could taste the bile as it rose in her throat and prayed that she wouldn't vomit.

"Now, I don't have to listen to any more of your shit."

He reached into his duffel bag and pulled out a bottle of

Ketamine and a syringe. He could see fear in both women's eyes as he slowly withdrew the liquid from the bottle. He held the syringe in front of their faces and pushed the plunger, squirting a stream of medicine into the air.

"I'll do you first, Arlene. That way I won't have to tape your mouth. Are you two wondering what this drug will do? You'll find out soon enough."

Geoffrey plunged the needle into Arlene's arm, and within seconds she slumped forward, almost totally unconscious.

Geoffrey grinned at Barbara. "Uh-oh, looks like I gave your friend a little too much sleepy juice. But it'll wear off soon and she won't miss out on the fun."

Barbara grimaced in pain as Geoffrey stomped on her wounded leg. "That hurts, doesn't it, bitch? Well, Angie hurt, too, just before she died in that awful wreck."

He turned back to Arlene and jerked her head up and stabbed her in the eyeball with the syringe, laughing as he did so. The pain brought her back to consciousness and she howled.

"I had planned to torture both of you some more, but I have to get back to Memphis to finish the job, so I'll just put you out of your misery after I leave my trademark on you."

Geoffrey Bockker then reverted to his days as the "Triangle Killer." He carefully carved the figure on Barbara's forehead and ripped the piece of skin from the flesh. When he had finished, he repeatedly stabbed her in the chest until she finally stopped breathing.

Arlene had watched the life drain from her friend and knew that she was next. Her heart pounded wildly and her brain spun out of control with fear. Her eye felt like someone had stuck a hot poker in it and she blinked repeatedly to try to make the pain go away.

"Okay, Mrs. Holcomb, it's your time. Oh, what's the matter? Does your eye hurt? I'm so sorry. Here, let me make it better."

Geoffrey cupped one hand under Arlene's chin and then gouged out her injured eye with his knife, laughing as it hung on her face, held only by several muscles. He severed them with his knife, and the eye slid down her cheek and landed on the floor like a peeled grape. Arlene fainted as Geoffrey spoke.

"Now, you're going to have to wear a badge of shame, too, just like Mrs. Atkins. I can't play favorites, can I?" After he had skinned off his triangular symbol from her forehead, he slit her throat with one swipe of the knife and laughed as the blood gushed down her body and pooled on the floor.

"Now, Angie, I have souvenirs from two of your murderers." He placed the pieces of skin in the jar of formaldehyde he had put in the refrigerator. "Soon two more will be joining them." Geoffrey walked toward the camera and clicked it off. "We've completed our masterpiece, Angie. I'll show it to you when I get back to Memphis."

This time he wouldn't have to worry about cleaning up the mess or getting rid of the bodies. Josiah and Agnes wouldn't be back from Cancun until the end of the week, and there was no telling when they might come out to check on the cabin. He would have a full two days because the four women weren't supposed to check out until sometime Monday morning. That would give him plenty of time to get back to Memphis.

The murders had taken their toll on Geoffrey. He went into the bathroom, took off his bloody clothes and stuffed them into a plastic bag. He turned on the shower as hot as he could stand it and let the pelting water cascade over his exhausted body. Afterwards, the rough texture of the towel made his skin tingle.

"Josiah, old man, I don't suppose you'll mind if I borrow some of your clothes," he said, as he opened a dresser drawer and grabbed some underwear and a T-shirt. Then he went to the closet and found some old running shoes and a pair of jeans. "Angie, baby, we're halfway home. I'll finish the job soon."

Geoffrey picked up the camera and stuffed it, the bag of clothes, all his other instruments, and the glass jar into the duffel bag and headed out the front door. As he was leaving, he smashed the front pane of the door to make it look as if an intruder had broken in and killed the two women. He calmly got into his car, turned on the radio, and headed back to Memphis.

41

By the time their plane had landed, Suzanne and Janine were already out of their seats and heading to the exit. The flight attendant rushed to the women and admonished them for getting out of their seats before the plane had come to a complete stop.

Suzanne cried frantically, "We've got to get off immediately! My daughter's been kidnapped. Oh God, I can't stand it. Let me go!"

The other passengers stared at the hysterical woman as the flight attendant tried to calm her down.

"I'll let you two get off as soon as possible. But please sit down or you might get hurt."

Suzanne stopped moving but refused to sit down. When the plane mercifully came to a complete halt, the two women were ushered off immediately. The minute she entered the airport, Suzanne rushed to the nearest phone. Janine held Suzanne's free hand tightly.

"Oh, God, please let Alicia answer," Suzanne whispered frantically. "Come on, baby, be at home."

Max picked up the phone and Suzanne recognized his voice.

"Max, this is Suzanne. Have you heard anything from Alicia?"

"No, Mrs. Carter. I've checked all the hospitals and the emergency rooms and called the police. But there's no sign of her. Oh, God, I'm so frightened. I just can't lose Alicia. She's the most important thing in the world to me. What are we going to do?"

"I just don't know, Max," Suzanne replied, fighting back tears. "I'm on my way home. Wait there. The only thing we can do now is to pray. That's all we've got left."

Geoffrey drove back to Memphis just slightly above the speed limit. He couldn't afford to be stopped by the police, not with what he was carrying in his duffel bag. Although he had two days' leeway before Barbara and Arlene would be missed, he knew that Suzanne would contact him when she got back to Memphis, and he wanted to be there when she called. Sure enough, when he walked into the door of his house, the phone message light was blinking. When he punched the button, he heard Suzanne's desperate voice.

"Bill, whenever you get back, call me. Alicia's disappeared and we can't find a trace of her anywhere."

He immediately dialed her number and knew that he wouldn't be pretending when he sympathized with Suzanne over her plight. He still regretted having killed Alicia, but he would have to put that out of his mind. He couldn't afford to arouse anyone's suspicions.

"Suzanne, it's Bill. What do you mean Alicia's disappeared? I thought that she and Max were going on a trip. I don't understand. She couldn't have just vanished."

"They were. Only Alicia must have gone somewhere else before she went to Max's to pick him up. She never showed up at his place. There's no trace of her anywhere. I thought maybe you might have heard something from her. Bill, we're desperate. Could you please come over? I really need you here now."

"Of course, Suzanne. I'll be there just as soon as I can. Now don't worry. I'm sure Alicia'll turn up any minute."

As he hung up, Geoffrey smiled. "But when she does, you'll wish you had never found her."

He changed clothes and headed to Suzanne's apartment, his heart filled with ambivalence. He really had fallen in love with her, yet his devotion to Angie was even more powerful. His head started that awful throbbing.

Oh, God, please not now. I've got to think straight. Do I need to make up an alibi for not being at home? If she called just that once, I won't need one. What if she called from Columbus? Damnit. Why didn't I check to see if I had any more messages before I called her? Wait a minute. I remember now. The machine said I had only one message. Whew, that's a relief.

Suzanne opened the door the moment the doorbell rang. "Oh, Bill, thank God you're here. I'm going crazy not knowing what's happened to my baby."

Geoffrey nodded solemnly to Max and Janine just as the phone rang and Suzanne rushed to answer it. Her heart sank when she heard an unfamiliar voice.

"Mrs. Carter, this is Captain Austin from the East Precinct. We've found your daughter's car in the parking lot in front of Oak Court Mall. The keys and her suitcases are still inside. We had the mall searched thoroughly, but there was no sign of her anywhere. We've taken the car to the impound lot so that the detectives can examine it for prints or other evidence. We'll call you as soon as we find out anything. At least there's still some hope."

From the look on Suzanne's face, the other three knew that the news was not good. She told them what had happened and then collapsed into Geoffrey's arms.

"Now I know that something terrible has happened to her," Suzanne cried. "Somebody must have taken her by force from the parking lot. She'd never go off and leave her car unlocked with the keys and all her luggage in it. I know my daughter."

"She might have left with a friend," Max offered.

"Max, you know that's not true. She wouldn't do that without calling you. Y'all were planning to leave on your trip as soon as she picked you up. No, something's happened to her."

"Well, I'm not going to believe it until I have more proof," Janine said, trying to console Suzanne and Max.

"Me either, Janine," Max said. "I'm sure there's some logical explanation."

"Yes, I'm sure there is," Geoffrey agreed, patting Suzanne's hands and holding them in his.

42

Jace Lundstrom was following his regular routine. This had been his day to scour the dumpsters in the southern part of the county. He was driving along Hack's Cross Road, stopping every so often to pick up old cans and bottles, or anything else he could find of value, to put into the back of his beat-up car. Jace's wardrobe for this particular day consisted of old tennis shoes and a dirty cardigan sweater and brown pants, which he had pilfered from a garbage bin a week ago. The only time he cleaned up was when he used the washrooms in the service stations where he stopped to buy gas or when he spent the night at one of the local homeless shelters. He noticed a dumpster just ahead and pulled in front of it. Perhaps this would be a lucky day after all. He excitedly lifted the cover with the stick he had fashioned for just that purpose. Most people would have been overwhelmed by the sickening odors emitted from the mixture of junk and garbage, but Jace was used to the smell. He hoisted himself to the edge of the container and was just about to put one leg over the side when he spotted an expensive-looking rug. He hurriedly crawled inside and unrolled the rug. To his horror, he came face to face with the body of a young woman. A corded pattern encircled her neck. He instinctively placed his fingers on the pressure point of her neck to search for a pulse. When he found none, a wave of nausea swept over him. In all his years of dumpster scouring, he'd heard stories that the police occasionally turned up a body part or two, sometimes a dead infant, in dumpsters. Still, he couldn't believe that he was now staring at an actual murder victim. When he moved the body, he noticed a glass vial and syringe. Instinctively, he picked them up, studying them carefully. He pushed in the plunger on the syringe to see if there was anything left in it. At that moment, a car full of teenagers turned off onto the road. They were screaming and shouting at the tops of their lungs, obviously drunk. When they got closer, they noticed Jace standing in the garbage bin.

"Hey, look at the old guy rooting in there. I guess he's going to add to his fashionable wardrobe. Old man, what you got in there?"

"You kids get away from here. Go on!"

"Well, we'll just see for ourselves."

One of the boys, obviously a weight lifter, easily bounded into the dumpster. When he saw the body, he screamed and lost his balance, falling backwards. At that moment, Jace threw down the vial and syringe and reached out and caught him.

"Don't touch me, old man. Don't kill me like you killed her," the boy warned. He pushed Jace's hand away, jumped out and ran toward the car. "Call the sheriff on the car phone, and tell him someone has just killed a girl and put her body in the dumpster just south of where Fleming and Stateline intersect."

"Get away from him, Bobby! He's liable to kill you, too."

Jace bounded out after the boy.

"Wait a minute, kids. I didn't kill the girl. I just got here and found her. I swear it."

"Sure, sure, old man. Just tell it to the cops. I hear 'em coming now."

"Bobby, we better get out of here ourselves. With all this beer, we'll get busted, too."

The teenagers squealed off and were out of sight by the time the deputies arrived. Jace walked toward his car but thought better of trying to escape. That would make him look even more guilty. He just stood by his car and hung his head when the deputies pulled up in front of the dumpster. Fred Triplett jumped out of the car and climbed in, almost knocking Jace down in his haste. He examined the body for signs of life but couldn't find any and turned to his partner.

"Oh, God, I bet it's that missing girl, the one whose car they found in front of Oak Court Mall today. Call the county homicide unit and tell 'em to send out detectives and the medical examiner." He climbed out, wiping off the garbage and other refuse from his uniform.

"Okay, old man, tell us what happened," Triplett said to Jace. "Obviously you don't have a cell phone in that piece of shit," nodding toward Jace's car. "Who called in the report?"

"A bunch of drunk teenagers pulled up just as I crawled in. When I got in there, I started unrolling the rug. I just found the girl's body when one of them got out of the car and jumped up in there with me. When he saw the body, he started screaming and yelling at me, saying I had killed her. Then he hollered for one of his friends to call you. They tore out of here when they heard your sirens and headed north. But I didn't kill that girl. I swear to God this is the way I found her."

"Okay, calm down. Give me your name and address and let me see some ID."

"Jace Lundstrom. Here's my driver's license. I don't have a real home any more, I just sort of ride around, looking for stuff to sell for food and gas. That's why I was out here. I spotted the dumpster and thought maybe there was something in it I could pawn or sell."

An ambulance and two cars roared up and screeched to a halt. Within minutes, deputies were cordoning off the area. Two detectives and a representative from the Shelby County Medical Examiner's Office got out of their cars and climbed into the dumpster, trying to be careful not to disturb the body any more than necessary. One of the deputies photographed the contents of the dumpster before the body was moved. As they were lifting the rug, he spotted the rope.

"Hey, guys, look at this."

The movement of the rope also uncovered the syringe and the vial of Ketamine. All the items were placed in separate bags and given to a deputy standing nearby.

"Looks like we might have found the murder weapon," Triplett said, turning to the medical examiner. "I bet when you examine the body, Dr. Anderson, you'll find some needle marks, too." Triplett looked at the poor dumpster scavenger. "We're going to have to take you in for questioning." Jace started to protest but realized it wouldn't do any good. He was handcuffed and put in the back seat of the patrol car.

There was no way Dr. Anderson could really tell much about the body in its present location. After he had finished his perfunctory examination of the victim, he said to Triplett, "It sure looks like a case of classic strangulation to me. The ligature marks around her neck run in a straight line and the blood vessels in her eyes are occluded. By the way, you were right about puncture marks. I found one on her upper left arm. She obviously wasn't killed here, but she sure hasn't been dead very long." Then he climbed into the ambulance to accompany the body back to the morgue.

43

When the phone rang, Suzanne automatically whispered a quick prayer. "Please God, please let my baby be okay." She picked up the receiver and said a frightened, "Yes?"

"Mrs. Carter, this is Captain Austin. We spoke earlier about your missing daughter. I'm afraid I have bad news. The county deputies found the body of a young woman who fits your daughter's description in a dumpster. I'm sorry but we'll have to ask you to come to the morgue at the County Medical Examiner's Office to identify—"

Suzanne dropped the phone and slumped forward screaming and sobbing. Max ran over and picked up the phone while Geoffrey and Janine grabbed Suzanne and helped her to the couch.

The captain repeated his message to Max, who turned ashen. "Thank you, Captain. We'll be there as soon as we can."

Geoffrey grabbed his keys and all four headed out the door. The drive felt like the longest one any of them had ever taken. A secretary ushered them into Dr. Anderson's office. He made his routine apologies and then escorted the group to the room where bodies were kept until they were carried to various funeral homes. Dr. Anderson slowly pulled a drawer open and lifted the rubber sheet back. All four gasped as they recognized Alicia's body.

Suzanne screamed, "Oh, God, my baby!" She lunged forward to caress the lifeless body of her child. Geoffrey, Max, and Janine sobbed quietly. Dr. Anderson leaned over and gently lifted Suzanne from her daughter's body.

"Since you've made a positive ID, I'll need to get on with my post mortem exam so that I can tell exactly how she was killed. From my preliminary exam I believe that she was strangled with the rope we found in the dumpster, but I have to check further to find out exactly what happened."

"Will you have to do an autopsy? I don't want my baby mutilated any more," Suzanne pleaded.

"Yes, m'am. The state of Tennessee requires that an autopsy be performed if the case is a suspected homicide. It'll help the police catch whoever did this. When the funeral home gets her fixed up, though, you won't be able to tell that an autopsy was done. I promise you that. If you all would take Mrs. Carter on home, I'll call you when I've finished and have given my findings to the police. Then I'll release the body for burial. I just want to tell you all how sorry I am that this has happened."

As the four grieving people made their way slowly to Geoffrey's car, he truly felt bad for what he had done. Seeing Alicia's body like that made him almost sorry for his actions, but then the inner voice reminded him that his beloved had once been in a morgue, too. His mind was now at war with itself. His head began pounding and blinding lights flashed in front of his eyes. He reached in his pocket and handed the keys to Max.

"I'm sorry to have to ask you to drive now. But I've got one of my migraines and I can't drive in this shape."

Max nodded numbly and got in on the driver's side. On the

way back the car echoed with silence except when Suzanne moaned and cried out, "Why? Why Alicia? She never did anything to hurt anyone! So help me God, I'll kill whoever is responsible." There was no consoling her as she fell against Janine's chest, sobbing. Janine cried with her.

"They'll catch the killer, the police will catch him," Janine said.

In the front seat, Geoffrey massaged his temples and Max tried to keep his eyes on the road, but his tears made it quite difficult.

As the four grief-stricken people got out of the car in front of Suzanne's apartment, local reporters descended on them.

"Look, Mrs. Carter doesn't feel like talking to anyone right now," Geoffrey said, doing his best to shield Suzanne from the horde that continued to press forward.

"Who are you and what's your connection?" asked one of the reporters, as she shoved the microphone directly into Geoffrey's face.

"I'm just a friend of the family. None of us have anything to say right now. Please, just leave us alone."

When they were finally able to get into the apartment building, they were met in the lobby by several policemen and a detective.

"Mrs. Carter," the detective said, "We think we have your daughter's killer in custody. Let's go to your apartment where we can talk."

Once inside the apartment, the detective handed Suzanne a Polaroid photo. "Have you ever seen this man before?"

Suzanne stared at the bearded and scarred face of Jace Lundstrom. She shook her head. "He doesn't look like anyone I've ever seen."

When she showed the picture to the others, all three shook their heads.

"Why do you think he ki—killed Alicia?" Suzanne could hardly get the words out.

The detective told them what had transpired at the dumpster.

"I want to go to the jail myself and ask him face to face if he killed my baby," Suzanne cried. "I'll know if he's lying. Let's go."

"Suzanne, they're not going to let you see him," Janine said softly as she put her arm around her friend.

"That's right, m'am," the detective said. "We haven't even charged him yet. There's still some evidence to go over and we have to search his car—"

"But what makes you think he might not have done it?" Geoffrey asked. "You said he was in the dumpster when the kids arrived. What other reason would he have had for being there?" Geoffrey hoped that no one had noticed the edginess in his voice.

"I can't say anymore right now. But I think there'll be enough evidence for the grand jury to indict him. We'll be in touch as soon as we have some more information. Mrs. Carter, if there's anything the department can do, just give me a call. Here's my card."

"Well, at least you have a suspect. That's better than I could have hoped for this soon," Suzanne said, her voice almost steady. She turned to Max who had just taken the ring box out of his pocket. He opened it so that everyone could see its contents.

"I was going to give this to Alicia in Gatlinburg." He broke down and wept angry tears.

"Oh, Max. It's beautiful. Alicia would have loved it," Suzanne said. She put her arms around Max and held him. "We'll just have to be strong for each other."

"I have to go," Max said, trying to compose himself. He put the box back into his pocket, hugged Suzanne tightly and nodded towards Janine and Geoffrey.

As soon as he walked out of the apartment, Geoffrey said, "Suzanne, would you like me to stay with y'all tonight?"

"No, Bill. Janine's here—oh my God, I've got to call Mom and Julie."

She turned around to dial the phone but noticed that the answering machine light was blinking. She hit the message button.

"Suzanne, this is Julie. We just heard on the radio about the police finding a girl's body in a dumpster. Please call and let us know something; we're frantic!"

Suzanne got her sister's husband, Terry, on the line. "Terry, let me speak to Julie."

"Suzanne, she and your mother are on their way to Memphis now. When you didn't call, they figured something terrible had happened."

Suzanne broke down as she told her brother-in-law the horrible news.

"They found Alicia's body in a dumpster and think some homeless guy did it. That's all we know." The doorbell rang and Geoffrey hurried to open it. "It's Julie and Mom," Suzanne said into the phone. "I'll have them call you later."

Suzanne collapsed into her mother's and sister's arms, and the three women began sobbing.

Margaret Yates had always been the strong one in the family, but she was totally devastated by the news about her oldest grandchild. She was now in her eighties and rather frail from past illnesses. Julie was worried about the effect the shock might have on her mother.

"Mother, do you need to take your medication? You know the doctor told you not to get too excited."

"Damnit, Julie, I'm old as hell, but I'm not helpless," Margaret Yates said with annoyance. "You tend to Suzanne.

She needs your attention more than I do."

Geoffrey got up to leave. He hugged Suzanne. "Call me if you need anything. I don't know what I'd do if anything happened to you."

44

A distraught Jace Lundstrom knew that he was really in trouble. He had no way of proving that the body was already in the dumpster when he got there. If those damn kids hadn't shown up, he could have just left and nobody would have ever known he had been there. At least the police hadn't charged him with any crime yet. And he knew he had the right to at least one phone call. The problem was he didn't know anyone to call. The door opened and a strapping man wearing a wrinkled brown suit swaggered in.

"Good afternoon, Jace. I'm Detective Steve Browning, and I'd like to ask you a few questions." Browning read Jace his Miranda rights and asked if he wanted a lawyer.

"I don't know any lawyers. I'll be glad to answer all your questions."

Browning flipped on a tape recorder. "Jace, tell me about yourself and how you happened to be at the dumpster. Take your time and don't be nervous."

Jace told of having been an adopted child who grew up in a loving home in Arkansas. He added that after high school he had received an appointment to the United States Military

Academy. "When I finished the Academy, I got married and we lived on different army bases for a few years. Along the way, we had a couple of kids. Then I went to Vietnam. Got a Silver Star and a Purple Heart. During my third tour of duty, my jeep was hit by enemy fire. I ended up with a skull fracture and some other wounds. By the time I got out of the hospital in Germany, the war was over so they sent me home. When I got back from 'Nam, things just sort of fell apart. My wife left me and took our kids to Birmingham. Her folks lived there. I just hit the road. I didn't have any family left, so there wasn't anybody else to turn to. The government wouldn't accept the fact that something was really wrong with us vets, and they didn't seem to care. You know how people treated us when we got back. They acted as if we were wrong for going over there in the first place. When the government finally tried to help, they sent me here to the VA for treatment. I got so tired of going back and forth to the hospital that I just quit going one day. It wasn't really doing me any good. Since then, I've just bummed around in this area."

Jace paused long enough to take a long swallow of the Coke that was on the table in front of him.

Browning nodded sympathetically. "What happened to you is terrible, Jace. Maybe we can get you some help. I know some folks over at the VA. I'll talk to them if you'd like."

"I'd really appreciate that, Detective. I hate having to go around like this."

Jace took another quick sip of Coke. "Well, I pulled up to the dumpster to see if I could find anything valuable. You'd be surprised what folks throw away. I had just climbed inside, when I noticed the rug. It looked like it could be Oriental, which meant it might be worth some money. I began to unroll it, and that's when I discovered that something was inside. When the body fell out, it scared me to death at first. I assumed that she was dead, but I took her pulse anyway. You see, I was a medic in 'Nam. Then I noticed the syringe. Like a fool, I picked it up. At that moment, a car full of kids pulled up, yelling and screaming—they had obviously been drinking. One kid got out of the car and climbed into the dumpster to see what I was looking at and saw the dead body. He screamed and jumped out and ran to the car. That's when they called the police on their car phone. Afterwards, they took off like a bunch of scalded cats. Then the police arrived. Detective Browning, I swear I didn't kill that lady."

"Jace, I really want to believe you, but look at things from my point of view. You were caught in the dumpster with the body and your prints were on the syringe."

"I just told you I picked it up and looked at it. I'm not trying to hide anything, I swear to God."

"Okay, Jace, just take it easy. We're checking your car now to see whether there's any evidence in it. Then we'll know soon enough if you're guilty. It's getting late. Let's call it a night. Oh, by the way, you and I are about the same size, and I've got an extra gym suit in my locker that would probably fit you. Since you're going to spend the night here and haven't been charged with anything yet, we'll let you take a hot shower first."

"Thanks, Detective Browning. I surely appreciate that. It's been a long time since I had a good hot shower and clean clothes. Do you happen to have a razor?"

"I'm sorry, but that's not allowed. You understand?"

Jace nodded. "Goodnight, Detective."

Browning went into the next room where several officers had filmed the interview with a TV camera.

"What do you guys think? I kinda believe him. It all could have happened the way he said it did."

"I don't know, Steve," replied one of the officers. "His story seems too pat, like he's practiced it a bunch of times before. He could be one smart cookie who's just pulling our chain."

"Have the guys found any incriminating evidence in his car?"

"No, Steve, but they're still going over it with a fine-tooth comb. If he had her body in the car, something will show up."

45

The next morning, Janine awoke early and turned on the TV. The account of Alicia's death dominated the news on all the Memphis stations. One of the reporters from Channel 5 had more information than just Alicia's death, however.

"This just in from Columbus, Mississippi. A prominent lawyer returned from a trip to Cancun, Mexico, and discovered the bodies of two middle-aged women in his cabin near Columbus. They had been brutally slain and both had been disfigured. A piece of skin shaped like a triangle was sliced from the forehead of each woman. The identification of the women is being withheld pending notification of their next of kin."

Chills ran through Janine's body. Barbara and Arlene were still in Columbus. Surely nothing had happened to them! They were probably in their room at the bed and breakfast. No events had been scheduled until 10:00 a.m. She dialed the inn and asked to be connected to Arlene and Barbara's room.

"I'm sorry but they don't answer," the woman at the front desk said. "In fact, it's kind of strange. They didn't come over for dinner last night or for breakfast this morning."

"Could you please check their room?" Janine asked, trying to keep her voice steady. "I just heard on TV about two women getting killed there in Columbus, and I'm worried about my friends."

"Of course, I'll check and call you right back."

Janine went into the room where Julie was sleeping fitfully. She shook her.

"Julie, wake up. The phone's going to be ringing any minute, and I don't want Suzanne to answer it. I just heard on the news that two women were murdered in Columbus last night. I called the bed and breakfast and the owner said that Barbara and Arlene phoned her early last evening and said they were going out for about an hour, but they never came in for supper or breakfast. She's checking their room now."

The phone rang, and Janine grabbed it before it could ring again. "Yes. They didn't? I agree. You'd better notify the police."

"Janine, what is it? What'd she say?" asked Julie.

"When she checked their room, their beds hadn't been slept in." She looked up and saw Suzanne standing in the doorway. "I'm sorry. Did the phone wake you up?"

"Yeah, was it the police? Do they know anything new?"

"No, it was the owner of the bed and breakfast in Columbus."

Janine told Suzanne the latest TV news report. "Oh, God, I haven't lost just my daughter—"

"Now, Suzanne, don't jump to conclusions. They're probably okay," Janine said, not convinced of anything she was saying.

The Channel 5 reporter broke in with a special bulletin. "We have just learned the identity of the two women who were murdered last night in Columbus, Mississippi. They are Arlene Harris Holcomb of Tampa, Florida, and Barbara Flowers

Atkins of Center City, Mississippi. The women were in Columbus to attend their class reunion at Mississippi University for Women. No other details are available at this time. Meanwhile, in an unrelated incident, the police have a suspect in custody for the brutal slaying of Alicia Carter, but he has not yet been charged with the crime."

All three women stared at the screen in disbelief and horror.

"My God, my God," Suzanne and Janine said over and over again.

"What on earth is happening?" Julie asked. The phone rang and Suzanne grabbed it. She listened for a few seconds then slammed down the receiver and burst into tears.

"It was him, wasn't it?" Janine said in a fury.

"What did he say?" Julie asked.

"He hoped our reunion wasn't spoiled since two of our sisters had been killed, but that we would soon be joining them in hell," Suzanne cried.

This time when the phone rang, Julie grabbed it. "We know who you are, you monster. So do the police!"

"Wait—it's me, Bill. I just saw the TV news. Tell Suzanne I'll be right over."

"Oh, Bill, sorry. I guess you know about the maniac who keeps calling my sister. He just called again and told Suzanne that she and Janine would be next. I'm scared for them. I thought he was just some creep playing a fiendish prank, but now I know he means business."

"Yes, yes," Geoffrey said. "I wish I could get my hands on the sonofabitch. I'll see you all in a few minutes."

The ringing of the doorbell startled all three women. Suzanne opened the door to find Max standing there. He hadn't shaved, his eyes were swollen, and he'd been up all night. Suzanne hugged him and said, "I guess you saw the news about Barbara and Arlene. And we just got another one of our calls.

Max, he made good on part of his threat! He says Janine and I are next."

Max nodded and sat down. "I've been thinking. Maybe there's a connection between Alicia's murder and the murders of Barbara and Arlene. Depending on when the crimes were committed, the guy could have killed Barbara and Arlene, then driven back here and killed Alicia. It's a possibility. I don't know, though. He'd have to have been pretty quick."

Janine shook her head. "Max, he didn't mention anything about Alicia. Maybe her murder was just coincidental."

"Yeah, but he could have been trying to throw up a smoke-screen to confuse the police. Even though Alicia wasn't," Max took a deep breath, "mutilated like Arlene and Barbara, it still could have been the same person."

The doorbell rang again. Suzanne answered it to find Geoffrey standing there holding a large tray of donuts and containers of fresh coffee.

"Come on in, Bill."

As Geoffrey was passing around coffee and donuts to everyone, Margaret Yates walked into the den, rubbing her eyes. "What has happened—have they found—?"

Julie ran to her mother. "I'm sorry, Mom. We've just heard the news that Barbara and Arlene were found murdered in a cabin outside Columbus late last night."

"Oh, my God!" She looked at Suzanne. "How did it happen? Do they think it was connected with Alicia's murder?"

"We don't know, Mom. Maybe we'll hear something later. Bill brought over coffee and donuts. Or would you like me to fix you some breakfast?"

"No, this will be fine."

Geoffrey went over to Suzanne, hugged her tightly and kissed her on the cheek. "I'm sorry, but I have to leave. Some urgent research work to do in the library. I'll see you all tonight. I'll call later when I can take a break."

"We'll be okay," Suzanne said, steadying her voice, trying to be strong. "If we hear from the police, I'll call you and leave a message."

Geoffrey squeezed Suzanne a little tighter, then hurried out the door. The voice of a TV news reporter brought everyone's attention to the television set.

"This is the scene of last night's brutal double murder of Arlene Holcomb and Barbara Atkins, who had arrived in Columbus yesterday. The two women may have been the victims of a copycat murderer, who is reminiscent of Geoffrey Bockker, the so-called 'Triangle Killer' who stalked the 'W' campus in 1963. Bockker, seen here in a photograph taken during his arraignment, carved triangles on the foreheads of his victims and kept the skin as trophies. According to reports, he died of a heart attack last year. Officials at Parchman, however, will not reveal any details about his death. There is speculation, however, that Bockker might have been secretly released from prison, put in a witness protection program and given a new identity. At any rate, this new killer is on the loose and is considered extremely dangerous. Oh, here comes Sheriff Jake Conner. I'll try to get a statement from him. Sheriff Conner, would you mind answering a few questions?"

"I don't have time for questions right now. But I will say this. I'll bet my last dollar that Geoffrey Bockker is the killer."

"But I thought that Bockker had died."

"Yeah, that's what we were all supposed to believe. But sometimes you can't even trust the government." Conner immediately walked away from the reporter, who announced that as soon as there was any further news, she would be back on the air.

"Suzanne, did you get a close look at Geoffrey Bockker in that picture? I swear he looks a little like Bill," Janine said.

"Don't be ridiculous, Janine. You've been watching too many detective shows. What do you think, Max?"

"Maybe there's a resemblance in the eyes, but I really didn't get a good look."

At the same moment that Janine and the others were watching the news from Columbus, so was Dean Carl Frazier of the law school in Memphis. What he saw and heard make him sick to his stomach.

"Oh, my God! That looks like William Caldwell. He's aged but I could swear it's the same man."

Frazier ran to his desk and flipped through his address book until he came to Josiah Perkins' office number. He dialed with shaking hands and as soon as the secretary answered, he said, "This is Carl Frazier, and I'm the dean of the law school at Southwestern Tennessee University. I need to speak to Josiah. It's an emergency."

"I'm sorry he's not available right now. Something horrible has happened, and he's down at the police station."

"I know. That's why I'm calling. I think those two women were murdered by one of my law students."

"Dean Frazier, I'll call the police station right now and get your message to Mr. Perkins. You stay there. I'm sure he'll call you right back."

Carl Frazier waited anxiously by the phone. His heart began to race and his palms perspired. He jumped when the phone rang.

"Carl, this is Josiah. I was just getting ready to call you. Those women were murdered in my cabin. Agnes and I were on our way to the airport, but she got sick so we came back home. Early this morning, I had a strange feeling that I needed to check on the cabin and I found the two women. Oh God, it was terrible." He paused and took a deep breath. "I couldn't tell you the truth about Geoffrey because he had been put in the Witness

Protection Program. Why in the hell did he have to come back here? I swear to God I didn't think he would ever do such a thing. All the prison personnel agreed with me. Of course, his release was different from most others since the federal government was involved. They were so glad to have proof against that mobster Johnny Garofoli that they agreed to Geoffrey's release without the usual parole stipulations. That's the only way he was able to get a new identity."

"Josiah, that's not all," Frazier said, his voice barely under control. "One of my law students was also murdered the same day as the two women. I think it's possible that Geoffrey might have committed that murder as well. I checked around and they seemed to have been close friends."

"I'm going to let you talk to the sheriff. I'm sure he'd be interested in what you have to say."

"Hello, Dean Frazier. This is Jake Conner. Thanks for calling. Of course, we haven't officially released any information about the details of the crime. But since the media already know—one thing is true—the women did have triangles carved on their foreheads. Other than that, I can't reveal any more information. Now tell me about this law student of yours."

"He goes by the name of William Caldwell. I let him into law school because Josiah and I are old friends and I assumed his credentials were legitimate. I had no reason to suspect anything."

"Yeah, Josiah always loved those kind. He should have told you the truth about Bockker. To hell with the Witness Protection Program. Society needed protection from this monster. I was a deputy in Starkville when the sonofabitch killed those girls thirty years ago. It wouldn't surprise me if Geoffrey was behind these three murders. I'm gonna call the Memphis police and fax Geoffrey's photo to them. Josiah wants to talk to you again. Thanks for everything."

"Carl, I'm so sorry," Josiah said. "If Geoffrey did these things, I owe you a deep apology for getting you involved. I'm on my way to Memphis right now."

An angry Josiah Perkins realized that the Geoffrey Bockker he first encountered thirty years ago had probably never really existed. It had all been an act. Josiah hated the real Geoffrey when he realized how he had been manipulated all these years. The deaths of at least five people weighed heavily on his conscience. Sending Geoffrey to prison had been a terrible mistake. He was the same violent person he had always been. He probably would have been better off in a mental institution where he could have received treatment. At least it would have kept him away from society until the doctors thought he was cured. By God, he would do whatever was necessary to bring an end to Geoffrey's insane violence, even if it meant killing Geoffrey himself.

After Carl Frazier hung up the phone, he was furious. He and Josiah had been duped by the worst kind of criminal, one who used his intelligence for evil deeds. And now he felt responsible in a way for the poor girl's death since he had been the one who had admitted Geoffrey to law school.

Carl Frazier formulated a plan of action. He'd go down to the law school office and check Geoffrey's schedule in the computer to see what class he had next. Then he'd send for him and keep him until the police got there to arrest him. But he remembered it was Sunday. Well, maybe Geoffrey was studying in the law library. He'd check there.

Frazier lived only five minutes from the campus and drove there in three. He entered the library from the second floor of the law school building. He spotted Geoffrey at one of the study carrels and went over to him.

"Hello, Bill, I see you're really burning the midnight oil. Would you mind coming to my office with me?"

"Sure, Dean Frazier. Is something wrong?" Geoffrey responded with hesitation.

"No, I just wanted to discuss the poor Carter girl. I think we ought to have some sort of class memorial. She was a good friend of yours, I believe."

As they walked back to the dean's office, Geoffrey said, "Yes, yes. We'd gotten to be really good friends. I'm even dating her mother. I still can't believe she's dead. Her fiancé and I are taking turns staying over at their apartment. Her family is really broken up."

"I know they must be. Did you know that two of her mother's friends were killed in Columbus last night?"

"Yes, it was on the TV news when I went over there this morning."

"Just go on into my office," the dean said. "I have a phone call to make. I'll be there in just a minute."

Geoffrey was nervous. Did the dean know something and wasn't telling him, or was he really interested in planning a memorial for Alicia? Frazier had closed the door behind him, which made it impossible for Geoffrey to hear what he was saying. He looked down at the intercom on the dean's desk and then very carefully pushed the button down.

"Tell the detective that I have some information about Geoffrey Bockker..."

Damn. He knows everything. How in the hell did he find out? Shit, now I'm going to have to kill him, too.

Geoffrey carefully clicked off the intercom the minute he heard the dean hang up. He picked up a heavy marble bust from Frazier's desk and walked to the door so that he would be behind it when Frazier walked into the room.

"I'm sorry I took—"

These were the last words that Dean Frazier uttered before Geoffrey smashed his head with the marble bust. Frazier slumped to the floor immediately. Geoffrey didn't even take time to wipe his prints from the bust. He opened the door quietly and, seeing no one in the outer office, walked carefully to the back stairs. No one had seen them enter the dean's office, and he felt reasonably safe for a while. He knew that the police would be closing in on him soon, so he didn't have much time to make his move. He had to get Max out of Suzanne's apartment.

I hope that Julie and Mrs. Yates aren't still there. I'd have to kill them, too. I've got to get home to get my duffel bag. This is not going exactly as I planned, but it'll have to do. Surely the police haven't gotten to my house yet.

Geoffrey got in his car, picked up the cell phone and dialed Suzanne's number. Max answered, and Geoffrey disguised his voice.

"Mr. Quinn, this is Lt. Hopson. Would you come down to the East Precinct right away, please. We have some information, but we'd like to discuss it with you instead of Mrs. Carter."

This puzzled Max, but he agreed to go to the station. When he hung up, he told Suzanne he had to go out for a few minutes. "Lock the door behind me," he said.

"What's the matter, Max? Who was that on the phone?"

"Oh, it was somebody at work. I'll be right back."

Suzanne looked over at Janine. "Don't worry about us." Suzanne's mother and sister had left a few hours earlier at Suzanne's insistence. Her mother had a doctor's appointment the next morning and it could not be postponed. Since Alicia's murder, Margaret Yates' blood pressure had skyrocketed.

After Max had left, Suzanne locked and deadbolted the door. She knew that she and Janine couldn't be too careful, even if the apartment had the best security in Memphis.

When Geoffrey reached his house, he was relieved that there were no police anywhere around and that the street was fairly deserted. He changed clothes and gathered up the necessary objects and stuffed them in his duffel bag. Since he wouldn't have time to video the murders, he decided to leave the camera and tripod behind. Besides, they would only impede his movements in case he had to get away in a hurry. Now, if only Max would stay gone long enough.

Max reached the police station in record time. "Where's Lt. Hopson? I'm Max Quinn. He called and said he had some information about the Carter murder."

The officer at the front desk said, "Mr. Quinn, there must be some mistake. Are you sure it was Lt. Hopson?"

"Of course. He called Mrs. Carter's residence not thirty minutes ago." He was impatient and irritated.

"Mr. Quinn, Lt. Hopson couldn't have called you. He and his family left on vacation last night. But we do have some new information on the Carter case. The sheriff in Columbus just faxed us this picture."

Max almost fainted when he saw the photo up close. "My God, Janine was right! It is Bill Caldwell!"

"Wait a minute, where are you going?" the officer asked.

"I think Bill Caldwell's the man who called me. He's probably on his way to the apartment right now. Send some men over there immediately." He grabbed the phone and dialed. "Mrs. Carter, this is Max. Just act like you're talking to your mother or Julie. Don't say anything except yes or no. Is Bill there? He is. All right, now listen carefully. The police think he's the one who murdered Alicia, as well as Arlene and Barbara. Don't ask me to explain. Make up some excuse to leave the house. Don't let him catch you two off guard. The police are on their way. Just stay calm."

The moment Suzanne hung up, Geoffrey asked, "Who was

that on the phone? Suzanne, you're trembling. What's wrong?"

"N, nothing, Bill. It was something Julie told me about Mom that upset me. Listen, you stay here in case the phone rings. Janine and I need to go to the grocery store."

Janine gave Suzanne a confused look, but said nothing.

"I'm afraid I can't let you do that," Geoffrey said. He unzipped his duffel bag, took out the syringe and a vial of Ketamine and laid them on the table.

"Bill, what are you doing?"

"The name isn't Bill, Janine. It's Geoffrey, Geoffrey Bockker or, as I used to be called, the 'Triangle Killer.' Does that ring a bell with either of you?"

"What?" Janine gasped.

"I lost my Angie and our unborn baby and spent thirty years in Parchman because of you two and the two dead bitches. Now you're gonna join them."

Geoffrey reached down into his duffel bag and pulled out a pistol. Suzanne whirled around and picked up a porcelain vase and threw it at Geoffrey's head. The blow stunned him momentarily, but he still managed to squeeze the trigger. The bullet caught Suzanne in the right shoulder and she fell to her knees, writhing in pain. Janine rushed to Suzanne, but she, too, felt the sting of a bullet as it grazed her head. Wiping away the blood before it dripped into her eyes, she lunged toward Geoffrey. He pulled the trigger again, and all Janine could feel was the momentary impact of the bullet as it entered her left cheek. Everything went black and she was aware of only a floating, dreamlike sensation.

46

"Mrs. Beauregard, calm down. Take slow deliberate breaths. You've just come out of surgery. Everything's going to be alright."

Janine looked around and could barely make out the figure of a nurse standing over her. She reached up to touch her head and discovered that it was almost completely covered with bandages.

Because of her injuries, Janine was barely able to open her mouth to speak, and the effect of the intubation tube made it even more difficult.

"What happened? Where am I?"

"You're in intensive care at St.Mary's. That psychopath shot you in the face, and you lost consciousness. You were in surgery for eight hours. If you hadn't turned, the bullet would have struck the base of your brain stem. Somebody up there was watching over you. Do you feel like having some visitors? There are three mighty anxious people here to see you."

Janine looked up and through her uncovered eye was barely able to discern her husband and two daughters.

"Take it easy, honey," her husband said. "Just lie still and don't try to talk. It's gonna take a little while for your wounds to heal."

"I have to know what happened to me. The last thing I remember was Geoffrey pointing that gun. Oh, my God, what happened to Suzanne? I remember now...Bill, uh, Geoffrey, shot her—"

"She's going to be okay," Janine's older daughter said. "The bullet cracked her left collarbone."

"Where's Geoffrey—where's that bastard?" Janine was getting agitated.

Her husband said, "After he shot you, he got out his knife and left his calling card on your foreheads, but George Haynes, the security guard who had heard the police alert on his scanner rushed into the building and got on the elevator. When he got off on the third floor, he screamed out Suzanne's name. Geoffrey came running out of the apartment. George shot at him as Geoffrey ran toward him, but Geoffrey managed to knock George down as he ran to the emergency stairs. George knows he wounded Geoffrey because he saw him clutch his left shoulder. After Max and the police arrived, they searched all over the building and the surrounding area, but Geoffrey got away."

"What happens if he tries to come here and—"

"Don't worry, Mom," Janine's younger daughter said, holding her mother's hand. "Someone's outside both yours and Suzanne's rooms at all times."

Janine moaned in pain. The nurse asked the family to leave. As they reluctantly left the room, she gave Janine an injection of Demerol and she was finally able to get some much-needed sleep.

On a different floor, Suzanne's visitors were Max, her mother and sister. They were all in a state of shock, but at least they knew Suzanne was safe.

"It's so hard to believe that Bill and Geoffrey Bockker are the same person. We didn't go to the arraignment, so none of us could remember exactly what he looked like. That's why we didn't recognize him." Suzanne started to cry very softly. "I just don't understand why he killed Alicia."

"The police think that she found some evidence that proved who he really was," Max said. "To throw the police off his trail, he left Alicia's car at the mall and took the bus home. On the way to Columbus to kill Arlene and Barbara, he put Alicia's body in the dumpster."

"I knew that was Bill's car we passed outside of Tupelo. Why didn't I make Janine turn around?"

"He might have killed all four of you then," Julie said.

"What happened to that poor man they picked up at the dumpster?" Suzanne asked Max.

"I think the police were going to release him as soon as they got back to the station."

"I need to see Janine," Suzanne said, trying to climb out of the bed.

"Janine's going to be okay," Margaret Yates said. "It'll just take time. As soon as you're able, the plastic surgeon will do a skin graft and your forehead will heal."

Margaret Yates leaned over her daughter and kissed her lightly. "Take it easy. I couldn't stand to lose you, too. Come on, Julie. We need to head on home."

"You're right, Mother. Suzanne, I'll be back tomorrow, soon as I get Mom to the doctor. Max, take care."

After her mother and sister had left, Suzanne and Max had to discuss the inevitable, Alicia's funeral. They decided to have just a graveside service in Friar's Point. Of course, Johnny had been consulted. He had flown in when Suzanne had called him about Alicia's death. Things were still strained between Suzanne and her ex-husband, but at least they were civil to each other, and Johnny had had the decency not to bring his new wife.

During the next few days, Suzanne recovered enough to go home and attend her daughter's funeral. Just before they closed the coffin at the funeral home, a sobbing Max had placed Alicia's engagement ring on the ring finger of her left hand.

47

Janine's recovery was remarkable, and she was able to be moved into a private room after only a few days in the I.C.U. One night she awoke from a restless sleep. When she opened her eyes, she was staring into the face of a man who looked just like Geoffrey Bockker.

"Help!" she screamed and lashed out at the figure bending over her. The man turned and ran out of the room and down the hall.

"What's the matter, Mrs. Beauregard?" asked her guard as he came rushing into the room.

"I just saw Geoffrey Bockker! He was standing over my bed staring at me. Didn't you see him leave when you came in the room?"

"No, m'am. I had stepped down the hall for just a minute to get a drink of water when I heard you scream. I didn't see any-body. Go on back to sleep. Everything's okay."

"Oh, God, I guess I must have had another hallucination. But I could have sworn I felt the presence of evil in the room."

Geoffrey Bockker *had been* in Janine Beauregard's room. George Haynes had wounded him in the left shoulder, but he still had the strength to run away from the apartment complex. From his experience in the hospital at Parchman, Geoffrey had learned how to apply enough pressure to a wound to keep it from bleeding profusely, so the police had not been able to follow his trail. He had hidden out in a deserted building for several days until he felt it was safe to venture outside. Fortunately for him, the building still had running water and he was able to cleanse the wound and wash the blood out of his clothes.

Calling from various pay phones near the building, Geoffrey was able to find out which hospital Janine was in. One night when he felt strong enough, he sneaked into the basement of St. Mary's and found the laundry room. He stole a doctor's smock and pants and put them on before heading upstairs. He asked an orderly where Janine's room was and told the man that he had just been called in on the case. He lingered outside her room until the guard walked down the hall. He stood over his nemesis, staring at her until she opened her eyes. He ran out of the room when Janine screamed and ducked into the stairwell. When no one came looking for him, he wandered around until he found the doctors' lounge, where he stole a sweat suit. Geoffrey got on the elevator and rode to the first floor. Just as he was about to exit through the front door, he almost bumped into a young man. Geoffrey and Max both froze in their tracks momentarily when they recognized each other. Geoffrey turned around and ran down the hall and out the side door. Max immediately notified security that he had just seen Geoffrey Bockker, and the hospital was sealed off. By the time the police arrived, Geoffrey was across the street. He smiled as he observed the excitement that was taking place around the hospital.

"I guess they must have found out I paid a surprise visit to you, Janine, but now I'm nowhere to be found, or to put it another way, 'Elvis has left the building.'" He chuckled.

Janine was now fully awake as three policemen came into her room.

"What on earth is going on?"

One of the policemen said, "Geoffrey Bockker was spotted in the building, but we think he must have gotten away. Just to be on the safe side, someone will be here in the room with you and outside your door at all times."

Janine glared at the man who was supposed to have been keeping watch outside her door.

"Then he was here in the room! I knew I could sense that sonofabitch's presence."

"They'll catch him. There's an all-points-bulletin out on him. He can't possibly get out of town." The policeman's words did not reassure Janine.

48

Suzanne was at home watching television when the local news was interrupted by a special report.

The announcer told of Geoffrey Bockker's visit to the hospital followed by another escape. At that very moment the phone rang. Thinking it must be either Max or Julie, Suzanne picked up the receiver and was about to say she had been watching the news when the voice on the other end said, "Suzanne, I hope you're feeling better." Suzanne froze. It was Geoffrey Bockker. He went on. "I didn't really want to hurt you or Alicia, but I had no choice. I made a promise thirty years ago and I have to keep it. I'll tell you this, though. When I kill you, it will be painless. I can't say the same for Janine, because she has to suffer just like the others. Goodbye. I'll see you again one day. Don't bother calling the police. They can't trace this call. I'll be long gone before they can ever find me. By the way, I still love you."

Before Suzanne could say anything, Geoffrey hung up.

Geoffrey smiled and put the cell phone back into the pocket of his sweat suit. "Talk about luck," he said quietly as he pulled out an envelope and thumbed through its contents once again.

According to the tax forms, the suit belonged to Dr. Avril Henley and the money had come from one of the Tunica casinos just down the road. Geoffrey knew the police were looking for him but if he stayed on the back streets, people would assume he was just a jogger out for some exercise. But it probably wouldn't hurt to change his appearance again. Geoffrey went back to the deserted building and opened his duffel bag.

He found just what he was looking for—hair dye, a moustache, and a different pair of glasses. After making the changes, he lay down and went to sleep. The next morning he awoke stiff and hungry. *I don't think I can stay around here much longer. I've gotta get out of town. But how? They've probably assigned police to the bus and train stations, as well as the airport. I'll have to leave by car. But I can't risk going back to my house to get mine. Anyway, they've got a description of it. I need to be among a whole group of people so that I won't stand out. There's got to be some place here in Memphis where there's always a lot of people.* He looked down the street at a guitar-shaped restaurant sign and slapped the heel of his hand to his forehead. *Graceland—that's it. I can take a bus there and mingle with the crowd. The only security guards out there are those hired by Graceland and they surely won't have been notified about my escape. Once I get there, I can hitch a ride with somebody from out of town and then steal the car.*

He picked up his duffel bag, crossed the street and waited patiently at the stop until the right bus came along. He got on the MATA bus and went as far to the back as he could. The bus pulled up across from the mansion at 3734 Elvis Presley Boulevard. He bought a ticket at the booth and went to one of the restaurants where he wolfed down a real breakfast for the first time in days. The shuttle pulled up in front of the restaurant and he boarded the bus along with other Elvis fans. As soon as Geoffrey sat down, a fat woman in a light blue polyester pants outfit plopped down beside him and immediately struck up a conversation.

"Is this your first visit to Graceland? It's my fifteenth. I try to come at least once a year. But sometimes I can't make it. My husband isn't real well and this is the first time I've been able to leave him in months. Did you ever see the King in person? I met him once and he was so nice. Of course, I wasn't this big then. When I was a young girl, I was really attractive. By the way, my name's Henrietta Harrison? What's yours?"

"Uh, Robert Jefferson."

"I'm from Marietta, Georgia. Where are you from?"

"What a coincidence. You're from Marietta? I'm from near Macon. Say, I wonder if, oh, never mind. It's too much to ask."

Geoffrey pretended embarrassment.

"Go ahead, honey. You can't get the answer if you don't ask the question."

"Well, I was wondering if maybe I could get a ride back with you to Marietta. You see, I came over on the bus and I don't have enough money for a ticket back. I spent more here in Memphis than I planned to. I'm so embarrassed. Look, just forget it."

"Of course, I'll be glad to give you a ride back. You look like a nice man. Besides, all Elvis fans have a special kinship. Come on now, let's just enjoy our tour. You don't need to get one of those silly tapes. I know more than the narrator does."

Geoffrey followed Henrietta around like a puppy, putting up with her incessant conversation. When the tour finally ended, he felt as if he could have won an Elvis trivia contest. They got on the shuttle bus and rode back to the parking lot. Geoffrey couldn't have been more excited when he discovered that Henrietta had an RV. He could kill her and then put her body in the back until he could find a place to dispose of it. They pulled out of the parking lot around noon. Henrietta prattled on until

Geoffrey thought he couldn't take any more.

"I'm sorry, but do you mind if I take a nap? I haven't slept real good in several days."

Geoffrey fell asleep with his head almost lying against the back of Henrietta's chair. She couldn't help noticing the odor emanating from Geoffrey's left shoulder. She gently touched his forehead and realized that he was burning up with fever. As soon as she reached the next exit, she pulled the RV into the parking lot of a convenience store. The lurch of the vehicle coming to a halt woke Geoffrey, and he rubbed his eyes and stretched.

"Honey, you need to take care of whatever's happened to your shoulder."

"I had an accident the other day and just got out of the hospital," Geoffrey hastily explained. "I'll be okay. I don't need a doctor, but I sure could use some painkillers. Do you happen to have any? I'm really hurting bad."

Henrietta was puzzled by his response. How could he have been in the hospital if he had just gotten to Memphis? She felt, however, in this situation *some* questions were best left unasked.

"Sure, honey. Just go in the back and look in the medicine cabinet in the bathroom. I've got a veritable drugstore in there. Between the two of us, my husband and I need a lot of medicine. Get some water from the refrigerator."

Geoffrey went to the back and found exactly what he needed—some strong aspirin, some tetracyclines, and even some antibiotic ointment to rub on the wound.

"Would you like to lie down back there and take a nap?" Henrietta offered. "The bed's pretty comfortable and you look like you really need the rest. There are some of my husband's clothes in the closet. Feel free to wash up and change into them. I'm sure he wouldn't mind. I'll wake you when we have to stop for gas."

"That's a good idea. Don't forget to wake me when we stop, though."

Henrietta was beginning to think she had made a huge mistake. Why on earth had she picked up a total stranger? Calvin was always telling her that this habit would get her in trouble one day. But what could she do now? Besides, he hadn't done anything suspicious except lie about being in the hospital. Although she did wonder how he had gotten his injury. Shaking her head, Henrietta slowly pulled out of the rest area and merged onto Highway 78, heading toward Birmingham. She turned on the radio, kept the volume down low and flipped from station to station. She finally found what she liked, Elvis's "Are You Lonesome Tonight?" Suddenly, in the middle of the song, the announcer broke in with a news bulletin. "The Memphis Police Department has asked all motorists to be on the lookout for Geoffrey Bockker. He has killed three women—one in Memphis and two in Columbus, Mississippi—as well as the dean of the law school at Southwestern Tennessee University. Authorities believe that Bockker has a gunshot wound in the left shoulder. He was last seen leaving St. Mary's hospital, wearing a blue sweat suit. Bockker's six feet tall, weighs about a hundred seventy pounds, and has short-cropped brown hair and gray eyes. Call the MPD if you see anyone fitting this description. Their number is 901-789-6543. Do not try to apprehend him yourself."

Henrietta froze with fear. Although her passenger had dark hair and a moustache and wore glasses, he did have a wound in his left shoulder.

Henrietta reached over to her mobile phone and dialed 911. Before she could say anything, she sensed that someone was behind her and looked in the mirror. Geoffrey was hovering over her.

"Hi, are you feeling better?" she asked, trying to stay calm. "I thought I'd give Calvin a call to let him know when to expect me home. He worries if I don't check in with him regularly. 'Bye, honey. See you in about six hours." She hung up and smiled at Geoffrey.

"I feel like a new person, thanks to your medicine," Geoffrey said with a smile. "Would you like me to drive a while, so you can rest?"

"No, I'm fine, but you can stay up here and keep me company if you want to." Henrietta tried desperately to hide her fear.

"Sure, it was kind of lonesome back there anyway."

They rode in silence for a few miles. As they rounded a curve, Geoffrey screamed out, "Henrietta, stop! I just saw a little girl down there trying to climb up the ravine. There must have been an accident. Turn around and let's go back."

For a moment, Henrietta forgot who her passenger was. She swerved around to go back to the spot where he claimed to have seen the child. When they reached the area, there was no one there.

"I'll go down a little ways and look for her."

After he had opened the door, he turned and said, "Henrietta, do you have any rope? She could have fallen back down the ravine and I might need it to pull her up."

"Sure, Geo—uh, Robert. I'll go get it for you. We have a hardware store as well as a drugstore back there. But you'd never find it."

Henrietta turned the ignition off and headed to the back. She prayed that Geoffrey hadn't caught her slip-up with his name. But he had. When she reached into the storage cabinet next to the bed for the rope and her gun, he lunged at her, knocking her onto the bed. He grabbed the rope and started to tie her up. She screamed just before he silenced her with a blow from the butt of the .38 Smith and Wesson revolver he had already found in the cabinet.

Jace Lundstrom was walking back to his car. He had stretched his legs and had relieved himself. He had been on Highway 78 for three hours, and his legs were cramping. When he came to a deserted side road, he drove down far enough so that passing traffic wouldn't see him. He thought about the strange turn of events that had led to this moment. When the police had received the picture of Geoffrey Bockker over the fax, they knew Jace hadn't killed Alicia Carter, although he did bear a striking resemblance to Bockker. Steve Browning had come back to his cell to give him the good news and to tell him that he had gotten him an appointment at the VA that afternoon.

"They're going to evaluate you and run some tests. It'll probably take a few days. Be sure to come by here after you get out. I want to know your plans."

Five days later, Jace was sitting in Lt. Browning's office.

"I just came to say goodbye," Jace said, his voice filled with emotion. "You were the first person in a long time who treated me like a human being. I can just imagine how that poor girl's family must feel. This whole situation has taught me just how precious your family is. I'm going to drive to Birmingham to find my wife and kids. Maybe I can convince her that I'm a different person. I appreciate all your help with the VA. I'm going to come back to Memphis on a regular basis to receive my treatment."

"Good for you, Jace. I have a feeling you're going to make it. Do you need anything before you leave?"

"Only the directions to Birmingham."

"That's easy. You follow this street and turn right on Lamar, which becomes Highway 78 when you get out of town. That highway takes you directly into Birmingham. Good luck."

Jace took Steve Browning's extended hand and shook it

warmly. "Thanks, you'll be hearing from me soon."

The sound of a muffled scream brought Jace back to reality, and he ran to the end of road. He saw the RV turned at an angle with its passenger door open. Believing that someone could be in danger, he went to help. He knocked on the door, but when no one answered, he stepped inside. Two people were on the bed, one kneeling over the other. Before Jace could get any farther, Geoffrey whirled around to see who had entered the vehicle. He picked up the pistol and pointed it directly at the intruder's chest. Jace was momentarily caught off guard when he looked into the face of the man pointing the gun at him. Before Jace could move, Geoffrey pulled the trigger. The blow stopped Jace in his tracks and he crumpled to the floor, unconscious and bleeding. Geoffrey removed the remaining bullets from the chamber and put the gun in his pocket. He walked over to where Jace lay and discovered that he was barely breathing. He went to the bed and picked up the still unconscious Henrietta and took her to the front of the van and placed her body in the driver's seat. He put the gun in Henrietta's hand to get her fingerprints on it just as he had done with the knife in North Carolina. Then he took the gun from her hand and placed the barrel in Jace's so that his fingerprints would also be on the gun. Another devious idea occurred to him. He took out his own wallet and swapped with Jace. Now, when the police found the body, they would identify the dead person as William Caldwell. This would buy him more time to escape. He cranked the engine and grabbed his duffel bag. Then he quickly jumped out of the passenger door just before the RV careened down the embankment. He watched it gradually roll out of sight. He had committed the perfect crime. *If the bodies are intact, I hope the investigators will assume that Henrietta shot her assailant and that he ripped the gun from her hand with a final surge of energy and smashed her skull with the butt of the gun when he dis-*

covered there were no bullets in the chamber.

Geoffrey didn't waste any time admiring his handiwork. He knew that the stranger must have had a car close by, so he walked up the highway until he came to the deserted road. Sure enough, there sat a beat-up old Dodge. Now he had a new identity and a car. He felt elated when he heard a muffled explosion from the bottom of the ravine. Geoffrey slid behind the steering wheel and headed off to a new life and freedom. He was going back to the beloved mountains of North Carolina to stay there until he felt it was safe enough for him to finish the job he still intended to do.

I think I'll take a look at my new identity. I might need to get out my disguise kit and make some major changes in my appearance.

He reached into his back pocket and pulled out the wallet belonging to the man he'd left to die. Flipping the wallet open, he gasped, slammed on the brakes, and pulled off onto the shoulder of the road. His hands trembled as he stared into the face of a man whose features were identical to his. He scanned the information on the driver's license and was astonished to find that the stranger's birth date and description fit him perfectly. He threw the wallet down on the seat as if it were a hot coal.

He began to heave and jerked open the door and vomited. Gasping for breath, Geoffrey Bockker came to the only conclusion that made any sense: He and Jace Lundstrom were twins. Why hadn't his mother told him the truth? He buried his head in his hands and cried tears of remorse—he had just destroyed his own flesh and blood.

"Hey, it's not your fault. If the idiot had minded his own business, he wouldn't be dead. Besides, what difference does it make? You two may have been blood kin, but he didn't mean jack shit to you. Just forget about him and go on back to North

Carolina. Remember we've still got two more people to kill."

As usual, Geoffrey gave in to the voice. He pulled back onto the road and headed the car north once again, not giving another thought to the twin he had left behind.

Fifteen minutes after Geoffrey had left the scene of the accident, a motorist driving along the highway noticed smoke coming from the bottom of the ravine. He hurriedly called for help on his cell phone. In a few minutes, the Jasper Fire Department arrived. The firefighters fought gallantly and finally brought the blaze under control. Fortunately, the company had installed safety features on the RV. Although both the diesel fuel and the propane had leaked, causing a terrific explosion and fire, the passengers were not burned as critically as they could have been. Henrietta and Jace were airlifted to the Callaway Burn Center at the University of Alabama in Birmingham. During the flight, the paramedics had to work diligently just to keep Jace alive. Both victims were comatose when they arrived at the hospital.

The Jasper Police Department had been called in to investigate the accident since one of the victims had a gunshot wound. They found the RV's serial number stamped on the lip of the glove compartment and called the Tracker RV Company, which informed the police that the vehicle had been sold to Mr. and Mrs. Calvin Harrison of Marietta, Georgia.

"Is this the Harrison residence?"

"Yes, this is Calvin Harrison speaking."

"Mr. Harrison, I'm from the Jasper, Alabama, Police Department."

"Has something happened to Henrietta? I'm just getting over surgery, and I didn't feel like making that long trip. I begged her not to go on alone, but she insisted."

"Mr. Harrison, there's been an accident. Your vehicle ran off into a ravine, and Mrs. Harrison received serious injuries and has been taken to a burn center in Birmingham. She's unconscious, so right now we don't really know how badly she's hurt. There's a car on the way right now to take you the airport where we've chartered a plane to fly you to Birmingham."

"Thank God, she's still alive. I'll be ready when they get here."

"By the way, Mr. Harrison, do you have a recent picture of your wife that we could borrow? We need to send it to the Memphis Police Department. That might help us confirm the identity of her male passenger."

"Yes, I have one. But she didn't have a passenger. Oh, Lord, I bet she picked up another Elvis fan and brought him with her. I've warned her hundreds of times not to pick up hitchhikers, but she never paid attention to me. This time I reckon it almost cost her her life. Excuse me, but I've got to answer the door. It must be the police to get the picture. Thank you for everything."

When the Memphis Police Department received the photograph of Henrietta Harrison, they had no idea that two mysteries would be solved instead of just one. Lt. Ron Hopson went out to investigate. Since anyone going through a tour of Graceland would have to purchase a ticket first, he went to the booth.

"Do you remember seeing this lady here in the last few days?" he asked, showing the photo to the man on duty.

"Of course, that's Henrietta Harrison. She's one of our regulars. Guess she comes up about once a year. I remember seeing her yesterday. It's the first time that Mr. Harrison didn't come with her. He must not have been feeling well enough to make the trip. I did see her talking to this guy in a blue sweat suit. In fact, he got in her RV and left with her."

Something clicked in Lt. Hopson's brain when he heard the words "blue sweat suit." That's what Geoffrey Bockker had stolen from the doctors' lounge before he left the hospital after "visiting" Janine.

"Is this the man who left with Mrs. Harrison?"

"It looks kinda like him except that he had darker hair and a moustache. Oh yeah, and glasses. Why do you have a picture of him? Has he done something?"

"I'm afraid he's wanted for at least four murders and he's been on the run for almost a week. Yesterday, Mrs. Harrison's RV was found down in a ravine near Jasper, Alabama. She and her passenger were badly burned. Thanks a lot. You've been a tremendous help."

Lt. Hopson ran to his car and called into headquarters.

"Get the captain on the phone right now. I have great news for him. Captain, one of the workers out here at Graceland positively ID'd Mrs. Harrison. Guess what else? The man who left with her in her RV was probably Geoffrey Bockker. Fate may have taken care of the bastard for us."

"Damn! I hope it's true. If it is, the sonofabitch got just what he deserved. I sure hope that poor woman doesn't have to die in the process. Somebody notify the Jasper authorities and then call Sheriff Jake Connor in Columbus. He'll want to hear about this, too."

Henrietta Harrison was still in a coma and lying in a Kinair bed helped to heal her damaged skin faster. Her head was bandaged and she looked lifeless. A ventilator controlled her breathing and a monitor constantly checked her vital signs. A young, heavyset doctor walked over to Calvin Harrison and shook his hand warmly.

"Mr. Harrison, things aren't as bad as they look. Your wife received excellent medical treatment at the scene of the accident. Her burns are serious, but her greatest danger comes from a skull fracture. She received a severe blow to her head. Of course, with this type of injury, you never know what may happen. We just have to take things day by day and hope for the best."

"Do you think she'll suffer any permanent brain damage?" Calvin asked.

"Right now, we can't tell. But if she comes out of the coma within the next few days or few weeks, I don't think she will."

Calvin nodded sadly and mumbled his thanks, then asked, "Can I stay with her for a little while?"

"Of course, Mr. Harrison, and talk to her just as if she were awake. We have theories that comatose patients can actually hear what's going on around them. Just have me paged if you need anything. Your wife's one tough lady."

Calvin held his wife's hand firmly. "Henrietta, baby, it's Calvin. Now, you've got to get well. We'll get a new RV and I promise you a trip to Graceland as soon as you feel like going."

Calvin swore that he felt Henrietta squeeze his hand when he made her the promise.

The chief of the Memphis Police Department sent a message to the Jasper Police Department informing them of the real identity of Henrietta Harrison's passenger.

When the fax line rang at the Jasper precinct, a young lieutenant snatched the paper from the machine and carried it to the chief, who quickly read the fax.

"Damn! This says that the guy hurt in the RV accident was actually a killer named Geoffrey Bockker," the chief said excitedly. "Contact the Birmingham police right now and give them this information."

After receiving the message, the Birmingham Police Department went into action and placed a call to the hospital burn center. The captain waited impatiently, then finally heard "Burn Center, Nurse Gist speaking."

"You have a patient there named William Caldwell. What's his status right now?"

"I'm sorry but I cannot give out any information about our patients."

"Damnit, this is Capt. Maxey of the BPD. That man's real identity is Geoffrey Bockker. He's wanted for multiple murders in Tennessee and Mississippi."

"If that's the situation, I can give you the information. That patient is still in critical condition. He hasn't regained consciousness yet. He just got out of surgery, but his prognosis isn't good."

"Get hospital security to guard Bockker until some of my men get there," Maxey instructed. "Don't let anyone go in that room by themselves until the police arrive."

"Yes, sir. Anything else?"

"No, just tell your people to use every precaution."

"Thank you very much for letting me know." Jake Conner hung up the phone, slapped the top of his desk and yelled, "Shit! They've finally caught up with Geoffrey Bockker."

"You're kidding! How'd they catch him?" Conner's chief deputy asked.

"Seems he tried to kill some woman and steal her RV, but she shot him first. They're both in the burn center in Birmingham. I'm not going to be satisfied until I see that bastard face to face. Somebody get me a damn reservation on the next plane to Birmingham. I'm going over there just to prove to myself that it's really Bockker."

The burn center was bristling with activity when Jake Conner arrived. Round-the-clock guards stood outside the cubicle housing the man everyone believed to be Geoffrey

Bockker. Conner entered the state-of-the-art room and stared at the body lying on a bed especially designed for burn victims. With the special wrappings for his burned body and the bandages covering his chest wound, Jace resembled a mummy. Tubes of all sorts snaked from his body.

"You sure this guy is Bockker? Did y'all run any tests?"

"Yes, sir. His hands were burned so badly that we couldn't take any fingerprints, but when we sent his DNA in for testing, it was a perfect match."

Although Jace's eyes were closed, Conner reached over and gently opened one of the lids. Even though a rheumy film covered the orb, Conner smiled and said, "It's him all right. Nobody else has eyes that could stare through a brick wall. Well, Bockker, you sonofabitch, looks like you won't be killing anybody ever again. As I told you before, I wish to God I could rip those tubes from your damn body. Nothing would give me more pleasure than watching you take your last breath."

Nobody else in the room uttered a word. Conner glared at the still figure for a few more minutes and then slowly turned around and walked out of the room.

49

When the news of Bockker's accident hit the papers, Suzanne was visiting Janine in the hospital. Janine had Suzanne read her the entire story, and they both savored every minute of it. After she had finished reading, tears trickled down Suzanne's cheeks. Both women prayed that he would die.

In a deserted cabin he had found far back in the mountains of North Carolina, Geoffrey Bockker rejoiced in the fact that he had gotten away with his most recent murders. Even if Jace did happen to survive, there was no way he could prove that he wasn't Geoffrey Bockker since, in all probability, they were twin brothers. However, the desire for revenge still burned deep within Geoffrey's soul. The smoldering fire would not be quenched until he killed the final two members of the group who had destroyed his life.

50

September 1996

Suzanne and Janine were once again headed to a reunion at their beloved "W." Although things would never be the same without the other two members of the "Big Four," they were determined to make the best of the situation. Obviously, their hearts were not in the trip, but they felt compelled to go since both of them were being honored as Co-Outstanding Alumnae of the Year for their tireless efforts on behalf of the various charities each one had so generously supported.

Much had happened to Suzanne and Janine in the two years since the horror. After Suzanne had gotten home from the hospital, George Haynes didn't waste any time in telling her exactly how he felt. He had almost lost her once and was determined not to let anything happen to her again. He told her how he had loved her since she had moved into the building. Suzanne felt a tremendous debt of gratitude to George for saving her life, and over time, gradually fell in love with him. They married a year later and moved to a home in Cordova, Tennessee. Time had begun to heal Suzanne's broken heart and she had turned to charity work to help ease the burden of her pain. She now felt that she had finally put her sorrows behind her. But the empty place in her heart caused by the loss of her daughter would never be filled.

Although Janine's injuries had not been fatal, the effect of the gunshot had caused extensive damage. Reconstructive surgery had repaired the fractured cheekbone, but it had been necessary to perform a mastoidectomy of her left ear. Further plastic surgery was required to help fill in the hollow left by the track of the bullet. Unfortunately, Janine's encounters with Bockker added to the already unhappy relationship between her and her husband. Divorce was now inevitable, and they finally ended a marriage that had been disintegrating for a long time. Her older daughter blamed her mother for the divorce and they had become estranged. The younger daughter lived in St. Louis and was working for the *Post Dispatch*. Suzanne insisted that Janine move in with her and George, at least during the difficult months of recuperation and rehabilitation. Janine gratefully accepted the offer. Ever since the tragic events, the two women had become like sisters and vowed never to let anything or anyone come between them. With the last of her surgeries finally behind her, Janine felt that she, too, could face the future.

To pass the time on the drive to Columbus, the two women practiced their speeches. The cell phone rang and Suzanne automatically pressed the button to allow both of them to listen to the caller. Almost before she could say hello, an all too familiar voice said, "You're going to die. I told you that nothing could keep me from killing you." A deafening silence followed by a click ended the call.

Janine and Suzanne froze in absolute fear. Geoffrey Bockker had returned from hell.

"Oh my God, Janine, Bockker can't be calling us! The

police assured us he was still in a coma in the rehab center in Birmingham."

"Obviously, they made a big mistake, or they weren't telling us the truth. Want to turn around and go home? It's up to you."

"Hell no! Let's call the Lowndes County Sheriff's office and let them know what just happened. They'll tell us what to do."

Two hours later, Janine pulled into a parking space in front of a new two-story brick building. The two women nervously got out of the car and went in through the double glass doors. They went directly up to the officer on duty at the front desk.

"I'm Janine Beauregard and this is Suzanne Haynes. We called a couple of hours ago about a threat we received on our cell phone," Janine said.

"Yes, m'am. Y'all come on back here. Sheriff Conner's waitin' for you in his office."

Jake Conner was still the epitome of a redneck. Even though he was now the sheriff of Lowndes County, he was just as crass as he had been when he was only a deputy in Oktibbeha County. He was leaning back in his chair, both feet propped up on his desk with a big cigar stuck in the left side of his mouth.

Not even bothering to get up, he pushed the cigar to the other side and spat out particles of tobacco.

"So you're the two ladies who think you've been contacted by Geoffrey Bockker. I don't know who called you, but it sure as hell wasn't Bockker. There's no way that sonofabitch could be here. He's still in a coma and has round-the-clock guards."

"Don't you think we'd recognize the voice of the man who's hunted us down like dogs all these years?" Suzanne said, her indignation rising. "The man on the phone was Geoffrey Bockker, whether you believe us or not."

Conner's face reddened and he glared at both women. "If you ladies don't mind, I have some work to do."

"But what are we going to do if it was Bockker? You can't just dismiss us," Janine insisted.

"Well, I'm sorry, but I can't spare any officers right now. We've got a big political rally coming up."

"Thanks for nothing. I'll bet you're running for re-election, aren't you? Come on, Suzanne. Let's get out of here. We'll just have to protect ourselves."

The two women stormed out of the sheriff's office and got back into Suzanne's car. "Let's don't say anything about the call. We'll just have to be extra careful. Suzanne, do you remember how to get to the Delta house? Aren't we supposed to have a meeting there first?" Janine was looking around as they drove.

"Suzanne, just take a left here off College Avenue. I think it's the next right. Oh, here we are. Gosh, the campus has really changed. They've even renovated our house."

A perky young woman at the desk eagerly greeted the two women as if they were celebrities. "You must be Mrs. Beauregard and Mrs. Haynes. It's an honor to meet y'all. Oh, a few of your classmates want you to join them earlier out at Carrier Lodge."

"Sheriff Conner's office. How can I help you?"

"This is Special Agent Casey of the Alabama Bureau of Investigation. Put Conner on the phone right now." There was a three-second pause and then Conner said, "What can I do for you?"

The agent replied, "Conner, get your butt in gear. I don't have much time to explain, but Geoffrey Bockker's on the loose. The man over here in Alabama in rehab turned out to be someone named Jace Lundstrom. We think he and Bockker must have been identical twins."

Conner turned pale. *Aw shit, those women were right.* "I've got to get off the phone. I think Bockker's already in the area."

Conner moved with the speed of a crazed man. "Charley, get your ass up out of that chair. Geoffrey Bockker's on his way here right now."

"But, Sheriff—"

"Shut up your damn mouth and get moving. Janie, call over at the 'W' and find out where they're having some sort of Delta Social Club reunion."

"It's out at Carrier Lodge, sir." Janie said. "One of my mom's friends is going to it."

Conner raced out of the office with his deputies in pursuit. He turned on his siren and sped down Highway 7 toward the lodge, a trip that would take at least thirty minutes, even if he broke the speed limit.

It took Suzanne and Janine about thirty-five minutes to get to their destination. They pulled up in front of the building and took a few minutes to repair their makeup. "I don't see anyone around. Maybe we got the time wrong. Let's go in and look at the decorations. In fifteen minutes, if no one has shown up, we'll go to the hotel and check in."

The two women got out of their car and started walking toward the lodge.

"Suzanne, wait a minute. There's a car pulling up. Let's find out who it is."

When the driver got out, Suzanne screamed, "Oh, my God, it's Bockker! Run, Janine."

But the two women weren't fast enough for the agile man. He pulled out a gun and fired a shot into the air, then ordered them to lie down on the ground. After he had tied them up, he put Suzanne up front with him and Janine in the back seat.

"Now your time has come. You're gonna die the same way that Angie did, in a burst of flames."

He cranked up the car and headed south.

"Where're we going?" Janine asked.

"Just shut the hell up. You'll know soon enough."

Geoffrey wound his way down an almost deserted road and pulled the car to a stop amid a maze of brambles and dense trees.

"Get out. We're almost there."

Unseen by Geoffrey, Janine had loosened her ropes enough to pick up a small spiral notepad lying on the seat next to her and slipped it inside the waistband of her pants.

After the three had pushed aside the thick vegetation, the two women were startled when they realized they were standing directly behind the cabin where their two best friends had been murdered.

Despite the protestations of his wife, Josiah Perkins had refused to destroy the cabin after the murders of Arlene and Barbara. It had such sentimental value to him because his great-grandfather and grandfather had built it with their own hands. Although he knew that he'd never set foot inside the cabin again because of the atrocities that had been committed there, he felt it best to simply abandon the building and leave it to the ravages of time.

Geoffrey chuckled and shoved the women inside the cabin. A musty odor permeated the room, and the sun reflected on the myriad spider webs that decorated the corners and windows. Broken chairs and dried blood indicated the very spot where Arlene and Barbara had met their deaths.

"You bastard!" Suzanne cried out. "You think we're just going to let you kill us like you did our friends?" Lunging forward, Suzanne managed to grab a piece of broken chair and swung as hard as she could. Geoffrey was faster and ducked out of the way a fraction of a second before she could make contact. Suzanne lost her balance and fell to the floor.

Bockker pointed his pistol toward the two women and reached to his left and picked up a red can. He walked toward them, dribbling a trail of liquid. The pungent odor of gasoline soon filled the room. He glared at the women as he slowly backed away, still keeping the pistol pointed at them. In a blurred motion, he threw down the can and pulled a cigarette lighter from his jacket pocket and clicked the wheel. He bent over and held the flame to the liquid.

A whoosh and a gunshot occurred at exactly the same time. Geoffrey clutched his chest and stumbled in the direction of the back door. George Haynes rushed through the front door and frantically dragged the two women outside just as the cabin erupted into flames. There was no way he could go back in for Geoffrey. The three people felt the heat from the fire and grimaced when they heard Geoffrey's screams as they headed toward George's car.

Only when they were safely inside was Suzanne able to speak. "Oh, George, how on earth did you manage to find us?"

"Honey, I know you and Janine can take care of yourselves but something kept telling me that I needed to go to Columbus. I got to the 'W' and the nice young lady told me about the reunion at the Carrier Lodge. When I pulled up in the driveway and saw your car, I knew something was wrong. I called the sheriff's office and told them what I had found. They said that Sheriff Conner was already on his way to the lodge. They patched me through to Conner and when I told him that your deserted car was at the lodge, he figured Bockker had taken y'all to the cabin where he had killed Barbara and Arlene. He gave me the directions and here I am."

"Here comes Conner now," Suzanne said, pointing to the approaching police cars.

"Those jerks. They wouldn't listen to us when we told them about the phone call," Janine said angrily.

"What call, Janine?"

"Bockker called us when we were in Tupelo. We went to the sheriff's office in Columbus, but that doofus sheriff, Jake Conner, didn't think we knew what we were talking about."

"Damn! I ought to beat the crap out of him," George said. "If y'all had been killed, it would have been his fault." George slammed on the brakes and flagged down the first car.

"George, don't do anything stupid," Suzanne pleaded. "We're okay now."

"Yeah, but I'm still going to give him a piece of my mind. You two stay here. I'll be right back."

They couldn't hear what George was saying but they could see his six-foot- four muscular frame towering over Conner. He poked his finger right in the sheriff's chest and talked non-stop to him for five minutes. Afterwards, Conner had a sheepish look on his face as he slowly walked toward their car.

George signaled for Suzanne to let the window down. "Ladies, I think Mr. Conner has something he'd like to say to you."

Conner bent his head down toward the open car window. "I'm real sorry about what happened at my office. I shouldn't have ignored what you told me." He could barely make eye contact with the women.

"Next time don't act like such a male chauvinist when two women try to tell you something," Suzanne said.

"Yes'm, Mrs. Haynes. Uh, I've got to get to that cabin to see what happened to Bockker."

Conner stalked back to his patrol car and headed toward the

cabin.

Suzanne turned to her friend and noticed something strange. "Janine, what's that sticking out of the waist of your pants?"

"Oh God, I forgot about this." She pulled out the spiral notepad and opened it to the first page. Her eyes grew wide with fright, and a look of disgust crossed her face. "It's that bastard's diary. He's written down everything that's happened since 1963."

"Let me see it," Suzanne said.

Tears formed in her eyes as she read the contents. She handed the notepad back to her friend.

"You keep it," she said, choking back sobs. "I just want to forget that Geoffrey Bockker ever existed."

As he drove toward the cabin, Jake Conner was still in a foul mood. That jerk had really humiliated him in front of his men, but none of them had dared to open their mouths. He screeched to a halt when he reached the cabin. There was nothing left of the structure but a few pieces of smoldering timbers.

Conner couldn't walk into the area yet so he went around back. He saw footprints coming from a deserted path. He followed the prints until they stopped next to a car with North Carolina license plates. He drew out his pistol and walked around the car. He looked inside and then turned back toward the cabin, his pistol still drawn. Just inside what must have been the back door lay the remains of a charred body. Next to the body was a red can with a spout. Conner bent down and sniffed the can. *So, Bockker, we meet again. I wish to hell I could have killed you myself, but at least I have the satisfaction of knowing you're finally dead.* Conner called to one of his men to phone the medical examiner. "I want to wrap this up as soon as possible. Better call the paramedics and the county fire marshal, too. He'll want to see this."

A few minutes later, the deputy returned to say that the medical examiner was on vacation so he had called Doc Jamieson.

"Even though he's retired, he can still sign the death certificate. Was that okay?" the deputy asked.

"Yeah, we know it's Bockker anyway," Conner replied. "Has to be. There's no sign of anyone else having been around here."

The paramedics arrived and helped the old doctor out of the ambulance. He was now in his eighties and could barely see or hear.

"Doc—!" Conner shouted. "I need you to sign this death certificate. You remember Geoffrey Bockker, don't you? Well, here he is, dead at last."

Jamieson tugged on his ear and drawled, "Don't you think we ought to go through the proper channels and send the remains to Jackson just to make sure?"

"Hell no! That'd take too much time. Just sign here. If anything happens, I'll take the blame. Okay?"

"It's against my better judgment, but I'll do it. I guess you've got to get ready for that big campaign rally."

After Doc Jamieson had signed the certificate, the paramedics put on their protective gear and loaded up the remains of the body. Just then the fire trucks pulled up, and the chief came over to Conner.

"Have you got any idea what happened?"

"Yeah, Geoffrey Bockker did it. I found a can of gasoline near the body."

"Where should we take the body, Sheriff?" the paramedic asked.

"I'll call Memorial and tell them you're on your way."

Conner replied. "After they embalm what's left of him, we'll stick his sorry-ass carcass in Friendship as soon as possible. I don't want to make a big thing out of this and have half the newspapers in the state comin' down on us. Hey, have any of you seen old Eddie? He sometimes spends the night in the cabin. I don't see any sign of his old Chevy pickup either. Guess he's found a new home."

By that night, the whole town had heard of Bockker's death, and Conner was more than willing to take the credit. He was glad-handed and slapped on the back so many times that he was actually happy to see the night come to an end.

The next afternoon, a group of people stood around the pauper's section of Friendship Cemetery to watch Geoffrey Bockker being lowered into the ground. Guards had been posted at the entrance to the cemetery to keep out the gawkers who had come to see for themselves that the "Triangle Killer" had indeed met his Maker.

"At last the world is rid of this monster," Jake Conner said. "Let's go home. We'll all sleep better at night knowing the sonofabitch'll burn in hell for the rest of eternity."

After the others had left, Josiah bowed his head and thanked God that the monster's reign of terror had finally come to an end. *Geoffrey, I'm sorry that I never got to tell you how I really feel. You used me and the whole judicial system to help you do your dirty work. Nothing that happened to you could ever justify the pain and anguish you inflicted on your victims and their families. I only wish that I could have been the one who caused your death. The deaths of your victims will be on my conscience the rest of my life. I hope that Jake Conner was right and that you really are burning in hell.* With tears in his eyes, Josiah turned away from the grave of the man he had once thought was his friend and slowly walked back to his car.

At the same time that Jake Conner and the group of "mourn-ers" thought they were burying Geoffrey Bockker, a man driv-ing a beat-up old Chevy pickup was smiling. He looked over at the Kelvar jacket and patted it gently. *My chest hurts like hell, but the bullet didn't do any damage. My only regret is not knowing for certain the fate of Suzanne and Janine. And my diary. It wasn't in the back seat of my car. That bitch Janine must have taken it. If she's alive, I'll get it back when I finish the job.*

The next morning Conner strutted into his office. Two men in business suits and dark glasses were seated in the waiting area. Conner grinned and stuck out his hand. "I suppose you guys are reporters who've come to interview me about Geoffrey Bockker. Come on in and I'll give you all the details."

The men stood up and followed the sheriff into his office. The taller man closed the door and drew the blinds.

"My name's Gomez, and this is my partner, Collins. We're U.S Marshals, not some friggin' reporters. Your ass is in deep shit. You were warned before about Bockker, but you just couldn't keep your nose clean. Why in the hell didn't you get an autopsy done before you took it upon yourself to identify the body as Bockker's?"

Conner squirmed in his chair and perspiration formed on his upper lip. "They, they called me from Birmingham and told me the guy in the hospital wasn't Bockker and that he was proba-bly on his way over here." Conner rubbed his hand across his lip and leaned forward, the palms of his hands resting on his desk. "I think y'all have got some explaining to do, too. Why the hell did the government let Bockker out in the first place? They knew what he'd done."

Gomez stuck a folded piece of paper in Conner's face. "That's beside the point. We've got a court order to have the body exhumed. For your sake, the guy in the grave had better be Geoffrey Bockker. Come on. Let's head out to the cemetery. We've arranged for somebody to meet us."

The jaws of the backhoe ate the earth in huge gulps and the cheap fiberboard casket soon came into view. Gomez and Collins peered into the grave and then stood back and watched as the cemetery crew attached a chain around the coffin and signaled to the crane operator to hoist it into the air. The man gently laid Bockker's casket on the ground. The funeral home director and his assistants, along with the two U.S. Marshals and Conner, picked up the coffin and slid it into the open doors of the hearse.

"Let's go," Collins said. "The state medical examiner is waiting for us at the funeral home. We can't afford to waste any time if this isn't Bockker's body."

He glared at Conner who tucked his head and tried to bury himself in the seat.

After two hours, the autopsy was finished, and the state medical examiner said, "It'll take me a few days to get the results. I'll fax them to you as soon as I finish. It'll take longer for the DNA results to come in, though. Fortunately, I was able to make a dental impression. The man's hands were burned so badly that I was able to get only a partial print from one finger."

"That's okay," Gomez said. "We'll get them to the FBI so they can match them up with Bockker's records. That'll be quicker than waiting for the DNA. It'll just be icing on the cake, though. Collins, get out your laptop and scan the print and dental impressions and download them. We'll have our answer in a few minutes."

The deafening silence was broken by the squawking of the fax machine. Conner nervously chewed on a cigar as the fax snaked out of the machine.

"Just what I suspected," Gomez said. "Neither the print nor the dental records match. This man definitely isn't Geoffrey Bockker. Looks like you screwed up big time, Sheriff."

Conner turned around and stormed out of the room. A few seconds later, he peeled off in his squad car, leaving the two marshals to get back the best way they could.

When Conner walked into the jail, no one said a word to him. They knew by the look on their boss's face that he was not a man to be crossed. Conner had two calls to make. He put off the task as long as he could. Then he jabbed at the buttons on his phone and chewed on the cigar while he waited for someone to answer. "Mrs. Beauregard, I'm afraid I've got bad news..."

51

Somewhere deep in the secluded mountain woods of North Carolina, Geoffrey Bockker stood and looked out the window of the rustic cabin. In the distance the Blue Ridge Mountains loomed like watchtowers. He reached down to a table and picked up a worn and faded picture of a beautiful young girl and clutched it to his breast. Shifting his gaze to a picture of four smiling girls, he seethed aloud, "I haven't forgotten about you, but right now I've got to take care of some other unfinished business."

He laid the picture back down on the table and ran his fingers through his bushy mane of hair and pulled on the wispy strands of his beard. From the time he had returned from Mississippi, something had been eating away at him. He nodded his head and sighed. "I can't put this off any longer."

Reaching for his jacket, he opened the wooden door and headed down the mountain. He checked to make sure his trip wires were still set and grinned. *Even Jake Conner couldn't find me up here. That stupid shit.*

After two hours of making his way down the mountain through the dense forest, Geoffrey came to the edge of a town.

His destination was the pay phone inside an old general store, the kind that existed only in the memories of most people. Inside the store, a cluster of men whose clothing and appearances strongly resembled Geoffrey's sat huddled around an old pot-bellied stove playing checkers and drinking homemade brew. When Geoffrey walked in the front door, the men stopped long enough to acknowledge his presence, then went right back to their game. They were the last of their kind, old men who still defied the law by making and selling their special brand of moonshine. Government agents, however, had given up their pursuit of these fossils in order to concentrate on the younger generation of criminals—the ones who sold a far more lethal brand of illegal drugs. This old generation of wrongdoers was a society of "live and let live" and they had accepted the stranger into their midst without asking any questions. Geoffrey had lived among them off and on for the past two years, and they had never once questioned his activities.

Geoffrey pulled out a worn card from his pocket and inserted a bevy of coins into the machine. His fingers trembled as he dialed the number, and he had to clear his throat several times before he could speak when a familiar voice answered the phone.

"Liz, this is your old friend from Mississippi. How are you?"

"My God, Geoffrey, I never expected to hear your voice again."

"I've been thinking over what you told me. I've just got to meet my son."

"I'm not so sure that's a good idea. He still doesn't suspect anything. I'm sorry I even told you about him."

"It's too late now." Geoffrey felt frustration rise up inside him and he gritted his jaw. "All, all, I want to do is just see the boy once. I promise I'll leave you two alone after that. Please,

Liz."

"Look, my husband died recently and Rex's been having some emotional problems ever since. He's been seeing a psychiatrist. I don't want to do anything that might set him over the edge."

Geoffrey stammered, "Maybe, maybe I can help him. Psychiatrists are a bunch of idiots. They can't really do any good. Come on, Liz. It couldn't hurt."

"Okay. You can see him, but just this once. How long will it take you to get here? I don't even know where you are."

Geoffrey hesitated a few seconds before answering. "I can be there Tuesday. You pick the time and place."

"How about two o'clock at the front desk of the library in downtown Eureka City? It's in the two hundred block of Main Street."

"That suits me fine. Are you going to tell Rex the truth beforehand?"

"No, I'll just tell him we're meeting an old friend. I'll see you Tuesday."

"Okay. And thanks, Liz."

Liz Anderson's breath came in short gasps after she had hung up the phone. Her body quivered with excitement at the prospect of seeing the only man for whom she had ever felt real passion, but her mind was filled with misgivings.

She walked over to her desk, opened a drawer and took out a yellowed envelope labeled *Mississippi*. Inside was a folder containing newspaper clippings dating back to 1963. Tears ran down her cheeks as she scanned the articles. Her hands trembled as she reread the last two articles. The first one told of Geoffrey's death in a remote area outside Columbus, Mississippi. The final article refuted the first by stating that the real person killed in the fire was an old man named Eddie Spinkston. Her face hardened as she reread the last line.

"Geoffrey Bockker has seemingly vanished into thin air."

After putting everything back into the envelope, she placed it at the bottom of the drawer. Then she walked to the foot of the stairs. "Rex, could you come down a minute?"

Geoffrey had hung up the phone and walked over to where the old men were sitting. "Would one of you fellows mind if I borrowed your truck for a couple of days? I need to tend to some business in Eureka City."

"Sure, Jack, you can take mine," said one of the grizzly-faced checker players as he smiled up at Geoffrey, revealing several missing teeth. "Come on by anytime. It's always full of gas. Never know when I might need to get away in a hurry. Right, fellas?" His buddies nodded in agreement and laughed.

52

Geoffrey was pacing nervously inside the Eureka City library when he glanced out the front door. His heart flip-flopped when he saw a petite blonde and a young man get out of a car and head toward the building. He swallowed hard when he noticed the striking resemblance between the young man and himself. When the couple entered the building, Geoffrey stood up and walked toward them with outstretched arms. He hugged the woman.

"Liz, it's great to see you again." Then he glanced over at the young man. "You must be Rex. I'm Jack Ingram. Your mom and I go back a long way."

Rex began to tremble. "Mother, you and Geoffrey don't have to pretend anymore. I found the articles one day while I was looking for something in your desk. I'm the spitting image of the guy in the pictures. One of my buddies who works at the hospital did some investigating and found that the reason I couldn't donate my kidney to Dad was because there was no compatibility at all. Come on. I'm twenty years old. For God's sake, tell me the truth."

Liz's face turned ashen and she stammered, "Al—alright,

Rex, I guess it's time you knew." Liz nodded toward an empty table in the corner and the three went over to it and sat down.

Rex sat across from his mother and this stranger who had just been identified as his biological father. When Liz had finished her story, Rex just shook his head. "Why didn't you tell me this before now? I could have handled it."

"I know how much you loved your dad. I was afraid the news would have devastated you."

"So you thought living a lie was okay? What about you, Geoffrey? Why did you wait until now to want to see me?"

"Rex, I didn't know you existed until a couple of years ago. At that time I was so caught up in something else that I just pushed your existence into the back of my mind. The other day I finally realized I had to see you. I promised your mother I wouldn't bother y'all anymore, though. I think it's best that I leave now."

"Wait a minute. You can't just come into my life one minute and then disappear the next. I, I want to get to know you."

"Rex, you've read about all the terrible things I've done. The authorities are still looking for me. The best thing is for me to get out of your lives completely."

"Wait, Geoffrey," Liz pleaded. "Those things you did—you thought you had a reason. You were sick. Let me get you some professional help."

"No, Liz. I won't go to any damned shrink. As long as I don't listen to my voice, things are okay. But, Rex, if you really want us to get better acquainted, I'll take you back with me for a few days. That is, if it's okay with your mother."

Rex looked at his mother. "Mom?"

Liz hesitated momentarily. She felt that Geoffrey would never deliberately do anything to hurt her or Rex. Yet she knew that Geoffrey had killed at least four more people. When she didn't give her answer immediately, Geoffrey stood up and walked over to her. He reached down and cupped her chin in his hand, staring down at her with his mesmerizing eyes. He gave her the same look he had given the woman outside the Biltmore House who thought she had recognized him. He gently squeezed her chin and grinned.

"Please, Liz, let me have this brief visit with him."

Liz felt herself grow weak. Whatever resolve she might have had completely evaporated and she stammered, "Okay, but just for a few days. Have him back on Sunday. Rex will show you how to get to our house. How can I reach you?"

"My phone's not working right now, but I'll have him phone you every day from a friend's house. I promise."

"What about clothes?"

"We'll pick him up some on the way."

Liz bit her lip as her son kissed her on the cheek and reached over and picked up his backpack. Tears filled her eyes as she watched the two men stride out the door.

"Let me carry that backpack for you, Rex. It looks heavy. What's in there?"

"No, that's okay. It's just some textbooks. I'm getting a degree in theater at State. I just finished a course on make-up techniques. I've got this neat book that explains how to make latex masks. Maybe we could get the ingredients and practice making one."

Geoffrey looked at his son and smiled. "Sure, I've always been interested in disguises and stuff like that."

After the boy and his father had left, Liz collapsed into the nearest chair. A chill worked its way up her spine and she shuddered. For the first time, she began to wonder if Rex's problems might stem from being the child of a psychopath. She went over to the nearest computer and hurriedly clicked in the topics she wanted to look up and nervously awaited the results. Forty titles appeared and she printed out their names and took the list to the librarian.

"We don't subscribe to all of these magazines, but I'll check off the ones we have and show you where to find the bound copies."

With an armload of books, Liz sat down to determine the validity of her fears. She prayed she was wrong. Her eyes widened in horror as the facts seemed to leap from the pages. Although Rex had never been abused, he did exhibit two of the childhood characteristics of men who had become serial killers. He had wet the bed until he was almost fifteen years old. He also had enjoyed torturing small helpless animals. She and Harry had taken Rex to a urologist who had diagnosed his problem as a weak sphincter muscle. In time the bed-wetting had stopped. Harry had shrugged off the fact that Rex enjoyed killing small animals by arguing that most little boys went through that stage. He told Liz that he and his friends used to torture frogs by sticking firecrackers in their butts and watching them blow up. Now, she was sure that these had been signs of an impending propensity to see other creatures suffer. As she read further, she realized that Rex's troubles in school had just been part of a developing pattern. Harry's death and discovering that Geoffrey was probably his biological father had been the catalysts that really caused Rex's problems to erupt. Why hadn't she seen it coming? How stupid she had been when all the signs were so obvious. At least he'd never done anything really serious. Maybe the stable influences of living with normal parents had been stronger than Rex's genetic makeup. She knew one thing: she had made a huge mistake in letting Geoffrey take their son. As soon as Rex phoned, she'd make Geoffrey bring him home or tell her where to come get him.

When they got back, she'd place him under the care of a competent psychiatrist who might be able to thwart his inclinations toward evil.

Liz hurriedly returned the books to the main desk and gathered up her notes. She would go home and busy herself with more research until she heard from her son.

53

On the way back to Geoffrey's mountain cabin, he glanced over toward his son. *Those bitches killed my first child, but no one can ever take you away from me. Even though their actions denied me the pleasure of seeing you grow up, at least now I'll be able to make up for lost time.*

Rex turned toward his father and started to say something, but could tell that Geoffrey was deep in thought.

When they pulled up in front of the general store, Geoffrey said, "Rex, the folks up here know me as Jack Ingram, so let's just keep my real name between the two of us. Let's go in and call your mom. She's probably worried to death. And I've got to give the truck keys back to their owner."

"Now, Liz. Don't be so upset. You know I'll take care of Rex. I'll bring him back home Sunday. I understand your feelings, but just remember that I love him as much as I love you."

Despite her misgivings, Liz reluctantly gave in and agreed to let Rex stay until Sunday.

As the two men stood in front of the general store, Geoffrey said, "I hope you're up to a long hike. It's straight up that mountain to my cabin."

"Sure, my friends and I hike in the mountains all the time. Let's go."

Two hours later, Rex looked out the window of Geoffrey's cabin and felt the same thrill Geoffrey did when he surveyed the majesty surrounding them.

As he ambled through his father's cabin, Rex spotted Angie's pictures and looked at his father. "This is the girl you loved enough to kill all those people?"

Geoffrey's eyes moistened and he said in a soft voice, "She's the only person I ever loved until I met your mother. Those bitches in that picture with the writing on it—they're responsible for Angie's death. They took her away from me. But I guess, in a way, they brought your mom and me together. But I wasn't destined to have lasting happiness with either one."

"Why don't you and Mom and me go off somewhere so we can always be together?"

"It's not that simple, Rex. The authorities are still after me. It wouldn't be fair to you or your mother. No matter where we went, I'd always be looking back over my shoulder. That's no life for you and Liz."

An angry look came over Rex's face. "You sure got screwed, didn't you, Geoffrey? I hate those women for what they did to you. What happened to the other two? From what I read in the newspaper clippings, you only killed Arlene and Barbara."

"Oh, Janine and Suzanne are still around I suppose. I don't want to dwell on the past, and we can't do anything about the future. Let's just make the best of the few days we have together. I want to make up for all our lost time. Tell me about yourself. I want to get to know you."

The next few days rushed by. Geoffrey and his new-found

son spent hours hiking, fishing, and swimming in mountain streams as father and son got to know each other.

Rex showed Geoffrey how to make latex masks. They laughed when Geoffrey tried on a Dracula mask they had just finished. "I vant to drink your blood," Geoffrey said in his best Bela Lugosi imitation. He took off the mask and glanced at Angie's picture. "Is it possible to make a mask of a picture?" he asked Rex.

"Sure, you've just got to construct a clay mold and then make a plaster cast from the mold. What'd you have in mind?"

"Uh, nothing. I just wondered if it could be done."

As Sunday approached, both Geoffrey and Rex were in a melancholy mood. Neither one wanted Rex to leave.

"Dad, please don't make me go back just yet. Let me stay a few days longer."

Geoffrey's heart melted when Rex called him "Dad." "I'd love for you to, Rex, but we promised you mother. You know how worried she was when we called her to let her know that we'd gotten here. Come on, let's head to the store. I'll borrow my buddy's truck again."

Four hours later, Geoffrey pulled up in front of Rex's house. Liz came running out and threw her arms around her son.

"Rex, I've missed you so much."

Geoffrey winked at Liz and gave her a disarming grin. "Thanks for letting me spend some time with him."

"Dad, I want to visit you some more when the next session of school is over. Can I?"

"That's up to your mother, Rex. She's the boss."

Liz put her arm around her son's shoulder, squeezing it slightly. "Let's go inside and you can tell me all about your weekend. I'd ask you to come in, Geoffrey, but I—I don't think it's such a good idea." She hesitated nervously.

"I understand," Geoffrey said. He waved and pulled out of

the driveway.

When they got inside the house, Liz Anderson could see a change in her son. His mannerisms had become more like Geoffrey's and he sounded just like him when he talked. She prayed those were the only similarities.

"Rex, I've got something very important to say to you. Just let me get through before you say anything."

Liz briefly explained to her son what she had read in the articles. She told him that she had contacted a specialist who thought he could help. Then with tears in her eyes, she said that it would be best if he never saw his father again.

"Damnit, Mom. I don't need to see a psychiatrist. There's nothing wrong with me. You certainly can't stop me from seeing my dad. I'm old enough to make up my own mind."

Rex jumped up from the table and ran out the front door. Liz just sat there sobbing, her head clasped in her hands. "Oh God, what am I going to do?"

As Geoffrey was heading back home, he relived the past few days with his son. *We had such a good time, but I worry about Rex. We're so much alike. I sure don't want him to turn out like me. Maybe it's best if we don't ever see each other again.*

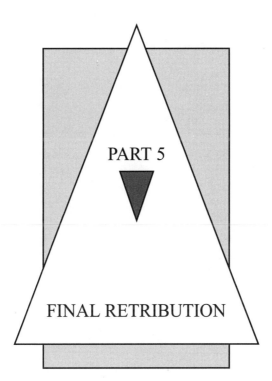

PART 5

FINAL RETRIBUTION

54

August 1999

Janine Beauregard brushed the sweat from her forehead. The window unit was on full blast, but it did little good against the oppressive humidity of a sultry August day.

"Why the hell didn't I put in central air like everybody said to?" she mumbled as she continued with the dusting.

Her younger daughter was due in later in the week and the house had to be spotless, but Janine had put off the cleaning until the last minute. Her arthritic knees ached with every move. As she caught a glimpse of herself in the oval mirror above the piano, she shuddered.

"Lord, how did I ever let myself get in this shape?"

Janine stopped her work for a moment and sat down in her father's old recliner to rest. After the divorce, she had moved into her parents' empty house and had gradually begun to make a new life for herself. For the past three years, neither she nor Suzanne had heard a word from Geoffrey Bockker, but his specter remained a real presence in her life. Her reverie was broken by the ringing of the doorbell. When she peeked out the curtain, she saw an old, gray-haired man standing on the porch.

"I'll be there in a minute."

"Jan, it's Sarah," Janine's oldest daughter said into the phone. "I know you aren't supposed to leave until Thursday, but something awful's happened. Mom's in the hospital, and you've got to get home right away."

"Oh, my God! What happened?"

"When I phoned her last night to see if she needed any help cleaning the house, no one answered. I called Cousin Sally and asked her to check on Mom. When she got there, the car was in the garage, but the front door was wide open. She found Mom lying on the living room floor covered with blood. Somebody had stabbed her and slashed her throat. Sally called 911 and then Dad. Jan, they don't know if she's going to survive."

55

Jan Beauregard walked fearfully into her mother's hospital cubicle in the critical care unit of the North Central Medical Center. She had been a homicide detective for the St. Louis Metropolitan Police and presently worked as an investigative reporter for the *St.Louis Post Dispatch*, but nothing in her past prepared her for the sight of her mother trapped in a bed surrounded by all sorts of life-saving equipment. The eerie stillness of the room was interrupted by the hissing of the ventilator that forced oxygen into her mother's lungs and by the incessant clicking of a variety of pumps. These pumps controlled the flow of the fluids that dripped into tubes snaking out of her mother's discolored and swollen hands and arms. A monitor indicated the condition of Janine's vital signs. A tube had been inserted through her nose, down her throat, through her stomach, and into her intestines. A liquid goop resembling a green milkshake eased its way from the bag down through the tube. On the side of the bed hung a Foley catheter that measured Janine's output of urine. A bandage encircled Janine's throat. Thoughts of revenge crept into the grieving daughter's mind and with them one name: Geoffrey Bockker.

Jan leaned over and kissed her mother tenderly. "I promise you, Mom, I'll get the bastard."

After a few minutes, Janine's nurse entered the room and walked over toward Jan. "I hate to make you leave, but your mother needs her rest now. You can come back in two hours."

"Okay, I'll just be down the hall in the waiting room. By the way, where are Sarah and my father? I thought they'd still be here."

"They stayed all night. Sarah went home to change clothes and your dad had to go to the sheriff's office to get a little work done."

Jan kept vigil that day. In the afternoon, her sister arrived. Jan immediately got up and rushed to Sarah.

"Why don't you go on home?" Sarah said. "I'll stay here for the rest of the day. Dad'll be in and out. I think he's planning on coming home for dinner. Y'all can have a good visit. Then both of you can come over together."

"I guess you're right," Jan reluctantly agreed. "I could use some rest. But promise me you'll call if there's any change in Mom's condition."

The two sisters hugged and both began to cry.

56

A tall, gaunt man wearing a blue sweat suit approached the cowering girl. When he was close enough for her to stare into his steel-gray eyes, he raised his arm. The moonlight reflected off the switchblade he clutched in his hand. The girl tried to turn and run, but she seemed to be frozen in place. No sound came from her mouth, although she made an attempt to scream. In that fleeting instant between dream world and reality, Jan Beauregard forced herself to wake up and discovered that she was gasping for breath. She lay in the bed a few moments, letting the panic attack subside. She looked over at the clock and jumped up. Her father would be there in a few minutes and she had to fix supper for him. The shrill ringing of the phone echoed in the quietness. Her gut knotted up, and she knew what had happened before she even put the phone to her ear.

"Jan, it's me, Sarah. Mom just died."

"Do you need me to come to the hospital?" asked Jan, praying that her sister's answer would be no.

Sarah responded icily, "I'll handle everything here. Besides, Dad's on his way. We'll be home as soon as we can, but first we've got to stop off at the funeral home to make all the arrangements. Do you want to meet us there?"

Panic set in again, and Jan began to take in short quick breaths. Her legs and arms tingled and she broke out in a cold sweat. Her heart raced wildly.

"No, I'm sure you and Dad can handle everything."

Jan let the phone slip out of her hand as she sank to the floor. Tears streamed down her face.

After she had calmed down, Jan went into the kitchen and began working on supper. At least that would help occupy her mind for a while and keep her busy.

An hour later, Jan heard the front door open. She walked into the living room and automatically hugged her sister. Then she began sobbing and grasped her father tightly. His face was strained, but seemed to be devoid of emotion.

For the rest of the evening a steady stream of neighbors kept coming over with food and calling to offer their condolences.

57

The next morning, after they had finished eating breakfast and their father had gone down to his office to see if any new information regarding the attack on Janine had arrived from Jackson, Sarah and Jan sat drinking coffee. Sarah reached out and patted her sister's hand gently. "You go to the house and pick out something to bury Mother in. After all, you were really closer to her."

Jan jumped up from the table, almost knocking it over. "Damnit, Sarah. Cut the jealousy crap! Mom's dead now."

She grabbed her purse from the counter and slammed the door as she left, hoping that Sarah had gotten the message.

Some of Jan's happiest times had been spent at her grandparents' house, which was located on a hill overlooking part of the two thousand acres her grandfather had amassed over the years. But as she pulled up to the driveway, she was overwhelmed with sadness. Her grandparents had been dead for two years, and now her mother was gone. She felt totally alone. Not even the sight of the beautiful ante-bellum home nestled among a cluster of stately magnolia trees could remove the pall that enveloped her. She hesitatingly got out of the car and walked up the sidewalk and the steep concrete steps. She lifted the police barrier tape and unlocked the front door. Entering the house, she detected the faint fragrance of White Shoulders, her mother's favorite perfume. She could almost feel her mother's presence as she made her way from room to room, hoping that somehow her mother's death had just been a bad dream and that she would walk in at any moment. Every room Jan entered was still in shambles and she became livid as she imagined someone going through her mother's possessions so indifferently. When she came to the living room, where her mother had been attacked, she shivered. The stench of blood still permeated the room. Dried bloodstains and fingerprint powder seemed to be everywhere. There was even a hole in the cream-colored carpet where her dad and his deputies had removed a sample to send to the state crime lab in Jackson. Next to the hole was a taped outline showing the exact spot where Sally had found Janine's unconscious body. A sudden onset of nausea overwhelmed her, and she had to swallow several times to keep from vomiting. After the nausea had subsided, she instinctively went to the antique mahogany desk and pulled out the top drawer. Behind a small panel, known only to Jan and her mother, was the secret place where they kept items important only to the two of them. She pressed a worn place in the wood, causing a spring to allow the panel to slide to the left. Jan reached in and pulled out their treasures—toys from her childhood, some of her grandmother's old costume jewelry and a few old photographs. She cried as she clutched the precious objects to her chest. When she went to put them back, her hand touched something unfamiliar. She bent down and saw that it was a red and gray stationery box. She removed it from the cubicle and noticed the words *For Jan* written in her mother's unique handwriting. Curiosity got the best of her, and she opened the box. Its contents consisted of old newspaper clippings and two books, one a yellowed spiral tablet and the other a maroon leather diary with the name *Janine Walton Beauregard* imprinted in gold foil.

Jan sat down on the floor, putting the box beside her, and began pouring over the items. The articles were about Geoffrey Bockker, beginning with the murders of the two "W" students and ending with his supposed death in Columbus. She finally realized the horror her mother must have gone through during the past thirty-five years. As ghastly as the newspaper accounts of Geoffrey's reign of terror had been, nothing could have prepared her for the information she gleaned from the tablet. Her eyes widened as she read the actual words of a cold-blooded psychopath. As she laid the tablet down on the floor, her hands trembled and her stomach churned with revulsion. *Bockker, you bastard. You'll rot in hell before I'm through with you.*

She picked up the diary and rubbed her fingers lightly over the gold foil imprint as if it were a magic lamp. Opening the book, she held it up to her nose and breathed in. White Shoulders. Tears streamed down her face. She eagerly turned the pages and was taken on a journey of the highlights of the past thirty-five years of her mother's life—her wedding, births, deaths, vacations, and her parents' breakup. In the very back of the book, there was an envelope addressed to Jan. She meticulously opened the envelope and removed the sheets of blue vellum stationery. It would be the last letter her mother would ever write to her.

Dear Little Janine,

I hope you don't mind my using your pet name, but you'll always be my little girl. I know that since you are reading this, I am no longer with you in body, but my love for you will endure forever. Please take care of Sarah and your dad. I love them both so much. I'm sorry for the way things turned out. I didn't mean to hurt them. The awful things Geoffrey Bockker did to my friends and me caused irreparable damage between your dad and myself. Sarah, naturally, took his side. She could never understand the special affinity I had for you. Because we almost lost you at birth, I guess I always went out of my way to protect you. This attention made Sarah think I didn't love her anymore and she turned to your father for consolation.

If my death is from natural causes, so be it. However, if there are strange circumstances surrounding my demise, please do a thorough investigation. Although Suzanne and I haven't heard from Geoffrey Bockker in more than two years, I know he is still out there just waiting for the opportunity to kill us. He must be destroyed. He will stop at nothing to harm us or our families. Hunt the bastard down until he is dead. My soul will not be able to rest in peace until the monster is burning in the fires of hell. But be careful. He is capable of anything. I love you.
Mom

From the quiet of the empty house there suddenly boomed forth eleven chimes from the old grandfather clock. The echo of the chimes made Jan gasp. She had been so engrossed in her reading that she hadn't even noticed the tolling of the previous hours. When the phone rang, she instinctively knew that it was Sarah calling to berate her for taking so long. To her surprise, a man's voice was on the other end of the line.

"Who is this? Where's Janine?"

"This is her daughter. Janine died yesterday. What do you want with her?"

"That's too bad. She has something that belongs to me, and I want it back. Do you understand? I want it back."

"Who is this?"

"It's none of your business. She has a book, a spiral notepad that she took from me. Have you seen it? Answer me. Have you seen it?"

Realizing that she was talking to Geoffrey Bockker, Jan

gulped and said resolutely, "I don't know what the hell you're talking about."

"I know it's there somewhere." Then he abruptly hung up.

Jan pondered the conversation and decided that the best thing to do was to take the box home for safekeeping. If Bockker thought the notebook was still in the house, he might be back. She hurriedly picked out her mother's favorite blue print dress and matching shoes. Just before she left the house, she locked all the doors and set the alarm. At least the security company would be alerted if anyone tried to get in the house. Jan put the clothes and the box in the car and drove home to face her irate sister.

Sarah was sitting in the living room with an angry frown on her face. "What the hell took you so long? I could have been there and back in forty minutes. You've been gone over four hours."

Jan didn't feel like getting into a fight with her sister so she just hung her head. "I'm sorry, Sarah, but I got tied up with something."

Jan took the lid off the box and showed Sarah its contents. When she told her about the phone call, her sister's anger seemed to dissipate and a look of horror came to her face.

"Oh, my God! Bockker's still alive. But we haven't heard anything from him in over two years. The sonofabitch finally made good on his threat. Jan, I loved Mother so much, but after her experiences with Bockker, she'd never let me get close to her. She just wanted to withdraw into her own private world. You were the only person she seemed to care about. I'm sorry I've acted like such a jerk."

Jan put her arms around her sister. "Okay, Sarah, we'll work on this a little at a time, but right now we've got to figure out what to do about Bockker." Then she looked her sister straight in the eye and said, "We'll stop him. Don't worry."

"Jan, you've got to be careful. That monster always seemed to do the impossible." Sarah bit her lip to keep from crying. "Dad wants to have a closed casket at the visitation and funeral. Is that alright with you?"

Jan said haltingly, "That's, that's a good idea. Mom never liked to look at dead people. I know she wouldn't want them gawking at her and saying, 'Oh, doesn't she look good.' " Jan let out an ironic little laugh and Sarah did too. They hugged each other tighter and let their tears flow.

58

The next night after the three mourners had returned from the visitation, Sarah and Jan's father told his daughters how he planned to catch Janine's killer.

"I think Bockker will be curious enough to come to either the funeral or the burial," he said. "I'm going to post some of my men at the different entrances to the church. They can hand out the programs. That way a stranger won't realize they're law enforcement officers. If Bockker tries to get in, we can apprehend him. Just in case he gets by them, I'll put someone in the balcony to video the funeral. I've also assigned some plainclothes detectives to keep an eye out for him. If he shows up at the burial service, we can nab him before he leaves the cemetery."

Letting go of her mother was the hardest thing Jan had ever endured. Sitting in the little church she had grown up in brought back so many childhood memories. The service was sweet but not overly sentimental. Afterwards, the crowd of mourners wound their way from the church to the cemetery in a solemn funeral procession, passing all the landmarks of Jan's childhood. The cemetery sat on an Indian mound surrounded by a grove of majestic oak trees. Her mother had carefully selected a spot that overlooked both Highway 61 and the Illinois Central railroad tracks because she loved to travel and to hear the lonesome whistle of the trains as they made their way through the remote areas of the Delta. After the burial service had ended and everyone else had left, Jan knelt by her mother's casket to tell her goodbye for the last time. Then she went to the car where Sarah and her father were waiting.

They had all gone over to their cousin Sally's house where food and drinks were being served to all the mourners. After everyone had left, Sarah and Jan's father sat around talking to his daughters and Sally. "None of my guys saw Bockker at either service, so let's see what the video shows." Emotionally, Jan wasn't up to looking at the film, but for her mother's sake, she knew it was necessary. As the camera panned the church, Sarah suddenly cried out, "Stop it right there! Now, go back a few more frames. Oh, dear God in heaven. That's him. I know it is."

"But, Sarah, you can't be right. That's just a kid. He's no more that twenty years old. We're looking for a man in his late fifties," her father said.

"I don't care what you say, Dad. Listen to me. That's Geoffrey Bockker." She held up one of the old newspaper clippings that Jan had found and jabbed her finger in Bockker's face. "Look at this photograph taken at his arraignment. It's the same man."

"It looks a lot like him, but I still say there's no way the guy in the video is in his fifties."

"Maybe Bockker has had plastic surgery," Jan said. "I don't know, but I think Sarah's got a point. Sally, what's your take on all this?"

"I agree with Sarah. The guy does look like the man in this

picture, but, Beau, your argument makes sense, too."

"Why don't I run the rest of the video and we'll see if we notice anyone else who resembles Bockker."

Beau ran the video through once and then ran it several more times, but no one except the one young man even remotely resembled Bockker. Sarah and her father were both adamant in their opinions.

"This isn't getting us anywhere," Jan said. "Dad, let me borrow your copy of the police report and the coroner's findings. I'm going to take my forensics kit out to the house to see if I might be able to pick up on something."

"I don't think you'll find anything, but go ahead. Sarah and I'll head on back to town."

On the way to the house, Jan glanced over at the forensics kit. Her father had given it to her the day she had gotten her Master's degree. As a freshman in undergraduate school, she had been torn between a career in journalism and criminology. Her grandmother was an amateur mystery writer and had encouraged her to enter that field, but her father had wanted her to follow in his footsteps. She had compromised by getting a double major. When the St. Louis Metropolitan Police Department offered her a job, she immediately jumped at the opportunity. The pay was excellent, and she would be only five or six hours from home. However, after working in the department for a few years, she developed a serious problem that jeopardized her police career. For some unknown reason, she began having debilitating panic attacks. She could never predict when an attack would occur so, by mutual agreement, she resigned from the department with the understanding that she would be rehired if she ever got the attacks under control. She decided to switch to what she thought might be a less stressful career and accepted a job with the *St. Louis Post Dispatch* as an investigative reporter.

Jan loved working for the paper, and the job left her with enough time to get to see the Cardinals, the team she and her mother followed religiously. During the '98 season, she kept her mother posted each night on McGuire's and Sosa's home run record chase. Janine watched most of the Cardinal games on television but loved to hear Jan's first-hand accounts of the games. The night McGuire hit his sixty-second, Jan had called her mother. They both screamed with excitement. One of Janine's most prized possessions was an autographed picture of the whole team.

All these memories flooded back as Jan pulled up to the driveway. The barrier tape hadn't been disturbed and the alarm was still on. As far as she could tell, Bockker hadn't been back. Jan entered the house, but she really didn't know what she was looking for. She went to the living room and sat down in her grandfather's favorite chair. She opened the forensics kit and got out the reports to see if she might be able to pick up on something. She didn't notice anything unusual until she came to the coroner's report. One statement signaled a red flag: "Bits of latex found under the fingernails of the right hand." Jan wondered how on earth her mother could have come in contact with something that contained latex. According to the reports, no foreign prints had been lifted from her mother's body or from any objects in the house. Jan picked up her kit and began searching around the room. Her search proved futile, and she was about to shrug off her idea as wishful thinking when something told her to check the closet in her mother's junk room. Her intuition proved to be right. When she opened the door, she spotted her mother's blue and white striped Delta dress with the triangle pin still on the collar. *Maybe Bockker took off his gloves and touched the pin since it would have held so much significance for him.*

Jan placed four bottles of powder—black, white, gray, and

red, her special order fiberglass brush, some pressure-wound tape, and a lifting card next to the dress that she had laid out on the bed. She got out her flashlight and shined it on the pin to see if any latent print might be visible. With a smile of satisfaction, she put the flashlight back into her case and twirled the brush between her fingers to make the bristles more fluffy, enabling the powder to adhere to them better.

Normally, fingerprint retrieval was a very tedious and boring process, but this time Jan was not merely going through the motions. She dipped only the tip of the brush into the red powder and very lightly dusted the spot where the light had revealed the print to be. As if by magic, a print began to take shape, and Jan carefully placed a strip of the pressure-wound tape directly across the print, making sure that there were no air pockets underneath. She pressed her thumb down on the tape as hard as she could and then quickly removed the tape from the print. Afterwards, she placed the tape on the edge of the lifting card and cut the tape from the roll with her knife. She labeled the card with her initials and noted where it had been found. *Okay, we have someone's right thumb print. If this is Bockker's then we're in business. Bockker's prints should still be in the FBI's IAFS (Integrated Automatic Fingerprint System).*

Jan quickly reset the alarm, locked the door, and jumped into her car.

"Dad, Sarah, look what I found," she said, excitedly, waving the card as she entered her father's house. A few minutes later, Jan and her father were on their way to his office.

Jan had worried about how the guys at the sheriff's department might feel about her horning in on their investigation, but they were thrilled when Beau showed them the print.

"Way to go, Jan," one of the detectives said.

Beau nervously faxed the print and a letter explaining its circumstances to the IAFS. The whole group stood fidgeting in front of the machine until their fax number rang. They waited impatiently until the reply came back positive.

"Yes!" Beau yelled as he pumped his fist in the air. "This print belongs to none other than Geoffrey Paul Bockker. I guess a triangle started all his problems and a triangle will help bring him down. That's poetic justice."

"I'll call Sarah and let her know what we found out," said Jan excitedly.

Sarah didn't seem very thrilled when Jan told her the good news. "That's nice. When are you and Dad coming home? I'm real busy right now, and I can't talk." Then she abruptly hung up.

"What's wrong, Jan?" Beau asked when he saw the puzzled look on her face.

After Jan told him what Sarah had said, Beau yelled out, "We've got to get home now! Something's wrong."

As they pulled into the driveway, Jan was surprised to see an old man hurrying down the street and around the corner. As she and her father came into the house, a distraught Sarah rushed to them.

"My God, Sarah, what's wrong?" Beau asked.

"Oh, Daddy, some old man just walked in off the street and threatened to kill me."

"Did you recognize him?"

"No. He looked like an old bum."

Beau hurried out the door, but the man had disappeared.

"Did he hurt you, Sarah?"

"No, he just said he wouldn't stop until he got what he wanted, even if he had to kill Jan and me."

"The print matched Bockker's. So he definitely was in the house. But who on earth could that old man have been and why did he threaten you? Damn, I still can't figure out why the man in the video looked so young. There's got to be more than one person involved."

Beau and Jan calmed Sarah down and all three of them decided it was best to start fresh in the morning. But Jan couldn't sleep. She sat up in bed watching television, and as she flipped though the channels, she came upon a documentary on movie monsters. She had always been fascinated, yet frightened to death, by old horror films and decided to watch the program. But halfway through the show she found herself in that world between dream and consciousness, picking up a few words here and there. She sat straight up in bed when she heard the word "latex." Shaking her head, she willed herself awake enough to watch the rest of the program. *I've got it. I know why Mom had latex under her fingernails. There's only one killer. When Bockker attacked Mom, she lashed out at him with her right hand, but she got latex instead of skin. He must have made a mold of his face and then created latex masks to make himself appear older or younger.*

Jan jumped out of the bed and yelled, "Sarah, Dad, wake up!"

The two rushed out of their rooms.

"There aren't three separate people," said Jan. "There's only one fifty-five year old man who's worn latex masks to change his appearance."

She explained her reasons for her theory, and both agreed that they were certainly plausible.

"I think you should get out of town, Sarah. It's too dangerous for you here right now. Why don't you go to Memphis and stay with your friend Rena for a few days? Then we won't be worried about you. I could put a twenty-four-hour guard on the house, but knowing Bockker, that wouldn't stop him."

Sarah agreed to her father's plan and the next morning she left for Memphis.

Jan said, "Dad, I think I'll go back out to Nana and Paw-

Paw's house. Bockker called there once and he might call again. You follow me in an unmarked car and we'll keep in touch by radio."

Beau started to disagree, but he knew better. Once Jan had made up her mind, there was no changing it. Besides, he knew she could take care of herself.

59

The minute Jan walked in the door, the phone began to ring. She knew who was on the other end before she picked up the receiver.

"I still want what you have. You know, you and your sister have to die if I don't get it."

"Bockker, you bastard, you don't scare me. I swear on my mother's grave, you'll be dead or in jail before the week's over."

"Oh, listen to brave little Jan. Just like your bitchy mother. I'll have you and your sister begging me to kill you before I finish with you."

A clicking sound indicated that he had hung up. Beau arrived in a few minutes and checked the answering machine to identify the caller's number.

"Damn, he must have jammed the signal. That bastard! He manages to stay one step ahead. Always has."

"I've got an idea. Let's try to draw him out. He wants that notepad. I'll use it and myself as bait."

"Jan, that's easier said than done. What's your plan?"

"He's somewhere between here and town. Let's leave the

house unlocked tonight. You pretend to go home, and I'll stay here. I'll be willing to bet he'll call back. Then I'm going to make him an offer he can't resist. Go on over to Sally's. We'll keep in touch by radio."

"Okay, but be careful. He's been a killer for so long that murder's become second nature to him."

Beau drove his car to a neighbor's house and left it hidden in the garage. He got the neighbor to drive him over to Sally's house and let Jan know when he had arrived. She turned on the television to pass the time. The Cardinals were playing the Cubs, but Jan couldn't really keep her mind focused on the game. When the rookie phenom Tony Simpson hit his fifty-fifth home run putting him five ahead of McGwire's pace, she cheered with the rest of the fans and turned around to give her mother their customary high-five. Sadness suddenly over-whelmed her. Jan became even more resolute to bring Bockker's killing rampage to an end. The ringing of the phone startled her momentarily.

"Yes, this is Jan. Is that you, Bockker? I was expecting to hear from you."

"Good, then you know what I want. Have you got it?"

"No, but I'll get it and bring it to you. Where are you?"

"You think I'm stupid? Your daddy and his whole damn cav-alry would descend on me like Sherman on Georgia. No, we're going to play by my rules. Now just shut the hell up and listen to me. Put the notepad in a manila envelope. Then go to the Lady Luck Casino movie theater and put the envelope on the third seat of the back row on the left side. Then leave. Don't screw around with me or you'll be sorry."

Beau had heard the entire conversation and called as soon as Bockker had hung up. "Jan, I don't think it's such a good idea for you to go to the casino by yourself. It's too dangerous."

"Dad, he won't do anything in front of all those people, and

I won't be in the theater at the same time he is. I'll be okay."

Jan picked up the manila envelope and drove the eight miles to the casino.

Although she still had a permit to carry her pistol, she didn't want to bring any undue attention to herself, so she locked it in the glove compartment. Before the movie started, she had followed Bockker's directions about the manila folder and then went up to the projectionist's booth to wait until the movie was over. There were only four people in the theater, a family of three and an old gray-haired woman. Just before the movie ended, Jan headed downstairs to get the envelope since she hadn't recognized Bockker among the group. He had tricked her and hadn't shown up at all.

Damn it. The envelope's gone. Bockker must have been disguised as the old lady. I should have known he'd have other latex masks. Now I'll have to try to find him among the crowd.

At that instance, Jan recognized the group in front of her as the family who'd been in the theater. The little girl was clutching the envelope. Jan knew she had to act fast. She ran and caught up with the group.

"Excuse me, but I accidentally left that envelope in the theater. Please give it to me."

"No way. Finders keepers," said the little girl.

Then the little brat stuck out her tongue and ran off down the corridor. Fortunately, one of the security guards saw what was happening and took off after her. The child darted in and out among the crowd, but the guard was able to catch up with her. She picked up the screaming child and carried her back to where an angry and embarrassed Jan was standing. Jan grabbed the envelope from the child's hand and thanked the security guard. She sighed and headed toward the parking lot. She got into her car and was about to crank the engine when she felt a cold object sticking in the back of her neck. She knew instinctively that it was the point of a knife blade.

"Sorry about that mess-up, Jan. Now, if you'll just hand me the envelope without turning around, I'll be on my way."

She picked up the envelope and held her arm over her shoulder. She shifted her eyes and glanced into the mirror expecting to see the face of an old woman. Instead she saw the face of the young man in the video. She shuddered and quickly averted her eyes so that he wouldn't be able to see her reflection in the mirror.

"Here it is. Now leave Sarah and me alone."

The intruder didn't say a word but calmly opened the door and walked off toward one of the shuttle buses.

Jan cursed and headed back to town to Sally's house to see if her father was still there and to tell them what had happened. Something caused her to look in the direction of the old Franklin house. A strange light came from the basement. *That's weird. No one's lived there for years, and there's no electricity or water.* She decided to take a look for herself. This time she made sure that she had her Glock 19 with her but she forgot to take the radio. She carefully made her way across the yard, praying that she didn't step on some creature that might happen to be prowling in the ankle-high grass. The Franklin house was located on the banks of the Yazoo Pass, and it was not uncommon for all sorts of detestable things to lurk in the yards as well as inside the houses. Jan breathed a sigh of relief when she arrived at the side entrance to the house without an incident. She opened the dilapidated screen door as carefully as she could so that she wouldn't announce her presence. She tiptoed across the wooden floor trying to avoid any loose boards. She reached the basement door and slowly pulled it open. Hesitating at the top of the stairs, she drew a deep breath. She could taste the dank air and a plethora of unpleasant odors greeted her. With no warning, her heart suddenly began to race.

Please, God, don't let me have a panic attack now. She breathed in and out slowly, repeating her mantra: *calm.* The wild beating of her heart lessened, and she slid her left hand carefully along the rust-encrusted rail. She held her pistol out in front with her right hand and slowly inched down the stairs, praying that they wouldn't give way and send her crashing onto the concrete floor. As her eyes grew accustomed to the darkness, she looked around to determine the source of the glow that had first attracted her attention. On a rickety-looking table she spotted a circle of candles surrounding a group of photographs whose frames were cracked with age. The glimmering light from the candles cast an eerie glow, and Jan gasped when she saw what was sitting on the next table. At first she thought they were the heads of several decapitated people, but soon she realized that they were latex masks. Jan scrutinized the masks. One mask was that of a beautiful young girl who closely resembled the one in the pictures. Another was that of the old man whom she had seen in front of her parents' house. When she looked carefully at the face, anger boiled inside her. On the right cheek were marks showing where the mask had been repaired. This must have been the same one he wore when he attacked her mother. *But, there's no mask for the twenty-year-old man. Oh, yeah. He was wearing it at the casino.* She froze when she heard footsteps on the floor above her.

"I'm coming, my beloved. I got our diary back from the bitch's daughter. Soon our enemies will all be dead and you can rest in peace."

Jan looked around for a place to hide, but as she stepped forward she heard a sound that sent chills throughout her body— a low vibrating sound that could only come from the one thing she feared—a rattlesnake poised to strike. Instinctively, she raised her arm and squeezed the trigger just as the snake struck. Her aim was perfect, and she blew its head off in mid-air. But now a far worse monster had her trapped.

"Aha, so you've found my abode. This isn't exactly what I had in mind for you, but it will have to do. First, I want to collect my souvenir, though."

Bockker lunged toward Jan with his knife blade flashing in the candlelight. Another panic attack hit Jan and she couldn't will herself to squeeze the trigger again. Just as he brought the blade of the knife down toward her, he let out a blood-curdling scream. Jan had always heard that snakes traveled in pairs and was thankful that at least this time the old saying was true. The mate of the one she had killed had been lying on an overhead beam and struck Geoffrey in the face when he moved toward Jan. He fell to the floor with the snake still attached and injecting its venom. Desperately, Geoffrey dropped his knife and grabbed the snake with both hands, flinging it aside. Just as he bent down to pick up the knife, two shots rang out from the head of the steps. They had come from Beau's .457 Magnum. He and Sally had gotten worried when Jan hadn't called and had rushed to the Franklin house when they heard a gunshot. Beau raced down the steps and leaned over to check Geoffrey's pulse. He cursed when he discovered that Geoffrey was still breathing. Geoffrey looked up at them with his cold steel eyes and whispered, "Please don't call an ambulance. For God's sake, just let me die. Then I'll finally be able to rest. That damn voice won't hound me anymore." Then he lapsed into unconsciousness.

"As much as I'd like to comply with your request, Geoffrey, I'm obligated to try to save your monstrous life," Beau said.

The three people somehow managed to get Geoffrey up the steps and Beau called for help on his car radio. The whole area was soon awakened to the sound of what seemed like a hundred sirens. The paramedics did what they could and then placed Geoffrey in the ambulance.

"This man is still capable of murder no matter how seriously he appears to be wounded," Beau said as he got in the back with Geoffrey despite the protestations of the paramedics.

The detectives, who had arrived just after the paramedics, began collecting evidence to take back to town. Sally and Jan walked to Sally's house and called Sarah to tell her what had happened.

"Do you think it's finally over? I won't believe it until I see him for myself. He's just like a boxer beaten almost to the point of submission. Just when you think he's down, he somehow manages to stagger back up."

"I know, Sarah, but this time I think he's actually whipped. He took too much of a hit to recover."

"Maybe. It's too late to come home tonight, so I'll get there around nine in the morning."

A few minutes later, Beau called from town. "Bockker's still alive. We've placed him in the security ward of the hospital under armed guard. There's no way he can possibly escape."

Jan decided to spend the night with Sally. She was so keyed up from all the excitement that sleep came sporadically. Whenever she did manage to get a few minutes of rest, she would wake up in a cold sweat, imagining that she could see Bockker in the room leering at her like he had at her mother that night in the hospital in Memphis.

The next morning Sarah picked up Jan and they drove into town. For the first time in her life, Jan prayed for someone to die. When they arrived in Clarksdale, they drove to their father's house.

"Dad, I want to go the hospital to see Bockker for myself."

"Sarah, I don't think that's such a good idea."

His older daughter gave him a look of defiance and Beau reluctantly agreed.

"You two wait in the car. I need to use the bathroom," Sarah said.

When the three arrived at the hospital, it was surrounded by reporters from all over the state. The media had been covering Geoffrey Bockker since 1963 and they weren't going to quit now. Beau and his daughters ducked their heads and refused to answer any questions as they made their way through the horde of microphones and questions.

When they finally got inside, Beau took them to the elevators used only by hospital personnel. Both Sarah and Jan nervously bit their lips as their stomachs churned with anticipation. The doors opened, and Beau led them down the corridor to the right. Police officers milled around the floor. One of them came up and whispered something to Beau. He looked over to the right and saw a man holding court and grinning like a possum. It was Jake Conner, who had come to extract his pound of flesh from Geoffrey at last. Beau didn't feel like talking to the imbecile, so he waved him off when he saw Conner approaching them. The rebuffed man frowned and headed back to his group of admirers.

Sarah and Jan hesitated a moment when they arrived in front of Bockker's room. Sarah stared in through the glass in the door and drew a deep breath. "You stay here, Jan. I want to go in first," she said resolutely. Beau insisted on coming in with her and stood guard at the door. She walked over to the bed and stared down at Bockker, who opened his eyes to see who his visitor was. Before Beau realized what was happening, Sarah reached over as if she were going to pat Geoffrey on the head. Instead, she carved a triangle on his forehead with the knife she had picked up from the house. She quickly ripped the skin away and calmly placed it in her purse. Beau finally realized something was happening when he heard Bockker cry out. He rushed over to Sarah and grabbed the knife from her hand before she had a chance to stab him. But Sarah had accomplished her purpose. As Beau was leading her out of the room, Bockker gurgled something that sounded like "Thank you."

Then he closed his eyes, and his monitors went haywire. The Code Blue team rushed in and did their best to resuscitate him, but they were unsuccessful.

An hour later, Beau called a press conference and announced to the world that Geoffrey Bockker had succumbed to his wounds and had died at eleven o'clock that morning.

"How do you know that the man who died is really Geoffrey Bockker?" one of the reporters yelled out.

"We took fingerprints and sent them off to IAFS. They matched perfectly. I can say without any doubt at all that the man is Geoffrey Bockker."

As soon as Beau turned around to leave, Jake Conner horned his way to the microphone. "I'd like to make a few comments on the situation."

Beau's face turned red with anger and he rushed toward the microphone. "Conner, I called this press conference, and we don't need any of your bullshit. As I recall, your ineptness almost got my wife and her friend killed. Now get the hell out of here."

Conner jerked his cigar out of his mouth and started to speak, but the look on Beau's face let him know that the matter was over. The defeated man stomped off.

Beau went back into the hospital to find his two daughters. The exhausted trio then drove home. Sarah never said a word but headed directly to the kitchen. She came out carrying some Scotch tape and a Ziploc baggie. Reaching into her purse, she pulled out the triangle of skin she had removed from Bockker's forehead and put it in the baggie. One of the detectives had given Bockker's notepad to Beau and he had carried it home instead of putting it in the evidence room. The notepad lay on the coffee table and Sarah reached down and picked it up, turning to the last entry. She carefully taped the triangle to the bottom of the page. With a flourish she wrote the words *Geoffrey Bockker: Died August 14, 1999. THE END.* She placed the notepad in her astonished sister's hands and hugged her tightly.

"Now, Jan," Beau said, "we have one more place to go today. Come on and get into the car."

Jan sighed and put the notepad back on the table. "Okay, but I hope it's important. I'm so tired I could drop."

Twenty minutes later, Beau pulled up in front of a new two story red brick building. The sign in front read *Care Inn Convalescent Center.*

"What are we doing here?" Jan asked.

"Just wait and see," Beau and Sarah replied almost simultaneously.

The two secretive people led Jan down a long hallway and stopped in front of Room 337. They pushed open the door, and Jan let out a gasp of surprise. There lay her mother, still hooked up to various monitors and pumps, but she was breathing without the support of a respirator.

"I don't understand," Jan cried. She ran over to the bed and kissed her mother, whispering "I love you a bushel and a peck and a hug around the neck," the childhood answer to her mother's rhetorical question "How much do you love Mommy?"

Janine opened her eyes and smiled weakly at her younger daughter.

"What the hell's going on? Why did you make me and everyone else think Mom was dead?" Jan asked as she turned to face her father and sister.

"I'm sorry, Jan, but the only way we could protect Janine was to make Bockker think she was dead. We didn't know what had happened to the notepad until you found it that day."

"Well, why couldn't you have just told me the truth?"

"Because you have such a big mouth, and you've never been able to lie with a straight face. You'd have given everything away, and we might never have gotten Geoffrey Bockker."

Jan laughed. "I guess you're right. But who knew the truth besides y'all?"

"Larry at the funeral home and some of the hospital workers. We didn't have to tell Suzanne and George because they're on a cruise around the world. We're having the editor of the paper put an article in this afternoon's edition telling the truth about Janine. Then when she gets out of here, we're celebrating with an open house for her homecoming."

"That's why I had to act so cold to you about coming to the hospital. I prayed you wouldn't want to come to the funeral home either. We'd have been forced to tell you the truth then," Sarah added.

After an emotional visit, Beau put his arm around Jan and said, "We'd better leave now. Your mom needs her rest. We'll come back tomorrow."

Jan leaned over and kissed her mother. Janine reached out and stroked her daughter's cheek. "I love you, little Janine."

"Me, too, Mom. By the way Tony Simpson hit another home run last night." Janine smiled, relaxed, and fell asleep.

A bereaved Josiah Perkins waited around until everyone else had left. He had rushed to Clarksdale when he heard the news about Geoffrey. His final act of friendship would be to claim Geoffrey's body.

"Okay, Perkins," said the Coahoma County coroner, "he's all yours. You can sit here in the hospital morgue with the body while you wait for the hearse to get here."

Josiah sat down in a chair and thought about his last moments with Geoffrey. He had entered the hospital room of the dying man with a mixture of emotions. Although he still hated Geoffrey for having used him as a pawn to accomplish his evil, when he saw the pitiful sight lying in the bed, tears rolled down his cheeks.

He walked over to the bed and looked into the face of the man he had once loved like a member of his own family. Geoffrey blinked his eyes and a half-smile came across his face when he recognized Josiah. He moved his lips, but his voice was so faint and weak that Josiah had to lean over to hear what he was saying.

"I'm sorry for what I did to you and those other people, Josiah. I tried so hard to make the evil voice go away, but it was just too powerful. Please forgive me."

Josiah didn't really know how to feel. Maybe Geoffrey was still manipulating him, but then what would he have to gain by lying? Yet he had seen guilty prisoners go to their deaths still protesting their innocence. He placed his hand on top of Geoffrey's and patted it gently and whispered, "If only you'd lived by the Bible verse 'Vengeance is mine...saith the Lord.' "

Geoffrey closed his eyes and before he drifted back into unconsciousness, Josiah heard him repeat softly, " 'Vengeance is mine...' "

Josiah continued to look down at the man in the bed and wept openly.

"Mr. Perkins," the coroner said when he came back into the morgue, "the hearse is here. You can wait down the hall while we get the body ready."

Josiah nodded and walked out into the hallway. He sat down in a chair and put his face in his hands. Whether or not he could forgive Geoffrey was immaterial. He had made up his mind to have Geoffrey's body cremated and to scatter the ashes in the Blue Ridge Mountains of North Carolina, the only place Geoffrey had ever felt truly free.

60

A week later Jan sat in her rented car ready to head to the airport. Sarah and Beau were on the verge of tears. Some matters still remained unsettled, but things were looking up. She gave her father and sister a farewell wave and headed toward Memphis. As she passed the cemetery, Jan said a silent prayer of thanks that her mother was alive.

It took Jan ninety minutes to reach the rental agency. She returned the car and took the shuttle to the TWA departure area. After she had picked up her ticket, she walked briskly to the gate. While she was sitting in the airport, she thought about everything that had happened lately. Had she looked across the waiting area, she would have noticed a distinguished looking older man staring at her. He, too, was headed for St. Louis, but she was so engrossed in thought that she never looked in his direction. When the reservation attendant called for the passengers in rows twenty-five to thirty to board, Jan picked up her briefcase and walked through the jet bridge, sad to be leaving her family but excited to be heading back to work. She took her seat toward the back of the plane and leaned back to relax. Several minutes later, when the remainder of the passengers were given the okay to board, the man who had been staring at her made his way to his seat. Jan was so absorbed in the magazine she was reading that she never even noticed him. After the plane had taken off, Jan's mind once again replayed the strange events of the last few weeks. She harbored the hope that her father and mother might be able to work things out, especially now that Geoffrey Bockker's specter no longer loomed on the horizon. After the plane had landed in St. Louis, Jan walked out of the terminal and hailed a cab. Meanwhile, the older man, who had been watching her every move, waited inside the building until he saw her cab leave.

The red light flashing on her answering machine caught Jan's attention the minute she entered her apartment. For some reason, the light brought back memories of her childhood when she and her grandfather would sit on the front porch on summer evenings listening to the Cardinal games. The fire on the end of his Lucky Strikes glowed in the dark like embers in a fireplace. Jan casually punched the button, fully expecting the message to be from her family or from someone at work. "You have something that belongs to me. If I don't get it back, you will die," said a man's voice. The message sent chills up and down Jan's spine, as she collapsed into the nearest chair, hoping to avoid a full-blown panic attack. Two blocks away, Rex Anderson stood in front of the bathroom mirror in the hotel room he had rented for a week. He reached up and wiped away the residue of the latex mask he had just peeled from his face.